"This is the saga of a black family. It is not the black experience, for there is no such thing. Each living soul, black and white, has a unique life experience."
—Eva Rutland

This story centers on Ann Elizabeth Carter, who was bred and pampered in the privileged segregated society of Atlanta's black elite, back in the 1930s.

This is the dramatic, emotionally charged story of one black family who lived through a period of remarkable change—from the Second World War to the years of John F. Kennedy and Martin Luther King, Jr. From the era of marches and demonstrations to the very end of the century.

This is a story for every reader, of every race and background. A story about overcoming the worst and finding the best, in life and in people.

EVA RUTLAND

NO CRYSTAL STAIR

MIRA

MIRA®

ISBN 1-55166-519-0

NO CRYSTAL STAIR

Visit us at www.mirabooks.com

Printed in U.S.A.

With love to my husband, whose wit, humor and life experiences are so much a part of this book.

With deep appreciation to:
My agent, Denise Marcil, who was with this novel
from the first thirty pages with its ninety-two
typographical errors. My editor, Paula Eykelhof, who,
with wisdom and keen perception, always manages to
flush out the flaws and enhance my work.

Many thanks to the following persons who have
shared experience and/or expertise:

Herman "Ace" Lawson (now deceased) and
George Isle, who kindly allowed me to fictionalize
some of their experiences as Tuskegee Airmen
during World War II

Rosemary Braxton
Patsy Sandefur
Deborah Gordon
Oscar Grant
Dr. Asa Yancey
Dr. Arthur Trent

This is a work of fiction. Characters, except for the
mention of well-known public figures, are fictitious,
and any relationship to persons, living or dead, is
purely coincidental. Fact does overshadow fiction
when one public figure, Herbert Jenkins, makes a
brief appearance in this book. I have never met this
man, but I have always admired him for his
renowned honesty, fairness and compassion in
Keeping the Peace, about his career from
rookie cop to Atlanta's Chief of Police.

Dear Reader,

My own life has been full of joy. I was fortunate to be born to a family who met the challenge of an unfair world with dignity and hard work and a zest for both laughter and love.

This story centers on Ann Elizabeth Carter—but I was not Ann Elizabeth. She was who I wanted to be (living in a two-story house with central heat, preferably on the West Side where the bulk of Atlanta Negroes lived). I, too, was bred in that privileged segregated world, so cherished and protected that I was proud to be me. I rode in the back of the bus, climbed to the Jim Crow section in the theater and shopped where I could not dine, scarcely giving a thought to what I was missing. My real world existed in the "colored" section. I attended colored schools, my colored church, socialized with my colored friends and roamed the blocks of "Sweet Auburn," which held the nucleus of Negro business, and where you went if you wanted to know what was happening. Like Ann Elizabeth, I was thrust from that private fenced-in world, and forced to face the problems of a multiracial society in a much wider and imperfect world. Like Ann Elizabeth, I met many people, black and white, good and evil, who played their own roles in the continuing clash over color, creed or class.

This story is based on fact, recounting, to some extent, the remarkable evolution that has occurred during my lifetime, from blatant segregation to a degree of integration that I would never have believed possible. As I reflect upon these changes, I have hope that we have learned…that as the multitude of people from different countries and different cultures pours into the United States, we will truly become a country of people who live, love and let live, free from the grip of yesterday's wrongs and that divisive taint of ethnic pride that is causing so much havoc and bloodshed throughout today's world.

This is the story of one black family who lived and learned during this period of remarkable change. I hope you enjoy it.

Eva Rutland

1

It was a Sunday morning, and a gentle breeze drifted through the stiff organdy curtains of the breakfast room at 2201 Hunter Road in Atlanta, Georgia. Ann Elizabeth Carter, still wearing her pink velvet robe, breathed in the fresh spring scent of pine needles and magnolia blossoms. Then she heaped her plate with fried chicken, grits and gravy, hot buttered rolls and jam. She smiled at her mother and her aunt Sophie, removed her napkin from its silver napkin ring, curled her toes around the rung of her chair and began to eat with unladylike relish.

Aunt Sophie, whose flowered chiffon dress did nothing to conceal her too-plump curves, sighed. "How you can eat like a horse and still retain that figure is beyond me."

The dimple at the corner of Ann Elizabeth's mouth danced. "Survival, Aunt Sophie. I starve all week at the dorm. Food at the dining hall is inedible."

"Silliest thing I ever heard of, making seniors live in, especially when you're practically next door to the college," Julia Belle snapped.

"Just one more month and I'll be free!" Ann Elizabeth knew that her mother's irritation had nothing to do with her boarding at school; it was about her attending Spelman at all. Julia Belle was an Atlanta University alumna and had never been reconciled to the affiliation of the three major Negro colleges, although the merger had occurred years before. Atlanta University had become the graduate school; Morehouse remained a men's college, and Spelman a women's college. Ann Elizabeth had a discomfiting thought. Would Mother insist on graduate school just so she could get that Atlanta University stamp? Except...

"Guess what," she said suddenly. "Last night Dan asked me to marry him."

Julia Belle Washington Carter paused in the midst of pouring herself a second cup of coffee, put down the pot and beamed. "Ann Elizabeth, how wonderful!"

"Mother, I—"

Sophie sat up, eyes wide. "Well, I do declare! Here I send Helen Rose to Fisk, way up in Nashville, so she can snatch one of those Meharry Medical School students, and you land a full-fledged doctor right under our noses! Not that it was unexpected—isn't that right, Julia Belle?"

"Yes, I think he was just waiting for the proper time. Now that she's graduating—"

"Well, it's too late for a June wedding, Julia Belle."

"August is better, anyway. Not as likely to rain and we can have the reception on the lawn." Julia Belle produced a pad and pencil. "Why didn't you wake me last night, Ann Elizabeth? I could have spoken to Reverend Hawkins after church this morning."

"Mother, I—"

"How many bridesmaids?" Sophie asked. "I know Helen Rose will be maid of honor. Yellow... No, not

good with her pale complexion. Deep rose, and the
other girls could wear pale pink. Good combination.
What do you think, Julia Belle?''

Julia Belle was studying a calendar. ''We'll have to
decide on a date immediately. I'll have to call Henry
about the catering. He's so busy these days. Even with
a war on, you wouldn't believe how—''

''Mother, Aunt Sophie, stop it!'' Ann Elizabeth's
voice was sharp.

Both women stared at her.

''I...I haven't decided.''

''Of course not. There are so *many* things to decide.
To schedule.'' Julia Belle made rapid notes. ''Let's see.
I'll call the bridal consultant at Rich's tomorrow
and—''

''It's not that.'' Ann Elizabeth drew a deep breath.
''It's Dan. I haven't decided about him.''

''What do you mean?'' Julia Belle's voice dropped
to a whisper.

''Dan. Marriage. It seems so...final. I just don't
know.''

''Good Lord, girl!'' Sophie's voice rose. ''How can
you sit there nibbling on a chicken bone and casually
announce that you've just turned down the most eligible
bachelor in town?''

''I...'' Ann Elizabeth hesitated. Looked at the two
women closest to her in all the world. She wanted,
needed to talk with someone. To sort out her feelings.
But this wasn't a discussion; this was a confrontation.
She sighed. ''I didn't turn him down,'' she said. ''Not
exactly.''

''Well, thank God for that!'' Julia Belle seemed relieved but still apprehensive. ''What exactly did you say
to him?''

"That I needed time."

"Time!" Sophie rolled her eyes. "Most girls would trade their souls for a *date* with him and she wants time to think about marrying him!"

"I'm not sure I love him." Surely, she thought, you ought to have a special feeling for the man you were going to marry. More special than the way she felt about Dan. She liked Dan. He—

"What do you know about love? You're only nineteen!" Julia Belle scoffed. "Love isn't what you read about in those trashy books Sophie brings from the drugstore."

"Oh, Mother—"

"Don't 'Oh, Mother' me! This is the most important decision of your life and you want to dillydally about it. You think you have to hear bells ringing or see sparks flying or some such foolishness!"

"No, Mother, it's not that. It's—"

"You'd better believe it's not that. Marriage is more than feeling like a lovesick cow! It's a good home, a decent family, standing in the community."

"And linen and crystal on the table?" Ann Elizabeth's eyes flashed toward the pink linen mats, the crystal vase holding the long-stemmed rose. Things! Nothing to do with *feelings*.

"Ann Elizabeth!"

"Well, that's what you mean, isn't it, Mother?" Ann Elizabeth was breathing hard now. She felt rebellious. Felt as though she was being pushed into something she wasn't quite sure she wanted. "You think I should marry a rich doctor and do it quickly while I have the chance."

Sophie's charm bracelet jangled. "Few girls get that chance."

"Not unless they pass the high-yellow fine-tooth-comb test," Ann Elizabeth said, an impish gleam in her eyes. It was conceded that once a Negro man gained professional status, he could marry his reward—the whitest colored woman he could find. Her mother and aunt fit the category. Julia Belle was tall and slender and Sophie was inclined to be fat, but both had complexions as fair as a Caucasian. Sophie's fine reddish curls, as well as Julia Belle's crop of silky black hair, slipped easily through a fine-tooth comb. Both had married professionals, Julia Belle a doctor and Aunt Sophie a pharmacist—a successful one who owned two drug-stores.

Ann Elizabeth giggled. She'd flunk the test herself. As Ed Sanford had pointed out in his brutal teasing way, "You got the keen features and the blow hair, Ann Elizabeth, but you're a mite too tan. Now, if your ma's white skin hadn't been tainted by your pa's dark brown…"

Thinking about it, Ann Elizabeth touched her auburn brown hair—and smiled. It wasn't as straight as Julia Belle's, but it was soft enough to be stirred by a breeze.

Julia Belle frowned. "Why are you grinning? Of course a professional man desires a wife with the right qualifications. He needs a woman who has a background and social niceties commensurate with his standing in the community."

Ann Elizabeth considered her father. He couldn't care less about his "standing in the community." And he probably cared no more about Mother's blow hair than he did about her background—daughter of Professor James L. Washington, among the elite of Atlanta's Negro society. The Washingtons were one of the few families with their own pew in the First Congregational

Church, right under the stained-glass window commemorating Grandfather. Dad might sit in the pew the occasional time he attended church, but it sure didn't mean as much to him as it did to Mother and Aunt Sophie, who reveled in such things. Symbols of their place in the black elite.

And why, Ann Elizabeth wondered, was she sitting here thinking stupid thoughts that had absolutely nothing to do with how she felt about Dan Trent?

Because she didn't *know* how she felt about Dan. She supposed she loved him. Ought to anyway, according to Mother and Aunt Sophie. Another involuntary giggle erupted.

"Ann Elizabeth, do be serious!" Her mother spoke curtly. "You need to think this through very carefully."

"I *said* I'd think about it!"

"Well, while you're thinking, think this!" Sophie said. "Herb gets all of Dan Trent's prescriptions, and he says Dan's practice is flourishing."

"I know Dan makes pretty good money, Aunt Sophie."

"Well, you'd know how important that is if you'd had to pinch pennies like we did when we were young. Wouldn't she, Julia Belle?"

"I do know," Ann Elizabeth said quickly. She knew her mother hated to be reminded of her penny-pinching days. She touched her aunt's hand and turned to her mother with a sigh. "I haven't said no," she reminded her. "Where's Dad?"

"At the hospital. Said he'd be back to drive you to the college. Ann Elizabeth—"

"Please, Mother, can't we talk later? I'm not even dressed yet. And I have to cram for a final." She gave both women a kiss and fled.

Upstairs in the bathtub she tried to dissolve her thoughts in the steamy scented water. Why did she feel so confused? She knew she'd probably marry Dan.

He'd come to Atlanta three years ago after his internship at Freedman's in D.C. Dad had taken him under his wing. "I like him," her father had said—and continued to say. "He's serious about his work."

Dan had been busy building up his practice. Busy dating, too, for every house in town was open to the charming handsome single doctor. From his lofty twenty-nine years, he'd always treated her like an impressionable younger sister.

And now... When had Dan's regard changed from brotherly affection to romantic interest? Had he, as Mother said, just been waiting for her to mature? He said he loved her. Seemed eager to please her. Goodness, he'd already bought a piece of land in that area being acquired by Negroes.

He'd driven her out there last night. He'd parked on the crest of a hill and pointed. "Five acres. Do you think it's a good site?"

She had leaned against his shoulder and gazed into the night. In the pale light of a full moon she could detect the faint outline of trees. A spring breeze freshened the air, tickling her nostrils with the heady aroma of pine needles.

"It seems perfect," she'd said.

"Say yes and we'll plan the house together. One big enough for our children and for all the parties you'll give."

Her future had spread like a lush carpet before her. Mrs. Daniel Trent, in a house built for children and lavish parties. She'd seen herself as a replica of her mother and hadn't known why the image disturbed her.

And Dan had already chosen the place for their home and bought her a ring. Was that what she'd resented? That he'd taken her consent for granted and made these decisions without consulting her? Now he—rather than Julia Belle—would choose for her.

Well, hadn't she always been happy with Mother's choices? Even as a child she'd felt so proud in those crisp organdy dresses and patent leather Mary Janes, her reddish-brown hair in the curls her mother fashioned by brushing her wet hair around a piece of broom handle. She had liked going to the private elementary school, to birthday parties and the dolls' club with her special group of friends.

Until high school... She chuckled. Lord, what a blowup there'd been! One, now that she thought about it, she'd actually prompted herself. She clearly remembered the morning they'd been driving to her private school and had witnessed a fight near the public high school. She'd been frightened when her father drew to the curb and jumped out of the car. He could get hurt! But Dr. Carter, in his commanding way, had stopped the fight and dispersed the crowd. He'd then tended the wounds of the two combatants, somehow managing to resolve their differences as he did so.

She'd observed the motley group of youngsters and, with the insight of her twelve years, made a hasty judgment. "They're bad," she'd said when her father returned to the car. "Not our kind of people."

She'd never forgotten the look her father had given her. And that he hadn't called her by his pet name "Kitten." But all he'd said was, "People are alike, Ann Elizabeth. Some just have more advantages than others."

That night had marked the beginning of a long series

of bitter arguments between her parents. Dad won. The following autumn, both she and Randy had been enrolled at Washington High, the one public high school for colored kids in the city of Atlanta. To her surprise she'd enjoyed those four years. She'd liked the homeroom devotional, where she first heard the beautiful old spirituals never sung in the Congregational Church. She'd liked being on the debating team and dancing in the operettas with her new school chums. Of course, Mother had seen to it that she maintained a tight connection with her old group, but as Dad wished, she'd made many new and different friends. In high school Sadie Clayton had been her best friend. Mother hadn't liked that because Sadie's father was a garbage man, and they lived in Beaver Slide, a far less genteel neighborhood.

Ann Elizabeth climbed out of the tub, toweled off and went into her room to dress, all the while reflecting that her friendship with Sadie had been her only rebellion against Mother. Unlike Randy, her brother, two years older and never as compliant. With him there had always been ripples of discontent—getting home late, making the wrong friends. And, come to think of it, Sadie. Randy had been immediately attracted to Sadie, and for a while they'd been pretty close. But neither she nor Randy had seen much of Sadie since she'd started nursing school.

Now Sadie's a full-fledged nurse, she thought, and I'm still wondering which way I'm going. I must remember to call her. I'd like her to see the play I'm in, show her I'm still performing. Lord, what fun we had, all those hours rehearsing operettas! I want her to come to my debut.

She hoped Randy would make it from Tuskegee. She

smiled. Another rebellion. Randy's fascination with airplanes, like a bolt from the blue, had disrupted their
parents' plans for him. Despite his disagreements with
them, Randy had been following their chosen path.
He'd completed his college requirements and was already registered in medical school. Pearl Harbor and the
U.S. entry into the war hadn't disrupted these plans,
since medical students weren't being drafted; it was
Randy himself who rebelled.

Ann Elizabeth sat on her bed to slip on her pumps,
remembering the day Randy had come in waving that
newspaper with the headlines in bold type: ARMY TO
ATTEMPT TO TRAIN NEGRO PILOTS. He read the
article aloud. "Disastrous mistake…some Army planes
fly at two hundred miles an hour, and it is well-known
that Negroes can't think that fast."

They had been indignant. Not Randy. He had howled
with laughter, his eyes bright with challenge. "We'll
show them!"

"We?" Dr. Carter's question had been an apprehensive gasp.

"I'm enlisting, Dad."

"But what about medical school?"

"Saving you a bundle. The Army will pay for medical school…after they've taught me to fly!"

Her mother had cried. Her father had tried reason,
and Ann Elizabeth's heart had ached for him. He'd been
counting on his son to join him in practice.

But Randy had been adamant. Determined.

Dr. Carter had tapped a finger to the paper. "Such a
waste. They'll take our best, our finest and brightest.
And they'll never know what they have!" He'd shaken
his head sadly.

But Randy had been excited, eager. He couldn't

waste time being hurt or angry or confused. He was simply going to do what he'd always wanted.

Downstairs she heard the phone ring, and a moment later her mother called up to say her father was delayed at the hospital. Did she want Aunt Sophie to drop her?

"No, thanks," Ann Elizabeth called back. She wanted no more advice. "I'll study up here and wait for Dad." Then she curled up on the window seat and opened her sociology book.

When she heard her father's car in the driveway several hours later, she gathered her things and rushed downstairs. She gave her mother a quick kiss and went out to the car. Her father stood holding open the passenger door, and as always she thought how handsome he was. Ann Elizabeth loved everything about her father. She loved his keen dark eyes, the rich brown of his complexion, the few strands of silver in the kinky black hair. Dr. William Randolph Carter was a tall man with a powerful build. The well-cut black suit so carefully selected by his wife was rumpled and the pockets bulged. He took a heavy gold watch from his vest pocket and glanced at it.

He smiled as he helped her into the car. "I'll have to stop by the hospital again, but we have plenty of time."

"Oh, Dad, Lynn can take me, then."

"I want to take you. Besides, Lynn's studying. Biology exam tomorrow."

How did he know? But then, her father always knew each detail of the life of whatever college boy occupied the room over the garage. He always took an interest, gave them pocket money and advice. Advice far more valuable than the room and board they received in exchange for household chores, firing the furnace, mowing the lawn and such.

"Something bothering you, kitten?" her father asked as the car turned into the street.

"Do you think I should marry Dan?"

His laughter rang out. "So, Dan popped the question, did he? That's Dan. Trust him to pick the best for himself."

"I think...he says he loves me."

"Of course he does. How could he help it?" He threw her a brief appraising look. "How do you feel about him?"

"I...I don't know. I like Dan. Love him, I guess. We're good friends."

"Marriage is more than friendship, honey."

"Mother thinks that I—"

"That you should snap him up before someone else does."

She returned his smile. "Yes. Something like that. You know Mother."

They both did. And they both knew what the town said about her. That Julia Belle Washington Carter was proudest of three things—her Washington heritage, her fair skin and her husband's medical degree. They might snicker behind her back, but oh, how they catered to her. They smiled and sought to be included in her clubs, her parties. To be accepted by her was to belong.

Dr. Carter touched his daughter's hand. "Don't be too hard on your mother. There's more to her than shows on the surface."

"I know." People forgot certain facts, like how hard Mother and Aunt Sophie had worked to establish a home for Negro orphans.

"She only wants the best for you."

"I know. But Mother's so caught up in…in things."

"Yes, I guess that's true." He hesitated as he parked the car in front of the modest Negro hospital, usually referred to as simply "Carter's." "You know, kitten, you've never been poor. Never had to do without."

She was silent, watching him. "Sometimes 'things' make a difference." He glanced at the one-story house he and some of his colleagues had converted into a hospital. "I've watched death, disease and poverty come in and out of this place day after day. I'd go crazy if I couldn't withdraw."

"Withdraw?"

He nodded. "Your mother has made me a comfortable retreat. I like the touch of elegance, the pretty table, my big leather chair. Hell, I even enjoy her parties."

That surprised Ann Elizabeth. She'd always believed that he never noticed, or, at best, merely tolerated those events. *A comfortable retreat.* Would she supply that for Dan? Could she? Was that enough?

"Now listen, kitten. Don't worry about what your mother says or what I say or anybody else, for that matter. Only *you* can know what's best for you. And you'll make the right decision. You're definitely your mother's daughter."

She stared at him, eyes wide.

He laughed. "Oh, yes. You've got that same streak. That same core of inner pride, that sense of knowing you're somebody. And that's not a bad thing to have, Ann Elizabeth. It's the kind of confidence no outsider can shake. And when you're that sure of yourself, you're not likely to make the wrong decision."

She watched her father disappear into the small hospital. She smiled at a woman who passed, waved to a boy on a bike. The boy was delivering medicine from her uncle's drugstore. This was her world, this West Side where the majority of Atlanta's Negroes lived. She felt comfortable within it. Reluctantly she opened her sociology book to do a little more studying. But she hadn't finished even a paragraph when she heard the car door open. She looked up, startled to see her father returning so quickly, his face tense and anxious.

"There's been an accident, Ann Elizabeth. I've got to go there right away." He started the car and headed down Hunter Street. At first she thought he was going toward Auburn, but instead, he skirted town and drove in the opposite direction through streets unfamiliar to her. Rain had begun to fall, and the day was growing as dark and dismal as her father's face.

"What happened, Dad?"

"It's Mr. Suber's boys. They've been in a fight." He spoke as he always did of his patients. As if she knew them and would be as concerned as he. She had no idea who Mr. Suber was. *He cares so much for all of them....* She gazed out at the road in silence and felt the jolting as he turned down a cobblestone hill. Shortly after, he turned right into a dirt alley and stopped in front of a run-down house. He got a flashlight from the glove compartment and picked up his bag.

"Come along, Ann Elizabeth. I may need help."

The door of the house opened before they reached it and a man emerged holding a kerosene lamp. "I'm glad you're here, Doc. I'm scared. Zeke's bleeding to death. Come this way."

Ann Elizabeth followed her father and the faint glow of the lamp through one dim room into another, where she almost stumbled over a tin washtub that appeared to be filled with blood. A wave of nausea swept over her as she was confronted by the smell of blood and cooking cabbage and a spectacle too hard to grasp. A young man—no, a boy—was lying on a couch and a woman was kneeling beside him, stanching a gaping wound in his neck with a cloth she dipped repeatedly in the tub.

So much blood! Ann Elizabeth swallowed and tried to hold her breath. She mustn't be sick. The woman moved aside and began to mumble almost incoherently.

"Oh, Dr. Carter, please! Please save my boy. They cut Zeke. He wasn't doin' nothin'. Lenny—he's the feisty one—he turned back to help. I told them both they shoulda run."

"There, there, Mrs. Suber. Try to be calm. You've done the right thing." While she'd been talking, Dr. Carter had removed his coat and opened his bag. "Come over here, Ann Elizabeth." He handed her the flashlight. "Hold this."

Ann Elizabeth swallowed again, trying to keep from retching, and shone the light full into the boy's face. Wide frightened eyes stared up at her. He couldn't be more than sixteen.

"I got good boys, Dr. Carter. They was coming home from work. Always come right home and bring me their money. That bunch of white trash had some firecrackers, and they threw one and tore up Lenny's pant leg. And they just laughed. Lenny was gonna jump 'em 'cause he thinks he oughtta fight back."

"Ann Elizabeth," Dr. Carter said sharply, "hold it this way. Steady now." Her father touched her hand, concentrating on the torn flesh. Ann Elizabeth stood mute, one hand over her mouth, the other holding the light steady. Dr. Carter worked quickly and efficiently, all the while speaking soothingly to the woman. "It's going to be all right, Mrs. Suber. We're lucky. They missed the jugular. It looks worse than it is. Zeke's going to be fine.''

In a few minutes he'd finished stitching and turned to the other boy, Lenny. Ann Elizabeth had hardly been aware of him. Mr. Suber had been sitting by Lenny and dabbing at the cuts on his son's face while her father attended Zeke. Now Ann Elizabeth moved as directed to focus the light on the other boy. Two slashes, but not as deep as Zeke's. Lenny was obviously younger, and the look in his eyes wasn't fear, but anger. As Dr. Carter cleansed his wounds, he echoed his mother. ''We wasn't doin' nothin','' he said, ''but mindin' our business. And they jumped us. They was hangin' around down on Pryor Street, whole bunch of peckerwoods. If I'd had a knife or a gun—''

''Calm down, Lenny. I can't work when you talk. Just keep quiet so I can stitch this.''

The boy stopped talking, but the anger was still there. Ann Elizabeth could see it banked behind those brown eyes. Suddenly there was a heavy pounding on the front door. It shook the whole house. ''Open up. Atlanta police!''

Terror. She felt it invade the room. There was a hush broken only by Mrs. Suber's, ''Oh, my God! Oh, my God! They'll take my boys.''

''Shine the light this way, Ann Elizabeth.'' Amazingly she did so while her father worked and Mr. Suber scurried to the door.

''Where are they? You trying to hide them boys?'' She heard the question, loud and vicious, in an unmistakable cracker twang.

Then she heard Mr. Suber. ''No, sir. We ain't trying to hide nobody. My boys...they got hurt.''

Then they were in the room. Two uniformed policemen, big, red-faced and burly, their billy clubs, hand-cuffs and guns menacing.

"Hold it steady, Ann Elizabeth." Dr. Carter hadn't turned around but continued to work. She kept a firm grip on the flashlight, but couldn't take her eyes from the policemen. One walked a little ahead of the other and seemed to grin with satisfaction when he saw the condition of the boys.

"We're taking 'em in," he said.

It was then that Dr. Carter stood up. He looked rather small facing the big policeman, and when he spoke his voice was different. Ann Elizabeth had never heard him speak that way before. Penitent. Almost obsequious. "Excuse me, sir. But I'm afraid these boys shouldn't be moved."

"Why the hell not?" the first officer bellowed.

"Sir, they've lost a lot of blood. If you take them downtown, I fear at least one of them might die."

Now the officer rounded on Dr. Carter. "They gonna die, anyway! They done jumped some white boys down on Pryor Street."

Lenny started up from his chair. "They jumped *us!* We wasn't—"

Dr. Carter whirled around. "Sit down, Lenny. Don't you talk to this officer like that. He's here to do his duty."

Lenny's eyes blazed, but he obeyed the doctor, who turned back to the officer. "Sir, the boys here tell a different story. They say the other boys started the fight."

"That's a lie!" The policeman moved belligerently toward Dr. Carter, and Ann Elizabeth's heart pounded with fear.

Suddenly the other officer spoke. "That you, Carter?"

Ann Elizabeth watched her father turn toward him and saw something pass between them she didn't understand. Something. Just a flicker. Recognition?

No. How could Dad know this…this… Coherent thought deserted her as the burly man, loaded with the instruments of death, loomed over her. They were closed in. Trapped.

Dimly, through the suffocating terror, she heard her father's voice. "Good evening, Officer Malloy." He spoke quietly, his tone carefully respectful as he added, "It's good to see you again, sir."

"Can you vouch for these boys, Carter?" Ann Elizabeth was amazed by the same tone of respect in the officer's voice. Hope stirred within her.

"Yes, sir, Officer Malloy. I certainly can. They're fine boys."

"That's good enough for me. Come on, Joe. Let's go."

"Now, looka here, Frank. We can't let these niggers get away with this."

"Take a look at these boys, Fred." Malloy waved a hand toward the injured boys. "The Gregorys didn't have a scratch. Not so much as a stubbed toe. Let's go," he said decisively.

As the officers departed, Ann Elizabeth expelled a breath. Quiet descended on the room; everybody was staring at her father. Mrs. Suber was the first to break the silence. "Praise the Lord! And thank God you were here, Dr. Carter," she muttered as her knees gave way and she sank into a chair.

"Did you hear him, Daddy? He talked right up to that policeman," Lenny said.

Mr. Suber clasped Dr. Carter's hand, fervently nodding his own thanks.

Ann Elizabeth, too, looked at her father in awe. This was a part of his life she'd never seen. He had his arm around Mrs. Suber and was telling her how to care for her sons' wounds when she expressed a worry that the policemen might come back.

"No," he said. "You can depend on Officer Malloy. If you have any trouble, call me."

Ann Elizabeth followed her father out into the fresh night air, leaving behind the smell of blood, cooking cabbage and fear. Once in the car she broke into tears she could no longer control. "Oh, Dad, it was horrible! All that blood and those policemen. I was so scared."

"Hush, kitten. You did a good job."

"No. You did." She thought of him, never pausing, continuing to tend the boys even as the policemen burst in on them. And later, just as young Lenny had said, talking right up to that policeman. "You know him, Dad? That...what was his name? Malloy?"

"Yes, I know him."

"Where? How?"

"It's the nature of things, child. Strangers meet in stranger places." He shook his head, a faraway look in his eyes. "And that doesn't matter. Just thank God he was one of the officers here tonight."

Yes, thank God. If he hadn't been... She shuddered as the horror swept over her again.

"Hush, child, it's over." He held her as he'd always held her, lending her reassurance and strength. Yet he had seemed so small, so vulnerable, standing in front of that hulk of a policeman. And he had humbled himself. She'd never seen him in that role before. She knew now that it had been necessary to protect the boys. The fierce pride she felt for her father battled with embarrassment at his humiliation.

"I love you, Dad," she whispered.

A few blocks from the Suber house, Frank Malloy still argued with his partner. They had pulled their squad car to the curb.

"I called it like I saw it, Joe. Be honest and admit you saw it, too."

"I saw nothing, Frank. 'Cept an old boy so pussy drunk he can't see straight. That nigger wench of yours must have a mink lined under yonder."

Frank Malloy whirled and grabbed the other man with both hands. "Leave her out of this!"

"Okay, okay."

"Okay, shit!" Frank's hold tightened. "I'm warning you. Another crack like that, and I'll—"

"Lay off. You're ch-cho…"

Frank released his grip. Damn! What was he doing? This was Joe. His partner. If it hadn't been for him he would've been up shit creek wid no paddle—just last night, when that pimp had come at him with a switchblade. "Sorry, Joe," he muttered. "It's been a hard day. And, well, you know about Gussie."

"Yeah." Joe straightened his shirt and didn't add, as he usually did, "Better watch that pussy trap, boy!" He just gave Frank an uncertain glance and said, "I know."

But he *doesn't* know, Frank thought as he drove away. He knows about Gussie. Knows about that ruckus on Decatur Street where we picked her up. Knows I drove her home, instead of to jail. Kind of trade-off that happens all the time.

But he doesn't know about the two years since. God, has it been that long?

Oh, he knows I check her out now and again. But he doesn't know how often I sneak into that little house on Glen Street.

And he doesn't know how it is between Gussie and me. How it is sitting in that kitchen at the back of the house, laughing with her and her grandma, eating her grandma's collard greens and custard-cream pie. Heap better'n boozing it up with the boys. First feel of home since I left Waycross. I was only fifteen, but Ma had died and all the love I'd ever known was gone.

Until Gussie. When she looks at me like I'm the Lord God Almighty himself, and when she lies beside me... No, Joe doesn't know I love her. I didn't know it myself until the night Luke was born. Until I thought I was going to lose her. She was having a hard time, and her grandma called me. She told me I didn't have to come, she'd called a doctor, but wild horses couldn't have kept me away.

They'd called that nigger doctor. Carter. I'll never forget him. I was still in uniform, but it was like he didn't care that I was white and Gussie black. Like he was just there to save our baby. He did, too. Stayed most of the night to do it—a long one. I'll never forget how he placed Luke in my arms. All he said was "You have a fine healthy boy, sir." And it was like he was handing me my life on a silver platter.

Yep, there are a lot of things Joe doesn't know.

And it's better that way, Frank decided, as he drove toward the station house in silence.

The chapel bell was tolling as Ann Elizabeth and her father drove through the lush campus with its old imposing brick buildings. It was as if they'd entered another world. Although it was a world familiar to her, tonight she seemed to be seeing it for the first time.

Dr. Carter stopped near the chapel, and she put her arms around him, loving his clean antiseptic smell. One of his favorite quotations flitted through her mind— ''Life for me ain't been no crystal stair.'' He'd said it a thousand times, but only tonight did she begin to get a glimmer of what it meant. She kissed his cheek, glad he could return to the quiet serenity of his home. Glad her mother would probably have a bridge game arranged. It would help him forget. She realized now that she was glad, too, that President Read insisted all seniors live on campus. It was good to slip back into campus life, leaving the horror she'd witnessed behind. Study for the exam tonight. Rehearsal tomorrow afternoon. She joined the girls hurrying into the stately Sisters Chapel for vespers. She passed through the tall marble columns to the sanctuary, slipped into her assigned seat between Jennie Lou and Josephine and lost herself in the soothing tones pouring from the organ, singing the words softly under her breath. ''This is my Father's world/ He shines in all that's fair....''

2

That afternoon, Sophie stood quietly at the window as she watched Dr. Carter depart with his daughter. "Ann Elizabeth's quiet but stubborn, Julia Belle. You can't handle this one as easily as you did Randy."

"Randy? What are you talking about?"

"That girl—what was her name? You said her father was a garbage man."

Abruptly Julia Belle got up to nosily stack dishes. "Goodness, that was just a high-school thing." Public high school! The only one in Atlanta for Negroes. Full of all kinds of youngsters, some of them from nowhere. Will had insisted on it. "They need to meet different people," he'd said. He was wrong.

"Careful, Julia Belle, you'll break that dish. Here, let me help you," Sophie said, gathering up silver.

Easy for her to be complacent, Julia Belle thought. Helen Rose was still in private school, while hers... Well, it was difficult to keep them from becoming too intimate with the wrong people. Ann Elizabeth still kept in touch with that Clayton girl.

"Sadie. Sadie Clayton," Sophie mused. "That was her name, wasn't it? Lord, was that boy besotted! And I sure can't tell why. Nothing to look at—coal-black with that real nappy hair. What would their children have looked like? No matter which gets the color, it's always the girl who gets the kinky hair.''

"Their children? Sophie, what in Sam Hill are you thinking? They'd never—"

"Well, he was that far gone. He could have married her.''

"Don't be ridiculous! He was only eighteen."

"Eighteen, and full of wild oats. What if he'd *had* to marry her?''

"Sophie! There was nothing like that going on."

"Don't get so huffy. These things do happen and you know it. I don't blame you for getting rid of Sadie."

"Sending her to nursing school was not getting rid of her.''

"Yes, it was. Away from the college—and Randy."

"She wasn't headed for college. And she would've been more out of Randy's reach as a live-in maid at the Grants' estate. That's where her father wanted to place her as soon as she graduated from high school.''

"No!"

"Yes. He called it a great opportunity. I guess it was, from his perspective.''

Sophie nodded. "Sure, sure. At least she'd be out of Beaver Slide and living high. If you have to work as a maid, best to do it for rich folks.''

"Well, I'm glad I talked him out of it."

"Paid her tuition, too, didn't you?"

Julia Belle shrugged. "Wasn't much. Sadie has a good mind. I'd hate to see it wasted on other people's toilets.''

Sophie chuckled. "So you did her a favor, as well as yourself. Where is she now?''

"Working at Grady where she trained."

Sophie shook her head. "Strange, isn't it? A Negro

doctor can't get near the county hospital. Yet they train colored nurses.''

''Nothing strange about it. Can you see white nurses handing out bedpans to Negroes in the colored wards?''

''Not likely,'' Sophie said, and they both laughed. ''Still,'' she added, ''I understand colored nurses are also permitted to tend patients in the white wing.''

''Nothing strange about that, either. Haven't coloreds been waiting on whites all their lives?''

''That's the God's truth. Anyway, I'm glad the girl's doing well. Guess something good comes out of everything. And I'd better be getting home. Herb will be wondering. I hope you can talk some sense into Ann Elizabeth. Negro professionals are few and far between.''

''Oh, I'm not worried. She'll marry Dan. She just needs time to think about it.''

Alone, Julia Belle tried to reassure herself. But despite the heat of the kitchen, a chill of apprehension persisted. Why was Ann Elizabeth hesitant? Surely she wasn't thinking of refusing Dan! He could give her…''linen and crystal on the table! That's what you mean, isn't it, Mother?''

No, Ann Elizabeth. It's more than that. Much more.

Julia Belle picked up a napkin ring from the table and held the silver circle in her hand, turning it over and over, seeing in its place the old bent one she'd held so long ago. Oh, Mama, you tried so hard. Secondhand napkin rings and frayed napkins. It wasn't easy on Papa's small teaching salary.

Even now Julia Belle could hear her mother's voice. ''The napkin goes on the left, and the glass is above the knife here on the right, see? Take your elbows off the table, Julia Belle. You ain't no field nigger—you're quality!''

Quality. Lord, how Mama drummed that word into us. Quality—clearly distinguished from field niggers and poor white trash. Julia Belle could almost see her mother now, small and wiry, wielding that heavy iron, running it across Papa's carefully starched shirt. "Some folks think if you look white you got quality," she'd explain. "And that's how Madame Walker, with her straightening comb, and Dr. Palmer, with his skin-whitening cream, done got themselves rich. But quality ain't black or white. It's who you are and how you act! Straighten up your shoulders, Sophie. And, Jimmy, don't go out of here looking like a tramp! Go back and get your coat and tie."

Julia Belle smiled as she plunged her hands into the dish water. Papa might have been the revered professor, but it was her uneducated down-to-earth mother who ruled the roost.

Lord! If I had as much control over my own children! Mama sure kept us in tow with her strict rules and strange admonitions. "Manners will get you where money won't." "Lie down with dogs and you'll get fleas." And "You Professor Washington's daughter and don't you forget it! What are you doing with that field nigger?"

"Mama, nobody works in the fields here," Julia Belle had said. "He's a bellhop down at—"

"Same thing. Beholden to white folks, ain't he?"

Mama had one firm rule about white folks: "Stay away from them. Long as you working for white folks, they let you get mighty close. Let you cook their food, nurse their babies, have their babies. That's why we got so many white niggers that don't know where they come from!''

Where had Mama come from? Pretty blue-eyed red-headed Mama. So quiet about herself. So proud of her husband—Professor James Washington. Everybody knew where *he'd* come from—a slave, son of the farmer who'd owned him. Julia Belle recalled how, as a child, she would be taken to visit Grandma Evvie, who lived in East Atlanta in a small house on Mr. Washington's back lot. Old man Washington, a big white man with a heavy cane, would come down sometimes to watch them play and he would pass out peppermint sticks.

Yes, there was no secret about Papa. Mr. Washington had given him his name, sent him north to school and provided for Grandma Evvie until she died. Maybe, Julia Belle thought now, it had been a real love match.

Not in Mama's case, though. Evidently Mama's father had also been white, but that wasn't talked about. Julia Belle knew almost nothing about her mother's background, just bits and pieces here and there. Mama's mother had died when Mama was a teenager. ''I started to work in the same house where my Ma had been a cook. After that I worked in a lot of big houses.'' Cleaning. Dusting. Placing the fork in the right place! For other people.

Mama had learned all the proper etiquette. But she'd learned something else, too. Something that caused the bitter line around her mouth and drew from her another admonition. ''No, siree! You can't take a job at that tearoom. You'll have to make do with that old dress of Sophie's. You ain't working in no white man's kitchen. I been there. Would still be there if I hadn't had the good luck and the good sense to marry your father!''

That was another thing. ''Be careful who you marry.

Someone who'll keep you from contact. White men ain't got no respect for colored women."

Mama hadn't liked Will Carter when Julia Belle brought him to the house that first day. "He's coal-black, Julia Belle! And did you say he's a dining-car waiter?"

"Just part-time, Mama. To pay for medical school."

"Oh." Mama had smiled. "Going to be a doctor, eh?" Will Carter had immediately become quality. "Doctoring's a good calling for a black man, Julia Belle." Mama's blue eyes had brightened with a knowing look. "Like I told you, the white man don't care how close he gets when you're serving him. But he don't like to serve you. He'll take the black man's money as long as he don't have to touch him. He don't want to doctor, beautify or bury you. He gonna leave that to black folks." Mama had laughed. "So, honey, you just marry yourself a doctor or a funeral director. He ain't gonna be on no salary and he ain't relying on no white man for his money. He's independent."

Independent. Not beholden. Julia Belle thought of her brother, Jimmy. He was a doctor in that little Georgia town and he didn't allow his wife to go to the grocery store. "Don't want her to have to deal with those white clerks." Protecting her from contact.

Julia Belle chuckled to herself. It was highly probable that the middle-class Negro woman was the most protected woman in the country.

She sighed. Ann Elizabeth was completely unaware of how vulnerable she was. She had always been protected and had always lived in a completely segregated environment. Except for shopping downtown. But even there, although they were banned from the tearooms and rest rooms, they were treated with respect. Because they were spending money earned by Dr. William Carter.

It's more than linen and crystal, Ann Elizabeth. It's much more. It's security, protection, even a little respect. If you marry Dan... *If.* Oh, she was being ridiculous. Of course Ann Elizabeth was going to marry Dan.

And such a wedding we'll have, Julia Belle thought. Even grander than the one Ada Simpson had for her daughter. Ada will be green with envy.

Julia Belle felt a little irritated. All this dillydallying! She wanted to get cracking with lists and invitations and...goodness! The dresses will have to be ordered and no telling how long that'll take. She must have another talk with Ann Elizabeth as soon as possible. Wouldn't it be wonderful if they could make the announcement at her debut?

Dan Trent. The catch of the season. She could just see the jealousy in Sally Richards's face. Sally had been trying for months to match Dan with her Jennie Lou.

If only Ann Elizabeth wouldn't fool around! Oh, she was just being coquettish. And she had so many things on her mind. Graduation. Rehearsals for that play. Well, she'd talk with her soon—next week—and they'd start making plans.

Julia Belle's thoughts reverted to her husband. He'd looked tired when he drove off with Ann Elizabeth. A bridge game always relaxed him. She would call Ada. Maybe she and her husband could come over. Julia Belle went into the hall and picked up the phone.

"I love you, Mrs. Moonlight, very very dearly." Ed Sanford spoke the words in a loud stage whisper as he leaned solicitously over Ann Elizabeth, a few bits of

powder from his simulated gray hair making tiny spots
on her blue satin gown.

Ann Elizabeth gazed at him adoringly, lifting her
hand to gently caress his cheek, then let it fall. She
sighed heavily, closed her eyes and very gracefully
died.

The curtains swept together amid a crescendo of clapping hands. Ed helped Ann Elizabeth to her feet and
she stood, her hand in his, as the curtain opened again
and the other players hurried back onstage to receive
the applause. Then she and Ed were left for a standing
ovation.

Ann Elizabeth knew her face was flushed with exhilaration. She loved acting, pretending to be somebody
else for a moment. Mrs. Moonlight wasn't one of her
favorites—some fantasy about a beautiful woman who
never wanted to grow old. Her wish was granted, but
when she saw her husband growing old without her, she
was ashamed and ran away. Years later she returned to
die in his arms. Silly.

Someone thrust a bouquet of roses at her. She selected a bud and carefully placed it in the buttonhole of
Ed's old-fashioned coat. He kissed her cheek. "Thank
you, my wife, always and forever."

It was a standing joke. In how many plays had she
been his wife? Five? No, six. She'd been Juliet to his
Romeo, Desdemona to his Othello, Anne Hathaway to
his Shakespeare. Once, in a black play, she'd forgotten
her lines and he had prompted her, muttering, "Say
something, nigger woman." She had answered in kind
and their adlibbing brought such response from the audience that they'd kept the lines in.

Oh, this had been fun, rehearsing and performing and
the applause. She felt sad that it was over. Well, maybe

it wasn't. She'd been asked to remain with the University Players for the summer season.

Upstairs in the little dressing room over the stage, she read the note attached to the roses. "You were great. Love, Dan."

"Ann Elizabeth, there's someone here to see you."

"Thanks." *Dan.* She hurriedly wiped off all traces of makeup, leaving her face bright and shiny. She slipped on her skirt and a pullover cashmere sweater and left the dressing room. Was Dan still in the theater, or was he waiting downstairs in the lobby?

Sadie Clayton, descending the stairs to the lobby, tried to stem the wave of disappointment. It had only been a faint hope that Randy would be here to see his sister perform. Of course, he'd be occupied doing whatever those pilots did at Tuskegee while they were waiting to be called overseas. Possibly occupied with other interests, too, she thought with a flare of jealousy. She wished—

Good heavens! Would she rather have Randy overseas in combat, risking his life, than exposed to the flood of women who'd descended upon Tuskegee, as eager for one of the handsome new Negro pilots as for a job?

How long was it since she'd seen Randy, anyway? And it was longer still since they'd been close. So why couldn't she stop dreaming about him?

She'd almost reached the lobby when she spotted Dan, leaning against a wall, talking to a group of friends. He was a handsome man and was, as always, impeccably attired. His tan suit fit his almost too-slender form perfectly, lending him an air of sophistication that Ann Elizabeth said had attracted her the first time she saw him. His eyes brightened when he noticed Sadie, and excusing himself from the group, he came forward to join her.

"Sadie Clayton. Just the person I wanted to see."

"Hello, Doctor. And how are *you?*" she said, smiling. "And what do you want now?"

He grinned. "All right, hello. But I don't need to ask how you are. You look great. And, yeah, you know me too well. I do want something."

"At your service, sir."

"I read in the paper that at the AMA meeting here last week, there was an interesting seminar on hypertension, and I wondered if you could get hold of a copy of the transcript."

"I'll try," she said. If possible, she was always glad to do things like that for black doctors, who weren't privy to AMA meetings or special seminars at the hospital. Some doctors, black and white, were content to peddle pills, relying on what they'd learned to pass the Medical Board exams. But dedicated ones like Dan and Ann Elizabeth's father were eager to learn new techniques. Dr. Carter had once waited tables at an innovative seminar on diabetes and said he was quite pleased with what he'd learned.

"Dr. Basil attended that session on hypertension," she now said to Dan. "I'll see if he's willing to share his notes."

"Oh! Isn't he the head of your department?"

"Yeah. And he's not nearly as racist as some of them."

"Thanks. I'd sure appreciate it. How did you like the play? Wasn't Ann Elizabeth great?"

"She was, indeed," Sadie replied, wondering if Ann Elizabeth knew how much this man loved her. Or if she really appreciated what a prize he was. She doubted it. If you never had anything but the best all your life, you tended to think that was all you'd ever get.

And Ann Elizabeth was so *protected*. Her ma never let her visit me in Beaver Slide—might get her pretty little pumps dirty. And, my God, if she had to deal with a bunch of bigots like those crackers at Grady... It'll be tough going if she ever moves out of that seditty circle. Those high-society muckety-mucks who thought they were so much. Probably won't, though. Not if old lady Carter has her way. She'll push Dan down Ann Elizabeth's throat and clamp her mouth shut. She's not likely to let a rich nigger white-looking doctor get away.

Not that any of that would weigh with Ann Elizabeth. Besides, she may be dumb about real life, but she's all heart. That's why I like her and why I'm standing here about to make myself late for my shift, just waiting to tell her she was good in that dumb play.

It wasn't Dan who stood at the foot of the steps leading from the stage to the auditorium. This man was short, stocky, red-haired and freckled. He looked strangely familiar, but she was almost sure she didn't know him. Was he one of the students from Clark College? She knew most of the Morehouse boys. His smile was shy and rather hesitant.

"I just wanted to tell you I thought you did a spectacular job." It came out in a slow cracker drawl. Oh, he was white! Not one of those very fair-skinned Negroes.

"Why, thank you. That's very kind of you."

"You folks do a much more professional job than we do at Emory."

Emory. Atlanta's premier white university. Ann Elizabeth had once gone there with some of the other drama students when, surprisingly, they'd been invited to view a performance.

"I wouldn't say that," she objected. "I very much enjoyed your *Cyrano* production." A downright lie. It had been lousy. But she'd only seen the dress rehearsal. Heaven forbid that a group of Negro students should be allowed to sit among white spectators at a regular performance! Professor Rose had said, "Don't knock it. At least it's the beginning of getting together."

It hadn't felt like getting together. Segregated, in the balcony, at a dress rehearsal. Here in Rockefeller Hall at Spelman, white spectators were allowed to attend any show and sit anywhere they chose. Of course, that shouldn't seem strange. Half the teachers at Spelman were white, as were the president and dean.

She became aware that the young man was staring at her awkwardly, as if he wished to continue the conversation and didn't know how.

"Are you in drama at Emory?" she asked.

"Heck, no. I'm no good at that stuff. I'm in business administration. I saw you at one of the 'Let's Talk' seminars."

Oh. Now she remembered where she'd seen that red hair. Last fall some liberal professor at Emory had dreamed up the idea of arranging meetings between black students and white students. There had been two sessions, one at Morehouse, one at Emory. Ann Elizabeth had attended but hadn't become too involved, especially at Emory. Sitting in that stuffy classroom, she was only vaguely conscious of the anxious white professor standing next to Morehouse's Professor Lindsey. She hardly noticed the intense faces of her fellow black students and strange white ones. Hardly heard the strained, slightly discordant verbal exchange. The day before, she'd been chosen by the Morehouse boys to be their homecoming queen, and she was planning her outfit.

"I wish we had more of those sessions," the young man continued. "We don't get much chance to talk to people of, er, different backgrounds."

"Yes, I know." She smiled at him, feeling a deep sympathy for his confusion and concern. And suddenly she remembered. No wonder he looked familiar! At the Emory seminar he'd caught even her attention when he stood up and made an impassioned speech for social justice, followed by a rather pitiful appeal. How was he to reconcile his own attitude with his father's opposite one? he'd asked. Now she gazed at the serious face before her, wanting to reach out and tell him not to worry. *We're doing all right without your help.*

Impulsively she extended her hand. "I'm so glad you came. And I'm glad you enjoyed the play."

"Especially you." The hand gripping hers was warm and a little damp. "You were great. Are you going into the theater? You could be another Lena Horne. You even look like her."

She smiled. "Most people tell me I resemble Loretta Young."

"I didn't mean...that is, I only meant..." The deep red flush extended to the roots of his hair, and she was sorry for the dig. "That you're very beautiful," he finished.

"Thank you. And yes, I do love the theater. But I'm afraid it's not for me. You see, I don't sing." She didn't add that neither was she the Aunt Jemima type, but he seemed to get the message.

"I'm sorry," he said. "I wish things were different."

Again she felt the need to reassure him. "Not to worry." She laughed. "It's been fun, but I really have no wish to be a star of stage and screen."

"Red!" a voice called. "Are you coming? We're in the car."

"Coming," he answered over his shoulder. Then he said to Ann Elizabeth, "They call me Red. My name is Stanley Hutchinson."

She nodded. "Mine is—"

"I know." He held up the program. "Good night, Ann Elizabeth. I hope we meet again."

"Yes," she said, knowing there wasn't the remotest chance that they would.

In the lobby she found both Sadie and Dan.

"What took you so long?" Sadie scolded. "I'm about to be late for work, because I've been waiting to tell you that you were stupendous!"

"Thank you. Oh, Sadie, I'm so glad you came."

"Wouldn't have missed it."

Wouldn't have missed a possible chance to see Randy, Ann Elizabeth thought, and was sorry her brother hadn't made it.

"Well, don't miss the debut, either. Everybody will be there," she called as Sadie hurried off.

She smiled at Dan, who'd been patiently waiting. "Thank you for the roses," she said. "They're lovely."

"Almost as lovely as you."

"Flattery will get you everywhere!" she said, laughing.

They walked out and sat on a bench under an oak tree near Rockefeller Hall. There were other couples standing around, privileged to spend a few moments together because the boys had been at the play. Spelman was a women's college and Morehouse a men's, and never the twain should meet…at night. Daytime was a different matter. Classes and professors were exchanged. Half of Ann Elizabeth's classes were on the Morehouse campus across the street, on the other side of the library. The library was shared by both colleges and was said to have spawned more romances than master's theses.

"I'm going to miss all this," she told Dan. "Even Mr. Willshoot."

"Willshoot?"

Ann Elizabeth laughed. She sometimes forgot that Dan was relatively new to Atlanta. He was from Washington, D.C., and had attended Howard College before setting up his practice in Atlanta. "That's not his real name. The Morehouse boys just named him that because he's always insisting that he 'will shoot.' He's Spelman's security guard and it's his job to see that the boys say goodbye at the gate and don't accompany the girls to their dormitories."

She watched the lights going on one by one in the dorms, casting a faint glow through the trees. She listened to the laughter and chatter of the girls and the muted whispers of the couples around them. She became suddenly aware that this part of her life was almost over.

"I feel a little sad," she said. "Something is ending. And nothing's beginning."

"Something could begin. And I suggest it be with me."

"Dan…I'm not sure."

"We belong together, Ann Elizabeth."

"I know. But I'm just not sure I'm ready to begin a marriage."

"Okay, okay." He took a pack from his pocket and

drew out a cigarette. "Tell me. What *would* you like to begin?"

"That's just it. I don't know. I honestly don't know."

"Well, it's not over yet. There's graduation. And your debut."

"That's just part of the launching." But launching into what?

I majored in drama, she thought, just because I like it. Nothing I can do but teach it, maybe. She recalled her conversation with the redheaded boy. No yearning to be an actress, a movie star? Or was it simply that she knew she could never be one? The only thing she was suited for was marriage, she concluded. To someone like Dan.

Dan, his face illuminated by the flame from his lighter, stared down at her. "Well, Mrs. Moonlight, do you want time to stop? Do you want things to stay as they are forever?"

"No, no. Of course not. Guess I've got graduation blues."

The chapel bell tolled the curfew hour, and they walked slowly toward Morgan, her dormitory. At the foot of the steps he kissed her and she thought of her father. That same clean antiseptic smell, mingled with a slight odor of cigarette smoke.

Ann Elizabeth's room was on the third floor, and she made her way up the stairs, passing girls in various modes of attire. She borrowed a vase from the matron and stopped to arrange the roses, then continued to her room. She heard the giggling before she opened the door.

"Surprise!" Her crowd—Doris, Etta May, Jennie Lou and Millie. All seniors and all members of the Debutante Club, except Etta May who was from Brunswick, Georgia, and roomed with Doris.

"Moonlight feast for Mrs. Moonlight," announced Millie. "We even got permission."

Ann Elizabeth's eyes brightened at the sight of hot dogs and hot chocolate. "Mrs. Moonlight thanks you from the bottom of her starving heart."

"Lord, Ann Elizabeth, are you ever *not* hungry?"

"Yeah, when I'm asleep. Pass the mustard, please. This is great!"

"You were really very good, Ann Elizabeth," said Millie.

"*She* was good? What about Ed Sanford?" Etta May, her hair tied up for the night in a strange assortment of old socks, leaned over her hot dog and crooned, "'I love you, Mrs. Moonlight, very very dearly.' Oh, if he'd just say that to me!"

Millie chuckled. "Forget it, Etta May. He whispers to Ann Elizabeth onstage and to Eloise Jenkins off-stage."

"Don't see what you want with him, anyway." Doris poured herself another cup of chocolate. "He drinks too much."

"And when he's not lapping it up, he's quoting Shakespeare," Jennie Lou chimed in. "If he ever does make it out of college, he won't have two cents to rub together. Now, if I wanted to hook someone, I'd go after Dan Trent."

Doris fingered a button on her plaid robe and didn't look at Ann Elizabeth. "Yep, he's already established. Gonna be one rich nigger."

"Well—" Jennie Lou smirked "—you'd have to fight half of Atlanta to get him."

"Shut up, Jennie Lou!" Millie's voice was sharp.

"Well, I think Ann Elizabeth ought to know she's not the only pebble on the beach. He's a skirt-chaser."

"Maybe it's the skirts who chase him." Millie bristled and glanced protectively at Ann Elizabeth, who blew on her hot chocolate.

"Maybe." Jennie Lou, glamorous even at bedtime, tightened her silk scarf around her head. "Personally I can't stand the man."

"Good." Millie smiled. "Then it's lucky for you that you won't get a chance to marry him."

"Oh, I didn't say I wouldn't marry him. Just that I can't stand him. A girl would be a fool to turn him down. But take my word—he ain't the marrying kind."

All eyes swung to Ann Elizabeth. She looked up and smiled.

"Hey," she asked, "is anybody going to eat this other hot dog?"

3

June 1942

The debutante ball was held on the Roof Garden of the Odd Fellows Building, an impressive ten-story structure housing the offices of many black professionals. It was located on Auburn Avenue.

Auburn Avenue was across town, but as familiar to Ann Elizabeth as the West Side neighborhood in which she lived. How many times had she traversed the marble foyer of the Odd Fellows Building and mounted the marble steps or boarded the rickety old elevator to her father's office on the third floor? She'd run up and down the hall to visit and receive candy and gifts from the secretaries of other professionals. She'd enjoyed the soda fountain in Yates and Milton's drugstore on the corner of Butler and Auburn, stepped across the street to the Citizens' Trust Bank to make deposits for her father, learned to swim at the Colored YMCA, the neat little building where her father often played bridge with his cronies. She had dined at Mrs. Sutton's Café farther up Auburn and been sent flowers from Sanson's Florist shop. The Herndon Building, another site that housed Negro professionals, was across the street from the Odd Fellows. It was named after Norris Herndon, a family friend of the Carters. Ann Elizabeth seldom had occasion to visit the place, but in the next block stood the shiny new sandstone structure of the Negro Atlanta Life Insurance Company, founded by Herndon, where Ann Elizabeth had once had a summer job. Nearby was the office of Atlanta's Negro daily newspaper, the *Atlanta World.* On the corner was Big Bethel, the imposing edifice that housed the largest colored Baptist congregation in Atlanta. She had spent many hours in Bailey's Royal Theater, the only white-owned business in the area that catered exclusively to colored. Farther up Auburn at the colored branch of the Carnegie Library she had immersed herself in *The Five Little Peppers, The Secret Garden* and many other children's books. On her way to the library Ann Elizabeth passed another church, not as large as Big Bethel, where Reverend Martin Luther King preached the Baptist doctrine.

This was Sweet Auburn, the center of Atlanta's bustling black business district, on a Saturday night in late June 1942. Prominent Atlanta Negroes in formal attire took the elevator to the top floor and climbed the few remaining steps to the Odd Fellows Roof Garden for the debut.

Debut. Beginning. But this was no beginning, Ann Elizabeth thought. More like an end. An end to nineteen years of organized girlhood. The debutantes, all twelve of them, had been just out of the toddler stage when their mothers organized the Doll Club. Carefully selected girls from families of similar backgrounds, they had come to those first meetings clutching their mothers' hands and dragging their waxen dolls with blond curls. They ate cookies and sipped chocolate from tiny china cups until they tired of playing ladies. Then the dolls lay abandoned while their owners rollicked in games of hopscotch, jump rope and hide-and-seek. In high school they called themselves the Sophisticated Ladies and played bridge at their meetings, and danced to popular record music with specially chosen young males at Saturday-night socials under the watchful eyes of chaperoning parents. Now they were debutantes and this was their debut.

The Roof Garden, usually quite bare, really looked like a garden this evening, with branches of flowering dogwood and banks of flowers. The hors d'oeuvres table featured a centerpiece of summer blooms, set under the flickering light of tapered candles. In one corner two younger girls presided over a crystal punch bowl and a couple of waiters served champagne. The debutantes, looking like a rainbow in their different-colored formal gowns, stood in line from five-thirty to seven to be presented to people they had known all their lives.

Helen Rose, in a green crepe-de-chine dress that cleverly camouflaged her plump figure, surreptitiously slipped her foot out of the green satin pump and whispered to Ann Elizabeth, "How long, dear Lord? How long?"

Ann Elizabeth glanced at the tiny watch on her wrist. "Take heart, fellow sufferer. Only twenty minutes more." Then she stretched out a white-gloved hand to Colonel Dalton. "How nice to see you. I'm glad you could come." Had he really been a colonel? she wondered. An honorary title because he was a lawyer? A trick to confuse those who would never address him as Mr.? Funny, she hadn't thought of that before.

The receiving line was thinning out now. People were gathering in small groups to talk and sip their champagne. The band had arrived and instruments were being set up. The dancing was to begin at seven.

"There's Randy!" Helen Rose said.

"Oh, good. I was starting to worry that he wouldn't get here." Ann Elizabeth looked toward the door. Randy, his drab green officer's coat standing out against the black tuxedos, was bending over his mother.

"He's so handsome." Millie, on Ann Elizabeth's left, had also noticed his arrival.

"Yes… He's changed." This was the first time Ann Elizabeth had seen him in his officer's uniform. He *had* changed. From clowning carefree Randy into a serious second lieutenant, William Randolph Carter, Jr., pilot, U.S. Army Air Corps. A tug of sadness pulled on the pride. Something else was ending.

Another man, similarly clad, was with Randy, his eyes sweeping the room curiously as he waited to be presented to her parents. Ann Elizabeth saw her mother, elegant in pink chiffon, greet Randy's friend. Nudged by Helen Rose, Ann Elizabeth turned her attention to a late-arriving Mrs. Jamison. The lady oohed and aahed for several minutes, reminiscing about the time Ann Elizabeth had danced for her women's club.

"Such a darling tiny ballerina in those pink tights and pink ballet shoes. My, my, how the years do fly!"

So Ann Elizabeth missed the progress of her brother and his friend along the line of debutantes. She was rather startled when the officer appeared before her. Randy gave her a hug and told her she looked very pretty. Then he turned to his friend.

"Robert Metcalf, meet my sister, Ann Elizabeth."

Ann Elizabeth glanced up—and up. He was slender, but she was aware of taut muscles under the uniform. It was the face that held her—smooth chocolate-brown, as dark as her father's. His nose was straight, his hair black and close-cropped. He was smiling at her and his teeth were remarkably white against his dark skin. It was a strong face, she decided. But when he smiled, dimples in both cheeks recast the face in a boyish mold. He bent toward her with an athlete's easy grace, and she wasn't sure whether his quizzical smile was admiring or mocking.

She stood mesmerized, able only to utter the same words she'd been repeating all evening. "How nice to see you. I'm so glad you could come."

For some reason this made him laugh, a hearty uninhibited laugh.

"Didn't I tell you?" Randy asked.

"You did. You did. You were right." The mocking yet admiring eyes still held hers.

She wanted to ask him what he'd been told. But then she saw Dan coming across the floor to claim her for the first dance, which was for the debutantes and their escorts only. Dan exchanged warm greetings with Randy and his friend. Then, as the music started, he placed a possessive hand at Ann Elizabeth's waist.

"Our dance. Please excuse us. We'll talk later, Randy." Dan nodded to the two men and led Ann Elizabeth onto the dance floor.

She felt the stranger's gaze following her. She was glad that her lilac chiffon gown was so flattering to her figure, clinging to the knees, then cascading in full accordion pleats that swirled around her high-heeled sandals as they kept pace with the tempo of the music.

Another pair of eyes watched Randy's progress across the floor. Sadie Clayton held her breath. Of course he'd go to his sister first. But then…would he seek her out? Would he even know she was here?

Maybe I *shouldn't* be here, she thought uneasily as

she watched him, laughing and talking, so much at ease with them—those "high-yellow gals with white folks' hair."

She straightened. Of course she should be here. She'd received an invitation followed by a phone call from Ann Elizabeth. "Be sure to come. It's going to be fun. And," she'd added enticingly, "Randy's going to try to make it."

Randy. Once he had called her beautiful. A long time ago, but she'd never forgotten it. In her whole life, no one else had called her beautiful. Not her, with the kinky hair and very dark skin.

It wouldn't be so bad being a Negro, she told herself, if Negroes, like white folks, were mostly all the same color and had the same kind of hair. And if she wasn't the darkest anybody could get, shunned by both races. The guys all wanted girls with light skin and good hair. Downtown it was the high-yellow girls who got the best jobs—waiting tables at the tearooms or running the elevators. Only job she could get was cleaning rest rooms.

Not anymore! With a proud lift of her head she accepted a glass of champagne from a passing waiter. She was now a professional—a registered nurse. Thanks to Mrs. Washington, she thought with a touch of bitterness. Randy's snooty mother had done it not for her, but to get her out of his reach. The plan had worked. While she emptied bedpans, Randy went on to college, frat dances and other women.

The flicker of pride diminished. Something painful caught in her throat as she saw Randy bend toward Millie Thompson and playfully tug one of her curls.

Okay. She hadn't come to see Randy. It was for Ann Elizabeth that she'd trudged through the streets alone in her long dress.

Funny about Ann Elizabeth. That first day at Washington High, when she walked in straight from her highfalutin private school with her smart clothes and prissy manners, everybody in their home room was all set to give her a hard time. Thing was, she didn't know it. Just kept acting like she was queen of the May, so sweet and polite, asking the way to the lab, borrowing and lending. "Need a pencil? Here's one." Couldn't help but like her, though Sadie didn't really get to know her till the next year, when they had to share a locker. They'd been standing in the hall by their locker that day... Like a hot tide, the memory flooded through Sadie, shutting out the people around her, taking her back.

Randy. Blue slacks. Heavy blue sweater with the big white W emblazoned on it. Randy, tall and handsome with that one-sided grin, his blue eyes inspecting her. Speaking to Ann Elizabeth. "Sister dear, who is this little black beauty?"

His words had cut like a whip and she'd spun away. She remembered as if it were yesterday how she'd run along the hall, down the steps, out of the school building. She was on the street before she'd realized that his long legs were keeping pace. He didn't say anything until they'd passed the throng of students. "Hey, what's wrong? What's your hurry?"

She couldn't speak past the lump in her throat. She rushed on, eyes blurring.

"Just wait a cotton-pickin' minute." He stepped in front of her. She tried to step aside. He blocked her way. Every time. Laughing. Like it was some kind of game. "What's wrong? What did I do?"

"You know damn well what you did, you big-shot bully! And you got no right calling me names. You're a nigger, too. And funny-looking. Those blue eyes don't match your face!''

''Touché! You hurt my feelings.'' But he didn't seem hurt. He was laughing.

''Well, you look funny as hell.'' She spit it out, *wanting* to hurt him.

''And you've got a chip on your shoulder as big as a brick.''

''Get out of my way.'' She tried to move on, but the blocking continued.

''Hey, wait! Why are you so mad? I didn't call you names.''

''You did so. You said I was black.''

''You are black.''

''You didn't have to say so.''

''And you're beautiful.''

That stopped her cold. What had he said?

He seemed to be studying her. ''Black as coal. Smooth. Lovely.''

She stared at him, trying to untangle his words. Was he making fun of her?

He bent toward her. ''Don't you know how beautiful you are?''

She stepped back. Gulped. No one had ever called her beautiful. Not ever. Not in her whole life.

He touched her cheek. ''So smooth and even. I love the color of you. What's your name, pretty lady?''

Barely audible, she managed a weak ''Sadie.'' At the same time she was sifting his words, still wondering. Beautiful. *Was* he making fun of her?

''Well, come along, Sadie. I'll walk you home.''

That was the beginning. He had walked her home many times after that, even after he'd graduated and started college. Never minded if her mama had the ironing board up in the living room. Always polite to her papa, even if he was barefoot and in his undershirt. He was the only boyfriend she'd ever had. The only person who had ever called her beautiful.

Sadie sighed. They'd gone their separate ways and she'd seen him maybe twice in the past two years. But...

Yes, she confessed. She had come hoping to see him. She leaned down to touch the skirt of the turquoise dress that had cost her a fortune. Randy had taught her to wear color... "Why do you always stick to black or dark brown?" he'd asked. "You need color!" She hadn't believed him until he bought that pale-blue scarf for her one Christmas, wrapped it around her throat. "See how it brings out the radiance of your complexion!"

No one had ever called her complexion radiant.

"Here you are! Why are you hiding off in a corner by yourself?"

Randy! She'd been so immersed in her thoughts that she hadn't seen his approach. "I'm not hiding. I was just...just..." Speech failed in the whirlwind of emotions engulfing her. Joy set her heart pounding, her pulse racing. Randy. So handsome in his officer's uniform. Blue eyes so striking against his dark skin. Looking down at her with that lopsided grin. Exultation. He had sought her out.

He took the glass from her, stood back to study her. "Lovely. That dress is just the right color. You look radiant." Then he pulled her into his arms. "Let's dance, pretty lady."

Heaven, she thought. Randy is here and I'm in his arms. Thank you, God, for tonight.

* * *

Five dances passed before Randy's friend, the handsome officer, approached her. Ann Elizabeth determined to be bright and composed and tried to conceal her too-eager anticipation.

"Well, how is the Air Corps treating you?" she asked.

"Roughly."

"Don't you like it?"

"Love it."

"Where are you from?"

"Los Angeles."

This was going nowhere.

"Now it's your turn," she said.

"My turn?"

"To start the conversation. Ask me something."

"I don't need to."

"Oh? Why not?"

"I know all about you."

"What do you know?"

"You are a princess." Now she knew the smile was mocking. "You live in a grand castle surrounded by a high wall."

"No moat?"

"Oh, definitely a moat."

"How dreadful! I do hope there's a drawbridge so that a prince can ride across on his white charger to rescue me."

"Dear lady, you are sadly lacking in modern fairy-tale lore."

"Oh?" She raised an eyebrow.

"The modern prince drives a Cadillac."

"Really?" She traced with one finger the insignia on his shoulder. "I thought he came swooping from the clouds wearing a pair of silver wings." She felt his arms tighten about her. His look was penetrating, no hint of mockery in his eyes now. She couldn't stop staring into those eyes. She felt strangely exhilarated. Something was beginning.

The elation did not dim the whole week that Randy and his friend were in Atlanta on leave. Lieutenant Robert Metcalf. Robert. Rob. Ann Elizabeth moved through that week in a daze, helping Randy and Sadie, who seemed to be back in Randy's life, entertain Rob. Tennis at the college, sodas at the drugstore, dancing at the Negro country club. And for Ann Elizabeth, all the familiar activities took on an unfamiliar aura. Rob. She'd never known anyone quite like him. He had an adventurous competitive spirit, so evident in the way he played. Hard. At tennis, cards, whatever. She felt herself straining to keep up.

If he was an eager participant, he also had high expectations. "Hell, Randy. This isn't a golf course. It's a cow pasture," Rob said as he glanced over the roughly hewn nine-hole course that accommodated members of the Negro country club. "Do we have to play here?"

"We do." Randy's deep-blue eyes twinkled.

"What about that course we passed as we came into town? Fabulous fairways. Isn't it public?"

"It is."

"Well?"

Randy turned, grinning as he put down his golf bag. "Well, now, sonny, I know you've lived in our lovely South for only a few months. But mostly you've been caged up at the airfield learning to fly. You don't get around much." Randy thickened his Southern drawl. "Let me explain about the language down here. Down here, 'public' means 'white.' Now, do I tee off first or do you?''

Rob set his jaw, tightened his grip on the golf club and whacked the ball viciously.

That night Rob was again visibly annoyed when he and Ann Elizabeth went to see a film at the Fox Theater. The Fox was a beautiful building fashioned like an Egyptian palace. A wide stone staircase on the outside of the building led to the colored section. It was ornate, impressive—and steep.

Rob hesitated as he gazed up. ''Do we have to climb this?''

''We do.''

He pretended to pant as they climbed. ''Only for you,'' he said as they reached the top. ''Only for you.''

''But it's so lovely up here!'' Ann Elizabeth exclaimed, leaning against the waist-high balustrade and gesturing at the sky above.

''Lovely,'' Rob echoed. But he was looking at her.

The movie was a romance, and its mood followed them into the night. They walked down the steps holding hands, and on the drive back Ann Elizabeth sat close to Rob, her head on his shoulder. When he halted at a stop sign, his lips touched her hair and his finger brushed against her cheek. She felt warm, safe and loved.

As they drove off, a siren wailed behind them. Rob pulled to the curb and stopped. Ann Elizabeth sat up and looked at the police car that had pulled in behind them, its red light flashing. Fear churned in her stomach. She had never been stopped by the police, but Randy had. And others. The episode at the Subers' house flashed through her mind. The police could be quite…quite… Dear God, what had they done?

Two policemen sauntered to the car. One peered in at Rob.

"Why didn't you stop at that stop sign, boy?" The tone was belligerent, ugly.

"I did stop." Rob sounded puzzled. "Why—"

"Who the hell you talking to, nigger?"

Ann Elizabeth held her breath. Prayed.

"Well, I did stop!" Rob's voice was louder now and firm.

The policeman wrenched open the door, grabbed Rob by the collar. "On your feet, nigger! Don't you know how to talk to a white man?"

"I only said—" Rob protested as he was yanked out of the car. The policeman's fist shot out and connected with Rob's chin. The car rocked slightly as Rob fell against it.

Ann Elizabeth quickly slid over to the driver's seat and leaned out. "Oh, please, sir—"

"Hey, Bud, wait!" It was the other policeman who spoke.

"Wait, hell! Didn't you hear the way that nigger was talking to me?" The officer stepped toward Rob, his billy club raised.

"Oh, please, sir," Ann Elizabeth said, anxiously emphasizing the "sir." "He didn't mean any disrespect. He's not from down here, sir, and—"

"Oh, we got a Yankee nigger here, huh, girlie?" The policeman's eyes moved insinuatingly over her body. Rob stirred, and the officer turned back to him, his club raised. "Well, maybe we need to teach him a few things."

The other officer intervened, quickly pulling his partner away. Rob was still leaning against the car. Ann Elizabeth reached out and touched his arm. They

waited, hearing scattered words. "Military…trouble…
nigger club…nigger, ain't he?"

Then the first officer came back, rocking on his heels
as he looked at Rob. "What's your name, boy?"

Ann Elizabeth pressed Rob's arm hard.

"Robert Metcalf…sir."

The policeman grinned. "Lemme see your license."
Rob produced it.

"Humph! From that nigger airfield, huh?"

"Yes, sir."

"Think you'll ever fly one of them planes?"

"We try, sir."

"Well, just as long as you fly in your own territory,
hear?"

"Yes, sir."

"This here your car?"

"No, sir. Her brother's."

"You all going up to that nigger club?"

"Yes, sir."

"Uh-huh." The officer's glance traveled over Ann
Elizabeth again. "Gonna do a little smooching, huh?"

Ann Elizabeth tightened her grip on Rob's arm.

"Yes, sir."

"You know you didn't stop at that sign back there!"

"Sorry, sir. I didn't realize."

"Well, we're gonna let you off this time. But you
better be careful, boy. Watch where you going. You
ain't in one of them planes, you know. You can get in
a heap of trouble around here."

"Yes, sir."

Finally the policeman rejoined his partner, and
slowly, deliberately, the two walked toward the squad
car. Rob didn't move and Ann Elizabeth held her
breath. When they reached their car, the more belliger-

ant officer swiveled around to give them a searching look. Then he climbed inside, executed a U-turn and drove away in the opposite direction.

Rob picked up his hat, got into the car and sat with his head thrown back, breathing deeply. "Son of a bitch!" he muttered. "Goddamn son of—" He broke off. "I'm sorry," he said with an awkwardness that twisted her heart. She knew the apology was more for his helpless posture than for the profanity.

"Rob, I..." What could she say? It was like that time at the Subers' with her father. She felt his shame, his humiliation. "Rob, I was so proud of you."

He sat up and stared at her. "Proud? When I just stood there and let that—"

"That's just it. You restrained yourself."

"Those guns and billy clubs kind of influenced me."

"I know. They could have killed you and never looked back. If you'd made one move, one gesture. But you didn't. You backed down."

"Like a coward." Rob's voice was bitter.

"Like a sensible man who knows what a redneck bigot with a badge and a billy club can do." Tears filled her eyes. "Rob, I would have died. I couldn't stand it if anything happened to you." He was looking at her, his gaze intense. "I know it wasn't easy for you to back down. But I'm glad you did. I'm so proud of you."

"Ann Elizabeth, you are some kind of lady!" He tried to smile and winced.

She raised one hand and gingerly touched his chin, which was beginning to swell. "We'll have to put some ice on that. Let's get Randy and go home."

He regarded her steadily. "Ann Elizabeth, I love you."

"Oh, Rob!" She kissed him ever so gently on his

bruised lip, then pressed her face against the hollow of his throat. His arms wound around her, holding her close for a long long time.

Julia Belle Washington Carter didn't know it then, but she was to have her August wedding, after all.

4

August 1942

"Hey, Rob, you done made a mistake, man! You in the wrong place." Pete Peterson, Rob's best man, had cracked open the door of the pastor's study and was peering out into the chapel.

Rob stared at the back of Pete's head, at the sweat pouring down his neck, glistening on that red hair, so typical of his type, usually called "merino nigger." Pale skin, pale eyes, red woolly hair.

"What the hell do you mean, wrong place? This is the First Congregational Church, isn't it?"

Pete turned, a glint of mischief in his catlike eyes, and jerked a thumb over his shoulder. "Take a look. Nobody but us white folks here."

Too nervous to appreciate the joke, Rob obediently took Pete's place at the door and surveyed the elegant chapel with its stained-glass windows. A world away from the converted clapboard house back home that the deacons had fashioned into Shiloh Baptist, the church he had reluctantly attended as a boy. He strained his eyes trying to glimpse the few dark faces among the many fair-skinned wedding guests rapidly filling the church. There. That was Mrs. Smith. She'd given a party for them. And that big-shot Colonel somebody. He turned back to Pete.

"Oh, there's a few of us darkies here. Just us rich and powerful ones." He made a gesture, classing himself with Dr. Carter who was pacing the floor a few feet away and glancing at his watch every now and then. Probably wondering, Rob thought, if he'd have time to escort his daughter down the aisle before rushing off to the hospital to see some patient.

The pastor's study was warm and stuffy. Rob took out a handkerchief and mopped his brow. His full-dress uniform did nothing to repel the heat. He looked back into the chapel and saw another dark face, his mother's. Thelma Metcalf, neatly but plainly dressed, seemed strangely out of place amidst this throng of sophisticated Atlantans. She hesitated at the entrance, apparently confused, until Randy stepped quickly to her side and slipped her hand through his arm. He bent to whisper something in her ear that made her smile as he ushered her to a front pew.

Rob, seeing her settled, relaxed. His mother had been uncharacteristically silent all week. She was a bit overwhelmed by these rich Atlanta Negroes. Frugal by nature and necessity, Thelma was suspicious of colored people who lived "too high on the hog," who drove expensive cars and dressed "fit to kill." All her life she had contemptuously dismissed such people as "nigger rich." It was Thelma Metcalf's thrift that, after his father died, had saved the family home and seen Rob through high school and college.

Rob had been more than a little concerned about how his mother would be received by the Carters. They weren't exactly jumping with joy at the prospect of him as a son-in-law. But he'd been pleasantly surprised. Old

Mrs. High-and-Mighty had been most cordial to Mama, installing her in the guest room and carefully shepherding her through the bridge parties…"No, Mrs. Metcalf doesn't care to play, thank you"…the showers, and Lincoln Country Club dances—the social swirl naturally attendant on the nuptials of Julia Belle Washington Carter's only daughter. And not by word or gesture did she ever betray to the outside world how deeply disappointed she was by her daughter's choice of husband.

Rob blew his mother an unseen kiss, mopped his brow again and turned back into the study. Damn! He wished this thing was over. Wished he had Ann Elizabeth in Tuskegee away from all this. Alone. Thinking about Ann Elizabeth, he felt his heart skip a beat, stop, then tumble on rapidly. Pulsating, full of excitement, desire…apprehension.

Away from all this? To Tuskegee? Away from that ten-room mansion with its large acreage and towering trees to a tiny bedroom in Mrs. Anderson's shabby little house. Life on a lieutenant's salary of one hundred and ten dollars a month. She had no idea, no conception. If she had, would she have listened to her mother?

He knew Mrs. Carter wanted Ann Elizabeth to marry that smooth-talking pale-faced doctor. In fact, she could hardly restrain herself when they'd told her about their engagement.

"Oh, Ann Elizabeth, are you sure?" She had glanced at Rob, the keen aristocratic nose quivering, her blue eyes accusing.

"Yes, I'm sure." Ann Elizabeth's eyes had been warm and confident. God, how he loved her!

Julia Belle Carter had spoken through dry thin lips. "Ann Elizabeth, honey, you're so young. Don't you want to wait? Perhaps a year... Give yourself more time."

"We don't have any time. Don't you understand? Rob might be sent overseas any day."

Damn, if Julia Belle's eyes hadn't brightened at *that* prospect! "My goodness, he'll be back. You're both so young. You've known each other such a short while. You—"

"No, Mother. We don't want to wait."

"A wedding in August? That's not enough notice! We couldn't possibly manage to—"

"We don't need a wedding."

"Of course you need a wedding! Goodness, what would people think? My daughter—"

"I don't care what people think." Ann Elizabeth had laid a hand on her mother's arm. "We're talking about a marriage, not a wedding, Mother. We love each other and we want to be together." She had stood there in her white tennis shorts looking like a child. Talking like a woman.

Julia Belle's eyes had filled with tears. But she had yielded to her daughter's pleading. "Well, Rob will have to talk to your father."

Rob had approached the sedate Dr. Carter with more trepidation than he'd felt taking off on his first solo flight. Their talk had not gone exactly as he'd expected.

"Tell me about yourself." Dr. Carter had nodded, leaning back in his chair, the tips of his fingers touching. His body was relaxed, his eyes interested and patient—as if he had all the time in the world.

"Well, sir, you know I'm in the Army Air Corps. I make—"

"No, no. Before that. Where were you born?"

"In Los Angeles."

"Tell me about it."

"About Los Angeles?"

"Yes, and about you. Your people."

"Well…" Rob faltered. Damn, what was there to tell? His father had died. His mother worked. His own life—school, football, odd jobs. He found himself talking about his father. Joseph Metcalf had fought in Europe in the First World War. He'd come to California from Alabama because life for an uppity black veteran was not safe in the deep South. Originally he'd wanted to go to Detroit and find work in one of the new automobile factories. But when the riots broke out there in 1919, he took his pregnant wife west, instead. He'd been in Los Angeles only a few weeks when he stopped to help a man fix a broken-down car. Impressed with Joseph's mechanical abilities, the stranded motorist helped him get a job in the maintenance department of a trucking firm.

"My father could fix anything that moved, Dr. Carter." Rob spoke with an intensity that betrayed his pride. "He was always paid a little less than the whites on the job. But he didn't seem to care because he knew, and they all knew, that he was the best mechanic in the shop. Actually, for us, it was a handsome living."

Dr. Carter nodded. "Yes, I imagine so. For a black man in the twenties just before the dawn of the depression."

"Well, Mama was always careful with money, and they bought a duplex in a neighborhood that was turning colored. Mama still lives there." He told Dr. Carter that just as he was about to enter school his father had dropped dead of a heart attack. "Mama took a job as an aide at the county hospital and we managed okay. I did lots of odd jobs—washing dishes, selling papers. I waited tables during the summer and while I was at college.''

"I used to wait tables."

"You!" Rob could hardly believe this.

"Yes. Anything I could get that allowed me to continue my studies.'' The doctor's smile was reminiscent. "Learned the bones of the skeleton between train runs. Had a diagram tacked over my bed in Mrs. Butts's boarding house for dining-car waiters." He seemed to shake off the memory and asked Rob about school.

"UCLA engineering on a football scholarship. That's where I got my taste for flying. Joined the pilot-training course. Those who finished the course were invited to join the U.S. Army Air Corps and I..." He hesitated, swallowed and hurried on, blotting out the painful memory. "They weren't taking colored, so I finished out my senior year. Then I read about Tuskegee. And here I am."

"What happens after the war?" Dr. Carter asked.

Rob again hesitated. He had a dream but no answer that he knew would satisfy Dr. Carter. Rob wanted to design airplanes, but he only said, "With my engineering degree and my flying background I should be able to get a good job. Or maybe start my own business."

The doctor perked up at the latter idea. He told Rob he could count on a steady customer base if he considered setting up shop in Atlanta. "Lots of well-off Negroes here," he said.

The conversation drifted to Ann Elizabeth, about whom there was no disagreement. Each man basked in the other's love and pride.

"Ann Elizabeth is mighty precious to me. I want you to take good care of her."

"Yes, sir, I will."

Dr. Carter gazed at him steadily. "If, for any reason, things don't work out, bring her back to me."

The suggestion had rankled. *What kind of man does he think I am?* Now, in the study, he turned to look at Dr. Carter and discovered that he'd left. Maybe it was time for the wedding to start. He sure as hell hoped so.

Downstairs in the Sunday-school room, Ann Elizabeth—in shimmering clouds of white organza, tulle and fine lace—stood waiting patiently while her mother arranged and rearranged her veil, calling out instructions to the cousins Edwina and Helen Rose.

"No, honey. Put that over this way. That's right. Be careful, honey—don't let the train touch the floor."

Someone handed Ann Elizabeth a sealed envelope with her name scrawled across the front. She recognized the handwriting. Dan. How like him! Always flowers or a note to wish her success.

Dan had been so understanding the night she'd told him about Rob. She had asked him to come over and they'd sat outside on the glider. The air was warm and heavy with the scent of roses and honeysuckle.

"I wanted to tell you before Mother announces it, Dan. I'm engaged. I'm going to be married."

"That pilot?"

"Yes. Robert Metcalf."

Dan was silent. She'd tried to see his face, but it was too dark. She'd wanted to say something, but she didn't know what. *I'm sorry?* But she wasn't sorry. Her heart was singing over and over again, "Oh, Rob, I love you. I love you. I'm so happy." It was hard to subdue the joy, to keep her voice calm. She didn't want to hurt Dan. He was silent for so long that she was startled when he spoke.

"When?"

"August. Well, you know…the war. We didn't want to delay too long."

"I see."

"I wish…" Her mind groped for a soothing word.

"No, Ann Elizabeth. *I* wish. I wish things were different." His hand covered hers. "But I also wish you both happiness. Rob's a lucky guy."

"Thank you."

He had left abruptly soon afterward. She had not been alone with him since. She opened the envelope, expecting the usual best wishes.

Not so. As she read she tried to compose her face, mask the surprise, the…she wasn't quite sure *what* she felt.

"My darling Ann Elizabeth. Though I've told you many times, I don't think you really believe how much I love you. How much I will always love you. I do not mean to intrude upon the happiness of this very special day. Indeed it is my fond wish that this happiness will grow with every passing year. I just want you to know that, if the time should come, if you ever need me, I will be there. I will never marry. It would be unfair. No other woman can ever fill the space I have reserved for you. Be happy. All my love, Dan."

Ann Elizabeth felt tears welling in her eyes. Dear Dan. She did love him. Like a brother. Like Randy. Certainly not like she loved Rob.

The thought of Rob brought a smile to her face. There could be no one else. No one but Rob. Oh, Dan. I hope you'll find someone who loves you as much as I love Rob.

The letter. What on earth would she do with the letter? She certainly couldn't carry it under her bouquet as she walked down the aisle to marry another man.

And it wasn't for her mother's curious eyes. She looked around. Her mother was showing Penny, the little flower girl, how to carry the basket of rose petals. The other girls were combing their hair, powdering. Only Edwina stared curiously at her.

"Edwina, stand in front of me."

"What?"

"Oh, for Pete's sake, just stand there." Balancing herself against the wall, Ann Elizabeth lifted the voluminous folds of her wedding gown, took off one shoe and slipped the note inside.

Later Ann Elizabeth had no thought of Dan as she stood upstairs in the vestibule, listening to Sadie's clear soprano above the tones of the organ.

She smiled. Mother had been so afraid she'd ask Sadie to be a bridesmaid—"She wouldn't fit in, you know." She needn't have worried. Ann Elizabeth wanted her wedding to have the sweet sound of Sadie's voice, clearly enunciating every word she sang. Like a blessing. Moving her now just as it had whenever Sadie led the spiritual during their homeroom devotional in high school. She was glad Mother had insisted on a church wedding. This church was part of her life. Here she'd been christened, had taken her first communion, had participated in pageants for Christmas and Easter. Here she had sat nearly every Sunday of her life in the family pew, next to the window bearing her grandfather's name. How many times had she stared at the stained-glass image of Jesus on the mount and puzzled over the scripture "Blessed are the pure in heart..."

I don't know if my heart is pure. But I do know I love Rob. Please, dear God, help me. Let me be a good wife. Let me make him happy.

The tones of the organ resounded through the chapel,

paused, changed tempo and made a solid melodious announcement. "Here comes the bride!"

Ann Elizabeth Carter took her father's arm and walked down the aisle to the man she loved.

The spacious Carter lawn was ready for the reception. It had needed only a few potted plants from the florist to supplement the natural background of blooming crepe myrtle, roses, honeysuckle and hydrangea. The rented tables, scattered under the towering trees, were draped in white linen and held centerpieces of white gardenias and baby's breath, tied with silver ribbons. Two young students from Morehouse in white waiter's coats poured champagne or ladled punch from the bars set up at either end of the lawn. One large table was laden with dainty sandwiches and hors d'oeuvres. Another table held a five-tier wedding cake surrounded by small serving plates and tiny white paper napkins embossed in silver with "Ann E. and Rob."

"Well, Julia Belle, you've really outdone yourself this time!"

"Oh, Letty, no. I just wanted it to be special. Something for Ann Elizabeth to remember."

"Julia Belle, the wedding was beautiful. Never saw Ann Elizabeth look so lovely."

"Thank you, Dr. Thomas. And Marge. How nice to see you. Have you met Mrs. Metcalf, Rob's mother?" No one could have known that Julia Belle's heart was breaking. Such high hopes she'd had for Ann Elizabeth, and they'd come so close to being fulfilled. She could have married Dan, taken her place among Atlanta's finest. But instead, she was off to God knows where with a nobody. "Oh, no, they won't have time for a honeymoon. Rob, you know, is an officer in the Army Air

Corps. He's needed right back. Oh, how do you do, Mrs. Nelson? So glad you could come. Have you met Mrs. Metcalf, Rob's mother?"

She winced as she watched Thelma Metcalf extend a work-worn hand. She must remind Ann Elizabeth about rubber gloves.

"No, Mrs. Metcalf is from California... No, they'll be living in Tuskegee." In one room! And then what? Dan would have built her a beautiful home right here in Atlanta where she belonged. "How do you do? Yes, a lovely couple. Yes. So happy." Oh, Ann Elizabeth, you do look happy. I want you to stay happy. But why, oh, why...? Now Julia Belle felt a little bit of what her own mother must have felt when she married Will Carter. *He's so dark. What will your children look like?*

But at least Will Carter was a doctor. Robert Metcalf was a uniform with a pair of silver wings that would tarnish after the war. And then what?

"Oh, yes, they are a handsome couple. They're happy." I'm happy for you, Ann Elizabeth. I am, Julia Belle thought, but she could not still the cry in her tortured heart. Why, oh, why couldn't it have been Dan?

"Ann Elizabeth, honey, come on. You and Rob. Cut the wedding cake so you can change clothes. You need to leave soon. Where is the photographer?" Dear Lord, thank you for the sunshine. Don't know what we would've done if it had rained. "I'm glad we had the reception early so you can get to Tuskegee before dark. Ann Elizabeth, stand right here. Here's the cake knife. Wait, Rob. Now. Look down at Ann Elizabeth. Smile."

5

They did not get to Tuskegee before dark. They had started out early enough, the four of them—Randy, Pete, Ann Elizabeth and Rob—in Dr. Carter's big car. They could never have fit in Randy's little roadster, especially with Ann Elizabeth's luggage and the few gifts she'd decided to take, mostly linens and towels. Silver, china and all the rest of the fancier presents would be stored in her parents' attic.

Ann Elizabeth knew she looked attractive in her going-away outfit—pink linen sundress with matching jacket, white gloves and a wide leghorn hat. All for effect—and her mother's photographer. As soon as the car turned the corner, she shed hat, gloves and jacket. The boys also took off their jackets and relaxed for the three-hour drive, laughing and joking about the wedding and the wedding guests.

Randy and Pete, on the front seat, discussed the relative merits of the single girls.

"Couldn't get near most of 'em on account of this handsome fellow," Pete complained.

Ann Elizabeth smiled. Her brother *was* handsome in an odd sort of way with his blue eyes and tan skin.

"What about Helen Rose?" Randy asked. "I thought you liked her."

"Couldn't get near her on account of her mother."

Randy laughed. "Aunt Sophie's on the watch. You know how it goes—best man, maid of honor. That combination is known to lead to marriage."

"Marriage!" Pete shrieked as if frightened by the word. Then he glanced apologetically toward the back seat. "Nothing against the institution, you understand. Just wasn't what I had in mind."

"Well, it's what Aunt Sophie always has in mind," Randy said, chuckling. "But not for you, you lowly lieutenant. Her thinking runs more along the lines of doctors and lawyers."

"Stop it, Randy!" Ann Elizabeth laughed. "Don't worry, Pete. Rob and I will have Helen Rose down for a visit and you needn't be afraid to date her. I promise she won't ask you to marry her." She leaned back against Rob. *Rob and I.* That had a nice sound.

"Comfortable, Mrs. Metcalf?"

"Oh, yes." Mrs. Metcalf. Mrs. Robert Gerald Metcalf! She looked down at the plain gold band on her finger next to her engagement ring with its tiny diamond solitaire.

"All paid for," Rob had said. "A lucky night at poker!"

"Rob, do you gamble much?"

The two in the front seat whooped and Rob gave her a startled glance. "Whatever made you ask that?"

"I thought…well, I don't know. But…do you?" she persisted a little anxiously.

The creases in his face deepened as he smiled down at her. "Well, no. Not now that I have something more interesting to do on Saturday nights."

"Good!" said Randy. "With old lover boy out of the game maybe the rest of us will have a chance."

Lover boy. Tonight. What would it be like? Tonight,

alone with Rob. Her husband... "As natural as breathing," her father had said. "Making love is part of loving. If you really love Rob..."

She did love him. She truly did. On impulse she reached out to touch his chin. Quickly he dipped his head to kiss her hand, and the look in his eyes, the feel of his lips against her palm, made her blush. But the sense of excitement was tinged with anxiety, and she turned away to stare out the window.

They were past the city streets now and the lush green landscape that was rural Georgia swept by them. Rolling hills, tall pines, fields of corn and cotton. There, set back on a little mound, was a run-down house around which a group of black children played. The sight was familiar to Ann Elizabeth. Often while visiting in the country with her uncle Jimmy's family, she'd sat in his car outside just such a shack while he attended a patient inside.

Nostalgia gripped her as she remembered summer visits with Uncle Jimmy and Aunt Sarah in the small town of Monticello. Long sunny fun-filled days running free as a bird with her cousins. The pungent odor of the cedar tree as she sat high in its branches and watched a faraway train race by. The feel of warm earth on bare feet and the color of her bath water from the soil of red clay hills. The taste of fresh juicy peaches, watermelon, sweet corn on the cob, crisp fried chicken and rich warm milk brought straight from the cow and strained by Annie, the girl who came daily to help Aunt Sarah.

Now they were passing a field of cotton. She saw a lone black laborer digging among the plants where small balls of white were beginning to burst through the brownish leaves.

"You don't see many peach trees out this way," she said almost to herself.

"Uh-huh." Rob was leaning back against the seat, his eyes closed. Ann Elizabeth nestled close to him, caught up in her own thoughts.

Yes, during those summers in Jasper County she'd seen a few fields of cotton, but mostly she remembered the peach trees. Dwarf peach trees standing in stately rows as far as the eye could travel. But this was the same country atmosphere, she thought as hot humid air drifted through the open car window. The lush odor of fresh-turned earth, meadow grass and cow manure. The scent of open countryside, the countryside that made her feel exposed and vulnerable. She gave a tiny involuntary shudder.

Memories of the past were bittersweet. Something sinister and threatening lurked behind and nibbled at the peace of those carefree summers.

One day a man had been dragged from his shack. He'd been found the next morning hanging from a tree, his body riddled with bullets. Ann Elizabeth never knew what crime he had committed, but she'd heard Annie whisper to Mandy, who came to wash clothes and had the peculiar habit of eating dry starch, that he'd "talked back to Mr. Parsons." And she'd heard Uncle Jimmy whisper to his wife that he couldn't tell if the man had died from the hanging or the bullet wounds. "Painful either way…pitiful." Ann Elizabeth had never seen her uncle look so helpless. These kinds of conversations were always conducted in whispers when children were nearby.

One thing they talked about quite openly. Williams Farm. Maybe because it had happened so long ago, before she was born, and carried no threat of present danger.

Williams, a white farmer, would take black prisoners from the courthouse to work out their fines at his farm. But the fines were never worked out. The cruelly treated and forever enslaved prisoners were never released. Those who rebelled were simply killed and tossed into the river. Whispered rumors were ignored because the victims were black and Williams was a powerful man in Jasper County. But when eleven bodies chained together floated beyond the county line, the travesty could no longer be ignored. Only then, in another county, was Williams brought to trial and finally imprisoned. That was in 1924, Mama said, two years after Ann Elizabeth was born. She must have been about five when, with her parents and Uncle Jimmy, she'd viewed the abandoned farm. The sight still burned in her memory. The small broken-down boxlike cells, the remnants of heavy rusty chains, still hanging from the walls... Randy had jumped into one of the cells, draped a chain around himself and grinned at them. Mother had snatched him away, her face pale, and yelled at Uncle Jimmy, "I told you we should never have brought the children here!" Uncle Jimmy had laughed. "Oh, sis, don't be so upset. The kids don't even know what it's all about. And this kind of thing is over now—over and done with."

Over and done with. So why was she thinking about it today? The hanging chains, her mother's pale face and the Yellow River flowing swiftly by.

Ann Elizabeth gave herself a shake. Why was she recalling this now, on her wedding day? Why this sudden feeling of dread? As if she'd stepped from a safe familiar world into—what? The knowledge of what had happened was a specter buried deep inside. But always there. It made a body nervous, edgy, always balancing between the pleasure of the present moment and the fear of what could happen in the next.

It wasn't something a person talked about. But she knew the men felt it, too, the way they grew silent as they drove through the small towns. The way Randy drove slowly, carefully, past the neat houses with white picket fences and the storefronts where people lounged or ambled by.

When Randy stopped at a roadside gas station to fill the tank, Ann Elizabeth gazed longingly at the door marked Ladies. All that punch at the reception. She needed to go. But she knew better than to ask.

Helen Rose had asked last summer when she and Sidney Smith were driving to Uncle Jimmy's. Actually Helen Rose was fair enough to pass and sometimes did so to suit her convenience. She must have forgotten about Sid, who was indisputably black. Arrogant, too. When her request was rudely refused, Sid ordered the man to shut off the pump. "If we can't use your facilities, we don't need your gas." He paid the forty-two cents due and drove off. A hundred yards from the station he was stopped for "speeding" and taken to jail. If it hadn't been for Uncle Jimmy, who was well-known as the colored doctor in the county, there was no telling what could have happened to him. Even so, his fine was three hundred and fifty dollars.

"Stupid boy," Uncle Jimmy had said. "You have to be careful how you act in this area. He ought to know that."

"Stupid girl," Julia Belle had said. "Helen Rose knows better. Men!" she had declared, shaking her head. "Sometimes they feel a need to flex their muscles, especially for and in front of their women. It's your duty, Ann Elizabeth, never to force your man into a battle he hasn't the slightest chance of winning!''

"Another thing Helen Rose ought to know," she continued. "Playing white is a dangerous game. Like that time on Stone Mountain."

"They thought she was white, Mother," Ann Elizabeth had said. "She wasn't playing white."

"She was getting ready to. Like it was some kind of game. Lord! If she was found out, they could all have been lynched!"

Ann Elizabeth shuddered. If she hadn't been sick with a fever, she might have been with them that Sunday, and unlike her cousins, she was recognizably colored, as was Sidney Smith, who'd planned to meet them for a picnic. Her cousins—Helen Rose and Uncle Jimmy's kids, George, Ruth Mae, John and Edwina— were on their way. They were all high schoolers except George, who had graduated and was driving the secondhand Dodge, his graduation present from Uncle Jimmy. On the mountain they encountered a mob. The Ku Klux Klan was having a big rally.

"When that man stopped us," Ruth Mae had said later, "it scared the bejesus out of me! I tried to be cool when he just looked at us and invited us to join the rally. Then that silly Helen Rose pipes up with 'We'd love to,' and I almost peed in my pants! Thank goodness George was driving! He declined ever so politely and got us off that mountain as quick as he could."

"Yeah," Ruth Mae had continued. "We met Sid and the others, turned them back and had the picnic at Washington Park." She'd paused dramatically. "Just suppose we'd stayed and the Klan had seen us with Sid. You know how dark he is. We could've been in real danger!"

I'm in danger of wetting my pants right now, Ann Elizabeth thought as she watched the door open and an attractive woman in a red checkered dress emerge. She tossed her long blond hair, put a comb in her purse and walked to the car in front of theirs. She smiled at the man who was driving as she slipped into the seat beside him.

Ann Elizabeth felt a wave of pure envy. Such a simple thing. Comb your hair, refresh your lipstick, relieve yourself.

Oh, well, she could wait. When they came to a town with a depot... They always had facilities for colored at the railroad station.

As they drove into Alabama, there was a drastic change in the weather. Thunder roared and great bolts of lightning flashed across the sky. The rain came hard and heavy, and the windshield wipers struggled against the torrents. Luckily there were few cars on the road.

"Blessed is the bride the sun shines on," Pete teased.

"It was shining when I got married! Anyway, I like it." Somehow she felt safer as the rain pelted the car, closing them inside. "The rain now doesn't count, does it, Rob?"

"No, it doesn't, sweetheart. I promise that your path will be only roses and sunshine."

She smiled at him, rested her head against his shoulder and was soon fast asleep.

She was jolted awake when the car gave a sudden lurch, skidded and something went bump-bump-bump.

"What the...?" Randy braked to a stop. "Flat tire."

"Well, I'll be damned," Pete said. "I thought a car like this..."

"The bigger they are, the harder they fall," Randy assured him cheerfully. "Must have picked up a nail."

"That does it," Rob said. "Next time I get married I'm taking the train."

"Next time! Robert Metcalf, you...you..." She playfully beat his chest with her fists, and he laughed and kissed her.

"Hey, man, you're not going to stay under this tree, are you?" Pete asked. "One rule about lightning is to stay way from trees."

"I'm not moving until that tire is changed. You want to change it in this storm, be my guest." Randy leaned back in his seat and prepared to take a nap.

"Honey, go back to sleep," Rob said. "We've got a long wait."

By the time the rain had stopped and the men got out to change the tire, Ann Elizabeth felt as if her bladder would burst. She stood on the wet pavement and looked around. It was growing dark now.

"Randy," she called, glad that Rob and Pete were busy with the jack. "I gotta go," she whispered.

"Can't you wait?" he asked, glancing doubtfully toward the trees that bounded the road.

"No, I can't!"

"The ground's awfully wet."

"I know, and I don't plan to ruin my new sandals," she said as she took them off. "You just check behind that tree. I don't want to step on any snakes in my bare feet."

A few minutes later as she stood behind the dripping tree, she could hear the curses of the men and the clanking of their tools. They were having trouble with the lug nuts or something. But she couldn't care about that or their being only a few feet away. The dazzling bride of a few hours, her bare feet sinking into the mud, gave a great sigh as she pulled up her pink linen dress and squatted.

As she stood, she saw the headlights of an approaching car coming around the bend. She caught her breath as it slowed and stopped.

Dear God…not the police. Please. Surely they couldn't be doing anything wrong—just changing a tire. Were they parked where they shouldn't be? She heard the car door slam and peered anxiously around the tree. Not the police. But he was white. Tall and skinny with stringy blond hair, dirty overalls. Poor white trash. She held her breath. Worse than the police. A man with nothing to flaunt but his white skin could be the most vicious of bigots.

"What y'all doin', boys?" he asked in the familiar cracker drawl.

"Got a flat." That was Randy. "I think we picked up a nail."

Sir, Randy, say sir, Ann Elizabeth silently pleaded, her hand pressed against her mouth.

"Can't do nothin' with that little ol' wrench." The man spat out a huge wad of tobacco. "Ain't you got a lug wrench? That's what you need."

"'Fraid not." Randy grunted as he strained. "Damn! Can't move it."

"Here. I got a lug wrench. Just wait a minute. Y'all can't do nothin' with that."

Ann Elizabeth leaned against the tree, weak with relief. There was no trouble. He had stopped to help. Emerging from the shrubbery, she saw the white man shake his head in disgust. "Ain't you never used a lug wrench, boy? Move. Lemme have it," he said as he pushed Randy aside and got down to work.

Ann Elizabeth, recklessly wiping her feet with one of

the new gift towels, listened to the laughter and the jokes as together the men speedily changed the tire. On impulse she rummaged in the back for the large portion of wedding cake her mother had packed, then wrapped a generous slice in a napkin.

"Shucks!" The man shrugged off their thanks. "'Tweren't nothin'." But he grinned broadly, cleaning his hands on his overalls before he took the cake. "Well, now, that's right nice of you."

"It was kind of you to help," she said, glad he would never know the cake was more apology than thanks. Never again, she thought as he drove away, would she judge a man by his drawl or his skin or his poverty.

The three-hour trip had now turned into five, but Randy said they'd have to stop in Notasulga to get the tire repaired. He didn't plan to travel without a spare. It was quite dark now, and the air was muggy after the storm. Ann Elizabeth's skin felt clammy, and she was tired and hungry. While they waited at the gas station for the tire to be fixed, she stared at the lighted diner across the street. It looked clean and cozy.

Pete voiced her thoughts. "Damn! I sure could go for a sandwich and a cold drink."

"Well, just run across the street and get it," Rob said. "What was that you said in church about you white folks?"

"Trouble is," Pete answered, "my nappy hair just might give me away. And you know what they call a yellow colored boy in Alabama."

"What?" Ann Elizabeth asked.

"Nigger!"

They all laughed and Pete suggested Randy might do the honors since he had the highest rank. Surely they wouldn't refuse a first lieutenant of the United States

Army who just wanted to carry out a few sandwiches and—

Randy snorted. "You know what they call a colored general in Alabama? That is, if there ever was one..."

"Nigger!" they chorused, bursting with laughter.

"Honey?" Rob looked down at her. "Are you hungry? They might let us carry something out. I'll go over and see."

"Oh, no! No." Ann Elizabeth's voice was a little shrill as she placed a restraining hand on Rob's knee. *Never force your man into a battle he can't win.* She reached for the box of wedding cake. "Who needs bread when we have cake? Awfully expensive cake, too. You wouldn't believe what Mother paid for it." She talked rapidly. "Randy, why don't you buy some Cokes and—"

"Sure crowded over there," Pete interrupted. "Who are all those men lining up outside?"

"And all dressed alike," Randy observed.

"Well, I'll be damned!" Rob's voice was a whisper.

"What?"

"Don't you see that PW on their backs? They're prisoners of war."

"Hey!" Pete jerked his head and stared. "The enemy! I thought we'd have to go all the way to Germany to see them."

"Is there a prison camp near here?" Ann Elizabeth asked.

"Nope." Rob rubbed his chin with the back of his hand. "They're probably on their way to a camp. Just passing through and stopped to eat."

"Eat!" Pete sat up. "Ain't that some shit! They're serving German prisoners and we..."

"Well," Randy drawled, "don't you know what they call a German prisoner in Alabama?"

"A white man."

"You got it. Letting you fight him don't give you the right to set down and eat with him, boy! Don't let them bars on your shoulder get you in trouble!" Randy, with his exaggerated accent, was in excellent stride.

Ann Elizabeth laughed with the others. It was so crazy it was funny, even when you were wet and cold and on the butt end of the joke.

6

It was after midnight when they reached Tuskegee and drove straight to Mrs. Anderson's, where Rob had procured a room for himself and his bride. Apartments on the base—for military and civilian workers—were still in the planning stage. By the time they were ready, Rob knew he'd be overseas. He didn't mention this to Ann Elizabeth. He simply told her they'd be in good company. "Practically every married couple is renting a room from the colored homeowners in Tuskegee Institute, which is right beside the town of Tuskegee. It's one hundred-percent colored, and it houses the college. Even has its own postmark. It's completely distinct from Tuskegee itself, which is predominately white."

"I know." She'd smiled and he realized he'd been talking too much. "I've been there, Rob. Not recently, but several years ago with Dad. Some kind of medical meeting at the Veteran's Hospital."

"Oh." Of course she'd know. Tuskegee wasn't that far from Atlanta. But he still felt anxious. "Mrs. Anderson's a widow and works at the college. She'll be away during the day and you'll have the house to yourself. Anyway, she's very nice. It won't be too bad—living with her, I mean."

"I'll love it," she said. "You'll be there." She stood on tiptoes to give him a kiss that was almost reassuring.

But now, when they stopped in front of Mrs. Anderson's little house, the anxiety returned. How would Ann Elizabeth like sharing a bath, cooking in someone else's kitchen, with separate cabinet and refrigerator space apportioned to her?

After the men unloaded the luggage, Randy and Pete drove off. Rob lifted Ann Elizabeth over the threshold into the house. He kicked the door shut and felt some apprehension as he surveyed the living room for the first time through Ann Elizabeth's eyes. Too small for the overstuffed blue sofa and the two matching chairs, the shadow boxes on the wall, the clutter of mementos. So different from the spacious elegance she had left. Had he been wrong to bring her here?

"Welcome home, Mrs. Metcalf," he said through dry lips.

She slid to the floor and looked around. He held his breath.

"This is…nice," he heard her say. "So cozy and clean, and look, Rob! A gift." She pointed to the gaily wrapped package on the coffee table. "For us," she said, taking from it the attached envelope. "See? 'To Lt. and Mrs. Robert Metcalf.' Lt. and Mrs. Robert Metcalf," she repeated, turning to him with shining eyes. "I like the sound of that." She carefully unwrapped the package, revealing three fluffy white guest towels, a quilted red rose embossed on each. "Oh, Rob… It's such a beautiful and *symbolic* gift, don't you think?"

"Huh?"

"Guest towels for our mutual bathroom. Like she's saying we're welcome to share her home."

He nodded and smiled as he watched her open the envelope. "'The house is yours for tonight,'" she read.

"'Have a happy beginning. Love, Mamie Anderson.'"
Ann Elizabeth glanced up.

"Wasn't that thoughtful of her!" she exclaimed. "I
like her already. I can tell she's a very perceptive, very
sweet person."

"You're sweet," he said, taking her in his arms. Everything was going to be all right.

As Rob approached their bedroom door, the delicate
spicy-sweet aroma he'd come to associate with Ann
Elizabeth permeated the air. His pulse quickened and
his hand tightened on the champagne bottle.

He paused in the doorway to gaze at his bride.

The light from the shaded lamp cast a soft glow on
Ann Elizabeth. She wore a white silk negligee and
looked so fresh and pretty that his heart leapt with desire. Her face was flushed, her hair damp and curling
from the steamy bath. One hand timidly touched the
ruffled lace collar of her robe. The ruffle stirred slightly
in the breeze.

Breeze? There was no breeze!

It was Ann Elizabeth trembling. She was looking not
at him but at the bed. Her eyes were wide and frightened.

Quietly he withdrew.

When he returned, she was sitting on the edge of the
bed, stiffly and primly, like a child. She turned to smile
up at him.

He set the tray with two steaming mugs of hot chocolate on the bedside table.

"You had a long day," he said, and kissed her lightly
on the lips. "I brought you a nightcap."

"How nice! Thank you, Rob." She sounded polite.
Distant.

He sat in the big chair across from her and regarded her thoughtfully as he sipped his chocolate. She clutched her mug with both hands, holding on for dear life.

"This is so good. How did you know this is just what I wanted? We used to make hot cocoa in the dorm. I remember before my graduation—it was a surprise party…" She spoke rapidly as she always did when she was nervous. As she had done tonight, making sure he wouldn't attempt to go into that diner. Trying to distract them.

How I love her. He stood up, took the empty mug from her and placed it on the tray with his. Then he turned and pulled her to her feet. One feathered slipper fell from her foot as he lifted her. Returning to his chair, he cradled her in his lap and kissed the top of her head.

"Tell me about it."

"About what?" Her voice was a small whisper against his chest.

"About the surprise party," he said, trying to quell the passion rising within him at the feel of her firm body under the thin silk.

"Oh." She sounded relieved. "It was Doris, Millie and Jennie Lou. And Etta May. They surprised me. I'd been in this play."

"Oh?"

"About this silly woman who wanted to stay young forever. It was nice, though."

"The play?"

"No. The surprise party. I was feeling kind of sad that night."

"Why?"

"I don't know exactly. I told Dan—"

"My competition."

"Oh, no!" she said quickly, and looked earnestly at him. "It was never Dan." She hesitated. "He was my friend...is my friend. But I love you."

He found himself wondering how Dan would have handled this night.

"Go on," he prompted. "You told Dan..."

"Well...that it felt like something was ending."

"And like the lady in the play, you wanted things to stay as they were forever?"

She laughed. "Funny. That's exactly what Dan asked. I told him it was more like everything was ending and nothing was beginning. And then..." She fingered a button on his pajama jacket. "Then I met you."

He could hardly restrain himself. To ease the tension he began to croon the lovely and romantic lyrics of "Blue Moon." Then he said softly, "You are my dream, Ann Elizabeth. You are my love."

She straightened his collar, and the touch of her fingers against his neck sent a wave of excitement through him.

"You have a beautiful voice, Rob. And I love that song. Sing it all," she urged, settling herself in his lap.

He swallowed hard and began again. "'Blue moon, you saw me...'"

He finished the last stanza and looked down at her. Her eyes were closed and her breath came softly, regularly. He watched her for a long time. Then resignedly, he untied the robe and let it slip to the floor. His breath caught as he gazed at the delicate curves of her slender body revealed so tantalizingly in the sheer low-cut negligee.

All the youthful energy of his twenty-two years welled up, combining with the love and desire, gripping him in an almost uncontrollable passion. He caressed one small breast through the silk. She stirred, trying to find a more comfortable resting place on his shoulder. He sighed heavily. Hopelessly. Then lifted her and tucked her tenderly into bed.

He frowned at his pajamas, stiff in their newness. Bought especially for tonight.

Hell, she was asleep. He might as well be comfortable. He shed the offending pajamas, switched off the light and climbed into bed beside his sleeping bride.

Ann Elizabeth stirred in her sleep, moving closer to the warmth. Basking in the rare peace and comfort, she almost drifted into sleep again. Then, startled by a movement beside her, she was instantly awake.

Rob!

It struck like a bolt of lightning. She'd fallen asleep on their wedding night! What must he think of her?

Stealthily she looked at the face on the pillow beside her. She had never noticed how long his lashes were. But then she'd never before seen him asleep. The chiseled features, the full lips, seemed even more handsome in repose. She reached out to touch his face, then drew back, consumed by guilt. She had not meant it to be like this.

She lay back and stared at the stiff white unfamiliar curtains, the soft rosy light of early dawn that filtered through the window. Her wedding night, and she'd fallen asleep! She tried to remember how it had happened.... He'd held her on his lap. She'd felt secure, nestled in his arms. She'd asked him to sing, and he had. And then she'd drifted off.

How could she! Vividly she recalled her father's words, words that had surprised and impressed her that night only a few weeks before her wedding. He'd sat on the glider beside her, touched her cheek.

"Ann Elizabeth, your education in some areas has been sadly neglected."

Puzzled, she'd asked what he meant.

He smiled. "Do you know the attributes of a perfect wife?"

She guessed she hadn't thought about it.

"Well, a perfect wife, my darling, is a lady in the parlor, a cook in the kitchen and a whore in the bedroom."

"Oh, Dad." She felt the hot color rush to her cheeks.

"And I think the last is ten times more important than the first two."

"Oh, Dad." That was all she could think to say.

"An old adage, kitten. It's trite but true. I think a husband will forgive anything—dirty house, dirty dishes, burnt roast—if he's happy in bed."

Ann Elizabeth had thought of her mother. The perfect lady. Was she...? She almost missed her father's next words.

Not that it mattered much, she thought now, a little crossly. He had given no instructions. Just advice and warnings.

"Don't believe that old saying about the way to a man's heart being through his stomach. Most marriages are made or broken in bed. Work on pleasing your husband there."

"How?"

On this he'd been vague. "As natural as breathing. If you really love Rob..."

She knew she loved Rob. And yes, in that way. His kisses thrilled her as no one else's ever had. But she felt so unsure. Afraid of not pleasing him. Was that why she'd gone to sleep? When she had planned to be so warm, so loving. She closed her eyes and the tears rolled down her cheeks.

"Darling!" Rob's voice startled her. "What is it? Why are you crying?"

Numbly she shook her head.

"Ann Elizabeth, tell me. What's troubling you?"

She wiped her face with her fist. "I'm so…so…" She choked. Stupid. "I don't know how."

"How?"

"How to be a whore."

"A *whore?* But, sweetheart, you're not! You could never be—"

"But I want to!" She was vehement. Angry.

"But…" Rob stared at her, not comprehending.

Haltingly, in jerky sentences, she told him what her father had said. "I didn't mean to go to sleep, Rob. I meant to be…like he said. I just don't know how. I…"

But Rob had flopped back on his pillow. His head rocked from side to side as he laughed uproariously.

"It's not funny!"

He couldn't seem to contain the laughter.

"Don't," she pleaded. "I'm sorry. I wanted to please you. And I was afraid I couldn't. That's why I went to sleep."

He sat up then, but the laughter remained in his eyes. "Darling, you went to sleep because you were tired. You had a long hard day and I expect the chocolate contributed."

She shook her head. "No, I was afraid I couldn't…"

"I thought you were afraid of *me*."

She turned to him quickly. "Afraid of you? Never! I love you. I just don't know…"

"How to be a whore?" He took her in his arms,

whispered against her ear, "Oh, my darling, let me teach you."

Much later Ann Elizabeth looked at Rob lying with one arm around her, his eyes closed.

Dear God, she hadn't known what love was. Until now. Never had she felt so fulfilled, so completely his. It was wonderful!

A thought struck her. Had it been so for him? Or had she been too eager, too grasping? She felt herself blush. She hadn't been able to resist touching him. Even now. With her forefinger she reached up, tracing the line of his jaw to his full lower lip.

Rob ducked his head, caught her finger between his teeth. "Gotcha!"

"Rob, I thought you were asleep."

"I would be if you could keep your hands off me!"

"Oh, Rob, am I too... Did I...?"

"Loved it!" He grinned. "Ann Elizabeth, can you cook?"

"Cook? Of course I can cook. I've been cooking since I was ten."

"Then relax, honey. You've made the grade."

"Grade?"

"Perfect wife."

7

First Lieutenant Robert Metcalf gently pulled back the stick and eased the throttle forward to lift the P-40 into the air. He felt the same thrill of excitement he always felt when the plane began to soar onward, upward, farther and farther from the red clay hills of Tuskegee, from the hangars and rooftops, the green trees and farmlands that dotted the landscape.

Release. Escape. An exhilarating sense of freedom coursed through him as the river became a band of ribbon, the trees like tiny shrubs. Alone, enclosed in his capsule, he was safe—far above petty jealousies and prejudices. Free!

He sent the plane forward at high speed, then turned sharply, moving in the opposite direction, looped, dived and just in time shot upward. Over and over, all the maneuvers he'd learned, and then he practiced new ones of his own making. Soaring, circling, somersaulting and loving every minute of it—the quick response of the plane to his touch, the sheer power.

The power. So vastly different from gliders, always subject to air currents. And why was he thinking of those gliders? It was more than six years since he'd built and flown gliders at Tech High. But that was where he'd first experienced the joy of flying. He had been even more fascinated by the structure and design of planes, had won a prize for a special design of his own.

Yep, it was the gliders that had started the urge to pilot engine-driven planes. Not that he'd ever expected to have the chance.

He supposed it was football that gave him the chance. His high-school coach had insisted on college prep courses. "You can get a scholarship just like that." He was right.

Fresno State had snapped Rob up. And in his junior year, Fresno was chosen as one of the colleges to implement the Civilian Pilot Training Course, sponsored by the U.S. Army Air Corps. Rob was one of the first to sign up.

He thought of those little planes in which he'd learned to fly. *Crop dusters! Couldn't touch you, baby!* He ran a loving hand across the instrument panel of the P-40. Still, it was in those fragile little planes that he got his first taste of flying. It had been fun, just as everything at college had been fun, particularly the football that was paying his tuition. More than tuition. Adulation, prestige—he was "Flash" Metcalf, Fresno's halfback and cocaptain of the team. He was also part of the team in the Civilian Pilot Training program, one of twenty who finished the course.

Part of the team. He felt a painful stirring deep in his chest as he remembered. He had been so stupid. So excited when the notice came from the Army. Joe Tillman, one of his teammates, had alerted him.

"Hey, Flash, you seen the bulletin board?"

Rob shook his head. He never checked the board except at exam time. "Gotta go, man. Late." He started running for his psychology class.

Joe tagged along. "You gotta see it. The Army wants to sign us up."

"Army?" Rob frowned, never missing a stride. "Who the hell wants to join the Army?"

"Air Corps," Joe panted. "Army Air Corps."

Rob stopped, faced him. "What?"

Joe nodded. "They'll take us as a team. We can all train together, even get in the same squadron." Joe went on to explain that an Army officer would be at the college the next week to interview those students who had completed the CPT course.

They went wild with excitement. The Army Air Corps! No more crop dusters. Real planes.

Rob again touched the instrument panel. Yes, it was the thought of this plane, this speedy little P-40, that had lured him into the conference room that cold rainy February day. A tall dark-haired man in U.S. Army dress, a major in rank, sat at the front desk, the American flag on his right and a lieutenant standing on his left. Rob and his buddies piled in, jostling, joking, kidding each other.

"You better forget it, shorty. Gotta pass a physical, you know."

"Oh, yeah? Well, you better gain a few pounds, skinny."

When the major stood to speak, the room fell quiet. He was articulate, well versed in his subject, and the words rolled off his tongue in a crisp New England accent. He spoke of the power and prestige of America. Opportunities and benefits of the Army Air Corps. Honor, duty, democracy. His words excited and inspired, got them keyed up, patriotic, anxious to serve.

As they stood in line to sign up, Joe touched Rob on his back. "Well, Flash, here we go again."

Rob nodded. It was good to be joining up with friends. When it was his turn, he stood in front of the major, smiling eagerly.

The major looked up and his eyes narrowed. "Just what the hell are you doing here?"

He hadn't understood. Somewhat surprised at the man's tone, he'd simply answered, "I...well, I'm here to sign up with the rest of the guys."

"The United States Army Air Corps is not looking for night fighters. Get out of this line."

Stunned, Rob stood silent.

The major's face reddened and he bellowed, "Move! Get the hell out of this line!"

Everyone had stopped talking. Rob was rooted to the spot. Humiliation burned in his face as he began to understand. Damn! How could he have been so naive? But when you didn't expect it...when you were sailing along, part of a group and—

"What's the matter with you? Can't you understand English? I told you to get out of this line."

The young lieutenant moved then, pulled Rob to one side of the room. "Listen, I'm sorry to have to tell you this, but the truth is...well, it's regulation. Negroes are not admitted to the Air Corps."

Several of the other guys had followed and crowded around them.

"What's the matter?"

"Why can't he get in?"

Rob walked away as the lieutenant began to explain. As he slammed out the door he heard their protests.

"Damn shame! America? Ain't that hell? Stinks, man!"

Joe ran after him. "Damn it, Flash, if you can't go, I'm not going."

"Don't be a fool. Go back in there." Not looking at Joe, Rob walked rapidly down the corridor to the outer door.

"Wait. Maybe we can talk to…to somebody," Joe said. "If we—"

"That's okay, Joe. Don't spoil your chance on my account."

Joe stood with his papers in his hand, staring after Rob as he strode from the building. Rob did not turn back. He walked rapidly, heedless of the rain. Glad of the rain. No one could tell he was crying.

Why, Rob wondered now as he took his plane through the various maneuvers, had he felt ashamed?

He gave an angry snort.

That was how they made you feel! Like something was wrong with you for being what you were. That was the way he'd felt long ago in Nevada when he'd gone in with the rest of the high-school football team to get a hamburger and that bastard had refused to serve him. That day the other guys had walked out with him, leaving their shakes and burgers behind.

He couldn't blame his Fresno classmates for not walking. There was more than hamburgers at stake. So it was not with resentment but with envy that Rob watched his teammates depart for their Air Corps careers.

Still, it had galled him. He was qualified. More qualified than some of them. And he wanted to fly.

He tried the Navy. They were only taking Negroes as mess personnel.

The Marines. They weren't taking Negroes at all.

His mother didn't understand. "Why are you trying

so hard to get in? Everybody says we'll soon be in the war."

"Do you know any other way I can learn to fly?" he asked, and added, "If we do enter the war, I'd rather be in the air than in the trenches."

So he wrote letters. To senators, congressmen, President Roosevelt, Mrs. Roosevelt. The answers, those he received, only confirmed that Negroes were not accepted in the Air Corps.

He felt very much alone, and was only dimly aware that other people like himself and other groups were also clamoring for the admittance of Negroes into all areas of the armed services. Nor did he realize that steps were being taken toward this purpose. He was both surprised and ecstatic when, early in May, an issue of the *Pittsburgh Courier,* a Negro newspaper, proclaimed in big headlines: NEGROES NOW ACCEPTED IN U.S. ARMY AIR CORPS.

Newspaper in hand, Rob rushed to the post office. The recruitment officer who, by this time, was well acquainted with him, grinned.

"That's good enough for me. I'll sign you up."

He did so, and a few weeks later, a jubilant Rob was ordered to report to Moffett Field in Sunnyvale, California. He was in.

Rob grimaced. Correction. He *thought* he was in.

At Moffett he passed his physical with flying colors. It was when he reported to a Major Johnson in Building 201 that he ran into trouble. Steely blue eyes regarded him coldly, studied his college transcript, turned coldly back to Rob.

"You don't have junior standing."

"Oh, yes, sir," Rob said. He knew that the requirement was two years of college. "I'm a senior. I've completed three years of college."

"It doesn't say you have junior standing. I don't see that anywhere here."

"But, sir, I have three years. That's more than—"

"Sorry." The major perused the papers in his hand. "I don't see anything here that says you have junior standing." He glared at Rob.

Rob stared back, trying to control the fury that was now pounding at his temples. Neither of them noticed the chubby young corporal at a nearby desk. He had listened intently to their conversation and now spoke.

"Sir, there's an exam he can take in lieu of the college requirement."

"Oh, we won't be giving that until sometime next year," the major answered.

"Oh, but sir," said the corporal. "There's going to be one next month."

Now the major turned his baleful glare on the corporal.

Rob, however, flashed him a grateful smile. "Sir?" he asked the major. "Do you have any material on this exam? I'd like to take it."

"Don't have a thing."

"But, sir," the young corporal said, "here's some." He reached into a drawer and handed Rob a stack of pamphlets.

If looks could kill, the corporal would have been dead on the spot. The major reddened, but said nothing. Rob took the papers and thanked the young man profusely. He fervently hoped the corporal wouldn't be busted.

Back home Rob studied the papers, heavy with trigonometry and calculus. He hoped he wouldn't have to take the exam. He explained his problem to the dean of the college.

"You could pass it, but you don't have to take it," the enraged dean declared. He took a sheet of college stationery and wrote in oversize letters: ROBERT MET-CALF HAS ATTAINED JUNIOR STATUS AT FRESNO STATE COLLEGE. He had the paper nota-rized and sent by certified mail to the major.

Several weeks passed and Rob heard nothing. Finally he appealed to a congressman who had answered one of his letters. The congressman promised to look into the matter. Eventually he wrote to Rob, saying he'd talked with army officials who were unable to find any records for a Robert Metcalf. After all the red tape had been unraveled, it was found that Rob's papers had been pigeonholed at Moffett. The major had simply declined to send his papers any farther. However, a letter from the congressman indicated that Rob would be taken into the Air Corps within the next month.

Now, high in his plane over Tuskegee, Rob laughed out loud, suddenly recalling one of the old spirituals his mother used to sing. "So high, you can't get over it/ So low, you can't get under it/ So wide, you can't get around it/ You must come in at the door."

Well, all right. So he had to come in the *back* door.

Back door, hell! A whole new facility for persistent niggers like himself—very separate and nothing like equal. There hadn't even been barracks when he first arrived. He and his fellow cadets had to sleep in tents. But most of the buildings were up now and the field was flourishing.

Candidates for the New Negro Air Corps were never a problem, and after Pearl Harbor, enrollment had

soared. Qualifications were high, but even so it was easier to get in than to stay in.

Rob's mouth twisted as he remembered the tense difficult months until he made it through to graduation.
More than two-thirds of the men washed out, sometimes
the day before graduation. Many never knew why. Attitude, a frequent disqualification, could mean anything
from a minor infraction of the dress code to being a bit
too cocky in dealing with one of the white administrative officers in charge of the base. Or, perhaps, a passing
remark, voicing exception to the picket fence that separated white from colored in the base cafeteria. The
prejudices that had so long barred them from the Air
Corps had followed them in.

Might keep us out of the damn war, Rob thought
now. If I were white, I would've been sent overseas two
weeks after my graduation. I bet Joe and the others have
been in the fight and come back by now. But here it is
February, nine months later, a promotion from second
to first lieutenant, and I'm still flying around and around
the Southeast U.S.

He executed a marvelous chandelle and grinned. Cut
the griping, nigger! You're flying, ain't you? And if
you'd taken off with your buddies from Fresno, you'd
have been in the cannon's mouth long ago and you'd
never have met Ann Elizabeth.

Ann Elizabeth. The thought of her sent warmth
through his whole being. Now he returned to earth with
an eagerness and anticipation he'd never felt before
she'd come here. He made a short detour to circle Mrs.
Anderson's house, swooped low and dipped his wings
to let her know he was heading home.

At the base he made his usual smooth landing,
shouted the usual greetings to the other airmen. His

steps quickened as he left the plane and headed for operations. He signed in and started down the hall. He stopped as he passed two rest rooms, one marked COLORED, the other WHITE.

He glanced around. The hall was deserted. Quickly he took the crew knife from his pocket and pried the signs from the doors. He shoved them into a nearby wastebasket, then walked away whistling.

Ann Elizabeth was waiting.

8

December 1942

"Me and brother Bill went huntin'…way up in eastern Maine…." The rhythmic beat of the band accompanied the wiry brown-skinned man who strutted across the stage belting out the silly catchy words. "As we were a-huntin'…"

It was Louis Armstrong at his best. The crowd roared its approval as the fiery little man took up his trumpet to join with the band before he dragged out the finale in a tempo that drove his audience wild.

Ann Elizabeth was as enthusiastic as anyone in the hangar. Never had she had so much fun. This was completely different from the sedate chaperoned socials of her girlhood or even the not-so-sedate frat dances that hired pretty good local bands. Never mind that she was standing in an aircraft hangar, no theater seats or polished dance floor. Planes had been wheeled outside to accommodate the crowd. Officers, enlisted personnel and civilians, anyone connected with the base, packed together to clap, stamp their feet and cheer the performer. Whistles and howls reverberated throughout the cavernous building. "Do it, Satchmo!" and "Blow, man, blow!"

Ann Elizabeth leaned closer to Rob and he slipped an arm around her. "Tired, honey?"

"Oh, no! Not at all!" Happy. Happier than she had ever been in her entire life. She was Rob's wife, and she loved every minute of it.

Nothing spoiled the joy. Not even the constant presence of their landlady, who occupied the other bedroom and kept a watchful eye on her tenants. Not the clutter of Mrs. Anderson's house—the overstuffed velour furniture that crowded the little living room, the ruffled curtains and ruffled shade on the lamp set in the middle of the crocheted ruffled doily. Shadow boxes loaded with bric-a-brac—tiny artificial flowers, birds, elephants with raised tusks. Clutter. Claustrophobic after Julia Belle's spacious elegance.

And of course there was the septic tank. Mamie Anderson, evidently unused to indoor plumbing, lived in constant fear that the septic tank would overflow. "Must you bathe every day, honey? Don't flush the toilet every time you use it. Use this pan for washing dishes, honey, and don't throw the water down the sink. Just throw it out the back door."

"At this rate," Rob had whispered to Ann Elizabeth, "we're likely to flood the backyard before the septic tank is half-full."

Rob. His quips, his light jaunty walk, the tunes he whistled under his breath. His love. There was nothing and no one but Rob when she closed the door of their uncluttered bedroom and wrapped her arms around him.

Sadie interrupted her thoughts. "That was really something," she said as the concert ended and they all filed out. She had been invited by Randy for the weekend. "Do you get all the big-time entertainers here?"

"Oh, yes," said Ann Elizabeth. "Last week Lena Horne was here."

"And last month Cab Calloway," put in Pete, who was moving with their group toward the Officers' Club while most of the departing crowd scattered toward the barracks or their autos for the ride home.

"Lucky you," said Sadie.

"Ain't it the truth." This was from Fran, Pete's current girlfriend. "Imagine! A CAF-1 and all this, too! Better than living on Broadway."

"Sure beats the hell out of a dogfight over Germany!" Randy chuckled as he took hold of Sadie and danced a little jig on the pavement. "Me and brother Bill went huntin'..." Others joined in to imitate the inimitable Satchmo, singing merrily as they trooped through the sultry starlit night.

Ann Elizabeth couldn't sing. The words stuck in her throat, choked by Randy's "dogfight over Germany." That was where they all wanted to go. Oh, yes, they were ready. Six classes had graduated from the Tuskegee base. Expert pilots, trained for combat, anxious for the call to war. Not she. She didn't want any of them, especially Rob and Randy, to go.

She wasn't alone. White commanders, engaged in heavy fighting overseas, had no confidence in an all-Negro squadron. Her father had said it: "They'll take our best and never know what they have."

The best. They'd come from all over the United States, this group of Negro airmen. Healthy, handsome, intelligent men, most of them college graduates. More than once she'd heard comments on the high caliber of the military personnel at Tuskegee. No drunkenness or brawling, no complaints from the townspeople. Almost no need for military police. The guardhouse remained empty.

They'll never know what they have. True. Cancellation after cancellation followed one alert after another. Orders were issued and reissued, changed and canceled, while the War Department vacillated, pondering over what to do with all those Negroes. The Negro press kept up its questions and demands, pointing out the speed with which white units were sent overseas, many with only a minimal amount of training.

Randy, in his slow ironic drawl, explained. "Well now, you just don't understand. White folks know better how to die. You see, dying takes a certain finesse. That's something about patriotism you niggers ain't learned yet."

But that night, as they crowded into the Officers' Club, they weren't thinking of patriotism or war or dying. Jubilant, in the aftermath of a great concert, they were just having fun.

Randy drew Sadie away from the others. "Let's sit a minute. It's kinda nice out here."

Sadie sat beside him on the steps. She'd sit in a swamp with him if he asked. But it's not so muggy, she thought, testing the hair at the nape of her neck, relieved to find it holding. Anyway, if Randy didn't care about her kinky hair, why should she?

"This may be the last time," he said.

"Last time?" Even in the moonlight she could discern that his face was sober. More sober than she'd ever seen it.

"Being together like this. I have a feeling they'll be sending us over soon."

Dear God, forgive me. I've been thinking of my hair while he... Peaceful, fun-loving, take-it-easy Randy.

She couldn't imagine him fighting, killing. Being killed. A chill pierced her spine. She reached for his hand.

He entwined his fingers with hers and abruptly changed the subject.

"You like working at Carter's?"

"Yes." She'd been working at the colored hospital for a month.

"Different from Grady, huh?"

"Yes." Very different, she thought, comparing its inadequate facilities with those in even the colored wing at Grady.

"I'm glad you're there. It's like…well, I can see you. Envision where you are while I'm away."

"Oh, Randy." Did he know she'd changed jobs because working with his father made her feel closer to *him*?

"Will you still be there when I come back?"

"Of course. Where else?"

"What I mean is—" he took her by the shoulders and looked down at her "—will you be waiting?"

She held her breath. "Waiting?"

"For me. Oh, Sadie, do you know how special you are to me? So steady, so lovable. I know it's not fair to ask. But I don't want to lose you again." He pulled her to him, spoke into her ear. "That night, when I saw you at Ann Elizabeth's big to-do, it was like I'd truly come home. And these last few weeks, being with you…it's like walking on air, but holding on to something solid. Do you know what I mean?"

"For you, too? Oh, Randy, Randy." She buried her face in his shoulder.

"Oh, shucks, I meant to do this right," he said, as he leaned back to reach into his pocket and took out a small box. "Will you marry me? The minute I get back?"

She managed a dazed nod. The world rocked, the silver crescent moon tilted, the stars twirled, tumbled and shone—but not quite as brightly as the little diamond he was slipping onto her finger. Not a spur-of-the-moment thing. He had planned to ask her, bought the ring. Randy loved her, wanted her to be his wife. "I must be dreaming," she whispered, almost to herself. "I've loved you for so long. I never believed someone like you could want me. Could love me."

He laughed. "I'm not such a prize, honey. Coming home will be like starting all over again. Medical school. Interning. It won't be easy."

"I don't care. I'll help you." She was a nurse. She could work wherever he trained.

He kissed her on the nose. "Just warning you. It won't be easy."

No, it wouldn't be easy. But she was thinking of something else. "Your mother won't like it."

"Mom? Heck, she didn't like Ann Elizabeth marrying Rob, either. Don't worry about Mom. She'll come around. She has a way of taking things in stride."

"Yes. Like you."

"Like me!"

"You needn't look so shocked. I mean the way you both—" she screwed up her face "—seem to feel comfortable wherever you are. That day she came to my house—"

"Wait a minute. My mother came to your house—in Beaver Slide?"

"Yep," she said, a chuckle escaping her lips. "Walked right in, pushed aside Mom's ironing and sat at the table like she was in some tearoom. And she talked right up to Papa.''

"Talked…about what?''

"About sending me to nursing school. I couldn't believe it. You know how loud and cantankerous Papa can be. But he was so befuddled he just sat there quiet as a mouse when she looked him straight in the eye.'' Sadie straightened and assumed Julia Belle's precise tones. "Mr. Clayton, do you mean to tell me you're willing to commit your daughter to domestic service and ten dollars a week for the rest of her life? What are you thinking of? When she could have a profession that would open up all kinds of doors.''

Randy roared. "You sound just like her.''

"Pa looked like he was under a spell. And when he started saying how long he'd been supporting me and all, she said she'd—'' Sadie broke off, her heart swelling as she recalled. "Your mother paid my tuition at Grady, Randy. Bought my uniforms and everything. I thought you knew.''

It was his turn to be dazed. "I didn't know.'' Then he smiled. "I *should* have known. My mother has a way of managing other people's lives.''

"Well, I sure like the way she managed mine. I'm paying her back. Every penny. But what she did…I could never pay back. It was like she gave me a brand new life.'' No matter why she did it, Sadie decided. Silently she sent a wholehearted thanks to Julia Belle and forgave her in the same breath. "I'll never forget it.''

"Just don't forget me, pretty lady,'' he said, tilting her chin to press his lips to hers.

She clung to him, reveling in this moment, the happiest moment of her life. It was a long time before they joined the others.

When they did, they found everyone settled in what were obviously familiar surroundings to them, the comfortable lounge of the Officers' Club. "This is nice," she said.

"Another advantage, ladies, of being a CAF-1 at good old Tuskegee Army Air Field—or TAAF as we fondly call it," Fran said. "'Course it doesn't come with the territory. You have to cozy up to a guy who has those little bars on his shoulder. Ain't that right, honey?" She tweaked Pete's ear as she sank onto the sofa beside him and kicked off her shoes.

"Right," Pete said, grinning. "Special place for special people, baby. So you better be nice to me."

"Tell me," Sadie whispered to Randy, "what on earth is a CAF-1?"

He laughed. "Isn't Fran a kick? It's just a classification for a government worker, which Fran is. She's a typist in the civilian personnel office, I think. Don't ask me what the initials stand for, but the CAFs go up and up. CAF-1 is the lowest—twelve hundred and sixty dollars a year."

"You're kidding!" Sadie stared openmouthed.

Randy grinned. "Yep. Niggers are suddenly making more money than they ever thought possible. I guess there's something to be said for having a war."

"Don't say that!" She placed trembling fingers on his mouth.

He took her hand and squeezed it reassuringly. "It will end, you know. And we'll make up for lost time when I get back."

She held on to his promise like a precious unbelievable secret, too unbelievable to be shared. But when she was alone with Ann Elizabeth in the ladies' room, she thrust out her hand. "Look!"

Ann Elizabeth's eyes sparkled. "Randy?"

Sadie nodded, feeling strangely shy.

"Oh, Sadie, I'm so glad." Ann Elizabeth hugged her. "Randy's a lucky guy. And now I've got a sister. You! I'm so happy."

"Me, too," Sadie said, but her eyes filled with tears. "I only wish…"

Ann Elizabeth hugged her again, knowing what she wished. No war. No waiting. "But the waiting will be easier with everything settled between you." Now at least they were engaged. She knew how much Randy loved Sadie, but he'd said it would be unfair to marry her when things were so unstable.

Ann Elizabeth was glad Rob hadn't felt that way. Funny that carefree lighthearted Randy did. One day she'd asked him about it. "If you love Sadie…" she'd begun.

"Love her too much to ask her to start something she might not be able to finish."

"What do you mean?"

"I mean if I didn't come back—and that's a possibility, sister dear. It would be harder for her to have a new life with someone else."

The idea was devastating. If Rob didn't come back, could *she* have a life with someone else? She blocked out the thought. Rob was her life.

Back in the lounge they found the others indulging in potato chips and pretzels, beer and soda pop, with Randy center stage as usual. From his antics Ann Elizabeth gathered that he was mocking the base commander, who'd held an officers' meeting the night before. First time on record, Rob said, of a meeting with white officers and black officers assembled together. The commander was irate. Someone had been tampering with the WHITE and COLORED signs posted throughout the base.

Randy stood by a table, his face austere and serious, as he spoke in that slow Southern drawl he could imitate so well. "Gentlemen, it has come to my attention that someone is destroying government property, namely the signs marked WHITE and COLORED. I called you in here today to make one thing clear." Randy leveled an accusing finger at his howling audience. "The United States Army Air Corps adheres strictly to the separation of the races. I want you all to understand that not only is segregation a policy of this state, it is also a policy of the Air Corps." At this point Randy slapped his hand hard on the table and glared belligerently. "No damn fool with a screwdriver is going to change that policy. I run this base! Anyone not adhering to regulations or vandalizing signs pertaining to same will be busted, *and* he'll be court-martialed."

Randy's delivery, according to Rob, was dead on. After the colonel made his speech the previous evening, Rob said, he had not been challenged. Everybody had listened politely before being dismissed and filing quietly out.

Next, Ted Watson, who had been valedictorian of Randy's graduating class at Morehouse, rose to carry the mockery a bit further. Amid gales of laughter, he stood up, assuming a quavering high-pitched voice. "I think it's a shame, sir. I really do. If I catch anyone tampering with signs that have guided me throughout my life, I'll sure turn him in. Court-martial! He ought to be horsewhipped. You done let us have this nice base with them neat signs and that pretty little picket fence in the cafeteria to keep us in our place. You let us fly them planes and wear these fine uniforms.'' He paused to shine the bar on his shoulder. ''And some damn fool is trying to mess it up! All I gotta say is he better not let me catch him.'' Ted gave a suspicious glance around the room, as if searching for the culprit.

Randy, trying hard to suppress a grin, beamed in solemn approval. ''Spoken like an officer and a gentleman, Lt. Watson. One, I believe, in line for a promotion,'' he added.

Rob stood and held up a hand. ''I wish to commend Lt. Watson for his patriotic spirit, sir, and add my name to the roll for this sacred duty. If we're diligent and keep our eyes open, I'm sure we'll soon run the culprit down.''

''Toast,'' said Pete, lifting his beer bottle. ''To the pursuit!''

Accompanied by several *Hear, hears* and the clinking of Coke and beer bottles, Randy—still impersonating the colonel—expressed his appreciation to those who understood his grievances. Pounding on the table, he listed things Ann Elizabeth was sure the colonel felt but dared not say. ''The pain and peril of being assigned to this godforsaken nigger base, the humiliation of seeing white enlisted men salute nigger officers, witnessing the degradation of a white soldier requesting permission to attend and sit with niggers at the base theater...''

Ann Elizabeth curled up beside Rob, feeling a little sleepy as the anecdotes rolled on and on.

It was Pete who told the one about the white flight officer who got hurt in a plane crash and was rushed to the Tuskegee Army Air Field Hospital for treatment. This really had happened. According to Pete, the officer became concerned and asked the Negro medic to check—was he getting black blood? The medic promised to do so. He returned, looking puzzled. "We got a problem, sir. Damned if this blood ain't all red."

Ann Elizabeth was unaware when the banter subsided and the talk became serious. She awoke to the sound of Ted's voice loudly outlining the progress of the war.

"What do you mean we're beating the pants off them?" he shouted, evidently in response to some remark from Pete. "The Brits might be holding their own in Africa, but Hitler has invaded Russia." He went on about which army unit was where and what had or had not been accomplished. Ann Elizabeth had always known Ted was brilliant. Everybody said he would be an even better lawyer than his father. But he was usually very low-key and very funny. Amazing that he should know in such detail what was happening overseas.

"Your predictions sound gloomy, Ted," Sadie murmured. "Do you really think we could lose?"

"Anything's possible, kid," was Ted's answer. To a storm of protest from the others, he began to argue. "Look how fast the Germans have moved through Europe. And they're pounding the hell out of England. Fact is, the Japs did the Brits a favor when they bombed Pearl Harbor. If we hadn't come in, they might've been wiped out by now. Hitler has built up a powerful war machine in the last few years. He's either lucky or pretty smart."

"He's crazy!" Sadie sounded so indignant they all turned to her. "Have any of you read *Mein Kampf*?"

None of them had.

"Well, I have," she said. "And I tell you it was written by a man with a diseased mind. If somebody doesn't stop him, we're all in big trouble!"

She looked so distressed that Pete reached over and

touched her hand. "Cheer up, honey. Don't pay any attention to Ted. We're winning. The U.S. Eighth Air Force is daylight-bombing Germany and—"

"And Hitler is launching massive retaliation on England," Ted said. "He ain't just sitting still!"

"Like we are," Rob said rather quietly. Ann Elizabeth sat up, surprised at the bitterness in his voice as he went on.

"Fighter pilots sorely needed and here we are—six classes of airmen, three squadrons' worth, eighteen aircraft each, pilots and crewmen languishing in south-central Alabama."

"Don't knock it, boy." Randy chuckled. "I kinda like this languishing. Ain't hankering to be over there. I don't relish the idea of them antiaircraft guns pointing at me."

The group laughed at his sally, but Ann Elizabeth shuddered while Ted chided, "Shit, man! Here you are with over one hundred and fifty flying hours and you ain't learned how to dodge them bullets? All you do is..." He made an upward swoop of his arm. "Quick, before—"

"Never mind the demonstrations." Randy laughed and sang a plaintive tune. "Please, sir, I don't want to go. I ain't no expert like my friend Ted."

"Don't be 'shamed, buddy, don't be 'shamed! Ain't many can aspire to the heights of First Lieutenant Ted Watson."

There followed a chorus of boos and a verbal contest about who could outfly whom. Ann Elizabeth and the other women listened and laughed on cue, not understanding any of it—chandelles, figure eights, immelmanns and "on the deck."

Ted was the loudest, contending that he "could fly the boxes the planes come in."

"Didn't see you make it under the bridge," Pete said.

Ted bristled. "Didn't see you make it, either."

"And you ain't going to," Pete answered. "I can't quite fly the crates the planes come in. And I ain't planning to dive into the river or buy a farm."

Ann Elizabeth knew about the bridge that rose high above the Tallapoosa River, near Tallassee. She knew that some of these foolish bragging men, trying to prove themselves, had actually flown their P-40s under it. But "buy a farm"? Timidly she asked, "What's with that buy-the-farm business?"

Several of the men answered. "A crash."

Then Randy explained. "When an aircraft crashes anywhere other than its airfield, it's generally on farmland, which the government then has to pay for."

"Really?" Sadie asked. "They have to pay for a crash?"

"Sure. When a plane crashes and burns, the damage to the land is extensive."

But there's no way to pay for a life, Ann Elizabeth thought, shuddering again. "Let's talk about something else. Okay?" As if in answer to her prayer, in walked Louis Armstrong with a few of his band members. He was greeted with enthusiastic shouts of praise and soon they all gathered around the piano for another concert, this one impromptu and private.

On a sunny Sunday morning two weeks later Ann Elizabeth lay in bed, almost bursting with what she had to tell her husband.

Beside her, Rob yawned. "So you're being lazy today?" he said. "I'm glad."

"Oh?"

"Yeah." He frowned at her. "Sometimes, sweetheart, I think you're a bit too much like my mom."

"How so?"

"On Sundays when you bug me to get up and go to church!"

She laughed. "Just trying to save your sinful soul." Often she did persuade him to accompany her to the college chapel. But not today. Today she'd—

"But not this morning, my sweet? Got something else in mind?" He nibbled her ear, his hand cupped her breast, his thumb gently teasing the nipple. The familiar urgent desire sprang to life at his touch. If he didn't stop...

"Wait!" She clutched his hand, held it still. "I have a surprise for you."

"Mm." Not interested, he continued his intimate caressing.

"Robert Metcalf, listen to me! I'm pregnant."

"Preg—?"

She grinned up at him. She had his attention now! "We're going to have a baby," she said, firmly placing his hand on her stomach.

Quickly he lifted it away from her body. "Careful. We don't want to...to..."

"Don't be silly. You can't hurt the baby by touching me." She chuckled. "If so, it would've happened before now. Carl said I'm six weeks already. At the clinic yesterday, he—"

"Ann Elizabeth, you never told me!"

"I didn't know it myself. Really. I was as surprised as you are right now," she said, speaking rapidly. "Never suspected until last week. And then I wanted to be sure and I saved it to tell you today." So they could savor the news on the one whole day they always spent together. "Oh, Rob, are you glad?"

"Almost as glad as I was when you said you'd marry me. Just...bowled over, I guess. And scared. You...are you all right?"

"Of course I'm all right. Being pregnant is normal, silly. And the doctor says I'm fine. He says—"

But whatever else the doctor said was muffled against Rob's chest. He held her close, but carefully as if she was fragile and precious. "We're going to be a family," he gloated, rocking her back and forth, telling her how much he loved her. "You'll be the mother of my child."

"And you'll be the father of mine," she whispered, wrapping her arms around him. This time it was she who coaxed. "It's all right. It's okay to love us both," she wheedled as she touched and teased. And smiled when he groaned in submission.

Afterward they showered and dressed, then went out to stroll through the campus.

"I love this town," she said, referring to Tuskegee Institute, named in honor of the college and quite separate from the town of Tuskegee, where the whites lived. "I guess Booker T. Washington had a point when he urged Negroes to 'let down your buckets where you are.'"

"You're talking about the great compromiser, old Mr. separate-but-equal Uncle Tom himself? You agree with him?"

"All I know is that I like being here. It's a little country town, but way different from towns like Monticello where my uncle Jimmy lives. Negroes there live in dire poverty. Here they live well, thanks to the institute and the veterans' hospital, neither of which would exist if it hadn't been for Washington.''

''Right.''

''And face it, Rob. If the school hadn't been here, neither would the Army Air Corps base. And neither would you.''

''Right. Still separate but not quite equal. Flying round and round, going nowhere.''

Ann Elizabeth's heart lurched. Why did they want to go where bombs burst and bullets flew? Not only Rob, but all of them. All those handsome virile black pilots at the base. So anxious to go to war. Didn't they ever think about dying?

She saw the muscle twitch in Rob's cheek, and her heart ached for him. She felt a twinge of guilt. She wanted him here. Right here. Flying round and round, going nowhere. Not in Germany...

She couldn't help it. She didn't care if they never sent the black pilots overseas. She wanted Rob right here beside her, planning for their baby.

She touched his arm. ''Let's go across the street for a burger. I'm kinda hungry.''

''You...or my baby?'' Rob smiled and reached around her waist to touch her still-flat belly.

''Both of us. And behave yourself!'' She slapped his hand, glad she'd diverted him.

On Monday Ann Elizabeth took the bus to the base and shopped at the commissary. She left her groceries to be picked up later. They would borrow Randy's car to haul them into town. She stopped at the base cafeteria for a hamburger and soda, sharing a table with Fran and some other base employees. When they left to go back to work, Ann Elizabeth walked to the Officers' Club to wait for Rob.

The Officers' Club was quiet. There were three officers at the bar rolling dice with the bartender. Two women seated at a table—Doris, married to one of the pilots, George somebody, and another woman. They were involved in such a deep private conversation she dared not disturb them. She greeted them cordially, retreated to the lounge and settled into one of the sofas with a magazine.

She heard the siren of an emergency vehicle, but it seemed far, far away. Sounded as if it came from the direction of Tallassee. Not to worry.

Two articles later she heard a commotion in the bar. She looked up to see the three officers rushing out, heard them cursing.

The bartender was about to follow, but Ann Elizabeth stopped him. "What's wrong?" she asked, clutching the sleeve of his white jacket.

"Somebody's bought the farm."

Ann Elizabeth's whole being plummeted. Her heart raced. Her head throbbed. She heard Doris exclaim, "No! No! Not George. It can't be George."

Ann Elizabeth silently echoed the plea. Not Rob. Not Randy. Please, God. Finally she managed some coordination between mouth and brain and was able to whisper, "Who?" Not Randy. Not Rob. Please, God.

The bartender, who had returned to his post, answered, "We don't know. We'll just have to wait." He poured brandy for the women and tried to reassure them. "We'll know soon. It might not be one of us. Could be somebody from Maxwell or Dothan."

Ann Elizabeth knew those bases were adjacent to Tuskegee. Forgive me, God. It's wrong to wish for some unknown person's death—someone from another base.

It seemed forever that the four of them sat in the bar. Hoping, praying. Scared. Actually it wasn't quite an hour later that Ann Elizabeth looked up to see Rob, closely followed by Randy.

Thank you, God. Thank you, God. She rushed into Rob's arms.

But their faces were grim.

"One of us?" she asked, holding her breath.

"Ted," said Randy. "A slight miscalculation. Didn't quite make it under the bridge."

Ted. Ann Elizabeth hid her face against Rob's shoulder, unable to hold back the tears.

There was no service at the base, hardly any recognition of Ted's death at all. His body was shipped back to his home in Atlanta for burial.

Because of an alert at the base, none of the pilots could get leave to attend. But Ann Elizabeth, who'd known Ted all her life, returned to Atlanta for the service. She sat in the same church where her wedding had been held, remembering Ted as a young boy... The time he'd raced through the Sunday-school chapel and knocked over one of the urns. The time he'd been Joseph in the Christmas pageant... So many memories.

She felt a deep sympathy for Ted's sister and his grieving parents. Her own grief was almost as keen. She listened to Reverend Hawkins and others who spoke highly of Ted, but she couldn't see anything for the tears clouding her eyes.

In her mind she saw only Ted. Clearly, as he'd been that night at the club. Bragging, joking...*I can fly the boxes the planes come in.* Ted...flying under a bridge to prove it.

Funny, serious, brilliant Ted. That night it was Ted who'd explained what was really happening overseas. He should have been one of the strategists, planning the moves.

Again she thought of her father's words. *They'll take our best, and never know what they have.*

She thought about life—so fragile.

About death—as sudden and unpredictable flying round and round over Tuskegee as in a dogfight over Germany.

9

April 1943

With a leaden heart Ann Elizabeth realized it was happening. The troops were going to be moved. For real this time. Furloughs canceled. Combat training sped up.

On the morning of April 3, when Rob's troop boarded the train at the Cheehaw station, Ann Elizabeth wasn't there.

"I want you settled in Atlanta before I leave," Rob had said, "where I know you and our baby will have the best of care." She'd protested, but he'd insisted. So it was she who left him.

Seated in the stuffy jim crow car, her face against the window, she watched Rob, standing straight, tall and handsome, the creases in his cheeks deepening with his smile. The train pulled slowly away and she could no longer see him. She'd never felt so alone in her life.

She paid little attention to the other occupants of the car, but kept her face pressed to the window, watching the landscape slip past. Trees, rivers, farms. Cows grazing in a meadow. Houses. In the neat backyard of one small cottage she saw a child swinging, a woman holding a baby. She rested both hands against her stomach, holding her own unborn child. If only she and Rob could have a house like that. Peaceful. No separation. No killing or dying. No war.

Not even the antics of the jaunty little porter could lift her depression. The short slight brown man in the trim blue uniform was a familiar figure to her. On their frequent trips to Atlanta, she and Rob had always laughed at his cheerful banter as he paraded through the car, never calling a station without a witty comment. "Opelika, Opelika. Come along, girl, don't be 'shame!... Notasulga, Notasulga, all out for Notasulga. Give me your hand and God your heart, and don't forget your parasol." Today, as they pulled into the big city, he announced, "Atlanta, Atlanta now. You been long hearin' talk about it. Atlanta now!" Grinning widely, he took her baggage and helped her down. "Give me your hand and God your heart, but leave your pocket-book behind!" he added with a big guffaw.

Ann Elizabeth managed an answering smile, but her eyes brimmed with tears as she tumbled into her father's waiting arms.

As it turned out, Rob and Randy weren't immediately sent overseas. They went with some others to Oscoda, Michigan, for special combat training. When they did leave to join their squadron, they were put on a troop train and sent to Miami. From there they would board a plane for a circuitous route through Brazil to their destination.

The troop train was filled with soldiers, only four of them Negro. It didn't seem to matter. They were all U.S. soldiers, comrades.

However, when they arrived in Miami, they traveled by bus for an overnight stay in hotels, and there they were separated. The four Negroes were deposited at a small motel in the colored section of town.

Early, before breakfast the next morning, the bus returned to pick them up. The driver, a white corporal, greeted them cordially before proceeding to a hotel by the beach where the white soldiers were waiting.

Rob stared at the plush hotel as the white soldiers filed into the bus. "Looks like the palefaces had better accommodations than we did," he said, remembering the mosquito-infested room he'd shared with Randy.

"Wonder if they ate," was Randy's only comment. "I'm hungry."

They hadn't eaten yet. There was a table already set for them at Miami's International Airport dining room. The men, laughing and talking, eagerly seated themselves.

However, before they could be served, a colored waiter rapidly removed all the place settings in front of the four Negroes.

"Wait a minute!" One of the white officers jumped up. "What's going on here?"

"What's going on is discrimination," Rob said quietly.

The officer turned to the waiter, who looked embarrassed. "I was told to…that is, they're not supposed to eat in here," he said.

The white officer was now turning red. "Call the manager," he bellowed. "I want to speak to him." When a man who said he was the assistant manager appeared, the officer accosted him. "Why can't these men be served?"

"They're colored. And coloreds eat in that room over there. Didn't you see the sign?" He pointed. The sign proclaimed in several languages: COLORED DINING ROOM. "Coloreds eat over there."

"I'm not going in there," Rob declared.

Randy tugged at his sleeve. "Come on, man. Don't be so touchy. I'm hungry."

"I'm not eating in there," Rob repeated.

The assistant manager shrugged. "Suit yourself. You're not eating in here."

"Why the hell not?" Another white officer stood up. "These are officers in the United States Army," he said. "On their way to fight for this country. May lose their lives."

"Don't matter to me. I don't give a damn if they never come back. They ain't eating in here." His voice was smug as he added, "It's against the law. They can't eat in here."

Meanwhile the waiter, though obviously curious about these proceedings, was carrying out his duties. Plates loaded with steak, eggs and fried potatoes were being placed on the table.

Randy transferred his gaze from the appetizing food to the waiter. "Hey, we getting the same food in there?"

The waiter nodded vigorously, giving him an I'll-take-care-of-you sign.

Randy turned to Rob, who had been joined by more white officers and was still arguing with the assistant manager. "Look, man, I'm hungry. Think I'll just go along in there and eat while you, er, discuss this matter."

"I'm going with you," said Bo Martin, one of the other black pilots.

The fourth Negro, Charlie, remained with Rob, both

staunchly insisting they wouldn't eat in the segregated dining room.

Though a few of the white pilots had begun to eat, ignoring the altercation, a number had stood up to argue with the assistant manager, who stoutly refused to serve the black men.

Finally the corporal who had driven the bus approached Rob. "Look, you don't have to eat here. I'll take you back to the hotel."

Rob looked at him and hesitated. He was mad as hell and he sure wanted no food in that flea-ridden motel. But the situation was getting out of hand. These white guys were rallying to his cause, but their food was growing cold.

The corporal, noting his indecision, persisted. "Look, we don't want to cause a scene. Come on. I'll take you back. I'll get you some food."

"Go ahead and eat your breakfast, fellows," Rob said to the others. He nodded toward the corporal. "He's gonna take care of us." Then he and Charlie quietly left with the corporal.

To their surprise, he drove them back to the plush hotel by the beach. After the corporal briefly conferred with someone, they were admitted to a coffee shop where they were seated and served hot coffee and sandwiches.

"White folks sure are funny," Charlie whispered to Rob. "First they wouldn't let us stay here. Now they're feeding us."

Well, Rob thought to himself, it's some kind of victory.

But he was thoroughly disgusted with the two who'd deserted. "Ratfink!" he said to Randy when they were seated on the plane.

Randy only laughed. "Did you get fed in nice proper style at a nice proper place?" He gaped when Rob named the plush hotel. "Well, that's sure enough a proper place. I'm right sorry I couldn't join you guys. But I was too hungry to wait. What did you eat?"

"We had coffee and sandwiches."

"Coffee and sandwiches, huh?"

"Yeah."

Randy's lips twitched. "Well, now, you know, I wasn't quite eating in the proper place, but I sure was eating good while you was fighting the black war. I'm mighty glad you won, though. I'm mighty glad you won!"

"Oh, shut up!" Rob pulled his cap over his eyes, slid back in his seat and went to sleep as the plane roared on toward another war.

10

August 1943

The kitchen door slammed and Aunt Sophie came across the driveway. The glider shifted as she settled her ample form beside Ann Elizabeth.

"Ann Elizabeth, do you mind? Would it be all right if Helen Rose wore your wedding gown?"

"Why, of course." Ann Elizabeth put down her book and smiled at her aunt. "You know I'd be glad to have her wear it."

"Good. You're both the same size, or at least you were. And heaven knows, you both picked the hottest time of year to get married in." She took a magazine from the nearby table and began to fan herself. "I declare it's a real bother in all this heat."

"Now, Aunt Sophie," Ann Elizabeth chided, "you know you're happy. You like Clyde." Helen Rose's sojourn at Fisk University had indeed been successful. She'd gotten her doctor. A dentist, really, and just graduating. But he had the title and the potential. Aunt Sophie couldn't have been more pleased.

"You're right, Ann Elizabeth. Such a nice young man. And I do want Helen Rose to have a nice wedding.

I guess it's worth all the trouble. Oh, honey, I do wish you could be matron of honor."

"Wouldn't I look great, floating down the aisle like an oversize balloon! Besides, my baby might decide to arrive in the middle of the ceremony." She patted her stomach proudly as Rob had often done.

Rob. She missed him. Without him, nothing was the same. Yet, everything *was* the same, here in Atlanta. The city hadn't changed. Well, not much. Her friend Delia and Jump Hawkins had married very quietly. Delia was attending the Atlanta School of Social Work, and Jump was working at the bank. During vacation from her elementary-school classes, Millie had started on her master's degree at Atlanta University's summer session. Jennie Lou, like Millie, taught in the public school and, if rumor could be trusted, was chasing Dan Trent like crazy. Many of the Atlanta boys were away at war or at camp, and there was meat and gas rationing. But for the most part, life went on as before. Luncheons and bridge parties, and lazy afternoons in the glider under the magnolia tree. Ann Elizabeth attended a few plays on the campus. If she hadn't been pregnant, she probably would have worked with the Atlanta University Players herself. The parties had sped up with Helen Rose's engagement. Ann Elizabeth and Julia Belle were planning a linen shower for her.

The screen door slammed again and Julia Belle came out, carrying a tray with three tall glasses of iced tea. Ann Elizabeth glanced at her mother's still-youthful figure with something like...well, if not envy, at least a fervent hope that her own figure would return to normal after the baby's birth. Julia Belle's dark hair was piled high on her head, and she looked cool and crisp in the blue linen dress that matched her eyes. She set the tray of iced tea on the wrought-iron table that surrounded the magnolia tree, then turned to Ann Elizabeth. "Another letter from Rob."

Ann Elizabeth beamed as she reached for the envelope that signaled he was still alive and well, wherever he was—a military secret, but somewhere in Italy, she thought.

"Let me know what he says about Randy," Julia Belle said. "I declare that boy hardly writes."

Ann Elizabeth, devouring her letter, only nodded. She lived for these letters, written in Rob's large irregular scrawl. As tender and ardent as Rob himself, they brought him closer to her and made the war seem far away. "The only thing that matters is that you are there and I am here without you," she read. "I think about the way you smile, I recall your touch...." The words seeped into her heart and warmed her. And he always ended with the message, "Take care of my baby."

That was the hardest part. He wouldn't be here when the baby was born.

"Well—" Julia Belle could contain herself no longer "—what did he say about Randy?"

"Oh, that he's still clowning around. Says he can mimic everybody in the whole squadron and keeps them in stitches."

"Now, isn't that just like Randy?" Aunt Sophie chuckled. "Clowning through the war. I declare, that boy ought to be in show business."

"He ought not." Julia Belle's voice was firm. "He's going to be a doctor."

"Well, he's got the bedside manner, all right. He could charm the..." Their voices faded as Ann Elizabeth disappeared into the house. Upstairs in her room, she read Rob's letter over and over again.

The luncheon shower for Helen Rose, arranged with Julia Belle's usual painstaking precision, was a beautiful affair. Ann Elizabeth conducted the games and handed out the prizes, prettily packaged in green paper and tied with yellow ribbon. She had also fashioned the center-piece for the dining table—a lovely arrangement of magnolia leaves, baby's breath and yellow roses. After feasting on shrimp salad, lime sherbet and lemon-frosted cakes, the guests returned to the living room to watch Helen Rose open her gifts.

Ann Elizabeth, busily recording—for Helen Rose's thank-you notes—the donor of each gift as it was opened, at first ignored the dull ache that started in the small of her back. But it became more intense, recurring at more frequent intervals. By the time she saw Millie and Delia, the last of the departing guests, out the door, she could ignore it no longer.

"The baby's not due for a couple of weeks," she said. "But these pains…"

Julia Belle immediately picked up the phone and, a couple of minutes later, sent Helen Rose upstairs to get Ann Elizabeth's overnight bag, which was already packed. Within ten minutes she was helping Ann Elizabeth into the car and instructing Sophie and Helen Rose not to bother cleaning up. "Call Lynn to come in from the garage. He'll do the dishes and put everything back in place." As they pulled out of the driveway, she said to Ann Elizabeth, "Don't fret, honey. Everything's going to be all right. Dan will meet us at the hospital."

Ann Elizabeth wasn't fretting. Of course everything would be all right. Wasn't she going to her own father's hospital? He and her mother would be with her. And Dan. When she'd arrived home from Tuskegee, she'd thought that Dr. Fox, who'd removed her tonsils years before, would deliver her baby.

"Not on your life!" her father had said. "None of us old fogies. You'll have Dan Trent."

"Do you think that's wise, Will?" her mother had asked. "He's a personal friend and—"

"Do you know any doctor in town who's not a personal friend?" he'd responded. "Anyway, Dan's the best. Keeps up with the latest developments. Always off to some seminar while the rest of these new youngsters are sitting on their backsides."

So Dan it was. The first time she'd gone to his office she'd felt awkward. She hadn't seen him since her wedding day and she thought of the letter.... Now here she was, all out of shape, her feet swollen, her face puffy. She'd hated letting him see her like this.

"Dr. Trent is ready for you, Mrs. Metcalf." The nurse had led her into his office and left, shutting the door.

Dan had come straight to her, taken both her hands in his and looked down at her as if he could devour her. His voice had been a fervent whisper. "Oh, Ann Elizabeth, Ann Elizabeth, you cheated me! You should have married me."

She was so relieved she almost laughed. But seeing his ardent expression, she reached up and touched his cheek. "Bless you, Dan. Here I am, looking like a big fat cow, and you... Never mind that you shouldn't have said it. You made my day."

He'd laughed with her then, and the tension had disappeared. But the ardent look was still on his face as he'd added, "Silly woman! You never realized how much I love you."

"Don't, Dan. Please, if I'm to be your patient. And

I do want to be. Dad says you're the best doctor in town.''

"Of course you're going to be my patient. I couldn't trust anyone else to take care of you."

"Then you'll have to behave yourself, Dan. I'm a happily married woman. I really am," she'd said. "And I want you to be happy too. Maybe if you let yourself get caught by one of those ladies who are chasing you. Jennie Lou—'' She stopped. *I didn't say I wouldn't marry him. Just that I can't stand him,* Jennie Lou had said. Okay, not her. Ann Elizabeth swallowed. "Someday you'll find just the right person for you, Dan. Someone who'll love you for the fine person you are. You just have to keep looking."

He'd shrugged. "Guess I'm too busy to look. Sit here, Ann Elizabeth. I need to ask you a few questions before I call the nurse in and examine you.''

It was as if the air between them had been cleared that day and both could relax. From then on he was the perfect doctor, as well as a good friend, never once going beyond that.

Today—coming here to deliver her baby—was the first time since her tonsillectomy that she'd been in her father's hospital as a patient. But it was all so familiar, the place and the people. Leanna Collins, behind the reception desk, greeted her immediately. "Hi, Ann Elizabeth. It's time, huh? Dr. Trent phoned instructions to get you ready."

Emma Watkins, who'd known Ann Elizabeth since she was a baby, took complete charge. "Might have known you'd be early. Always was one to get ahead of the game. Come along. I'm going to put you in the back room. Nice and cool."

Before she was settled in bed, Sadie came in, looking

very professional in her starched uniform and cap.
"How about this?" She grinned. "I'm going to help
deliver my own niece or nephew! I can't wait to tell
Randy." She and Ann Elizabeth began to compare news
from their letters. Despite the increasing pain, Ann Elizabeth felt contented. She and her baby were secure, in
the care of old and competent friends.

Dr. Carter and Dan arrived, agreed that, yes, the baby
was on the way and left. Julia Belle and the nurses
fussed over her during the long hot afternoon. When
Dan returned, late in the evening, he advised Dr. Carter
to take his wife home.

"Nothing's going to happen before morning," he
said. "And I'll be right here."

So it was Dan who sat with her throughout the night,
laughing and joking, bathing her face when the hard
pains came. "Don't hold your breath, Ann Elizabeth.
Just relax. Go with it. That's right. You're doing just
fine."

He surely doesn't do this for all his patients, she
thought, feeling a little guilty. But she was glad he was
there.

And it was Dan who gave her the happy news at
3:35 a.m. "A boy. Six and a half pounds."

A boy. She smiled. "Rob will be pleased," she murmured before falling into a deep sleep.

In the nursery Sadie watched Dan carefully enclose
the tiny baby in the oxygen tent. He turned a ravaged
face to her. "He's just not getting enough air and, and...
Oh God, we're so limited, Sadie, and he's so tiny. I
don't dare try a tracheotomy. But he can't survive long
like this. I'm going to contact Grady Hospital."

"No." She shook her head, detaining him. "Children's Hospital. They're specially equipped."

"They'd never take him," Dan said, reaching for the phone. "And we can't waste time."

She took the phone from him. "Let me try. If I can get hold of Dr. Benson..."

"Benson?"

"A pediatric surgeon. I've seen him work miracles. He was teaching at Grady. Transferred to Children's just before I left." She dialed as she talked, her heart in turmoil. Ann Elizabeth's baby, Randy's nephew. Please, God. She stiffened when the phone was answered. "Nurse Clayton here," she said with a ring of authority. No way would they know who she was. "Dr. Benson, please. Urgent." She covered the mouthpiece and spoke to Dan, who looked doubtful. "He'll come. He's not only skilled. He cares."

She had not yet seen her baby. Something was wrong. Ann Elizabeth felt it, even before Dan came in, looking haggard and worn. He must have been up all night. Her heart gave an anxious lurch, and she tried to focus on what he was saying. "We've called in a specialist."

"A specialist? What's wrong?" she whispered.

Dan took her hand and gently explained. "His vocal cords are a little too close together. This limits his breathing. We've got him on oxygen, which helps. But the problem has to be corrected surgically."

She tried to keep down the panic, forced herself to remain calm, speak rationally. "Is it safe? He's so tiny. Can you do it without...without harm?"

"Not I." Dan gave a wan smile. "But we're lucky, Ann Elizabeth. Dr. Benson, one of the few pediatric surgeons in the country who could perform that kind of surgery, is right here in Atlanta. At Children's Hospital." Children's Hospital. She remembered a gracious brick building; she'd seen it through the spokes of the wrought-iron fence that enclosed its grounds. One of the many for-white-only structures viewed from the outside, like the big hotels downtown.

Dan's voice seemed far away, muffled by the cloud of anxiety that engulfed her. "Sadie called him. She worked with him at Grady. She says he's fantastic."

He's white. "Will he come?" she asked.

"He'll come," Dan said. But the uncertainty in his voice pricked like a knife, and her fears that the doctor wouldn't come mounted.

Dr. Benson did come. He sat beside Ann Elizabeth's bed, a slight pale man with pale hair, thinning on top, keen gray eyes peering at her through horn-rimmed glasses, saying what Dan had already said. "It's fortunate that Dr. Trent diagnosed the problem and got him into an oxygen tent immediately. But I'll have to go in to correct the problem so he can breathe naturally, and I'll have to do it now."

She stared at him through wide frightened eyes. His smile was reassuring. He took her hand in his long slim surgeon's fingers. "Don't worry. Babies are my specialty."

"What will you need?" Dr. Carter asked.

"Need?" The surgeon turned a puzzled face to him.

"To operate? Instruments—"

"I'll just need a portable oxygen tent. I'm taking him to Children's Hospital."

"You're what?" Dr. Carter's voice was incredulous.

"He's a newborn baby. I couldn't possibly risk it here without my special equipment and staff." He picked up the phone beside Ann Elizabeth's bed and dialed. "Nurse Califf, please." He drummed his fingers impatiently on the table while he waited, then spoke into the phone. "Mrs. Califf? I've got a small problem for you. I want you to get the operating room ready. A newborn baby. Trachea. I'm bringing him over now. A little colored baby. He... Yes, that's what I said... Well, I'm gonna do it. You just get the room ready." A flush rose to his face, and his words came now in an angry explosive grunt. "That's not your problem, Mrs. Califf. You just get the room ready," he said before he slammed down the phone.

Ann Elizabeth's heart flooded with fear. Her baby, in the hands of nurses who didn't want him, who wouldn't care... She looked around for her father, but he and Dan had gone, probably to arrange for the portable tent. "Listen, Dr. Benson, maybe this isn't wise. If they don't want him—"

"Do I have to fight you, too?" His voice was curt and she winced.

"No. I just thought that if—"

"You want your baby to live, don't you?"

She nodded. If there was no choice... "I want to go with him."

For a moment he looked doubtful. Then he shrugged. "Of course."

Children's Hospital was located in a luxurious section of Atlanta seldom visited by Ann Elizabeth. But she had, on one or two occasions, caught a glimpse of the stately seven-story brick building set in a park, studded with trees and paved walks, and enclosed by a wrought-iron fence. On warm days, you might see children wheeled about in wheelchairs or walking with nurses. It had never occurred to any of the Carters that they'd ever be inside that structure. But at the moment Ann Elizabeth was hardly thinking of where she was or how she'd gotten there. She waited in the basement of the vast building, her mind focused on what was happening in an operating room somewhere far above her. Her father and Dan had been permitted to go up and view the operation from the observation room.

Take care of my baby. I'm trying, Rob. I'm trying.

Dr. Benson is trying. Please God, guide his hands. Please, God.

It seemed forever. Her mother was even more perturbed than she was, and Ann Elizabeth tried to reassure her. "He's going to be fine, Mother. Sadie says Dr. Benson can perform miracles." She began to talk faster, as she always did when she was worried. "We're lucky. I mean, Sadie being a nurse and all and working with him and knowing who to call. Strange how things happen, isn't it?"

"Yes," Julia Belle said. "Strange."

They waited in the basement room, Ann Elizabeth's eyes constantly straying to an empty crib with complicated equipment beside it.

Two hours later, the baby was brought in. Dr. Benson followed. He hardly glanced at them but went straight to the crib to see the baby settled in. Ann Elizabeth watched apprehensively as she saw all the tubes they attached to her tiny boy.

"Is he all right?" she asked Dr. Benson when he finally turned to them.

"He's fine. The operation went well."

"But all those tubes. He looks so..."

"Postoperative treatment is as important as surgery. I'm stationing a nurse in constant attendance," he said. The tiny tracheotomy tube would remain in the baby's throat until the trachea healed. The equipment she'd noticed was a suction pump. Whenever the baby coughed, the nurse would use its electrically powered syringe to suck out the phlegm threatening to choke him.

A much-relieved, still-apprehensive Ann Elizabeth tried to thank the doctor, but mere words seemed inadequate. "He's such a kind caring man," she said to her mother once he'd departed.

"Definitely a skilled surgeon," Julia Belle said.

Dan and her father confirmed this, full of praise about the excellent surgery they'd witnessed.

"I am so grateful to him," said Ann Elizabeth. "Both for the surgery and daring to bring us here. But also to Sadie and to you, Dan, for recognizing the problem." She smiled at him. "Dad was right. You *are* the best doctor in town."

"Not yet. Maybe the best colored doctor," he said. "But I mean to be right up there with the rest of them." His expression was a strange mixture of envy and grim determination. "If you've got the training...and the right arena, you can do anything. God, Ann Elizabeth, you should have seen that operating room!"

Robert Gerald Metcalf, Jr., thrived. How could he help it, with all the tender loving care he got from his white nurses?

"They treat him," said Dr. Benson, "like he was the king of Babylon. Always asking to get the shift down here. They adore the little booga."

It was true. The baby had benefited from the same efficient technology and received the same thoughtful care that would have been given to any white patient. The nurses were not in the least resentful, as she'd expected.

They were equally gentle and competent with her. It might have been Miss Emma bathing her, carefully handling the breast pump. "I know it's painful, honey. Try to relax. There. That wasn't too bad, was it?" They talked and laughed with her, shared experiences. Freida, the little redhead on the early-morning shift, was engaged to an intern, Oliver, and was planning her wedding in the fall. Kate, the older woman, had a son fighting overseas and a bedridden husband at home. Strange how they'd become like friends in such a short time.

Julia Belle came every day to see her grandson. "Little brown baby with sparkling eyes," she would croon whenever she visited. His eyes did sparkle. His skin was brown and he had thick black hair that lay in soft curls. "And he's got dimples, Ann Elizabeth, just like his father."

Ann Elizabeth smiled. She'd never thought of the creases in Rob's cheeks as dimples. But yes, he did look like Rob.

Rob. It was as if she'd put thoughts of him aside while their baby was in danger. She'd been afraid to tell him he was a father—until she could add "a beautiful healthy boy." Dr. Benson declared that Bobby was out of danger now, but still she waited. When she was sure, when all those ugly... No, not ugly! When all those wonderful health-giving tubes were removed. Then she'd take pictures and send Rob volumes about their boy.

She was thrilled when the tubes came out and she could hold her baby in her arms, so warm and...alive. "Thanks to you," she said over and over to Dr. Benson.

As always he shrugged off her thanks. "We'll keep him a few days longer to see how he progresses. Then you can both go home."

Ann Elizabeth became fully conscious of the magnitude of her debt to Dr. Benson the day the Negro maid who came to clean every morning confided in her.

"Lord a mercy, honey, you all done sure kicked up a ruckus!" It was the first day no white person had been in attendance, and the wiry dark-skinned maid deliberately put aside her mop and pail and prepared to say what she'd clearly been dying to say all week. "Yes, siree, you and that little fellow over there done blacked up the hallowed halls of this lily-white hospital. Lemme fluff up that pillow for you." The dark face bent over Ann Elizabeth, the gold crown on a front tooth flashing with her conspiratorial grin. "Never seen such carryin' on in all my born days. There, that's better."

"Thank you. I'm sorry, I didn't know how much trouble..." She hesitated. "Well, I did know, but..." Her whole mind had been absorbed with her baby.

"You musta knowed you the first colored patients we ever had. And I reckon you'll be the last if Dr. Sinclair has his say. Didn't know where to put you in the first place. Old Nurse Califf, soon as she seen Dr. Benson bound to bring you, she tell me to get down here and fix up this room in the basement. Ain't nothing else down here but supplies and X ray." She paused, hands on hips, and looked around. "Got it fixed up real nice, don't you think?"

"Yes. It's very comfortable. You did a fine job. Thank you."

"Shoot. No need to thank me. I meant for you to have everything them white folks upstairs has. I could see Nurse Califf was mad as a wet hen. Couldn't wait to tell Dr. Sinclair."

"Who's Dr. Sinclair?"

"He the head man, honey. And when he find out Dr.

Benson done operated on a colored baby, that's when the shit hit the fan!''

Ann Elizabeth remembered Dr. Benson's flushed face, his anger when he'd made the call to that nurse. She hadn't even thought of his predicament. "I hope we didn't cause him too much trouble," she said.

"Who? Doc Benson?" The little maid gave a hoot of laughter. "Don't nobody mess with him. Nurse Califf say he the best—"

"But you said—"

"Oh yeah, Doc Sinclair go up in smoke! Come into Dr. Benson's office for what he say gonna be a private talk. But he shouted so loud, I 'spect you could hear it down here."

"I'm sorry—"

"Sorry? Shit! Was all I could do to keep from bustin' out laughing. I was cleaning the washroom in Dr. Benson's office and they didn't know I was there. Cracked the door a mite and didn't miss a word. 'I like to know where you get off,' Dr. Sinclair say in that whine of his. He a doctor but he sure talk like a poor cracker. He ask Dr. Benson, 'What you mean, hauling anybody you please into this here hospital?'

"'Always bring my patients here,' Dr. Benson say, cool as a cucumber.

"'You know what I mean,' Dr. Sinclair shout. 'You know we don't 'low no pickaninnies in here.'

"Dr. Benson say as how he's a doctor and he wouldn't turn a dog down, much less a pickaninny.

"Then Dr. Sinclair ask do he expect white nurses to attend a black nigger baby.

"'They doing it,' say Dr. Benson.

"'What!' Dr. Sinclair shout. It was all I could do to keep from opening that door to see his face. Don't matter. I could *hear* it turnin' red. Sound like Dr. Benson was rustling some papers and he say kinda matter-of-fact, 'They all seem crazy about the little fella. Treat him like he's the king of Babylon.'"

"That's true," said Ann Elizabeth.

"That's 'cause he's about the cutest baby that ever been in this hospital." She bent over the crib and gazed down at the sleeping infant. "Look at him, all smooth and brown. Not pale and wrinkled up like them newborns upstairs."

"And healthy now. I'm so grateful. Everyone's been so kind."

"Oh, yeah, they real nice. Some of 'em." The maid swished the mop energetically across the floor, then put it with the pail outside. She returned to pick up Ann Elizabeth's breakfast tray. "This has been some goingon, I tell you. Wouldn't've missed it for the world!" The gold tooth flashed with another grin. "Well, got to get along. See you in the mornin'," she said before she went out, shutting the door behind her.

11

November 19, 1944

The day was misty and gray. A hint of winter chill lurked in the breeze that sent the colorful leaves scattering across the lawn.

In the Carter kitchen the air was warm, and rich with the sweet smell of holiday baking. Nutmeg, ginger and vanilla mingled with the lemon rind Julia Belle was grating for the lemon-iced cake Randy loved.

"Do you think they'll get this by Christmas?" Sophie, enveloped in a big white apron, looked up from the fruitcake batter she was mixing.

"They'd better." Julia Belle's mouth tightened. She had no patience with a war that dragged on and on, keeping her son, who shouldn't have been there in the first place, in constant danger.

"Usually takes six weeks. We should be in time if we get the boxes off this week. And don't let me forget—Sadie brought over some of her mother's fried peach tarts. She says Randy especially likes them." Ann Elizabeth licked her finger, sampling the frosting she was smoothing on the devil's food cake, Rob's favorite. She bent to offer a taste to Bobby, playing at her feet.

He pushed his building blocks aside and stood up, clutching his mother's skirt, clamoring for more.

"Now that was a mistake," Sophie cautioned. "You shouldn't encourage him to like sweets."

"Oh, Aunt Sophie, half the fun of the holidays when I was a girl was eating up the leftovers in Mother's mixing bowl—if I could get to them before Randy. Never did me any harm and it's not going to harm my healthy boy."

"Healthy is right." Julia Belle dumped the lemon rind into the double boiler, set the mixture on the stove and began to stir. "When I think how I sat in that room praying for him to stay alive, it seems like a miracle."

Because of quick and expert surgery, Ann Elizabeth thought. Strange, but not until she'd been at Children's Hospital did she realize how makeshift the Carter Hospital was. For the past six months, she'd been doing volunteer work there and had become fully cognizant of the inadequate facilities. Hardly more than a holding facility for the damaged children who were brought in needing special equipment and expert care. And weren't getting it. Bobby was lucky, thanks to Dan and Dr. Benson, who'd kept a careful watch on him for months. Only a tiny scar at the base of his throat remained from the ordeal at his birth. He was a happy active fifteen-month-old boy, and the adored center of the Carter household.

"He sure is cute, Ann Elizabeth," Sophie said. "Just like his dad with that chocolate skin and those dimples."

"Yes. I must have more pictures taken." For Rob. To send along with the goodies and other gifts. Hard to believe that pictures were all he'd seen of his boy. Rob. That happy time in Tuskegee seemed like a long-ago dream. "No more," she said to Bobby, who was still demanding more. "Sit down and let Mommy show you how to stack these blocks."

"Come over here, honey," Sophie entreated. "If your mom can spoil you, so can I. You want a taste of this?"

Bobby did. He deserted the blocks for Aunt Sophie, climbing on a chair to reach the table, almost upsetting the piles of nuts and dried fruit destined for the fruit-cake. Ann Elizabeth managed to catch him just in time.

"All right, you worked for it." Sophie chuckled as she held out a spoon with a bit of cake batter to Bobby, now squirming in his mother's arms. "Did you see him climbing, Julia Belle? I declare that boy's like a little monkey."

"You got that right." A breath of cool outside air cut through the baking smells as Dr. Carter entered the kitchen. "I tell Ann Elizabeth she'd better put a leash on him or she'll find him scampering along a branch of the magnolia tree one of these days. Come here to Grandpa." He took the boy from her and swung him to his shoulder. "Sit with me while I read about what your dad and his buddies are doing to those Krauts!" he said as he unfolded a copy of the *Pittsburgh Courier.*

Ann Elizabeth winced. The *Pittsburgh Courier,* the leading Negro paper, always carried full accounts of the activities of the Negro airmen, praising their perfor-mance, expertise and daring in the line of fire. But all she could think of was "line of fire." It had been bad enough in Tuskegee, when her heart turned over with every daring roll of Rob's plane. But now they had antiaircraft gunfire and German fighters aiming at them.

She tried not to listen as her father read, pride ringing in every word. "'The Ninty-ninth shoots down twelve

German fighters in two days... The 332nd Fighter Group gets the new P51-Ds.' Aha!'' Dr. Carter looked up from the paper. ''They're upgrading our boys' planes. Beginning to recognize their worth.''

''Randy said, 'We'll show them,''' commented Sophie. ''Those were his very words.''

''They're showing them, all right. Listen to this. 'Captain Edward Denton downs three Jerries on one mission with his new P51.'''

''Eddie Denton,'' said Julia Belle. ''Isn't that the chubby dark-skinned boy Randy brought with him one weekend? He and his wife. You remember, Ann Elizabeth. We took her shopping at Rich's.''

''Yes,'' Ann Elizabeth replied. ''Rose Denton. She's back in Ohio now with her folks.'' *Waiting, just as I'm waiting, for this horrible war to be over.* What was it all about, anyway? Wars were stupid. Good people, killing and being killed. Maybe she ought to feel patriotic and proud, hearing of their brave exploits. But she just felt a little sick. Hard to imagine Rob killing someone. Not her gentle Rob. Not happy-go-lucky Randy, who'd never hated anyone.

''Well, our boys are showing their mettle,'' Dr. Carter said. ''And thank God for the Negro press. Otherwise we wouldn't know a damn thing about it. Come along, Bobby, let's clip and paste all this good news in our scrapbook.''

Ann Elizabeth watched her father retreat with Bobby on his shoulder, glad he'd taken the newspaper with him. The newspaper that brought the war closer and filled her with fear. She was glad her mother and aunt were too busy mixing the fruitcake batter to continue the discussion. They'd begun to pour the mixture into half a dozen oblong pans she'd lined with well-oiled brown paper. She studied each pan carefully, directing the women's work. "That's enough in that one...too much in this one." She had found that if she concentrated hard on what she was doing—volunteering at the hospital, entertaining Bobby, portioning out cake dough—she sometimes forgot that she might never see Rob again. Might never hear his merry whistle, see him with Bobby, lie in his arms.

"Do you think I should, Ann Elizabeth?" Sophie asked.

"Should what?" She had tuned out their conversation.

"Ask Dan for Thanksgiving dinner. Helen Rose and Clyde are coming." Clyde was at the veterans' hospital in Tuskegee, an easy traveling distance.

Ann Elizabeth hesitated. "I suppose..."

"Of course you should ask him," said Julia Belle. "It'd be a shame for him to be alone on a holiday."

"Oh, I don't think there's any danger of that." Sophie gave a dry chuckle. "Plenty of invitations, which I understand he mostly refuses. I think you ought to know people are talking about the amount of time he's spent at the Carter household since Ann Elizabeth's return."

"Let them talk!" Julia Belle snapped. "He's Bobby's doctor, and you know he works with Will at the hospital."

"And still looks at Ann Elizabeth like he could eat her up."

"Oh, Sophie, don't go making too much of it. Of course he's fond of Ann Elizabeth, always has been. But Dan Trent's a gentleman and his visits here are open and aboveboard."

"Lordy, I know that. But other people don't. Fanny told me that Sally Richards said—"

"Sally Richards is a jealous bitch. She ought to know by now that if Dan wanted Jennie Lou he'd—"

"I'd better check on Bobby. It's his bedtime and he must be driving Dad crazy." Ann Elizabeth hurried from the room. She felt sorry for Dan. All these speculations. If and when and who he'd marry. Nothing about what an excellent doctor he was and how hard he worked. She'd never realized, until she worked with him at the hospital, how dedicated he was to his profession.

"Damn shame, Ann Elizabeth," he'd told her the other day, not hiding his frustration. "Folks come to us, paying for what they think is the best care, and they get shortchanged. And that's not our fault. Do you know there's not one black doctor in the state of Georgia who's qualified by the American Medical Association Board of Surgeons?"

She hadn't known. Had never thought about it.

"Not exactly our fault," Dan had said again. "There's not one accredited private hospital in the state where a black surgeon is permitted to practice." No, Carter Hospital wasn't accredited. A whole lot of money was needed for accreditation—adequate facilities, equipment, not to mention staff.

Something else she'd never thought about.

Dan had said other things. About what wasn't and what ought to be. Ann Elizabeth had listened and empathized. Of course there ought to be an accredited hospital for private black patients. Of course there ought to be qualified black surgeons. Yes, training took time and money. Yes, of course Dan should make that sacrifice. Only she and her father knew that Dan had applied to

Freedman's Hospital in Washington, D.C., to train under the eminent black doctor, Charles Drew, who had perfected the technique of preserving blood plasma, which was saving the lives of so many injured men overseas.

Ann Elizabeth liked Dan, admired him. All right, it was more than that. She enjoyed being with him, felt flattered that he confided in her, was glad to help him relax over a game of bridge with her parents. Sadie came to their home quite often, too, sometimes alone, sometimes with Dan. Funny, Ann Elizabeth thought. Her mother never alluded to Sadie and Randy's engagement; in fact, she seemed to shy away from the subject. But she did think Julia Belle had begun to enjoy Sadie's company. Perhaps she simply craved *any* company. Like Ann Elizabeth did. Keeping busy, having friends over, helped dull and sometimes banish the worry about Rob.

Rob. There were indications that the war was drawing to a close. He might be home soon. And then?

The rush of gladness was always impaled by that disquieting "and then?" Where would they live? They couldn't go back to that little room in Mrs. Anderson's house. Or to the Tuskegee base—standing in a hangar listening to jazz, dancing at the Officers' Club, watching the planes flying round and round. The war was almost over. And for the first time she realized that the whole two years of her married life had been built around a war.

Never mind. Rob would be home soon. They'd talk about it then. Where they would live. What he would do. She lifted Bobby from his bath, dried and powdered him, sang a little lullaby as she settled him in his crib.

Tomorrow she would have more pictures made to include with the Christmas gifts.

March 1, 1945
The early dawn of a beautiful day somewhere in Italy

Captain Robert Metcalf tucked the well-worn picture of his son into the pocket of his flight jacket and climbed into the cockpit of his P-40. He gave a good-luck salute to Randy, first in command on this mission to strafe a German airfield, then took off behind him in formation with the rest of the squadron.

It was a strange sight. All those German planes, row upon row of them, lined up like sitting ducks. A few bullets into the gas tanks and they'd burst into flames. Strange that not one of them took off.

"I'm going down," Randy signaled. "Cover for me." He peeled off from the others.

Rob, following directly behind, saw Randy's plane go into a sudden dive. He'd been hit!

"Eject!" he radioed. "Jump, Randy." He'd go down after him and… Even as his feverish brain registered the thought, he saw Randy's plane begin to roll over and over, slowly, making a complete circle. He gasped in horror as it plunged to the ground and exploded like a cannonball, igniting everything around it, smoke billowing and flames leaping in a wall of fire two blocks long. The forty-thousand-dollar coffin. With Randy inside it.

A wave of sickness swept over him. Randy. He didn't expect…didn't want to believe it. Not Randy.

A deafening explosion rent his ears and the sky lit with flames as the plane beside his blew up. Lawrence? God, it could've been him!

He forced himself to put feeling aside. Antiaircraft

fire from the ground was coming at them like mad. They were being peppered by tracer bullets that were picking them off like flies. Damn! Rob propelled his plane upward to escape the line of fire.

At eight thousand feet he paused to consider. With Randy gone, he was now in command of a squadron scattered by the most hellish ground fire he'd ever experienced. No German fighter planes, but the antiaircraft missiles had been hot and heavy. The Germans were trying to save their planes. And why weren't those damn planes blowing up? They'd shot at them, but nothing happened! It came to him. No gas. The Germans were running out of fuel. No gas to catch their planes on fire. No gas to lift those fighter planes into the air.

He started to laugh hysterically as he radioed and reassembled his scattered formation.

The battered squadron went down one more time, braving the still-heavy ground fire. They shot into the immobile planes, causing enough damage to render them useless. But how much damage, Rob wondered, was worth the men they'd lost?

Randy. God, how could he tell Ann Elizabeth?

They had done all they could. He signaled to the men "Mission completed. Return to base."

He pulled back the stick for an upward climb, but the plane refused to gain altitude. It had been damaged. He'd never make it back to Italy. He radioed to the others that he'd been hit and would try to get to Switzerland. But he knew as he turned in that direction that he could barely make it over the Alps. He was unsure of his location. Even now he was losing altitude. He was in real trouble.

He thought of bailing out. Too low. The plane responded slightly to his maneuvering, gaining a little altitude. He propelled it forward, searching desperately for a piece of level ground on which to land. There seemed to be nothing but trees. After about two minutes he spotted an open field. He circled twice, reducing his speed. Cut off his engine and bellied in. The plane thumped and lurched crazily over the rough ground, finally coming to rest in a field of brush that seemed to stretch for miles, glowing golden under the noonday sun.

It was so quiet. He couldn't believe the silence. Not after the roar of the planes, the guns.

The stillness. Absolutely no one around.

For a moment he just sat, trying to absorb the peace and quiet. Forgetting to be frightened.

Randy. He wanted to cry, but couldn't. He felt weighted down by a sense of loss, suffocated by a grief he couldn't release.

Randy. How could he tell Ann Elizabeth?

Yet he knew his own loss was as great as hers. Randy was his buddy, his confidant. It was Randy who'd joked and cajoled and bullied him through this damn war. Rob closed his eyes, seeing Randy, hearing him. "Now, look here, Robbie, old boy, for a guy who worked as hard as you to get in this-here war, you ought to enjoy it more!"

"How the hell can you enjoy a war?"

"How the hell else would you get to fly your own little private plane? All over Italy and Germany, too."

"Shit!"

"Now, if you stick with it and act like a good boy—" Randy, leaning toward him, that mocking grin on his face "—you just might get to see Paree. If you stop drawing pictures of them Messerschmitts and start

shooting at 'em, instead! Now, I know about them little
wheels and those sleek graceful bodies, but it's kinda
dangerous to be fooling around studying the design.''
When Rob tried to speak, Randy had bent over him, as
if imparting a grave secret. "You see, ol' boy, the object is to shoot them before they shoot you. Not to let
them get too close!''

Nobody knew him like Randy did—and what he'd
said was true. Even in the thick of the fighting, Rob
would find himself marveling at the little Messer-
schmitt, so sleek and swift as lightning. Hell! He didn't
forget he was in a fight. He could down them fast as
anybody. But there was always a tug at his conscience
when any plane went plunging to the ground. So graceful, so beautiful.

He couldn't help it. He wanted to build airplanes, not
destroy them. He wanted to work with pilots, not kill
them.

Randy understood this. Randy was gone.

He sat for a long time, missing Randy.

Something, a mouse perhaps, scurried through the
brush. Brought him to his senses.

The war was not over. He was in enemy territory. A
field somewhere in the middle of Germany. And he'd
better get the hell out.

Mechanically his training instructions came back to
him. Remove the survival kit. Destroy the plane.

He ran his hand lovingly across the panel. Destroy
this plane that had carried him so many miles, brought
him safely through so many missions?

It was no use. He couldn't do it. Besides, starting a
fire would alert the enemy to his whereabouts. He com-
promised by destroying the gun sight. Then he got out
and started walking toward what he hoped was Switzerland.

12

Dan had left. Accepted by Dr. Drew to begin his residency at Freedman's, Dan had lost no time getting his affairs in order. Philip Driscoll, a new black doctor in town who'd studied with him at Howard, was to take over his practice. No speculations about Driscoll. He already had a wife and two kids.

"I don't understand it," Julia Belle fretted. "Why must Dan go to Washington now? Just as he's gotten his practice so well established. He's already such a good doctor."

"He's determined to be a better one," said Dr. Carter.

Julia Belle shook her head. "I don't think his patients will trust Driscoll."

"Maybe they'll run to me."

"Oh, Will, that's nonsense. You have more people leaning on you than ever and it's too much! They think they own you, calling at all hours of the night for anything from a slight case of indigestion to a family problem. I wish you'd slow down and let some of these youngsters take over. If they can measure up to Dan, that is. I'll never forget how he took care of Bobby." She shook her head again. "He's going to be sorely missed."

Not only by his patients, Ann Elizabeth thought.

Dan's departure had left a void in her life. She felt a little guilty about this, as if enjoying Dan's company was a betrayal of Rob. But that was ridiculous. Nothing, no one, could replace Rob. It was just that she liked talking with Dan, sharing his problems. She missed him, but she was glad he'd be gaining desperately needed expertise.

There were few, if any, black specialists in Atlanta. Sometimes a white doctor could be called in for surgery or consultation. But many, like Dr. Benson, refused to work in such inadequate facilities. Although, unlike Dr. Benson, most wouldn't—or didn't—dare transfer these patients to their own hospitals.

Ann Elizabeth had come to realize that there should be a decent hospital for Negroes. And maybe it was putting the cart before the horse, but she was glad Dan had gone for further training. "I mean to pass the AMA Board of Surgery," he told her. She had no doubt he would.

Sometimes she wondered what it would be like if she'd married Dan. She would be in Washington with him now, probably taking a job at the hospital or the college, working to "put hubby through."

And why, for goodness' sake, was she daydreaming about what-if? She had plenty of other things to do. Taking care of Bobby, keeping him safe and happy for his father, who would certainly be home soon. There was still the work at the hospital, bridge with Millie and some of the other girls, and yes, the meeting at the college tonight. She'd been asked to participate with the University Players, and tonight they would discuss plays and casts for the forthcoming summer series.

It was going to be fun, Ann Elizabeth thought later, to be acting again. Sitting in the drugstore now, for an after-meeting snack, she felt like the schoolgirl she'd been two years before. Or she would have, if it weren't for Bobby, at home with her mother, and Rob's last letter, tucked snugly in her purse. "This mess is almost over. Home soon."

Home soon. Ann Elizabeth hugged his reassurance to herself. She felt happy. And hungry!

Eloise Jenkins stared enviously at her. "Hamburger, french fries and a double chocolate malt! Jeez, Ann Elizabeth!"

"Eloise, you were the one who suggested we stop for a snack."

"My snack is half a peach and a mound of cottage cheese. I'll probably gain ten pounds just smelling your french fries while you stay—"

"As slender and straight as a willow reed that blows gracefully in the wind," supplied Ed Sanford.

"Oh, shut up, I'm suffering enough," Eloise snapped. "And give me your wallet. We treated you last time," she said, seizing it from the protesting Ed.

"'Who steals my purse steals trash,'" he quoted. "''Twas mine, 'tis his, and has been slave to—'"

"Trash is right!" Eloise sighed as she peered into the wallet. "One thin dollar. Ann Elizabeth, have you got any money? This ratfink—"

Ed raised a hand, assuming an injured air. "'But he who filches my good name, takes that which not enriches him, but makes me poor indeed!'"

Eloise contended that he was poor in name, as well as purse, and if he didn't do less quoting and more promoting—like finding himself a job—he'd stay poor.

Ann Elizabeth laughed as she fished in her purse. It was like old times. The bantering. The penny-pinching. She was glad to be part of it.

She was glad, too, that she now fit so easily into her before-the-baby dresses. Rob would be pleased. *Home soon.*

An hour later, when she turned Randy's little car into the driveway, she noticed that all the lights were on downstairs. Bridge? She looked, but there were no other cars around. Well, Dad must have just come in from a late-night call.

The side door to the kitchen wasn't locked. She closed it gently behind her and fastened the latch. Then stopped short, her nostrils quivering. A sweet smell, vaguely familiar.

Aromatic spirits of ammonia. Dad always gave that to Mother when she was upset.

Upset? Bobby! Ann Elizabeth rushed across the kitchen to the breakfast room.

Julia Belle was sitting very straight, her hands folded on the table in front of her. Dr. Carter bent over her.

"Dad, Mother, what's wrong? Is Bobby—"

"Bobby's fine. Asleep upstairs." Julia Belle spoke through pale lips and lifted dazed eyes to Ann Elizabeth. To her husband. Then glanced at two yellow envelopes lying on the table.

Ann Elizabeth's gaze followed hers, fastened on the envelopes.

No! Oh, my God. No. Please. Don't let it be. She felt a crazy impulse to turn and run.

"Take it easy." Her father's arms were around her. She found herself clinging to him, so that her knees wouldn't give way.

"Now, kitten, it's not as bad as it could be," her father said. "They haven't been... We're not sure..."

"They?"

"Rob and Randy. They're missing in action."

"Both of them?"

He nodded. "Two telegrams. One to you, one to your mother and me."

She picked up the telegram addressed to her. "Regret to inform you...Captain Robert Gerald Metcalf..."

She put it down. She knew that hearts don't break. They hurt and hurt, and the hurting doesn't stop. She knew now how it felt—to want to die and yet keep on living.

"Here, kitten, drink this."

Aromatic spirits of ammonia. The first time she'd ever tasted it. Her father's hand, holding the glass, was shaking. She stared up at him. His eyes seemed tired and the gray at his temples was more pronounced. He was getting old. She'd never noticed before.

Dear God, why was she thinking such inconsequential things when Rob... And Randy! Again she felt the impulse to turn and run.

"Kitten, your mother..."

She looked down at Julia Belle, so quiet and pale. Moving quickly, she put her arms around her. "You've always told me never to think the worst. It just says missing. They could be...they're not...could be all right," Ann Elizabeth finished lamely, shutting out the picture of a burning plane, charred ashes, desolate impenetrable wilderness. She thought Julia Belle's eyes brightened a little and she tried to sound more cheerful. "The flyers have these survival kits, Rob told me. They could hide out for weeks in the German countryside. Can't you just see Randy..." Her voice broke, but she plodded on, conjuring up a picture of the two of them escaping through a forest while Randy joked about poor transportation routes.

It was a long time before they turned off the lights

and went up to bed. In her room Ann Elizabeth gazed at Bobby, safe in his crib, one hand under his chin, the other clutching the leg of a fuzzy teddy bear. So much like Rob, with the long lashes sweeping his cheek. She knew she shouldn't disturb him, but she couldn't help it. She picked him up and sat in the little chair by the window, holding him close and rocking.

The soft light of dawn was stealing through the window and the tears had dried on her cheeks by the time she placed the baby back in his crib and went downstairs. She plugged in the coffeepot and put in a call to Rob's mother. Then she called Sadie.

Because he'd selected flat ground on which to land, there was no place to hide when they came looking for him. He saw the truck coming and thought of that old spiritual—"Run to the rock to hide my face. The rock cried out no hiding place, no hiding place down here." As a boy, the song had always made him a little nervous, especially with his mother looking directly at him from her place in the church choir.

That was nothing compared to the panic churning in him now. Sure as hell no place to hide here. He surrendered to the German folk soldiers—two ruddy-faced teenagers, their long coats flapping about their legs. They seemed more curious than belligerent, but he could only shake his head at their guttural questions.

They took him back to the plane, examined it carefully, exclaimed excitedly over the damaged gun site. The town they finally drove him to was so small, he thought it probably wasn't even on the map. They found a farm girl who translated in broken high-school English.

The only identification on his flying jacket was his name and a pair of wings. *"Kanedische?"* she asked.

This he did understand. She was asking if he was Canadian, probably puzzled by his dark skin. He nodded, yet he wondered why he felt safer to be identified as a Canadian.

Canadian or American, he was now in the hands of the enemy. No will, no power of his own.

Two days' incarceration in the local jail. A three-day ride in a boxcar crowded with weary German soldiers. Almost as weary, as hungry, as helpless as he. Together, in a boxcar that swayed and rumbled in a never-ending trail of events.

It was when he was escorted by his two guards from the boxcar into the busy Frankfurt depot that hostility erupted. He could see the hatred in the tired anxious faces as he was deliberately jostled by the crowd. A woman spat at him and he almost toppled over as he was kicked in the backside by a heavy boot. He knew why when they emerged from the station and he saw the battle-scarred city.

Canadian or American, he was one of the airmen who dropped the bombs that were destroying their city.

Outside the station they waited, evidently for a street-car that was to carry them wherever they were going. A crowd began to gather and people shouted at him. The language was unintelligible, but the meaning was clear. He grunted as a woman's knapsack struck him in the chest. Another woman kicked him and a man slapped his face. The crowd was growing more irate and his guards maintained a detached silence. Rob fended off his attackers as best he could, his fear mounting. God! Had he escaped heavy artillery fire only to be lynched by a German street mob? Thankfully he was saved from that end by the timely arrival of the street-car.

Their destination proved to be the interrogation center at Oberereusel. At last a sense of order. Officialdom. Healthy well-fed Germans in sleek officers' uniforms, striding about and clicking their highly polished boots. Regular soldiers and secretaries scurrying after them, pads and pencils poised.

Here, at least, he was correctly identified. *"Nicht kanedische!"* the German officer scoffed, then proceeded to say in perfect English, "American nigger!"

Rob's interrogators were friendly, laughing at how he'd been able to conceal articles from his survival kit about his person, telling him more than he told them.

He told them nothing, as he'd been instructed: *If you're taken prisoner, keep your mouth shut. Intelligence-gathering is the Nazis' forte. So they'll have some facts. They'll feed them to you, along with what they only guess. Your reaction, just a gasp or a lift of your brow, might confirm or deny their guess. Your role is to keep mum and look dumb.*

Rob did just that, refusing to answer when questioned about his station or missions.

"Captain, you don't have to tell me," the officer finally conceded with a smug grin. "Let me tell you. You are with the American Ninety-ninth Squadron, currently located in Ramitelli, Italy." He then pulled out a book, labeled "99th Squadron Fighter Group," and read from it, quoting names, call signs, formations.

Rob, amazed at the amount of correct information, assumed an expression of indifference and tried to keep a straight face.

"Captain Robert Metcalf. Ah!" the officer continued.

"You have been nominated for the Distinguished Flying Service Award." He paused, a satisfied smile on his face. "Didn't know that, did you?"

Damn! Had he given himself away? But he'd had no idea...

"For what you did to our airfield at Porz Wahn. And, oh, yes—did you know that Captain Randolph Carter, of your squadron, has been promoted to major?"

That really hit him. Randy. Why did it hurt so much that Randy would never know? Randy wouldn't have cared about a promotion. The war, like life, was just a game to him.

But Randy was dead. Back came that lonely depressed feeling. Missing Randy...

He stared at the German officer, who didn't know Randy was dead. Nobody but he knew. At home they didn't know. Ann Elizabeth, his parents. They would have to be told.

"Will my name go out on a prisoner-of-war list?" he asked.

He was assured that it would and that he could send a letter.

A letter he didn't want to send.

Rob was transferred to the prisoner-of-war camp at Nuremberg, where he encountered two other black pilots, Andy Charles and Elroy Spencer.

"Where do we sleep?" he asked, looking at the almost empty barracks.

"The floor, nigger. Where else?"

Rob said he didn't know what he wanted most, a hot bath or a juicy steak.

"Don't worry," was Elroy's cheerful reply. "You ain't gonna have to decide about either one."

Someone slapped him hard on the back. "Well, old man, here we are. Together at last."

"Joe Tillman! Where did you come from?"

"Damn Krauts dragged me out of the river up near Cologne. After one of them SOB's crippled my plane and I had to ditch. But don't worry." Joe's fist formed into a pistol and he made a sharp shooting sound. "I took two of them with me. You can call me Ace, old buddy."

"Congratulations, Ace. And fancy meeting you here!"

"Yeah. Ain't it great."

It *was* great. And strange. Joe had been his buddy all through high school, college, all through football and pilot training. The military had separated them. *The United States Army Air Corps is not looking for night fighters... Get the hell out of this line.* Even now, Rob could feel the shame, the humiliation he'd felt when that white major had separated him from his white comrades. Strange that it was in this cold barren enemy prison camp that they could be buddies again.

Strange, too, that he should be thinking about this. Randy wouldn't have given it a second thought, except maybe to laugh or make some stupid joke.

Now, as always, Rob thought of Randy. Randy, eating steak in the colored section of the Miami Airport. He remembered the arrogant restaurant manager saying, *I don't give a damn if they never come back.*

Well, Randy wasn't coming back. Suddenly Rob was glad that Randy had enjoyed his steak and potatoes that day, had laughed at the maître d', had laughingly apologized to Rob. *I sure was eating good while you was fighting the black war.*

Yep, Randy's life had been short, but he'd loved

every minute. He had just ignored— No. Poked fun at discrimination, at prejudice. It occurred to Rob that maybe he should take a lesson from Randy.

Besides Americans, there were also British, Canadian and Australian prisoners in the camp. Rob conceded that the British were the best soldiers. Every time he looked at one, he was reminded of that old line "There's something about a soldier that is fine, fine, fine." Something about the way they stood. Their neatness. Their arrogance. And they were organized, efficient, alert. They had a little radio, which they took apart every night, distributing the parts among the various prisoners, then reassembled every evening to catch the BBC broadcast. The most important news received was "Don't try to escape. Sit tight. We're coming." This welcome news was passed from prisoner to prisoner and it made the flies, the filth, the thin soup fortified with weasel meat, easier to bear.

The guards were from the Wehrmacht, the regular German army, with only a few officers in charge. They were regimented, but reasonably tolerant and fair, making order out of the most disorder Rob had ever encountered.

Intermittently officers from the Gestapo would appear, the Nazi storm troopers. They were smartly clad in black knee britches, matching officer's coats and shining black boots. Usually they came, issued a few orders and disappeared. It was after one such visit that preparations were made and the order given. "March!"

The prisoners were not surprised. They had learned from their concealed radio that the Allies were near. Word got around that the march from Nuremberg would be to a prison camp near Munich. "A hell of a long walk," Elroy Spencer declared. "We'll be marching for weeks."

Rob didn't care. He'd rather be moving than sitting. He no longer even thought about a hot bath. He'd become immune to the stench of his own body and the bodies around him. As they marched, he grimly endured the dirt, the insects, his growing itching beard, and the flapping sole that had come loose from his left boot. If he could get hold of a tack or some glue... Wearily he flapped on and on. It was quite an orderly march, considering the great number of prisoners. So much mud. So little food.

Joe, eating with relish from his tin cup of barley soup, reckoned they "shouldn't complain about the diet. We're lucky they're sharing their slim rations with us."

"And lucky they didn't filch our Red Cross packets," said Rob.

Discipline was lax. The line of march was miles long, and the guards paid little attention. The men traveled in pairs. At night one of the buddies would prepare a place to sleep and the other might slip off to a nearby farm to beg or barter for food. The Red Cross rations came in handy. Two cigarettes for an egg, one for a potato. The farmers, whose homes had been relatively undisturbed, were not as hostile as the city people.

It always amazed Rob that they would open their doors and express no surprise, no fear to see a member of the enemy on the doorstep. Nor did they seem to care that the enemy was black. They were friendly and eager to trade their rations for the precious items from the Red Cross packet.

One night Joe and Rob went foraging together. When they knocked at the door of a farmhouse, it was opened by a short stocky woman, her gray hair wound in neat braids around her head. A clean white apron almost covered the frayed black dress beneath it. A warm appetizing smell wafted from behind her, and Rob reluctantly returned the cigarettes to his pocket. This neat German hausfrau would not want them.

The woman smiled. "Americans?" she asked. They nodded. "Hungry?" They almost laughed and couldn't believe it when she stepped back, inviting them in accented but perfect English to come inside.

Never had Rob felt so dirty, so unkempt, as he did entering that spotless kitchen, trailing mud on a floor scrubbed as clean as the round wooden table. There was a big iron stove with a roaring fire. The savory aroma drifted from a big black pot in which something bubbled and sizzled.

"Sit," the woman said, her eyes twinkling. The kindest eyes Rob had ever seen. The best stew he had ever tasted. It was mostly cabbage, onions and potatoes, and she served it with big hunks of black bread, advising them to "eat slowly."

Rob showed her the scuffed picture of Bobby sitting under the Christmas tree, clutching a ball. Joe talked of a girl named Tammy. She showed them a picture of her grandson, a freckle-faced youth in a folk soldier's makeshift uniform. It clearly identified him as among the Nazis' last-ditch recruitment; by this stage of the war, no man was considered too young or too old to carry a gun.

She touched his picture. "He should be here. It's planting time, and anyway, he didn't want to go." The kind eyes grew sad as she repeated his words. "'I don't want to kill anybody, and I don't want anybody to kill me.'" She prayed he was somewhere safe and Rob prayed that none of his gunfire had hit that boy.

They talked about the war. "A terrible waste," the woman said. "Nobody wins."

In a nearby city bullets whined and bombs struck, but the sounds were muffled in the little farmhouse kitchen.

Before they left, the women glued the sole back on Rob's boot. He was as grateful for that as for the food. It would be much easier to walk.

They didn't always escape the bombs. One evening, as the line of march crossed the railroad tracks in a big city, they heard the whine of the warning siren and simultaneously the roar of American planes.

"Shit!" Joe shouted. "Don't they know we're down here? Don't tell me I survived all those dogfights just to be killed by my own people!"

The guards, as frightened as the prisoners, began to bark out orders in German and halting English, ushering them to a nearby railroad tunnel. They joined the German civilians and soldiers rushing to the shelter, everyone pushing and shoving to get to safety. When the Germans discovered that enemy prisoners were also seeking space, their resentment flared in loud and violent protest. They struck out at the prisoners, refusing to let them enter. Rob, pushed forward by the crowd behind him, found himself face-to-face with a machine gun in the hands of an angry German. His shouts were unintelligible to Rob, but he read the hatred in the eyes and saw the shaking fingers on the trigger. He pushed back against the crowd, fright flowing through him.

He felt Joe's hand on his arm. "Duck!" Rob ducked and followed Joe's bulk through the oncoming crowd. Most of the prisoners, realizing it was useless to resist the enraged civilians, made a run for the hills, some distance away from the railyard, which was the prime target of the raiding planes. Bombs were falling now, and the ground heaved around them. The air was thick with dust and smoke. People screamed and scurried like frightened animals. Halfway across the tracks, Rob saw a woman carrying a baby and pulling a little boy behind her. The child stumbled and drew back, crying. They would never make it to the shelter.

"This way," Rob shouted as he instinctively scooped up the boy and made for the hills. The woman followed.

In comparative safety, they watched as the bombs dropped and the ground erupted. Near the railroad tunnel a great hurricane of fire roared, the dust and smoke so thick it was difficult to breathe. Far below they could hear the agonized cries and screams of those who hadn't made it.

The child in his arms whimpered and Rob looked down into wide frightened blue eyes. So young and innocent, only a little older than his Bobby. "It's okay," he soothed, urging the child close and wrapping his jacket around him. "You're safe. It'll soon be over."

But it wasn't over yet. The bombs dropped, the fires raged, the smoke and dust filled his lungs. His heart thudded with rage and pity and fear. He made a silent promise to himself and to his God. *I'll never drop another bomb as long as I live.*

At last the raid ended. The planes headed off, probably back to England. The all-clear sounded and people emerged from the tunnel, coughing and choking. Fires still burned and across the tracks lay the bodies of the dead. Hardly anyone in the crowd paid attention as they ran to their homes.

"*Danke,*" said the woman. She took the boy from Rob and hurried away.

The order was given and the long march continued. The men were strangely quiet as they trudged through dust, debris and death.

13

"**I** wish to hell the Allies would catch up with us," Joe said to Rob several days later during the midday rest stop.

Rob said he hoped so, too, but he said it rather absentmindedly. He was watching a woman, her long dirty-blond hair blowing in the wind as she ran across the road toward them.

"Roosevelt," she gasped. "Roosevelt *ist tot.*"

"What is she saying, Joe?"

"It's about President Roosevelt, I think."

The woman gestured with her hands at her throat and repeated, "*Der amerikanisch Praesident ist tot. Kaputt*—finish." Now they understood. The president of the United States was dead.

"Thank you," said Rob. He found it difficult to speak. Dead. The man who had been president for as long as he could remember, whose fireside chats had cheered his mother through difficult times. "The only thing we have to fear is fear itself." The man whose "alphabet" programs had directed Rob's life. Food on the table with Dad's WPA job, summer jobs at CCC camp, the NYA job during college years. His was a deep and personal grief, and he hardly heard the comments as word was passed along.

"Who's president now?"

"The vice, stupid."

"Who is?"

"Damned if I know."

"Truman. Harry Truman."

"Never heard of him. Damn! Just as we're about to win. What's going to happen now?"

On the seventeenth day of the march, they arrived at a prison camp near Munich, similar to the camp they'd left. With one difference. A barbed-wire fence separated them from another group—Russians. The Russians were well supplied with watches, which they would gladly trade for any American goodies, and much trading went on across the fence.

One morning Rob and Joe were striding together around the compound. They were some distance from the barracks when one of the German guards ran toward them, gesturing excitedly. "Run!" he shouted, giving Rob a violent shove. "*Schnell!* Hide!"

Rob stared, uncomprehending. This guard had always been friendly and... The guard turned to run toward the front of the compound, joined by other guards, their guns at the ready. Rob saw a convoy draw up and dispatch a group of Gestapo. Rob wasn't sure what was happening, but instinctively he grabbed Joe's arm. "Let's move!" he cried.

They ran, sped on by the sound of gunfire. They scrambled under the barracks and from this vantage point witnessed a strange sight. A gun battle between the Wehrmacht and the Gestapo, some of the prisoners being caught in the crossfire. The battle lasted only a few minutes. The members of the Gestapo, who had not expected such resistance, were greatly outnumbered and soon surrendered. Any survivors were allowed to leave.

It was days later that the prisoners learned the battle

had been fought over them. The Gestapo were attempting to carry out orders to execute all prisoners. The Wehrmacht, whether for humanitarian reasons or in fear of reprisal, had prevented it.

The Allies were coming. The prisoners knew this, not only from the British broadcast, but from the sound of artillery that got nearer and nearer. One day, a jeep drove through the compound, two flags flying—one white and one with stars and stripes. The men broke into wild cheering. The American officer waved, but drove on to the prison headquarters and soon drove out. The prisoners knew they would soon be released.

The next afternoon the tanks rolled in and there was more cheering and shouting as the Americans took over the camp. The men were told to stay put until arrangements could be made for their evacuation. The Russian prisoners disregarded this order, tore down the fence and moved into town. Some of the Americans followed suit, but Rob stayed put, glad that his food rations had improved. He started another letter to Ann Elizabeth, although he hoped to be home before it reached her.

When evacuation began, it was by rank. Joe, a colonel, was among the first to go. The next day, feeling restless, Rob went into the little town, a few miles from Munich. Wandering along the cobblestone streets through the business district, he passed a bakery. Outside was an American quartermaster's truck that almost blocked the narrow street. Leaning against the wall, arms folded, a Negro sergeant directed two privates, who were filling the truck with freshly baked bread. Rob and the sergeant greeted each other with the easy familiarity of two colored boys in an alien all-white land. They exchanged a few words and Rob moved on.

Most of the people he encountered were tankers and

some of his fellow ex-prisoners, and he wondered where all the German civilians were. Had they gone into hiding like the Gestapo, for whom some of his comrades were diligently searching?

The cobblestone street wound into a residential area, and Rob stopped to admire a neat white frame house. Strange after all the blood and turmoil to see flowers, bright red geraniums spilling from a window box—a bit of beauty and normalcy in a war-torn world. He heard screams and shouts as the door burst open. An old man tumbled down the steps, kicked by a laughing Russian, one of the prisoners he recognized from across the fence. Instinctively Rob helped the old man up. As he straightened he was almost knocked over himself, bumped in the chest by a woman who had been shoved down the steps by...yes, one of the American ex-prisoners. He got just a glimpse of fear-filled eyes, disheveled gray braids, before the frightened couple rushed away. The American soldier clapped his hands and howled with laughter. "That's right. Run and save your hides, you stinking Krauts!"

At that point Captain Robert Gerald Metcalf pulled rank. "At ease, soldier. Cease and desist. Now. That's an order. Understand?"

The soldier was stunned. And resentful. Others, all white, Russian and American, an even dozen by now, closed in. The nigger captain had no weapon. This was war. It would be their word against his, this black bastard who patronized and fraternized with the enemy. Rob read the message in the faces moving toward him. His heart pounded and his muscles tensed. This could be fatal.

"Back off, motherfuckers!"

Rob heard the order, saw his startled attackers move

cautiously backward. He turned to see that the order had
come from the black sergeant he'd met outside the bakery. He sprang from the truck that had just driven up.
Submachine gun in hand, he repeated the order. "Back
off! Or there'll be a lot of dead motherfuckers around
here!"

The sullen resentment remained in their faces, but the
group slowly began to disperse, none willing to do battle with a submachine gun.

"You better ride with me, Captain," the sergeant said
in low tones. "They're just waiting to tear you apart."

Rob, knowing he was right, hopped nimbly aboard
and the sergeant drove on. Rob looked back and saw
the soldiers returning to the house. The looting would
continue. "Damn shame," he muttered.

The sergeant glanced over his shoulder and back at
Rob. "Going into battle all by yourself, sir? And you
a Negro captain! Crackers are still crackers, sir."

Rob grinned. "Right." He glanced at the man's insignia. "Thank you, Sergeant Amos Searcy, for rescu-
ing me. Incidentally I'm Robert Metcalf."

"Well, if I was you, Captain Metcalf, I wouldn't get
so riled up about these fucking Krauts!"

Rob was shocked by his bitterness. "Oh, I know
they're the enemy and all. But I think most of them are
ordinary decent people, not mad at anybody. They're
caught up in this mess just like we—"

"You think so, huh?"

"Yeah. Look, one night this old woman took us in,
me and my buddy. She—" He broke off. That smell.
It was the same odor that had permeated their prison
camp, but stronger, diffusing the sweet aroma of the
freshly baked bread. Something burning. Something
dead—like the time he'd been forced to crawl under the

house to retrieve a dead rat. Only worse. Much worse. "What's that smell?" he asked.

"Dead bodies, sir." Searcy's voice was soft and sounded...sad. "They were burning them and the smell still lingers."

"You don't mean..." Rob couldn't finish the thought.

"Yeah. Human. Bodies of decent ordinary people who weren't mad at anybody. They just happened to be Jews."

Rob stared at him, stunned. He had heard rumors over the BBC that Jews were being mistreated, incarcerated, but—

"Being a Jew in Germany is like being a nigger in Georgia," said the sergeant. "But a lot worse. They kill 'em in droves here. By law."

When it was obvious that Rob didn't believe him, Searcy became incensed. "I think you need to have your eyes opened, buddy—sir!" he quickly amended. "Think I'll make a little detour. You need to see Dachau. All of it, Captain."

Rob fell silent. They were only a couple of miles from the town when they came upon a large building, a swastika engraved on the front. Several smaller buildings, neat and freshly painted. Green lawns, flowers, shrubbery. Near one of the smaller buildings a little tricycle lay on its side. There were now jeeps in front, and some American and British officials moving about. Still... "This is the camp?" he asked, rather surprised.

"Shit!" Searcy exclaimed. "This was for the bigwigs and goddamn guards. You ain't seen nothin' yet. Wait'll I get these food supplies unloaded." He drove around to the back of the large building, and service personnel quickly unloaded the loaves of bread and other rations.

"Now we'll take a little tour," the sergeant said, returning to the truck. "There's something you ought to know about these Krauts, sir." He drove on, circling the compound.

Rob still didn't want to believe it, but he was looking at it. The long line of boxcars on a track that led into the camp, cars stained with blood. "Some people never made it into camp," Searcy said. "We removed hundreds of bodies from these cars. And there were others. People who'd been gassed."

Dead bodies piled on top of one another, ready to be incinerated in the crematorium. "They were trying to get rid of them before we got here," said the sergeant. "Very efficient, these Germans, when it comes to getting rid of the dead. The evidence."

Rob hardly heard him. He closed his eyes, but couldn't shut out the pile of decaying flesh, the clear form of a child clutched in his mother's arms. He felt weak, and suddenly very sick. He stood by the truck and retched. Over and over again, as if he could vomit out the unspeakable horror.

"I'm sorry, Captain." The sergeant laid an apologetic hand on his shoulder. "But you were so...I thought you ought to know."

He didn't want to know. Couldn't believe that people would do this to other people. Even babies, innocent children.

But the evidence stared him in the face. Kindled a rage so wild he could hardly contain it. Hell, yes, he could drop bombs. He could fly over this whole damn country and wipe out every person in it! Anyone who could—

Anyone? Deep within him, memories surfaced....

Did they know? That couple being thrown out of their home?

Sure they did! So close, they were probably part of it. The woman had planted geraniums while this massacre was happening.

That guard who had saved his life? Did he know? The woman who'd fed him?

Suddenly Rob was laughing—or crying. He leaned against the truck and buried his face in his arms.

Searcy handed him a handkerchief. "Pull yourself together, sir." He helped him back into his seat and drove on, past the crematorium, which had been shut down. Past the workers doing what had to be done, identifying bodies as best they could.

Rob closed his eyes. All the questions... Who? And why?

He didn't know he'd asked them aloud, but he heard the sergeant answer, "Jews, mostly. They hated Jews. I don't know why."

Suddenly Rob was back at Tuskegee, hearing Sadie Clayton talking about some book she'd read. *A man with a diseased mind...*

More than one diseased mind, he thought.

Jews. His mother had once worked for some Jews, the Jacobsons. Nice people. Mr. Jacobson had given him their son's old bicycle.

"Have to take some medical supplies to the infirmary," Sergeant Searcy said as he stopped in front of the main camp. "We got word to share as much as we can with the survivors. The lucky ones who were able to hang on till we got here."

The lucky ones. Scarecrows of men and women, children, with sunken cheeks and swollen bellies, dazed eyes still holding the specter of what they had escaped.

Rob had never before felt such compassion. He had never before felt so helpless.

He did take one girl in his arms; she was maybe fifteen, and couldn't seem to stop crying. He just held her, rocking back and forth, muttering the same words he had to the little boy he'd held during the bombing. "There, there, it's over now. You're safe."

"Her *Mutter*," another woman told him, explaining in broken English that the girl's mother had been killed only two days before the Allies came. She motioned with her hands, and Rob understood she would try to coax her to eat something.

Rob was aware that some signal had sounded and the survivors were all going to the mess hall. He walked in the opposite direction, but he felt caught, a part of this miserable mob. In their ragged prison uniforms, they were even dirtier and more disheveled than he was. Some barefoot, some in worn shoes. His own boot was coming apart where the woman had glued it—the hausfrau who'd fed him. Again he wondered—did she know? Suddenly he was suffocating, gripped by a paralyzing panic. He had to get away. The sergeant. Infirmary. He forced his feet to move in the direction the sergeant had taken. He got a whiff of the clean antiseptic smell and he thought of the incongruity. An infirmary in a death camp.

The beds were lined up, only inches from each other. Attendants, some in crisp uniforms, some as ragged as he, moved among the patients. Perhaps he should—

"Here, hold him, soldier!" The words were English, the voice German. The man who pulled at his sleeve had a tattoo on his wrist. "Hold him," he said. "I've got to change these bandages."

Automatically Rob knelt by the bed, held down the

kicking legs and took the hand of a boy, about ten, who lay on his stomach and screamed. He watched the man carefully remove the sticky bandages on the boy's back. His stomach turned over at the long line of infested wounds, thick with pus and blood. He wanted to weep. He squeezed the boy's hand and spoke the soothing words "It'll soon be over. It's all right now. You're safe. You'll be all right." How many times had he said it?

"*Will* he be all right?" he asked the man. And when the man nodded, "Are you sure? His wounds look so...so..."

"I'm sure. Thank God you people got here in time," he said as he swabbed the wounds. The boy had grown quieter, and the man spoke to him in German, calling him Fritz. "The sedation is taking effect. He'll sleep now," he said to Rob.

A nurse hurried over and handed him a jar. "Here's the salve you wanted, Dr. Goldstein." He thanked her and she moved on.

Rob looked at the sunken cheeks, the thin arm, the tattoo. "You're a doctor?"

The man's smile was ironic, showing the gaps between stained teeth. "Dr. Herman Goldstein, formerly of Weisbaden," he said. He shook his head as he expertly applied salve and clean bandages. "Bad thing, barbed wire."

"That's what made these wounds?"

The man nodded, explaining that the boy had been late for roll call and the guard had thrown him, scraped him against the fence.

Rob closed his eyes, gripped by another rush of fury, of sickness.

He felt a hand on his shoulder. "It'll be all right. It's

over now." The same words he himself had used to
console. But was it over? Would it ever be over? How
had it happened?

Again he was unaware that he'd asked aloud, but he
heard the doctor answer, "A little bit at a time, son. A
little bit at a time."

He glanced up. The doctor stared over his head and
spoke in a musing voice. "You're living quietly with
your family, taking care of your patients, operating at
the hospital. You don't have time for politics, rum-
blings, rumors. One day they say don't operate in this
hospital. Do not bring your patients here. So you move
to another hospital. Then you are banned from that.
Then you send serious cases to other doctors, do simple
surgery in your office. One day they take your children
out of school…" The man's voice broke and he shuddered. "The synagogue is burned, your windows are
broken. Every day you say to yourself, 'tomorrow it will
be better'. Then it is too late. Your family is gone, you
don't know where, and you are in a boxcar being transported to…to this." He made a feeble gesture with his
hand. "And you ask yourself, how did it happen?"

He looked straight at Rob. "You are an American
Negro?"

"Yes."

Trembling fingers gripped Rob's arm. "Be careful,
my son. Don't let it happen to you."

14

July 1945

The war was over. Rob was home.

But the Rob Ann Elizabeth had seen off to war was not the Rob she welcomed home. He laughed and teased, rolled on the floor with little Bobby, who was almost two, and played bridge with her parents. But it was as if he wasn't quite there, as if part of him was far away.

Only at night was he really close—as if he wanted to lose himself in their lovemaking, in her. Yet he seemed somewhat out of place in her bedroom under that frilly canopy above the bed. She should have removed that stupid thing. Or maybe they should have taken Randy's room. But it had already been relegated to Bobby.

Randy.

They all missed Randy. When they received the official news of his death—long before Rob's return—it was Julia Belle who'd broken down. She'd held in her hand the tiny bronzed shoe that had been his.

"Do you remember?" she asked. "That Sunday we walked from the drugstore to Aunt Sophie's? He kept saying his foot hurt and I kept scolding him and made him walk on. I said he was just being his usual stubborn self. But when we got to Sophie's, Herb took his shoe off...'' Here her voice broke and her eyes filled. ''A tack was sticking up, right in the heel of his shoe.''

''Mother, you didn't know.''

''I should have known, should have looked. I made him walk all that way.'' She held the bronze shoe against her cheek. ''Oh, Randy, I'm sorry. I'm so sorry,'' she choked through the tears.

Strangely enough, Sadie was the one who'd been able to quiet her, holding her close. ''Hush, now. Can't you hear Randy—'Ah, Mom, cut it out. It wasn't the nail that got me!' And I'll tell you something else. Randy's not crying. He's laughing, wherever he is.'' Sadie tried to laugh herself, but Ann Elizabeth saw the tears. ''Have you ever seen him when he wasn't having fun...taking things in stride, laughing at life?''

''That's true.'' Julia Belle looked thoughtful. ''Randy always took a special joy in whatever he was doing...wherever he was.''

''You had a special son, Mrs. Carter, and you must have had a hand in making him what he was. Thank you. I... Oh, dear God, he made me so happy. I...we owe it to him to stay happy, don't we?'' Sadie, tears streaming down her face, silently rocked Julia Belle back and forth.

In the following weeks, Sadie always seemed to be there when Julia Belle needed her. To comfort or cajole. ''Let's have a game of bridge. Dr. Carter's had a hard day.'' Or, ''Mama's house plants are all dying. I wish you'd take a look.'' And Julia Belle would go with her to the house near the hospital, where Sadie had brought her mother to live after her father's death. Anything to keep Julia Belle busy. And gradually she'd seemed to accept Randy's loss. She centered her attention on Bobby and regained some of her cheerful composure.

Dr. Carter, however, did not bounce back. He was as diligent as ever with his patients, as solicitous and loving to his family. But the pride, the anticipation, was gone. "Randy," he often said, "would have been such a good doctor."

Something else bothered her father. Those bombs. "They never should have dropped them. They didn't on Germany. Why on Japan?" His mouth twisted. "A matter of color?"

Ann Elizabeth was surprised. This kind of bitterness was unlike her father.

Anyway, she was glad they hadn't dropped it on Germany. Rob had been there.

Still, she worried about her father, sometimes as remote and withdrawn now as Rob. Ann Elizabeth's heartbreak was just as great. She'd been very close to Randy. She, too, was depressed, and anxious about her husband.

The years of acting came in handy. Now it was Ann Elizabeth who hummed or whistled a little tune as she went about the house, folding clothes or arranging flowers. It was Ann Elizabeth who cajoled the family into a game, invited friends over, took Rob to the tennis court. It was her bright smile that kept them all going.

She didn't press Rob. She simply waited.

Late one night he told her. They lay in her old bed, and Rob wasn't looking at her. Just staring up at the white canopy.

"Ann Elizabeth, I'm scared."

"Scared? Of what?"

"Of everything. Where to go. What to do. Of life, I guess."

"Well, don't let life know it!" she said, and chuckled.

"I'm serious. I—"

"I know," she said, quickly apologetic. "It's just...well, you made me think about a play I was in. Ed Sanford was Life and I was this young girl, weak and scared of Life and—"

"Ann Elizabeth!" He sat up. "We need to talk. And not about plays."

"Of course." She sat up to face him, but couldn't get the play out of her mind. Lying helpless on the stage, with Ed Sanford wielding a whip over her. But Mabel, the strong woman, had sternly demanded, "Life, bring me a rose!" Ed, head bent, had scurried away to do her bidding. "Don't ever say you're scared, Rob. You have to demand what you want in life and—"

"You don't know a damn thing about life! You sure as hell aren't going to learn about it in plays."

"Well, you needn't talk to me like that!"

"I'm sorry, sweetheart." He pulled her to him, instantly contrite. "I'm not hitting at you. It's...well, honey, life ain't always fair. You can get caught where you don't want to be."

She looked up, seeing in his face things he'd only hinted at—a whole painful lifetime lived in the months he'd been away. She didn't like him being sad. If only she could make him laugh, as Randy had. Or say something to bring back her happy, confident husband. But... "You're right, Rob. I'm silly and naive."

"Untouched is how I'd put it," he said, and kissed her. "And I want you to stay that way. I want to take care of you and Bobby."

"You will. I've never doubted that. Even if you have to dig ditches."

"I don't want to dig ditches."

"Oh, you know I didn't mean that literally! What *do* you want to do?"

"I'm not sure. I just know I don't want to stay in the Air Corps."

"Then don't."

"I have to do something." Rob leaned against the headboard. "And that's what's bothering me. I didn't even finish college, you know. So anxious to fly one of those planes."

"That's easy. You can finish on the GI bill." She thought of Randy's words. *Saving you a bundle, Dad. The Army will pay for med school after they teach me to fly.*

Rob's eyes brightened. "I thought about that. I could go into aeronautics."

"Aeronautics?"

"I'd like to design airplanes."

She tried not to let her surprise show. But...she'd seen him touch Randy's old models, still in his room, high on the shelves out of Bobby's reach. "Did you make airplane models like Randy did when you were a kid?"

Rob laughed. "Heck no. We didn't have the money for that kind of stuff. Guess I got the itch fooling with those gliders at school. And even overseas, Randy was always riding me. Said I was going to get killed because I was always busy studying the design of the plane, instead of shooting at it. And then, he's the one..." He stopped, swallowed. "It seems so unfair. He—"

She placed a finger on his lips. "Don't. Don't feel guilty because it was Randy and not you. These decisions are made by God."

"Oh, Ann Elizabeth, Randy was so...so..."

"I know. I know what Randy was. You said it so beautifully in your letter. And Sadie's forever repeating it to Mother. He will always be what he was—joking and laughing, taking life as it comes. And you know something, Rob? He always did what he wanted to do. And you must do what *you* want to do."

"Pete says I should stay in, that I could make major. And jobs are scarce now. It'll take three years if I go into aeronautics." He grimaced. "Then when I finish I might not get a job. Pete says—"

The bed bounced as Ann Elizabeth got to her knees and faced her husband. "Rob," she began, "it's like in that play. You have to decide what you want from life and ask for exactly that. You have to ignore the doomsayers who'll tell you it can't be done."

He laughed. "Well, sometimes those doomsayers are right. You know what a heck of a time I had getting into the damn Air Corps, and that was like volunteering to die! Can you imagine the flack I'll get when I apply to those aircraft companies wanting to design—"

"Wait," said Ann Elizabeth. "I haven't finished. You have to *act* as if there's nothing stopping you. You can't expect failure. And if anyone predicts it, you just smile and continue on your own way."

Rob shook his head. "You make it sound so easy, honey. All I have to do is take charge of life and grin as I go about it!"

"Right."

"It won't be easy. I'd have to move back to L.A. to get into school."

She thought of her parents. They would miss Bobby. "I wish we could stay here."

"You know damn well they wouldn't let me into Georgia Tech."

"No, I guess not."

"And, honey, I'd have to get some kind of part-time job. We'd probably have to live with Mom. Her place in Watts is rather small. Would you mind?"

She traced the outline of his face, cupped his chin with her hand. "Whither thou goest…"

He kissed her finger. "I love you."

She smiled. "Let's go down and make hot chocolate."

Leaving her family that September was the hardest thing she'd ever had to do. Going so far across country, taking Bobby away from them… Bobby was their heart, in some way making up for the loss of Randy. She wished…

But Rob was her husband. She knew he was doubtful and apprehensive about their future.

She was apprehensive, too. She knew many doctors, teachers, some lawyers, a couple of successful businessmen. But aeronautics, even engineering, was an uncharted field for Negroes.

However, she didn't say one word when her father suggested that he finance a gas station for Rob. "Along with mechanics, you know, that could be quite lucrative." She didn't even look disappointed when Rob thanked him but refused the offer.

Whatever Rob wanted. Whatever would make him happy and confident again.

She smiled through all the preparations, the leave-taking. "We'll be back to visit often. And you must come to us. I'm sure you'll love California," she told her parents, and kept up a stream of cheerful chatter.

Only with Sadie did she share her tears and her fears.

*   *   *

Ann Elizabeth loved her mother-in-law, she really did. It was just that she didn't always understand her. Thelma Metcalf was an enigma. A puzzling combination of practical hardworking mature woman and fussy complaining child. She was especially proud of her duplex in Watts, which she'd purchased with the legal and financial assistance of her longtime employer, Mr. Tyler.

"That old house me and my husband bought was about to fall down on me, and when I told Mr. Tyler about this place, he said it was a good buy. The rental from the downstairs flat would take care of the payments, he said, and then, when I got too old to work, it'd all be paid for and I'd have a good income. But do you know I went down to that Housing Administration office three times and they kept turning me down and turning me down? Mr. Tyler, he say, 'Thelma, they just giving you the runaround,' and he went over there. And, honey, before the Lord got the news, they had them papers ready for me to sign. Been here about two years now. You like it?"

"Oh, yes. Very much." Ann Elizabeth's bright smile covered her dismay. Their bedroom was so small. The crib, bureau and bed took up all the space. "Such a beautiful spread!" she exclaimed, knowing that the spread, the crisp new curtains and the crib were Thelma's way of saying welcome.

Thelma beamed her satisfaction. "I'm so glad you like it. I didn't know about the colors, but I thought...well, if she don't like it, she can always change it. Now, honey, you just get comfortable. I'll help you unpack later. I want to take my grandson downstairs and show him to Lizzie and Hank—the Stevenses. They good tenants. Been here ever since I got the place. He's a fine boy. Just look at those curls. Come on here, honey child, come to Grandma." Ann Elizabeth was proud that Bobby went willingly. "Now I'll be right back. You just make yourself at home."

As Thelma's footsteps retreated, Rob looked anxiously at Ann Elizabeth. "All right?"

She smiled. "All right." And never, in the three years they lived there, did she show by word or action that it was not all right.

Rob enrolled at the University of Southern California and got a part-time job at the post office. With the GI bill for school, they managed fairly well. Actually the three of them managed *very* well under Thelma's direction.

"Truman ought to hire her," Rob declared, "to run the budget. She could show them how to make a dollar out of fifteen cents."

Ann Elizabeth learned a great deal from Thelma. How to comb the newspaper for bargains and where to shop. She always felt guilty if she ran out of milk and had to buy it from the corner store.

"Don't never buy nothin' from that old skinflint," Thelma told her. "Everything down here is overpriced." She bought all their groceries in Mr. Tyler's neighborhood. "They's cheaper and fresher where white folks live." She would lug groceries home every Friday evening and sit with Ann Elizabeth to carefully plan the week's menu.

Thelma's economizing did not extend to little Bobby. He must have the best and most expensive outfits, ready to be shown off at every occasion. And woe be unto those who didn't praise him. "She's one peculiar woman. Jealous! Just plain jealous! Did you notice she didn't say one word about my grandson? And him so cute with those curls and them big eyes, and looking so smart in that yellow outfit. She just jealous!''

One evening the whole family had to be taken out to the Tylers' home and inspected by them. Ann Elizabeth and Rob stood smiling and embarrassed while the Tylers exclaimed over and over again about Thelma's son and his family. "So fine-looking!"

Thelma was sweet and generous. And demanding. This wasn't particularly a problem for Ann Elizabeth, but Rob could be as stubborn and unyielding as his mother. When that happened, the little flat would rock as tempers flared and voices rose. One sore point was Rob's church attendance, or rather, lack of it. His schedule was pretty full with school and job. Privately Ann Elizabeth felt he deserved one day of relaxation, and he did so enjoy listening to the radio broadcast of football or baseball games on Sundays.

Thelma didn't agree. "You ought to be ashamed of yourself, Rob. Sitting there by that radio on the Lord's day. You ought to be in church, down on your knees, thanking the Lord for bringing you through that terrible war and giving you such a fine family."

Rob said he'd be more likely to find the Lord on the football field. This was a championship game.

"Don't you go blaspheming the Lord now! You in enough trouble. I never raised you to act like this. I always taught you to remember the Sabbath and keep it holy."

But Rob's attention was now on the radio, and Thelma's shouts went unheeded. She would leave, Ann Elizabeth and Bobby beside her, for Shiloh Baptist Church. There, with Thelma in the choir loft and Bobby in the nursery, Ann Elizabeth would sit alone, more confused than enlightened by what went on about her. It was so different.

Oh, she knew what they said about her Congregational Church in Atlanta. A "seditty" church. If your skin wasn't light and your hair wasn't straight, you couldn't get in. Jesus probably wouldn't be admitted because of his social standing. She knew that these charges were only slightly exaggerated. Yet she also knew that in certain ways, the sophisticated members of the Congregational Church, who sat quietly listening to their minister, had the same desires and beliefs as the exuberant, shouting members of Shiloh. They had the same cares and problems, the same yearning for truth, love and peace.

But there was no peace, Ann Elizabeth thought, in the preacher's hell-and-damnation sermons. The shouting and amens from the congregation were disturbing. The collections, long litanies and endless announcements, tiresome.

She loved the music, though. When the tones from the organ swelled and the answering chords sounded from the piano in that moving gospel rhythm, a kind of exhilaration would sweep through her and she would tap her foot and sing with the congregation. She hadn't sung the old spirituals since her days at Washington High.

Once again she felt glad her father had defied her mother and insisted she and Randy attend the public high school. There was no auditorium, cafeteria or gym. But every morning they'd had devotions in their individual homerooms. No organ or piano. But the beautiful deep voice of James Hughey or the high soprano of Sadie would lead them in a spiritual. There was something lovely and inspiring about the simple words and powerful beat. So unlike what her father called the la-di-da hymns of the Congregational Church and Spelman Chapel. If her father hadn't sent her to the public high school, she never would have learned these songs, so familiar to her now, and would have felt even more out of place at Shiloh Baptist Church.

The various church activities to which Thelma dragged her were just about the only social outlet Ann Elizabeth had. She saw so little of Rob. The time he wasn't in class or at work was usually spent at the library. There was no place to study at home. He did play basketball with a group of fellows every now and then. She approved of that; he needed the exercise. The only exercise Ann Elizabeth got was cleaning the apartment and lugging Bobby's stroller up and down the long stairs. She took him for a walk every afternoon up the street, past the grocery store and the local pool hall. The men, lolling about outside, always spoke politely and plied Bobby with chewing gum or candy, which she confiscated as soon as they'd gone around the corner. She would slowly circle the neighborhood, glad to be out of the apartment. The place was stifling; she felt closed in. The sofa and chairs in the living room were protected by heavy plastic covers, sticky and uncomfortable. She wanted to get a job or take a class at the university, but there was Bobby. She didn't like to ask Thelma to keep him after a long day at the Tylers'. Besides, she never knew when Thelma might be off to some church affair.

Ann Elizabeth tried not to be lonely. She taught at Sunday school and Bible school, and worked with the women's auxiliary. Spent long afternoons on the little enclosed patio with books Rob brought her from the library. *Gentlemen's Agreement* by Laura Hobson,

Daphne du Maurier's *The King's General*, Frank Yerby's *The Foxes of Harrrow*, and many others.

She desperately longed for a friend. Someone to talk to. Someone on her own level. She was ashamed of that thought. She was not a snob!

Twice a year her father sent her money for train tickets, and she would spend three glorious weeks in Atlanta. But home was where Rob was—the stuffy little house on Central Avenue in Los Angeles.

September 1948

Then Rob graduated. He was now a certified aeronautical engineer, and as soon as he found a job, they would move. Anywhere!

It would be wonderful. They would have a house of their own. A yard. Flowers. She could even send for her wedding gifts. The day of Rob's graduation she'd picked up the surprised four-year-old Bobby, swung him round and round. "We're moving! We're moving!"

She banished the thought that it was now three months past graduation and no job was in sight. There were so few aircraft companies and none of them seemed to want a Negro engineer. She shut her mind to Thelma's constant refrain. "You better go full-time at the post office. A nice respectable good-paying job. A bird in the hand is worth two in the bush! Ain't none of these big white companies gonna hire a nigger. They likes you down there and you just better stay where you is."

Ann Elizabeth crossed her fingers and prayed. This time, surely! The telegram from Benton Aircraft, somewhere near Seattle, had read, "Qualifications excellent. Interview at 9 a.m. Monday, September 1, 1948."

Please, she prayed. *Please.*

15

The sign outside the roadside motel near the Benton Aircraft plant flashed VACANCY. Rob pulled in. "Completely filled up," said the man behind the desk. His smirk said he knew Rob knew he was lying and could do nothing about it.

Rob wanted to bust him right between his squinty little eyes. But the man was right; he couldn't do a thing. Where would a brawl get him?

Besides, this one hadn't been as blunt as the guy in the other motel. "We don't serve colored."

Should've stopped in one of the bigger cities, Rob thought as he drove out past the flashing sign. Easier to find a place that would accommodate you. But he'd wanted to put up in the vicinity, so that in the morning he could shower and shave, be fresh for his interview. Fat chance. It was now past midnight. He'd been driving for six hours after a late shift at the post office, and he couldn't get a bed to sleep in. As for a shower and shave…well, he'd think about that in the morning.

He found a parking space by the side of a gas station and ate the last of the fried chicken his mother had packed. Then he climbed into the backseat of the car and tried to get some sleep. But his legs were long, his mind in turmoil. Why did he think this interview would be different?

On his application and résumé he had purposefully omitted that he was a Negro. That detail could erase those "excellent" qualifications—in the top ten of his class, letters of recommendation, his years as a pilot.

Hell, what would it gain him? He hadn't mentioned race on his application with Air-tech, and he'd made it to the interview stage. But as soon as they saw his black face, he was shown the door. He shifted position, tried to stifle his mounting anxiety.

This was a fast-growing company and they were hiring, had openings, needed people with his expertise. Experimentation with the new jet engines had landed them a contract with a major airline to build their large commercial airplanes. God, he'd like to be part of that!

When the station opened in the morning, he drove around to the gas tank. Leaving his car to be filled, he got the key for the men's toilet—at least no flack about that, thank God—and went in. He shaved, freshened up as best he could and changed clothes. Neat black suit, crisp white shirt, black tie. Ignoring the attendant's curious stare, he stored his gear in the trunk, paid his bill and drove away.

There was enough time but no place to get a cup of coffee before the interview. He doubted he could swallow anything, anyway. He was that nervous! And hot. Even this early in the morning, he could feel the relentless heat and humidity. He took off his coat, laid it on the back of the passenger seat and loosened his tie.

Despite his qualms, he felt a surge of anticipation as he drove through the entry gates at Benton Aircraft Corporation. The buzz of activity in and around the big office, manufacturing buildings and hangars was like a heartbeat. This was where it was all taking place. The construction of the big airliners, the travel mode of the future. He envied the few workers he saw who were already involved in it.

He parked in one of the unreserved spaces by the office building, adjusted his tie, put on his coat and resolutely entered the building.

Outside the personnel office, he hesitated. This was the last chance and he knew Ann Elizabeth was counting on it—a good job for him, a home of their own. He thought of Ann Elizabeth kneeling on that frilly bed of hers in Atlanta, tossing back her head, philosophizing about life.

Poor baby—so naive. But he chuckled, amused and strangely bolstered by the image.

Okay, Life. Just give me a job.

He approached the girl at the personnel reception desk, and it was like a newsreel that had been played over and over again. Her start of surprise when she saw him.

"Robert Metcalf. To see Mr. Stewart."

"You have an appointment?" Incredulity written on her face.

He produced the telegram.

"Just a minute." She went over and spoke to a man seated at a corner desk. He glanced at Rob, took the telegram and disappeared into a partitioned office to the left of the large room.

A bald man appeared at the door, looked at Rob and went back inside.

Rob sat on one of the chairs near the outer wall and waited. And waited.

The door from the hall opened, admitting a pleasant-faced young man with blue eyes and crewcut auburn hair. Similarly dressed—dark suit, crisp white shirt, tie. "Gordon Jones, to see Mr. Stewart," he said to the receptionist. She went over to the office and the man who'd been seated at the desk emerged.

"Oh, yes, Mr. Jones," he said to the young man. "Mr. Stewart is expecting you. This way, please." He led him to the wide double doors at the back of the office. Before the doors closed, Rob glimpsed thick carpeting and a large potted plant.

The clerk then turned his attention to Rob. "I'm sorry. There seems to be some kind of mix-up."

Rob stood. "Mix-up?"

"About your notification."

"The telegram stated specifically to report at 9 a.m. today, September first. This is the first, isn't it?"

"Yes. But the position— Er, your qualifications—"

"Are you Mr. Stewart?"

"No, but—"

"My interview is with Mr. Stewart. I've driven a long way to keep this appointment." Rob didn't intend to be fobbed off by some two-bit clerk.

He couldn't say it aloud, but the clerk seemed to get the message. He seemed embarrassed and confused. "Just a minute. I'll have to go check." He went back into the partitioned office.

A dark-haired girl came through the double doors. She glanced at Rob, then went over and whispered to the receptionist, who whispered back but didn't look at Rob.

Rob felt his ears burn. Deep down in the pit of his stomach, something began to seethe and boil. Something indefinable, something between hurt and hot anger. That old newsreel, playing over and over again. The smirks, the stuttering, the pussyfooting. While he waited. His job...no, his very life on the line.

He concentrated on a picture on the back wall. Joseph

Benton. Old-fashioned handlebar mustache, clear searching eyes.

This time the bald man came out. He was neither confused nor embarrassed. "Sorry, Metcalf. There've been some changes."

"Since Friday? This is only Monday."

"Things happen fast around here."

Rob kept a firm grip on himself. He might not get the job, but he sure as hell wasn't going to be stymied by some bastard with a brain as blank as his face. He looked toward the double doors. If he could only get—

As if by some signal, the doors opened and a rather handsome man in a smart gray suit walked out. He was talking to the young crewcut man, whom he led over to the dark-haired girl.

"This way, Mr. Jones," she said as she escorted the young man out of the office. Presumably, thought Rob, to where he would be placed. It seemed so easy if you were white.

The stabbing sensation cut deep. More poignant than the suffocating hurt was the seething anger. The envy.

Not that he wanted to be white. He just wanted to get through those doors. He wanted the opportunity to prove himself. He wanted... He moved determinedly toward the elusive Mr. Stewart.

"Excuse me, sir," he said before the man could retreat into his office. "Are you Mr. Stewart?"

The man turned, startled but polite. "Yes?"

"I'm Robert Metcalf. I have an appointment to meet with you."

The bald assistant moved as if to intervene. Stewart waved him away, giving an I'll-take-care-of-this nod. "Oh, Metcalf. Yes, indeed. Come in."

At last he was inside the thick-carpeted and luxuriously furnished office. Seated, facing the man behind the polished oak desk.

To no avail. He knew it from Stewart's first words. "It's regrettable that we weren't able to contact you in time to save you the trip, Metcalf." The somber face. A futile gesture, expressing regret. "These last-minute changes..." He shook his head. "There's been quite a shift, since the airline contract has been drastically changed. The project on which you were to be placed had to be eliminated."

"Oh?" Rob had to let Stewart know he recognized the lie. "Your clerk said there was some question about my qualifications."

"Oh, no. No, indeed." Shocked surprise. "He must have misunderstood. You have excellent qualifications. Yes." He took a folder from his basket and began to thumb through it. So the bastard *had* been expecting him! "Yes, indeed. An excellent record. Excellent war record, too. We here at Benton are aware of the combat performance of the all-colored Ninety-ninth. We provided tech reps for the Seventeenth Air Force in the Italian theater." He looked as if he expected some commendation for this support, which, incidentally, had put the damn company on its feet.

Rob said nothing.

Stewart cleared his throat. "But, as I say, the contract change killed the project we had in mind for your services. Business is business, Mr. Metcalf. No reflection on your qualifications."

"I'm glad to hear that. Perhaps there's an opening on one of your other projects where I could be—"

"Indeed, indeed. We'll keep your application on file. When and if something arises, we'll send for you."

That'll be a cold day in hell, Rob thought as Stewart

rose from his chair, indicating that the interview was over. Enough talk spent on you, nigger. Now get the hell out of here.

Rob turned and walked away. He got into his car, feeling very tired, the hot anger subdued by a crushing wave of disappointment. He hated to go home to face Ann Elizabeth. And his mother's "I told you so."

He drove past the cement buildings and hangars that, just for an instant, had held promise. He drove calmly, easily, as if there was no storm raging within him. Out the entry gates, through the little town. It had the feel of a country village, although it was within easy driving distance of Seattle. This was beautiful country. Early fall, and already the leaves were beginning to turn. A quiet town with neat well-kept houses, green lawns. In front of one house, a young woman fastened a toddler into a stroller and he thought of Ann Elizabeth and Bobby. One house, green with white shutters, had a For Sale sign in the yard. Ann Elizabeth would have loved it.

Cut the daydreams, nigger! You think they'd let you buy that place?

Then he saw it. A freshly painted white house, a window box with luscious red geraniums spilling from it. He panicked. He pulled to a stop, afraid he might lose control of the car as it all came flooding back. Germany. A white house, red geraniums, looting soldiers, the colored sergeant. Dachau. He could see him as clearly as if it were yesterday—the Jewish doctor with the sunken cheeks and missing teeth...

It happens a little bit at a time. They take away your job...take your children from school...ban you from this or that. Then, when it's too late...this.

A recurring nightmare that haunted, jerked him

awake, screaming and in a cold sweat. It alarmed Ann Elizabeth, but he'd never told her. Not all of it—the horror that would never leave him. The rotting corpses, the body of a child clinging to his dead mother, the decay, the blood...the unbelievable horror.

God, this was broad daylight, and he still saw it. He wanted to get out of the car and retch. He swallowed, fighting for control, hearing the doctor's words ringing in his ears. *Don't let it happen to you!*

How did you stop it? By grabbing a bald man by the throat and choking him until his face turned purple? By socking a fist straight into that smooth-talking Stewart's mouth?

By landing in jail? Besides, his fight was not with the bald man or the smooth-talking Stewart. It was with something bigger, something that wound through every fiber of his life, as surely as that river wound through this lush green countryside.

Two women strolling by eyed him curiously, suspiciously.

He switched on the engine and drove away. He drove calmly, easily, as if no storm raged within.

He had married a jewel. He knew how difficult the last three years had been for Ann Elizabeth. How cramped the apartment. How much she longed for a home of their own, more children, the kind of life she'd lived before. He knew she'd been counting on the Benton job more than he had. But by not one flicker of an eyelash did she let her disappointment show. That adorable inevitable dimple lurked at the corner of her mouth and her eyes sparkled with optimism.

"Well, maybe the good Lord's looking out for us. It gets awfully cold up there in Seattle."

She even silenced his mother. "Not now, Mama, he's had a long day. Let him eat his dinner. Come on, I've kept it warm."

While he ate, she talked of something else. A phone call from Pete—he and Fran were in town. "Some kind of air show. They'll be here for a couple of days. I invited them for dinner tomorrow. Is that okay with you?"

"Sure. Great."

"It'll be like old times. Do you realize we haven't seen them since their wedding?"

"Yeah." He'd been best man. At Lockbourne Field when what was left of the Ninety-ninth were just settling in.

"Oh. Pete's made major. Isn't that great?"

"Yeah. Great." He pushed his plate aside. Most of the guys who'd stayed in the Army Air Corps were moving up, slowly but surely. Just sitting around getting promoted while he'd been busting his brains and getting nowhere.

"Finished? Good. Save room for your mom's peach cobbler. I'll dish it up. Fran sounds just like her usual crazy self. I can hardly wait to see them. Maybe I'll make fried chicken, corn on the cob..." Not noticing— or perhaps ignoring—his lack of enthusiasm, she talked cheerfully on, while he wondered if he hadn't made one hell of a mistake, not staying in the damned military. *You forgot, didn't you, nigger? How hard it is to get in...anywhere.*

It was later, when they were alone in their bedroom, that she ventured to suggest alternatives. "Your mother's right about one thing, Rob. You're already in with the post office—and you could easily get on full-time." With his hands behind his head he stared into the dark. "A steady government job, and it's not a bad income, Rob."

He shifted. Just forget all you've learned about propellers, jets and everything. At least sorting mail's a hell of a lot easier than digging ditches.

"Just while you're waiting," she added quickly. "One day someone's going to figure out how smart you are and sign you on. What about that new company in Arizona? Have you sent them an application?"

He felt as if the room was closing in on him.

"And we wouldn't have to wait. To buy a house, I mean. Daddy wouldn't let me pay a cent when I was living with them, and we've still got all that allotment money. A hefty down payment. Why don't we go Sunday and look at that new development? It would be like an investment, and we could sell it when—"

"When what, Ann Elizabeth?"

"When you get—"

"When hell freezes over!"

"Oh, Rob, don't say that." She sat up in bed. "I know you're discouraged now. But you can't let it get you down. You can't let other people determine your fate. How does it go?" She began to quote from a favorite poem of hers, Rudyard Kipling's "If". "'If you can trust yourself...'" He stood it as long as he could, but when she got to "'Or being lied about, don't deal in lies,'" he blew.

"Shut up, Ann Elizabeth!"

"What?" He couldn't see her, but he heard the astonishment, the hurt. He didn't care.

"I said shut up with all the sweetness and light! You don't know what the hell you're talking about. What about when you're being lied to and you know it and they know you know it and there's not a damn thing you can do about it?'' He snatched his pants off the chair. "I've had it up to here with the bring-me-roses and all the rest of that crap! You need to know this is a shitty world we live in. And for niggers, it's double! So just forget all that poetic gibberish, Lady whoever-you're-playing-now!'' While he talked, he was dressing. He'd better get out before he smashed something.

Ann Elizabeth lay back on her pillow. Not moving. Stunned. Never before had Rob spoken to her like that. And he had no reason to. None at all. She'd just been trying to...trying to... How dare he speak to her like that! When all she'd been trying to do was...

What? Cheer him up? Or were you trying to figure some way to get out of this cramped little house with those stiff plastic covers that make the only place you can sit down so darn uncomfortable. To get away from his uncompromising, bossy, childish—okay, kind and generous mother—with all her church socials and prayer meetings and those thunderous boring come-to-Jesus sermons every Sunday of the year. Oh, it's fine for you, Robert Metcalf. You just don't go. But...

You don't have to go, Ann Elizabeth. No, but... Oh, God, she'd rather go than stand the fussing or the sulks or...

Darn it, she just wanted a place of her own. It didn't have to be a big place. Just a small separate house with no meddlesome tenants downstairs, without a hundred steps to climb down just to get a breath of fresh air, no pool hall practically next door. A yard big enough for Bobby to play in and where she could have a flower garden. And Rob with a regular job—not this studying and rushing to the post office and no time to do anything with each other.

I've put up with it for three years, just so he could do…be what he wanted to be. And now… She buried her face in the pillow to muffle her sobs. She couldn't bury the misery. It was a dead weight inside her.

It was after four in the morning when he returned. He was due at the post office at five. She pressed her face deeper into the pillow, feigning sleep, breathing deeply as he tiptoed about the room, collecting his things. She heard the shower in the bathroom, and later, the quiet shutting of the front door, his steps as he hurried out.

She wished she could sleep. Or just disappear.

Then she heard Thelma in the bathroom and that was when she remembered. Fran and Pete were coming to dinner tonight. Oh, God! Today of all days.

She couldn't call and cancel. What would she say? Rob and I had a big fight. Bobby's sick and… No. Lies like that sometimes came true.

They were coming. She'd have to get ready. She'd planned to take Rob to work so she could use the car to shop. Now what? Maybe she could ride out to Belair with Thelma, ask Liz downstairs to keep Bobby. She was sorry she'd called her meddlesome; the woman was always so obliging. Still, if she rode out with Thelma, how would she get back in time to clean the apartment and start dinner? Was there a bus?

Thelma solved the problem for her. She said she'd planned to leave work early today so she could help prepare for a social at the church tonight. If Ann Elizabeth didn't mind the wait, she'd drive her to the store now, and they could be back at the house about one.

The supermarket where Thelma dropped her was in a small shopping area that also contained a beauty parlor, a drugstore, a dress shop and a deli. Three hours to

kill. She decided not to pick up groceries yet. Almost
numb with depression, she moved like an alien among
the shoppers hurrying in and out of the drugstore or
beauty parlor, loading groceries into parked cars. She'd
been so happy when Fran called yesterday. So looking
forward to tonight, to the kind of fun they used to have,
a break from her usual monotonous routine. She tried
not to think about Rob, tried not to think about anything
as she wandered into the dress shop, poked through the
sale rack. A yellow sundress with a full skirt bordered
by embroidered orange chrysanthemums caught her eye.
She tried it on. It seemed made for her and she felt a
tiny surge of pleasure at the thought of the coming dinner party. Rather expensive, even on sale, but she
bought the dress.

In the drugstore she bought a few toilet articles and
a couple of magazines. She wasn't hungry, but she'd
better eat something. Lots to do to get ready for Fran
and Pete.

In the deli she ordered a Coke and club sandwich and
sat at a corner table. She tried to eat, tried to blank out
Rob and their quarrel, idly thumbed through the *Ladies
Home Journal.*

The column "Making Marriage Work" jumped out
at her. Perhaps there was some advice here. But no, this
advice was aimed at a wife who complained that her
husband was a slob. After he moved out she'd found
seventeen pairs of his socks under the bed. Ann Elizabeth giggled. What kind of wife would leave that many
socks under a bed that long? White folks sure didn't
have much to worry about.

When Thelma arrived she was ready with her bags
of luscious fruits and fresh vegetables.

"Nice," Thelma said when Ann Elizabeth put two

pots of orange chrysanthemums on the back floor of the car. "That'll sure brighten up the place. Did you get peaches? I'll have time to make you a cobbler before I leave for the church."

They got home a little after one, and with some relief, Ann Elizabeth noticed that Rob's car was parked in its usual place. At least he was home. Did he remember they were expecting company? He was stretched across their unmade bed, half-dressed, in a deep slumber.

"Let him rest," Thelma said. "I'll help you clean. He had that long drive yesterday." If she knew he'd also been out all night, she gave no indication.

Ann Elizabeth didn't dare ask that the plastic covers be removed, but when they'd polished everything to perfection, the apartment looked warm and welcoming. The flowers did brighten it up. She broke off three of them and a few fronds from Thelma's fern to make a low centerpiece for the table.

Finally everything was almost ready—Thelma's cobbler and the candied yams, string beans, crisp fried chicken in a big covered bowl, the corn ready to boil and the corn muffins to pop into the oven at the last minute. Thelma was off to her church social, and Ann Elizabeth bathed herself and Bobby. Then she went in to wake Rob.

It wasn't easy. He was still fast asleep and it wasn't until Bobby climbed up and pulled at him, "Daddy, Daddy, play with me," that he began to rouse. He sat up, his arm around Bobby, but still seemed dazed.

"Get up, Rob," she said. "Fran and Pete will be here in twenty minutes."

He looked at her, his focus sharpening as memory surfaced. "Ann Elizabeth..." He hesitated, his expression half defiant, half sheepish. "Listen, I—"

"Daddy," said Bobby, tugging away.

"That's right, Bobby," she said. "Get your daddy up. Company's coming."

"Ann Elizabeth—"

"Not now, Rob. There isn't time. Hurry and get dressed."

"Okay, buddy," he said to Bobby, lifting him high in the air before putting him down and hurrying in to shower.

"Don't mess up the bathroom," she called after him as she began to make the bed. Then she combed her hair, slipped into the new sundress and helped Bobby change into his pajamas.

But the pleasurable anticipation had been expelled by anxiety. With a heavy heart she wondered if they were going to be able to act natural. She wished Fran and Pete weren't coming. Not tonight.

16

How could you not be natural around Fran? She burst in like a ray of sunshine. "Ann Elizabeth!" she cried, hugging her. "I hate you. You're just as pretty and tiny as ever. More so. While I'm getting fat and flabby and I haven't even had a baby. And this is Bobby. Come here, you, and give your aunt Fran a kiss. Isn't he cute, Pete? Dimples, just like his dad." She handed Bobby to Pete and turned to hug Rob. "That's what I said—dimples. I always did like a man with dimples."

Rob took Bobby downstairs to the Stevenses, where he was going to spend the night, and then, as if they'd been together only yesterday, they settled into the old laughing teasing relaxed routine.

"My mouth's been watering all night, Ann Elizabeth," Pete said as he helped himself to his third piece of fried chicken. "I remembered what a good cook you are."

"That's my wife," said Rob, his gaze enveloping her, the colorful dress, the matching flowers on the table. "A cook in the kitchen, a lady in the parlor—"

"You sure got that right!" Fran broke in. "Ann Elizabeth's sure enough a lady. 'Cause she come from them seditty Atlanta folks, you know. Too bad for you Pete—you got this country bumpkin from Waycross. But I'm learning how to set a nice table like this with the pretty little flowers. I'm watching you, honey chile.'' She flashed her impish grin at Ann Elizabeth and rattled on.

But Ann Elizabeth was conscious only of Rob's steady gaze that signaled he was remembering the rest of the saying. She felt herself blush. ''Listen, do any of you want wine?'' she asked. ''It's been so hot. I thought that iced tea—''

''Delicious,'' said Fran. ''And so refreshing. Now, Pete, do you notice that little sprig of mint stuck in the slice of lemon? Make a note. That's one of those fancy touches us common folks must remember. Especially now that I'm Mrs. Major Peterson.''

They had already congratulated Pete on his promotion, but that started another round. Rob brought out the wine.

''Have to make a toast to my old buddy,'' he said as the cork popped out and he filled their glasses. ''It didn't come easy,'' he said, lifting his glass. ''Up and onward, old pal.''

''Onward is right,'' Pete said as they touched glasses. ''Did Fran tell you we're being transferred to Wright-Patterson next week?''

Rob stared at him. ''In Dayton? Are fighter squadrons based there? I thought that was the headquarters of the Materiel Command. Has there been a change?''

''No. It still is. I'm going to Area B where they invent and test-fly. Integration, buddy boy. Ain't you heard? Got to put us somewhere and they're scrambling like mad. This is election year, kid, and the catch phrase is civil rights.''

''Oh, yes,'' said Ann Elizabeth. ''I almost couldn't believe it when we heard Hubert Humphrey read the Democratic platform.'' Even now she could recall the thrill that had shot through her as she listened. "We watched the whole convention downstairs on the Stevenses' little television."

"We watched, too." Fran put down her ear of corn, wiped her hands on her napkin. "A whole bunch of us at the Officers' Club just jumped up and hollered when Truman thumbed his nose at the Dixiecrats!"

"And that took guts," Rob said, his eyes glowing. "We didn't know what we got—back in 'forty-five I mean. I was on the march to that prison camp when some German woman ran out to tell us Roosevelt was dead, and Truman was president, and somebody asked who's Truman! I knew he was the VP of course, but I didn't really know him."

"You know him now! When he took his seat, he put his money where his mouth was. Signed Executive Order 9981. Hallelujah!"

"He's reaching for the colored vote," Fran said.

"And he's sure got mine," Pete said. "As Rob put it, the man's got guts." Pete stood up and, with a great deal of poetic license, did an impersonation of the little man from Missouri. "Okay, boys, this is the way it is. Enough of this separate-but-equal shit. We're starting with the Armed Forces. Integrate. That's an order." Pete slammed his hand on the table, almost upsetting his wineglass, amid a chorus of amens.

"I bet the shit hit the fan then," said Rob. "You know how many rednecks there are in the Army."

"Oh, yeah, he got a whole lot of buckin' and kickin'. I can hear them now. 'This'll never work, Mr. President.' 'It's gonna work while I'm the commander.' 'Course under their breath they're saying, 'That won't be long.' And then he says, 'Any of you can't follow my orders can quit. I'll accept your resignation now. At that table right over there. Is that clear?'"

"Ain't many of 'em walking, either," said Fran. "They got bills and car payments just like we have."

"Truman." Rob looked very sober. "Like I said before, that took a lot of courage."

"Yeah, but it ain't all courage," said Pete. "It's politics. He's had a lot of pressure from the NAACP and the Negro press, and don't discount the Negro vote."

"Politics." Rob had almost forgotten. It was a congressman who'd untangled the red tape and finally got him into the Air Corps. "You don't think about it," he said, "or you get too busy to be involved. I remember a man in Germany said to me you just go along, doing your job, trying to take care of your family, not thinking much about politics…"

Ann Elizabeth saw the sad haunted expression that always scared her, and she hastily changed the subject. "Have you seen Jackie Robinson play?"

"Have we!" Fran grinned. "Every time there's a Dodgers game in Cincinnati, we're there."

"Worth it, too. Just to see him rattle the pitchers when he's on base. 'I'm gonna steal, I'm gonna steal.' And he does. Folks come just to see him outrun the throw between bases. I tell you that nigger's a clown."

"He can play ball," said Rob. "I know. Played against him when I was at Fresno and he was at UCLA. Sure took the big leagues a long time."

Ann Elizabeth relaxed as the talk moved to baseball. Fran said that now they were gradually moving in more colored players, the fans were as much fun to watch as the game. She said last time she was in Cincinnati, there was a fat colored woman behind her who had a jar of collard greens for lunch and a crush on the new catcher,

Roy Campanella. Fran said she kept waving her jar of collard greens and yelling, "Come on, Pomponelly!"

Talk drifted to other subjects. Who had gotten out of the corps and who had stayed in. Trace Wells had finished at Meharry and was setting up practice in Memphis. Bo and Lil had separated. Bo got into Yale Law School, you know. Yeah, he made it, but he was still trying to pass the bar in Atlanta.

When Ann Elizabeth led her to the bathroom, Fran confided that she wasn't looking forward to Wright-Patterson. "Living on the base, next door to white folks who ain't as much fun as we are and don't want you there, anyway." She sighed. "I know it's the right move and good for Pete. But I'm sure gonna miss the fun. Almost every night, we'd gather at the Officers' Club and, Lord, that Chappy James is a real kick. I hear he's moving to..."

Soon the evening was over. Fran and Pete were gone; Rob and Ann Elizabeth were alone. She stacked some of the dishes and took them into the kitchen. Rob followed, carrying several glasses. She emptied scraps into the garbage and went to the sink, turning on the water. Rob moved behind her and slid his arms around her.

"Ann Elizabeth, I'm sorry. So sorry."

"I know." She knew the hurt, the frustration he felt. Knew how hard it was to hold it in. How hard not to strike out at someone. She wanted to tell him she understood, but the words caught in her throat.

He buried his face in her hair. "I shouldn't... I mean I was kinda mad and I took it out on you. When it was me. I shoulda stayed in the damn Air Corps."

Tears filled her eyes. Yes, it was hard for him; she realized that. Congratulating Pete right after he himself had been turned down by every company he'd approached. "You didn't want to stay in, Rob. And we're all right. You've got a good job and…" She stopped. Sorting mail. He hated it. She turned to face him. "Get back in."

His brows went up. "Yeah. Excuse me, Colonel, sir, but I made a big mistake. If you'll just let me back in, I—"

"No. I mean as a civilian. All those airplanes? You wouldn't be designing them, but they must need engineers. And that Executive Order Pete mentioned. I've been reading about it. It includes federal employees, as well."

Rob seemed to consider her words. "Yeah. Not exactly what I want, but better than the post office. Let's face it—engineers are paid a lot more. But hell, Ann Elizabeth, that's the kind of position white folks reserve for themselves." His eyes grew hard. "It'll be just as difficult to get past some two-bit government clerk as it is to—"

She drew herself up. "I didn't say it would be easy, Robert Metcalf. Nothing is. One of my Daddy's favorite quotes goes, 'Life for me ain't been no crystal stair. It's—'" She closed her mouth, eyes wide.

"Oh, Ann Elizabeth, don't look at me like that! And don't stop. Don't ever stop." He crushed her to him, held her tight. "Never stop being you…playacting and quoting. It keeps me going. I love you, Ann Elizabeth. I love everything about you, my lady in the parlor. Do you know how proud I was tonight? After I'd gone off like a damn idiot and left you… I don't know how you managed with the house and the dinner, but you're some kind of lady, Ann Elizabeth. When I saw you tonight in this dress with matching flowers on the table and… Oh, God, I love you. I'll never stop loving you," he said, kissing her hair, her temples, her lips. "So. How does it go? Life ain't no crystal stair? Tell me. The end is always the best."

She grinned, happy that he was more like his old self. "Well, it's from a poem by Langston Hughes. A mother talking to her son, you see. She tells him about the hard time she's had, but she didn't give up and he mustn't, either. 'Don't you quit now. Don't you...'"

Rob smiled, thinking of his own mother.

September 10, 1948
Sacramento, California

The placement officer's glance skimmed over Rob briefly as he scanned the circle of new employees waiting in the reception area at McClellan. "Robert Metcalf?" he inquired.

Rob stood up. "Yes, sir."

The officer's head snapped back and his mouth fell open. He quickly recovered, but his face turned a pale shade of red as he ushered Rob into his office.

"Good morning, Mr. Metcalf," he said, waving toward a chair.

"Morning." Rob sat in the chair, a straight padded olive-green chair, in front of the olive-green desk. The nameplate facing Rob read James J. Green.

Green shuffled through the papers in Rob's file, cleared his throat. "Let's see. Robert Metcalf," he said rather dubiously. "CAF-9, $8500 per annum."

"Yes, sir." CAF-9 was his classification as a government employee. A relatively high classification, he knew.

Another shuffle of the papers. "Well, I see you had a great deal of experience, but it's as a rated flying officer. Not much on the engineering side of the house.''

''I was the engineering officer for my group for six months before I was shot down. Isn't that in there? And there's my degree in aeronautics.'' Why the hell was he explaining? ''I passed the exam. The telegram said report for duty.'' Not for a damn interview.

A frown furrowed Mr. Green's brow. ''It's just that at the CAF-9 level, three years of experience is preferred.''

''Oh?'' Rob's eyes narrowed. Another runaround by another two-bit clerk?

''Not to worry,'' Green said hastily. ''We'll find a space for you in Materiel Command. Something to fit your experience.''

''I see. Or maybe I don't.''

Green was quick to counter. ''It's okay. You're on the payroll as of today. But the exact position will have to be finalized. A new requisition will have to be written by the office you'll be assigned to, and that'll take a little time.''

''I see.'' Rob drew a carefully controlled breath. Here we go again. ''I am on the payroll, you said?''

''Yes, indeed.'' Green rose from his chair. ''Do you have friends in the Sacramento area?'' he asked.

''Not really. Why?''

''Well, Rob, it'll take a day or two, maybe a week, for the personnel requisition to be processed. And I thought you could visit or something. While you wait.''

Rob got the point—while they figured out where the hell they could put this nigger! ''I passed a golf course as I drove in this morning, and—''

Green interrupted. ''You play golf?''

Rob wanted to laugh at the man's unconcealed surprise, but he simply answered, "Yes. I play."

"That's excellent. Why don't you just go and play a round and come back tomorrow morning." Green rose in the age-old gesture of dismissal.

In the parking lot, Rob got into his car and looked over the data he'd been given. A temporary badge, a sticker for the front bumper that would allow him to pass through the gate, a booklet that said, "Welcome to the Materiel Command," which featured a picture of the commanding officer, a map of the base and other related data.

Okay, here's my passport, badge, sticker and all. So why do I feel like I've just been kicked out?

Relax, nigger. You're on the payroll. The man said so. Go find yourself a house and get your family up here.

Christ. A house. Where? Who'll sell to me? Another struggle I'm not up to facing just now.

The man made a good suggestion. Go play golf.

Rob smiled, remembering Green's surprise. He'd played golf since he was sixteen, when he first began to caddy at Los Angeles's poshest country club. Not only had he picked up an interest in the game, but he'd gotten a little practice and some great pointers, thanks to the pro, who was an all-right guy. Rob had continued to play—at any public course that didn't give Negroes the "no tee time" runaround.

He wondered about that as he approached the golf course, a beautiful eighteen-holer. But he was greeted affably by the man in the snack bar. Even the three men seated at a table gave friendly nods. All white. Not one Negro. Too bad. He'd been hoping to see someone who could direct him to the colored section of town, where he might be able to find a decent house.

Sure, he could rent clubs, the man at the bar told him, and pointed toward the pro shop. Rob got a bucket of balls, deciding to hit a few practice shots first. He knew he was rusty. Between school and work, he'd hardly touched a golf club in years.

Not bad, he thought later, as his third ball sailed true and straight to the range target.

He heard a low whistle and the jubilant echo "Not bad! Not bad at all!"

He turned to see that he'd been watched by a jaunty man in khaki shorts and T-shirt, one of the three who'd been sitting in the clubhouse.

"Hey, why don't you hook up with us?" the man suggested. "My partner didn't show. You and me, buddy. With that swing we can beat the socks off those guys."

He did. Had a good round. Won two beers and an invitation to play again. Nice guys. He'd learned that his partner was Hugh Bavin, a captain in the newly formed Air Force, no longer Army. Bavin was on leave until the next Monday, when he was to report to his new post at McClellan. He'd flown bombers in the war and they exchanged war stories. Bavin told of a rescue by the Ninety-ninth Fighter Squadron when he'd been under siege by Germans. "Never so glad of anything in my life when I heard that southern drawl on the radio band saying, 'Look out, man, he's right on your tail.' And a confident reply, equally Southern, 'I see the mother. Let him come on in! I got his ass in the middle of my gun sight.' The SU-109 started to smoke, sink and fall in a ball of fire. That might've been you, partner. Saved my life then, just like you're saving this damn game.''

Yeah, I guess it could've been me, thought Rob. Small world.

He phoned Ann Elizabeth as soon as he got back to the hotel. "We're in the money, honey. I'm all signed in."

"That's wonderful! How do you like it? Or is it too early to say?"

Much too early. He changed the subject. House hunting. "Sure you wouldn't like to come up to Sacramento and look?"

"Living in a hotel with Bobby? Dragging him around? No, thanks. I trust you. We'll come when you have a place for us."

Later, seated in the hotel dining room sipping a martini, Rob scanned the place for a colored person. All the patrons and hotel clerks were white, all the serving people Mexican.

Where are the Negroes? There must be some in this town.

After dinner it was still light. He stood in front of the hotel and stared across at the California state capitol building and the beautiful grounds surrounding it, vaguely admiring, liking the feel of this small city. Determined to find his own space within it, he turned his back on the capitol, going up Twelfth to K Street. He strolled east on K, passing the business district and entering a residential area. Trees, more trees and Victorian houses, all the way to Twenty-eighth Street. Occupants white. Not a brother in sight. Disconsolately he retraced his steps.

Back on Twelfth he passed the alley and saw a crew from the hotel disposing of garbage. He approached them and asked where could he find Negroes. They smiled and suggested he head for Seventh and P.

Aha! It was still early, eightish. So he walked down Tenth, alongside the capitol grounds toward P Street. He soon came upon houses and people—Chinese, he thought. Had the hotel people misunderstood?

No. Here he was at Seventh and P. The colored section. The drugstore, the Momo Black and Tan Club, Banjo's Barbecue, the taxi stand and brothers of every description.

Rob entered the drugstore. It was typical—a soda fountain and three small tables with wire-back chairs. A couple seated at one table. The pharmacist stood at the counter talking to a distinguished-looking brown-skinned man in a tan business suit. Rob seated himself at the soda fountain. An attractive girl took his order, a root-beer float.

A tall, very dark man sat on the next stool, ordered a banana split, then turned to Rob. "Hi. What's happenin'?"

"Not much. Just passing time. I'm new to this area."

"Me, too. Been here a couple months. Transferred from Dayton to work at McClellan. Civilian employee."

"Well, I'll be damned. I work at McClellan, too."

"Oh, yeah? Where? What division?"

"Don't know. I haven't been placed yet. But I'm on the payroll." He extended his hand. "I'm Robert Metcalf."

"Lonnie Drake." A grin split his face and his handclasp was firm and friendly.

A small world, Rob thought again as the two men—brothers in an alien land—exchanged personal information.

"So you ain't been placed yet," Lonnie said "But you been hired? What classification?"

"Engineer, CAF-9."

Lonnie gave a low whistle. "Man! No wonder you ain't been placed."

"Oh?"

"You way up there. They don't like that. You okay long as you totin', carryin' and followin' orders. But they don't like you *giving* orders, supervising some of them!" Rob's alarm must have shown, for Lonnie added hastily, "Don't worry 'bout it. You on the payroll. And...CAF-9! Man! Don't matter where they put you," he added with a satisfied chuckle.

Lonnie was a fount of information. "The man who was talking to the druggist? Oh, he's a dentist. Got a office on Eighth and P, next to a doctor's office. Huh? Oh, I don't know where he lives, but the doctor and his wife got digs over the office." He consulted his watch. "'Bout time for the Momo to open. Man, that joint's really jumpin'. Draws more whites than colored. Either for the music or the cocktail waitresses." He gave a loud cackle. "Prettiest gals in town...tan, tall and terrific! Wanna go?"

Rob said not tonight and pressed for more information. Where did Lonnie live?

"Me? I got a room over a funeral parlor—just temporary until this apartment farther down on P is vacant. In a couple of weeks. Then my wife's coming. Say, you looking for a place? There's another room over—"

Rob shook his head. A room over a funeral parlor didn't appeal to him. Nor did he want to put Ann Elizabeth in an apartment in the Negro business district, even if he could find a vacancy. He wanted tree-lined streets and gracious houses, like the ones he'd seen near the golf course or farther out K Street. He sighed. Did Lonnie know a colored Realtor?

Lonnie did. Rob took down the phone number.

The next day at the personnel office Mr. Green reared back, hands clasped over his ample waist, and greeted Rob with a hearty, "Morning, Metcalf. How was your game?"

"Okay." Rob regarded him steadily. *Where's my job?*

Green sat up, coughed. "Well, I have good news. And bad news. Good news first. Your requisition's been approved. But since it's a high-grade position, it has to go through the Twelfth Civil Service Region for approval. That'll take another day or two—which is the bad news."

Rob thought of Lonnie's words. "So what do I do in the meantime?"

"More good news. I've been authorized to let you play golf for another day. You can't beat that with a stick, can you?" he asked, smiling.

Rob accepted the humor with a wry smile of his own and said he hadn't planned to play golf, but if it was okay, he'd do a little house hunting, instead.

Green seemed delighted with the suggestion and told him he needn't come in the next day, but the day following.

That night Rob called Ann Elizabeth. "O.T. Jones is the only colored Realtor in town, I understand. His main interest seems to be 'How much money you got, Mr. Metcalf?' I asked him how much did I need and what's he got to show me. So far, nothing suitable. But I'm sticking with him and doing some looking on my own."

He had plenty of time to look, since every day he reported for work, Green hedged. He hadn't heard from some region or hadn't received some requisition. Rob could play golf, house hunt, whatever. "Administrative leave. Don't worry. You're on the payroll."

But after a week Rob *was* worried. Bigots or not, nobody was dumb enough to keep paying him to play golf. Or maybe they *were* that dumb! And when the shit hit the fan, he'd get fired for goofing off.

Damned if he would! He looked hard at the placement officer.

"Perhaps I should consult the Inspector General."

He saw the panic in the man's eyes even before the quick protest. "No. Don't do that. I'm sure you'll be placed directly."

When hell freezes over if I leave it to you! "When? And where? It's been more than a week and—"

"Soon. I've already spoken to Chuck Samples in engineering and he's—"

"Perhaps I should talk with him myself." Fight my own battle. This pussyfooting son of a bitch was no damn help!

"That's not a good idea. You see—"

"You'd prefer I speak with the Inspector General?" Rob knew he was being reckless, using this kind of blackmail, which might not mean anything, anyway. But his rage was boiling over. He braced himself to—

"No, no, no. That's not at all necessary." Again Rob saw the panic. Apprehension that someone high up might get on his tail for discrimination. "If…if you can convince… It might be a good thing for you to speak with Samples, after all." Now Rob sensed relief, as if Green had been given an out. Samples, not he, would be on the hot seat.

"Thank you," Rob said, adding "Mr. President" under his breath. But he couldn't prevent a feeling of trepidation as he was led to Samples's office. If the engineering officer was forced to hire him against his will, working with the man would be pure hell! Threats were no good. This time he had to sell himself.

Again he felt the burning rage. Why did a Negro always have to prove himself before... But Green was opening the door to Samples's office, and Rob told himself to stay cool.

Tired eyes and thinning blond hair revealed Chuck Samples to be about forty. His desk was piled high with papers, and he had a Do Not Disturb frown on his face.

Green ignored the frown. "Sorry to bother you, Chuck," he said, "but this is Mr. Metcalf. The engineer I spoke to you about. I, er, I thought you should talk with him yourself, discuss his, er, qualifications." He laid Rob's résumé on Samples's desk and, with a mumbled apology about some meeting he had to attend, backed out of the door, leaving the two of them alone.

Not for long. As soon as Green left, a woman rushed in with a stack of papers. "James wants an okay on these right away." Then there was a telephone call that prompted a tirade from Samples. "Don't know what those Warner Robbins idiots think they're doing. You sit on this, Bill!" Two men burst in, concerned with a problem about the fuselage on the F-104.

Watching Samples handle each matter with dispatch, Rob was impressed. This was a man concerned with getting the job done. Under the right circumstances an ideal man to work for.

Abruptly the interruptions ceased, and Samples looked across at Rob as if surprised to see him still there. "Well, Mr.—" he glanced around, found Rob's résumé. "—Metcalf. Let's see..." He perused the file, cleared his throat and started again, "Well, let's see.

All your papers are in order. Looks like you've passed everything—twice, it seems. But—''

"But I'm black." Rob said it softly, but resolutely.

"Ah, now, wait a minute. I didn't say that."

Rob held up his hands in agreement. "I'm not confronting you, sir. It's just that I've been sitting on my hands for two weeks, playing golf at government expense, and I'm sure this whole charade is about what should be done with me."

"Now, look, Metcalf, this has nothing to do with you personally. I have nothing against—"

"Maybe not. But you've got problems—like who's gonna work with me, perhaps how will your peers accept you, and—"

Samples tapped his pen on the desk signaling for a stop. Rob leaned toward him. "Let me finish, sir."

Samples gave a resigned "go ahead" shrug.

"I can do this job, Mr. Samples."

"I don't doubt that, but—"

"And I can get along with a rattlesnake if I have to."

"You'd damn well have to!" Samples gave a rueful smile. "And not just here. Georgia, Alabama. Lots of travel."

"I can deal with it. I've been colored all my life, sir."

There was a gleam of admiration in Samples's eyes. For a moment Rob's spirits lifted.

But Samples looked doubtful again. "I don't know." He rubbed his chin in reflection. "It wouldn't be easy, Metcalf. This is a tough job at best."

"I know. You're in the middle of the biggest arms race in history and industry's snatching your qualified people like crazy. Think about this. They won't snatch me!"

Samples's eyes sharpened. Then he smiled, this time a smile that was whole-hearted, even a bit conspiratorial. He picked up the phone and dialed. "Okay, Jim, you can come and get this requisition. I've signed it." He listened a moment, then added, "Thanks. I'll need it."

Rob knew the thanks was for the personnel officer's promise to comb the ranks to find employees who might condescend to work with a Negro, and it set his teeth on edge. All this fumbling pussyfooting bullshit to hire one colored man. So damn stupid!

Down, boy! You're in, aren't you? He shook Samples's outstretched hand. "Thank you, sir. I won't let you down," he said.

The very next day Rob was given a small cubicle and a title, T33 Engineering Specialist, CAF-9.

At least he was at work.

By now Rob was also exasperated with Mr. O.T. Jones, his riddles, his funny nasal whine and his rundown houses. "Mr. Jones, you haven't shown me a single house where there are other houses nearby. They're all next to some business or an overgrown empty lot full of trash."

"Well, Mr. Metcalf, how much money you got?"

"Not a dime for what you've shown me so far! Is that all *you've* got?" asked a thoroughly irritated Rob.

"Well, there's Del Paso," Jones whined.

Del Paso. Treeless. Arid. Junky. Washed-out stucco shacks. The prize site was one that had a three-foot-high chain-link fence and a concrete covered backyard, with a picnic table and a redwood bench on each side.

It looked, Rob decided, more like a honky-tonk joint than a residence. He didn't even go inside.

"Don't you have anything in the Curtis Park area?" he asked. He'd been driving around in that area, with its beautiful old homes on tree-lined streets. He'd heard that houses there might be available to nonwhites.

Jones was honest. His license didn't allow him to contract south of W and X streets. But he had a friend, a white Realtor, who might accommodate Rob. He gave Rob the man's card.

Rob thanked him. Now he understood. The juicy prospects, fairly decent areas opening up to colored, were reserved for white Realtors. He wasn't annoyed with Jones anymore. He felt sorry for him. What kind of business could you do with one hand tied behind your back?

He looked at the card. Ferdy. He drove back to where he'd seen that For Sale sign. A good neighborhood, tree-lined and quiet. Across the street a couple of Chinese children were at play.

It was an old house, but in its day it had been top of the line. A twenty-five-foot setback, big yard, front and back, a driveway to a rather rickety garage. It would probably do.

He drove to Mr. Ferdy's office. "Mr. O.T. Jones said you might have some houses I could see."

"I sure might. What are you looking for?"

Rob described the house he had just seen. "Your For Sale sign is in front."

Ferdy drove him out to inspect the house. Not bad, Rob thought when he was inside. Lots of dark wood paneling, a stone fireplace in the living room, wide windows in both the living room and adjoining dining room. Another room downstairs, which could be used as bedroom or study, plus a kitchen and bathroom. Two bedrooms upstairs.

Not bad. Well…okay, anyway. Torn linoleum in the kitchen, plaster crumbling in the bathroom and bedrooms, back steps falling down.

"It's not in the best shape," he said.

"Nothing that can't be fixed," Mr. Ferdy said. "We'll knock off a bit for that." He smiled at Rob. "It's still a good deal. I don't think you'll find a better one."

Rob understood. This house he could buy.

"Okay, I'll take it." The price was $11,500 with a down payment of two thousand dollars. They shook hands and went back to his office. Rob wrote the check. They signed papers and he gave Rob the keys to the front door.

Not quite an hour's work for Mr. Ferdy. Rob wondered if he would give O.T. Jones a small cut.

17

"No, Bobby. Don't put your hands in that gooey stuff. Sit over here and read me your book. As soon as I finish, we'll go outside and you can take your dump truck. Read to me about the three little pigs."

Five-year-old Bobby dutifully retired to a corner of the bathroom and, with the help of the pictures and the words he recognized, tried to recite the story. Ann Elizabeth smiled as she listened to the childish voice imitating her own dramatic interpretation while she frantically applied wet sticky filler. The man in the hardware store had said it would work. If she could get it to harden in the cracks of the crumbling wall above the bathtub, she would cover it with contact paper. It had worked above the sink in the kitchen.

Rob had painted the woodwork and put down new linoleum in the kitchen and bathroom. The contact paper would make the rooms bright and cheerful. There was still a lot to be done, but the house wasn't really bad, she thought. Built of sturdy redwood, it had needed no outside paint and looked quite presentable once Rob had pulled down all those vines. She liked the old-fashioned front porch and the big yard. Rob had had to haul away discarded cans and bottles and tear down that old garage.

There was shrubbery in the front around the porch. She had never worked in a garden in her life, but she hoped to plant some flowers in the spring. Right now she had to concentrate on the inside.

They'd opened an account at the furniture store, but hadn't had to buy much. Julia Belle had shipped the wedding presents and added her old dining-room set, studio couch, desk and other odds and ends more elegant than anything they could afford.

Ann Elizabeth worked hard to make the old house livable and beautiful. In this she had help from her only colored neighbor, Bertha Perkins. Bertha knew just what to do for rough floorboards, leaky faucets and crumbling plaster.

"You'd know what to do, too," she told Ann Elizabeth, "if you'd lived in one of them shit-ass company houses at the lumber camp. Damn things fall down if you don't know how to prop 'em up."

"How long did you live there?" Ann Elizabeth asked.

"Ten years. Took me that long to skim off enough from Sam's pay and his gambling for a down payment on something I could call my own. Some folks been living in them shit-ass shanties for twenty years and don't own a plank. I told Sam to hell with that!" The Perkinses were also beneficiaries of the "going colored" block. The down payment had been spent on the two-family house next door, and they were now converting it to its original one-family status. It was—or would be—big enough to house Bertha and their six children, and Sam who came home from the lumber camp on weekends.

Bertha was a small wiry woman who ruled her children and her tall husky husband with an iron hand. Although her conversation was punctuated with words that shocked Ann Elizabeth, Bertha would tolerate no cursing from her kids. "Thing I can't stand is a foul-mouthed young'un, specially one I'm feeding and clothing. Sammy Junior, get the hell outa them damn bushes 'fore I bust your butt!"

Despite obvious cultural differences, the two women got on well together. Bertha's practical know-how was more than complemented by Ann Elizabeth's inherent good taste in color and decoration. Roberta and Racine, Bertha's quiet respectable older girls, earned spending money by baby-sitting Bobby.

Another neighbor who extended a friendly greeting was Sue Imoto, the Japanese woman across the street. "I'm so glad to have a new playmate for my Tom," she said as they watched the boys at play and shared the coffee cake she'd brought over. Though most of the other neighbors simply ignored her, Ann Elizabeth soon felt at home on the quiet tree-shaded street in Sacramento. She enrolled Bobby in the cooperative nursery at the public school only four blocks away, took her turn one morning every week, met more of her neighbors at the semimonthly mothers' meeting. There were several Japanese and Chinese families, but only one other colored family—besides Bertha's—that she knew of in the entire area, and she was the only Negro mother who regularly participated in the PTA meetings and the cooperative nursery school.

"Don't you feel kind of funny?" Bertha asked. "Being the only one 'mong all them white folks?"

"Well, no," she answered. "Guess I haven't thought

about it.'' Then she chuckled. "But now that I *do* think about it, I realize I'm quite an asset."

"Oh?" Bertha looked skeptical.

"I'm the one who had the idea of labelling all the kids' boots and coats. Before that, you can't imagine how mixed up we got—after naps and getting them dressed to go out to the park or home. So many look-alike jackets and mostly the same size. And I'm the one," she said, puffing out her chest, "who wrote the skit we're performing at every PTA in town. So they ought to be glad to have me."

"Guess you're right," Bertha conceded, but her mouth twisted. "All the same, I bet some of them don't like your being there one little bit. I know white folks."

Strange, but Ann Elizabeth hadn't really thought of them as "white folks." Only concerned mothers like herself. And she enjoyed them, enjoyed acting in that silly play she'd written. A funny play, pointing out all the mistakes made by frustrated mothers, and of course the better way to handle problems. It had become quite a hit.

It was after a performance one night that she was reminded of what Bertha had said. Mary Gibson, one of the mothers she particularly liked, invited the participating women to her house afterward for cake and coffee. Mary turned to her and said pointedly, "You have to get home early, don't you, Ann? Sorry." Ann Elizabeth realized she wasn't invited. Some of the others looked shocked. But they all got the message. Later Ann Elizabeth wished she'd thought of a disdainful reply like, "You surprise me, Mary. I gave you credit for more intelligence." But a cutting remark, even in retaliation, wasn't her style. Besides, she was more amused than hurt by what she recognized as Mary's insecurity.

Suddenly she thought of what her father had said that day at the hospital. *Your mother's daughter with that same core of inner pride...a kind of confidence no outsider can shake.* She grinned. *Right, Daddy. I'm Ann Elizabeth Carter.* What do I care about having coffee at Mary Gibson's house?

However, the incident did open her eyes a little. Bertha was right about some white folks, and Ann Elizabeth became more aware of Rob's problems. He was being snubbed by certain people at work—where it mattered. But, she thought with pride, he was handling it. As for herself, the Mary Gibsons meant little. Unlike Rob at work, she could pick and choose her own friends. She also gained new friends from old ties. "Be sure to look up Laura Tinsley," Julia Belle wrote. "I saw her mother at church Sunday and she says Laura lives in Sacramento now. Her married name is Mason. You remember that she went to Howard. Met and married a law student there, who is now practicing in Sacramento. Oh, yes, and an old classmate of mine has lived there for years. Selina Chatwell. On her last Christmas card..."

Laura and Mrs. Chatwell took her to the Negro Congregational Church, formed, Selina said, after a couple of Negroes were refused admittance to the Congregational Church downtown. Services were held in an old renovated house, but the congregation was perfect. Her kind of people.

"Doctors, lawyers and Indian chiefs," was the way Rob described them. "Ann Elizabeth, you're a snob. You think if anyone comes from Spelman or Morehouse or marries someone you knew in Atlanta or—"

"Oh, hush up! You like them, too. I couldn't drag you away from Phil and Laura's the other night." Nothing wrong with seeking out the kind of friends you enjoy, she told herself.

But she felt a little guilty when she entertained the bridge club she'd joined with her new friends. What about Bertha? "Come for lunch, even if you can't play bridge," she invited her.

"Who you having? That lawyer's wife and her crowd?"

"Laura Mason, you mean?"

"Yeah. That's the one. Comes over here switching like a freshwater trout!"

"Well, Laura is…" What could she say? Bertha's description was apt.

"Just count me out. I don't have no truck with them highfalutin society broads who look at me like I was something the cat dragged in."

In the end Ann Elizabeth was relieved that Bertha persisted in her refusal. Bertha wouldn't fit in—particularly not her language.

Ann Elizabeth did enjoy her new friends. It was like having a little piece of Atlanta that she could wrap cozily around herself. Rob likes them, too, she thought, only vaguely aware that she and Rob were pulling in different directions. While she was grasping for a small secure world like the one she'd known in Atlanta, Rob was striving to enter a wider world. He was trying to gain a toehold in the economic reality dominated by whites, many of whom wanted no part of him. But at least his boss didn't feel that way.

"He might talk like a Georgia cracker, but he treats me like he does everyone else. Matter of fact, I seem to be in on more consultations than most. Can't figure out whether he's testing me or what," Rob told Ann Elizabeth.

"Probably knows you're smarter than he is."

"Not so sure about that, honey." Chuck Samples was a GS-13 deputy to Lieutenant Colonel Henry Marks, who headed the T-33 Weapons System Division. "It's true that he came up through the ranks with no engineering degree, but he's very respected. He's a hard worker, sharp as a tack and has no use for incompetents. I know he was pretty skeptical about me at first," Rob added. "I mean to cross every *t* and dot every *i* with precision."

She grinned at him. "You mean you'll perform the job with your usual brilliance?"

He smiled, wishing he could be as sure of himself as she was. He was smack in the middle of an enormous undertaking. The cold war between capitalism and communism simmered, boiled and threatened to explode. Planes had to be recycled or discarded, bought, maintained, peddled or donated to allies throughout the world. Aeronautical engineers were indispensable.

Chuck Samples might have no attitude about color, but he didn't play favorites. Like the other engineers, Rob was saddled with extensive travel and major consultations. Samples had been right. The job wasn't easy, particularly not for Rob. Some supervisors, like Samples, were only interested in getting the job done, but others clearly resented having to work with a Negro, and he had to quickly discern which was which and how best to deal with each. So this was more than a job. It was more encompassing than that—a challenge he tackled with vigor, expertise and, strangely enough, some amusement.

Consultations often spilled over into after-work

drinking sessions or golf games, and he made a point of participating.

"Sometimes playing golf with a guy is the best way to get to know him or let him get to know you," he told Ann Elizabeth. "I never lack for partners," he said with a wink. "I've got a low handicap."

Ann Elizabeth, remembering Mary Gibson, never complained about the long hours he spent on the golf course.

Rob enjoyed the games and he enjoyed his work. He wasn't designing the planes, but he played a major part in keeping them running and creating the innovations that would improve them. He discovered that both his bosses, the colonel and Samples, were good to work with.

So well did this team work together that the F-86 and F-94 weapons systems were added to their division. Marks went up to full colonel and Samples to CAF-14. Samples immediately put in a request for Rob's promotion to CAF-11. "You deserve it. We have you to thank for the modification and delivery, on time, of the F-86 Fire Control System."

"Not me alone," Rob said. As point man for the project he had worked with engineers, manufacturers and flyers at several bases. He was proud that he and his team had delivered a system that would allow the plane to hit a target on a collision course at supersonic speed, but his feelings were mixed. Hadn't he once vowed not to drop another bomb?

When he thanked Samples for the promotion, the other man chuckled. "It wasn't a favor, buddy. We need your black ass."

Rob grinned, aware that procedures had sometimes been delayed while participants got used to dealing with first a nigger, then the black guy and finally and respectfully Rob Metcalf.

What was most difficult was simple hotel accommodation. Once, in Mobile, the government vehicle sent to pick him up sped away as he walked toward it. The woman civilian driver had stopped just long enough to shout, "I ain't gonna drive no nigger!" Often he had to seek out a colored hotel or an acquaintance for housing, like the doctor in Virginia who'd been a classmate of Dr. Carter's.

It could be difficult for his companions, also. Chuck Samples had been working with him on the F-86 engine-power problem in Oklahoma City the time the base restaurant was closed. Directed to an establishment across the street, the two had been deep in discussion when the waitress placed Chuck's utensils and left.

Chuck beckoned to her and pointed to Rob. "You missed him."

It was then that the manager appeared and gruffly announced, "We don't serve niggers."

An irate Chuck rose to protest, but Rob grabbed his arm and hustled him out. "I don't want to eat here, anyway." Such incidents had become routine—needling interruptions that mustn't be allowed to interfere with the work at hand. And they weren't unique. He knew that other Negroes, beneficiaries of Truman's Executive Order, in both low-level jobs and the few-and-far-between high-level positions, were dealing with the same experiences. He was lucky to have the support of his immediate bosses.

Even so, he considered the relationship a purely business one and was quite surprised when Chuck said, "We need to celebrate. Can you and your wife come for dinner Friday night?"

When he relayed the invitation to Ann Elizabeth, she readily consented. Unlike coffee with Mary Gibson, dining with Rob's boss was important. She knew that Rob liked Samples. More important, Samples liked him, had shown neither prejudice nor favoritism in dealing with him. Obviously Rob had made a good impression. For his sake, Ann Elizabeth hoped that she would, too.

When she first entered the Samples home, she was assailed by a wave of pure envy. This was the kind of house that, except for the color bar, she and Rob could have bought. No crumbling walls, rotting linoleum, no rubbish to haul away. And no long daily drive for Rob. He would have been living near his work, among his co-workers in a shiny well-built house with lush carpets, smooth walls and freshly painted woodwork. She could smell the newness.

Ann Elizabeth Metcalf, you're a crybaby, she told herself, and pasted on a bright smile as she greeted their host.

He took her hand in a warm grasp. "I'm Chuck, your old man's sidekick."

"That's not quite the way *he* tells it," she said, liking him immediately. "I've heard good things about you, and I'm glad to meet you."

"And this is my wife, Cora."

"So nice of you to have us," Ann Elizabeth said, turning to a plump woman, who was obviously a nervous wreck. She looked as if she wasn't used to entertaining, but was anxious to do it right.

"My pleasure," she said. "Do have a seat. I'll be right back." Biting her lip, Cora returned to the kitchen; Ann Elizabeth wished she knew her well enough to offer help.

The Markses arrived, and more introductions were

made. Colonel Marks, a short hefty man with dark hair, was very affable. Hazel, his wife, seemed aloof, as if it were she and not her husband who wore the silver leaf.

The three men immediately plunged into shop talk, and she and Mrs. Marks exchanged chitchat over glasses of wine, while Cora Samples rushed back and forth serving canapés and seeing to dinner preparations. She seemed so flustered that Ann Elizabeth felt sorry for her. The men were on the other side of the room around a small bar, where Chuck was serving drinks, and she and the Marks woman were seated near the dining area, which led into the kitchen. Hazel Marks was telling her something about the Officers' Wives Club when Ann Elizabeth heard a crash and a gasp of dismay from the kitchen. She knew Hazel had heard it, too, and had decided to ignore it.

Ann Elizabeth couldn't. "Excuse me," she said, moving toward the kitchen.

She found Cora Samples in tears, staring down at the broken pieces of a gravy bowl and the splattered remains of gravy.

"What am I going to do?" Cora wailed. "There's hardly any gravy left and the biscuits are ready to come out of the oven and—"

"Never mind," Ann Elizabeth said, stooping to collect broken glass. "We'll fix it. Let's just get this mess cleaned up."

They managed to do that, but Cora couldn't hide her dismay. She said she'd decided to fix fried chicken with rice and gravy, because she usually had success with it. "But now the gravy's gone," she wailed.

"Onion soup," said Ann Elizabeth. "Do you have a can?"

It worked. The last bit of the gravy, mixed with the

onion soup, combined well with the rice. They piled it on a platter, sprinkled fresh parsley over it and placed the fried chicken around it. Everyone said it was delicious.

Later Cora spoke quietly to Ann Elizabeth. "I was in such a tizzy," she said. "And you made it all so simple. Thank you. I'd like to... Look, can we meet for lunch next week?"

It had been a small gesture, a natural inclination to help someone in distress, but it had won Ann Elizabeth a lifelong friend.

"Cora's too shy and warm-hearted to realize what a power she is," Ann Elizabeth told Rob a few weeks later.

"Power?" he'd asked. "What do you mean?"

"She's the wife of top executive Charles Samples, so Cora Samples is a power among the wives. And she doesn't even know it. She's sure made it easy for me to slip in."

He stared at her. "Into what? Parties? That's nonsense. It's you. All by yourself." He pulled her up from the sofa where she'd been sitting, rocked her in his arms. "I've watched you. You're so unintimidated and comfortable. You make others feel that way, too. And you're...well, you're delightful. Charming. Do you have any idea how proud I am to have you beside me?"

She kissed him. "I love you, too, Mr. Metcalf." But she knew it was Cora who had set the tone for her entry into that select circle, and she was grateful. She liked being there, liked hearing about Rob.

Oh, she knew about his promotions and increased paycheck. But it was at the small social functions that she learned of the liking and respect he had gained from the people with whom he worked. At a small dinner party, she heard Samples say, "Rob's got people savvy."

"You're right about that," an officer agreed. "Rob can make a mad dog lay a bone at his feet when he was all set to bite."

"So you're a master at handling people," she said as she and Rob drove home.

He grinned. "Have to be. People are more complex than planes, more of a challenge than fixing the bird."

The way he spoke, it sounded simple, straightforward—but she knew it wasn't. By this time, Rob was a supervising engineer with a staff of four, and was traveling even more extensively throughout Europe, Asia and the Middle East. He found it a little irksome that he was accommodated more easily outside the United States than inside it.

Ann Elizabeth was proud that Rob was doing so well. She kept herself busy, tried not to mind his frequent absences and never complained about them. But the house seemed empty without him. Empty without his quick light step, hearty laughter and those tunes he was always singing or whistling.

One day when he returned from a trip to Colorado Springs, he wasn't whistling or singing. He looked grim.

"Didn't the meeting go well?" she asked.

"Great!" he replied. "Mission approved in all aspects."

"So what's wrong?" she asked.

"I just did a damn-fool thing."

"Oh?" She felt a twinge of alarm. "Tell me."

"I impersonated a prince."

"You... *What* are you saying?"

"I'm saying I'm stupid. We were on a high. Great job. So. We—Walt, Colonel Bavin and I—felt like celebrating. We go to this posh restaurant in Colorado Springs. Mistake. They don't serve—guess who?"

"Oh, Rob..." She knew it hurt every time it happened.

He shrugged. "Bavin gets hot, but I calm him down and we go to the Officers' Club, where we should have gone in the first place. But Bavin's still stewing the next day when we're at the hotel in Denver, waiting for the shuttle to the airport. He spots this fancy bar across the street and decides we should pay them a visit. I'm burning from the night before and tell them to go ahead without me. But Bavin insists. You're going to be Prince Ahmed, he says, and we'll be your escorts."

"Prince Ahmed?"

"He said that an Arab monarch who was visiting the President in Washington had brought one of his sons—me!"

"Rob! You didn't!"

He nodded. "Fool that I am, I put on that lamb's wool fez I bought in Pakistan and marched right over."

"And what happened?"

"Royal welcome! Escorted to the best seats at the bar. Everybody sending drinks over and gaping at the 'prince.' Walt was in his element, downing the free drinks and spouting off about the prince's millions. Bavin was flirting with the waitress while I sat looking princely and muttering in French."

Ann Elizabeth, picturing the scene, laughed.

Rob's hand hit the table, startling her. "It's not funny! I was a blithering idiot to pull such a stupid stunt just to get into some stupid bar!"

"Don't be so hard on yourself. It's not like it hasn't

been done before. You know that. Any Negro can wrap
a rag around his head, start talking in gibberish and—''

"Tell me about it! It just proves that any foreigner
from any country in the world is treated better than any
Negro citizen in his own United States!"

Surprised by his bitterness, she was silent. She had
never thought of it in quite that way.

"And I had to go them one better. I impersonated a
real person. I masqueraded as the son of a royal Arab.
Do you know what would have happened if we got
caught? *Which we almost did.*"

"Oh, no!"

"Oh, yes. The owner of the bar comes over, bowing
and scraping, so honored to have royalty at his establishment and he's called the *Denver Post* and their cam-
eraman's gonna be there in ten minutes!"

"Rob!" Ann Elizabeth's hand flew to her mouth.
"What did you do?"

"Got out of there pretty damn quick. Bavin made
some excuse about me expecting a phone call, and said
we'd be right back. What we did was grab a cab to the
airport and hop the first plane headed this way."

"My, that *was* a narrow escape."

"Walt and Bavin were laughing fit to kill. But I was
shaking in my boots. If we'd been caught, they'd have
lost their commissions and I'd've been out in the street
on my black ass! That is, if I didn't go to jail."

"Goodness, I don't think…" Her voice trailed off.
She had never really appreciated how Rob weathered
such incidents, time after time. Negroes were still
banned at all kinds of places, but people usually knew
where they could or couldn't go. But for Rob, traveling
to different locations and with white companions it
was… Difficult. Embarrassing for his companions, too,

but she didn't care about that. Maybe it was good for them to see what it was like.

Episodes of discrimination were routine for Rob, and she suspected he usually found them more irritating than embarrassing, often a major distraction from the job at hand. She marveled that he kept whistling.

She took his hand. "Let's take Bobby and Bertha's little boy to the park. I'll fix sandwiches and a thermos of hot chocolate. We can have a picnic."

Thankfully there were no repercussions from the Prince Ahmed incident.

Well, just one. The story circulated and became a joke among his co-workers. He was often greeted as "Prince," and regaled with comments like "What does Your Royal Highness require?"

As the months flew by, Ann Elizabeth's life expanded far beyond the black elite circle she'd known in Atlanta. Hardly realizing it, she found herself stretching in several directions—the warm good-neighbor relationship with Bertha and Sue Imoto across the street, the PTA group, her Negro friends from the bridge club and the little Congregational Church, and the group at McCellan where often they were the only Negro couple at a function. Eligible now with his GS rating, Rob joined the Officers' Club, where he often had lunch with Ann Elizabeth. This was also where they attended the many social functions, seated up front as protocol required. He was always proud to have Ann Elizabeth beside him. Never intimidated by anyone, she was as much at ease with their white companions as she was with Laura or Bertha, and, small affair or large, was always a delightful guest. If she felt a twinge of envy for the shining new houses with the built-in dishwashers, she gave no sign.

And she made it easy for him to reciprocate. She'd worked hard with their old house, giving it a kind of style and elegance. When it was their turn to entertain, there was a fire in the stone fireplace, and their wedding china and silver glistened in the flickering light of the candles on her mother's Chippendale table. Ann Elizabeth, daughter of Julia Belle Washington Carter of Atlanta, was a charming hostess.

She enjoyed the visits from Julia Belle and Thelma. At different times, thank goodness, for what appealed to one would not have appealed to the other.

California, with its snowy slopes in the north and sunny beaches in the south, was a wonderful state to live in. There were so many interesting trips they could take. When her parents visited, Ann Elizabeth and Rob took them on a tour—Yosemite, Monterey and Fisherman's Wharf in San Francisco. "Best vacation I ever had," Dr. Carter declared. Julia Belle said that was because it was the only vacation he'd ever had.

Sadie had also come to visit for two weeks in September. They'd shopped in San Francisco and taken several short tours and, of course, spent hours just talking.

Ann Elizabeth was happy. Rob was a good husband. Bobby was a vigorous, healthy boy. She had her own home and good friends.

And now, in October 1951, she was pregnant again.

May 1952

It was when Margaret Ann was born that Julia Belle grew to love her son-in-law. A month before the baby was due, she sat in her dining room in Atlanta, holding

Ann Elizabeth's letter in her hand. Seated across from her were her sister, Sophie, and Claire Hastings, a wealthy Atlanta socialite who, like Julia Belle, sat on the board of regents of Atlanta University.

It seemed strange to some Negro Atlantans that Julia Belle Carter and "that white woman," Claire Hastings, had become such close friends. Nothing strange about it to Julia Belle, who was never intimidated by race or wealth. She was devoted to her alma mater and firm in her ideas about which direction the university should take. She had found an ally on the board in Claire Hastings. Moreover, Claire was intelligent and, like herself, born of quality folk. An equal.

Though Claire was more often at the Carter house, she had entertained Julia Belle in her own home. Once she'd taken her to lunch at her exclusive country club, explaining quite frankly, "You're so fair, no one will guess you're colored."

Now Claire regarded Julia Belle with troubled eyes. "What makes you think something's wrong? Her letter sounds so…so lighthearted."

"*Too* lighthearted," said Julia Belle.

"Yes," agreed Sophie. "Ann Elizabeth always puts on an unusually cheerful air when something's bothering her."

"Exactly. That husband of hers is always off somewhere, leaving her by herself. And she's pregnant. I'm calling for reservations right away."

"You're going this early?" Sophie asked. "It's four weeks before the baby's due. What'll you tell Will?"

"That I'd like to enjoy a little of California before the baby's born. And don't you tell him anything different. I don't want him to worry."

* * *

She didn't come a moment too soon. Julia Belle was appalled to learn that Ann Elizabeth had been confined to bed since the fourth month of her pregnancy.

"Something about the baby being in the wrong place," Rob explained. "Dr. Brady says she could easily miscarry. She can't exert herself or—"

"All this time! And you didn't tell me!"

"She insisted I not call you. Said you'd worry."

"Worry!" Julia Belle was irate. "I'm her *mother*. I should've been here. My poor child bedridden all this time without a soul here to help her. How could you!"

She was only slightly mollified when he explained he had engaged a woman to come in every day, and that Bertha, next door, was with her almost constantly.

"Not that he trusts any of us one little bit," Bertha told her later. "Got to see after her himself—as much as he can, what with work. He ain't done no traveling since she been like this. Hovering over her and carrying her up and down the stairs like she's a piece of china. And whistling and acting like everything's okay when you can tell he's worried to death."

Julia Belle was sick with worry herself, despite Ann Elizabeth's assurances. "For goodness' sake, Mother, I'm fine. I've done just what Dr. Brady said, and I haven't lost the baby and I've only got a few more weeks. I *knew* you'd worry. I wish Rob hadn't told you."

"He didn't tell me!" But he should have, she thought. Still, she hadn't told her own husband. Though she longed for Will's support and advice, she didn't want to upset him. Besides, Rob said that Dr. Brady, the white gynecologist who attended Ann Elizabeth, came highly recommended. And she did like him. He was a kindly man who seemed genuinely concerned for his patient, even making house calls because he felt it was too dangerous for Ann Elizabeth to come to him.

Though gratified by his careful attention, Julia Belle became even more concerned. Ann Elizabeth was too pale, with dark circles under her eyes. And far too thin. Nothing but swollen belly.

As that uncouth woman next door put it, "She ain't nothin' *but* baby! Don't eat enough to keep a bird alive. Didn't hardly touch that split-pea soup I brought over, and you know she need nourishment."

Julia Belle agreed. She piled in fresh fruit and vegetables, and made sure Ann Elizabeth ate plenty of each. She took her cue from Rob and acted as if the situation was completely normal, while doing everything in her power to make it so. She vacuumed, polished, drew the draperies against the summer heat, doctored the potted plants and filled bowls with cut flowers. The neglected house took on an air of cool serenity and elegance. She was gracious to the friends who called, and even gained a certain rapport with Bertha.

"I'm glad you're here," Ann Elizabeth admitted. "I feel like a little girl again."

I'm glad I'm here, too, Julia Belle thought, as she sat on Bobby's bed, directing him to make order out of the chaos that was his room.

Bobby. Her heart turned over every time she looked at her grubby grandson, almost nine years old. Ann Elizabeth said he resembled Rob, and of course there were the dimples and the eyes. But the coloring, those sturdy black curls, the lovable grin—that was Randy. Her Randy.

"Hey, Grandma, this is the pump that goes to my gas station. I'm gonna fix it right now."

"No. Not until you get this room straightened. Just

leave it over there. And let's stack the books on the shelf where they belong.''

"Aw, Grandma. Can't we quit now?''

"Not until we finish. Then I'm going to take those pants off you and put them in the washing machine and—''

"Jeez, Grandma. These are my cowboy jeans!''

"Well, they're going in the washing machine even if I have to put you in there with them.'' She smiled. "I bet if you gave me a big hug and a kiss, we'd have this room done in a jiffy. And then...guess what?''

"What?''

"I've got a surprise for you in the kitchen.''

"What surprise?''

"Where's my hug?''

He wound his arms around her and Julia Belle buried her face in his curls, savoring all his little-boy smells. He was a darling. A good-natured cheerful marvelous child. She could almost forgive Ann Elizabeth for marrying Rob. Somehow they'd produced this perfect piece of humanity. And to be fair, there was no doubt that Rob loved Ann Elizabeth. He was tender with her, yet strong and reassuring.

But at the crucial time, he faltered. Julia Belle could tell he was terrified when Dr. Brady ordered that Ann Elizabeth be taken to the hospital in an ambulance.

"She's overdue, and I don't like the baby's position. I plan to induce labor,'' the doctor said. "I'm worried.'' Pressed by Rob, he explained that there could be complications. "I have to be frank with you. If we delay too long...'' He hesitated. "Sometimes in a case like this—not always,'' he said hastily. "But sometimes the placenta comes first, and I want to prevent that at all costs.''

"If that happens?" Rob asked.

Dr. Brady took a deep breath. "The cord could wrap around the baby's throat and strangle him, and...well, we're in danger of losing both mother and child."

The words rang in Julia Belle's ears long after the doctor left them. She stood in the waiting room with Rob, but scarcely noticed him. "...danger of losing both mother and child." She was back in Atlanta that night so long ago, praying, as they waited in the basement of a white hospital to hear of Bobby's life—or death. What did it matter that they were now in a completely different place, a well-equipped integrated hospital in California, with two specialists attending Ann Elizabeth and her unborn child? Life and death were in the hands of God, not man.

Please, God, she begged, hoping the silent plea deep in her heart could reach Him. *You took Randy. Please...not Ann Elizabeth.*

A sound, a slight movement beside her...

She turned to see her own stark terror reflected in Rob's eyes, heard the anguish in his frightened whisper. "I couldn't live without Ann Elizabeth."

Her arms went around him, supporting him. Loving him.

"It's going to be fine," she said, giving him an assurance she didn't feel herself.

Fortunately everything *was* fine. After the tormented hours of waiting, a healthy beautiful five-and-a-half-pound baby girl lay squirming in the nursery, one tiny hand touching her cheek. Vanquishing, in the way babies have, all the terror and turmoil preceding her birth.

Ann Elizabeth wanted to call her Margaret; Rob wanted to name her after Ann Elizabeth. So she became Margaret Ann. But she would always be called Maggie,

Julia Belle thought, as she looked at the darling delicate girl who'd captured her heart as completely as Bobby had. There's something special about grandchildren, she reflected as she folded the soft white diapers still warm from the September sun.

And something special about a son-in-law who so obviously loves his wife. Funny how things work out. Ann Elizabeth's life wasn't as she'd envisioned it. She had wanted her married to Dan and enfolded in the kind of life she'd always lived in Atlanta. Protected. But Ann Elizabeth had chosen Rob and a life that was more... how should she put it? Exposed. Exposed, yes, but still protected. Rob was the one taking the hard knocks. Oh, he joked about it—like that Prince Ahmed caper. But under all the bantering Julia Belle sensed the humiliation he'd suffered under the barriers of prejudice that could and probably had stifled many a man. But Rob seemed to persevere. She had to admire him for that. Evidently others admired him, too, the way he was being sent to confer with and counsel people all over the world. Yes, she was proud of her son-in-law. Julia Belle smiled. She knew Ann Elizabeth loved Rob; she'd loved him when he was nothing but a pair of silver wings. Now...I wonder, Julia Belle thought, if she appreciates or even realizes what he's become and how lucky she is to have him.

Anyway, Ann Elizabeth was herself again, and Julia Belle could go back to Atlanta, leaving her in Rob's capable loving hands.

Ann Elizabeth did enjoy her life as the next several years rolled by. She didn't like Rob's being away so much, but she was proud of him. And her own life was full—her social life with Laura and others, either in their homes or at integrated tearooms and restaurants that, in California, she took for granted. PTA, Little League, dancing and swimming lessons for the kids, teaching Sunday and Bible school, tutoring Bertha's children, especially Racine, who was turning out to be a good writer with real potential. Yes, her private life was so full that she only took a vague interest in the world outside. But she was a proud and elated spectator when certain momentous events flooded the news and flashed on her television screen: 1954, in a unanimous vote, the Supreme Court declares separate but equal education unconstitutional; 1955, a woman named Rosa Parks is arrested because she refuses to give up her seat on a Montgomery, Alabama, bus, and a minister named Martin Luther King, Jr., heads a passive resistance boycott, which results in the integration of Montgomery buses in 1956; 1957, integration of Little Rock, Arkansas, schools under protection of troops sent by President Eisenhower.

Yes, life was changing, she believed. For everyone in this country. But especially if you were black.

18

January 1958

Rob pulled the covers tight around him and buried his head in the pillow. He was chilled to the bone, sweating like crazy, nauseated, and his head ached. Maybe he was dying. No. He knew it was just the flu. But having the flu in a Paris hotel was not exactly an ideal situation. Besides, he didn't have time to be sick.

He tried to think. How many places had they covered? He and Chuck had been sent on visits to all the countries that flew airplanes that were depot-maintained by McClellan. A worldwide and very important trip. And it was still in the first stages. Rob muddled through his aching head and tried to review the agenda. F-86s and T-33s in Norway, Denmark, Italy, Greece, Turkey, Iran, Ethiopia and Japan. No, he didn't have time to be sick. He hoped those pills Chuck got from the embassy would do the trick. Chuck had doctored Rob as best he could and had now gone to the American Embassy to pick up their visas.

Rob fell into a deep sleep and was just awakening when Chuck returned.

"How're you doing?" Chuck asked.

"Better, I think…hope," Rob murmured, shutting his eyes again.

"Well, I wish you'd get off your ass. You're getting to be a bit of a handicap. Here we are in gay Paree, all set to live it up and you—"

"Oh, shut up! Go out and live it up and let me sleep." Rob turned his back and buried his face in the pillow again.

"Yeah, quite a handicap. You get me kicked out of restaurants and now you're about to get me kicked out of a country."

Rob turned to face him. "What's the matter? Didn't you get the visas?"

"Got mine." Chuck held it up. "Not yours. No authorization for an American Negro second-class citizen, as they put it, to do state business with the Royal Ethiopian Air Force."

Rob sat up, wincing at the throb of pain in his head. "You're kidding."

"No."

Rob lay back down, too sick to care. "So you go to Ethiopia and I'll go on to—"

"No. I phoned the big boys back home and they're taking care of it. The American attaché will handle the problem, and you're to pick up your visa in Athens, Greece. We have to go there first, anyway."

A week later Rob was feeling much better and they proceeded to Greece. They concluded their business with the Royal Hellenic Air Force and stopped at the MAG, the Military Advisory Group, to pick up Rob's visa. No visa.

In the meantime a TWX was received, ordering Chuck to return to the States. Rob was to continue the tour alone. Sit tight, he was told. Your visa will be issued forthwith.

Three days later, the visa was issued and he boarded an Ethiopian airliner for the flight to Addis Ababa.

From the moment he got off the plane, he was astounded at the sea of black faces that surrounded him. The first country he'd visited where all the people looked like him. And, he thought ironically, the first country outside the United States where he was banned because of his race. Banned from doing government business!

However, he was billeted at the plush Ghion Hotel and utensils were not removed from his place setting when he went down to dinner. Maybe because, in this country, there was no way he could be recognized as second-class. He couldn't help grinning at that observation. The dining room was large and elegant, but rather sparse in clientele. He saw only the members of the crew who'd flown him in, and two other groups of four seated in the grand ballroom. The menu was in English, the food excellent, and they were elegantly entertained by a string quartet.

Later the American Military Advisory Commander called on him. A quiet affable man, he told Rob a pickup had been ordered at eight in the morning and they were to meet with General Asifa at nine.

The next morning, as he was driven to the meeting site, Rob felt somewhat frustrated and a little disgruntled. According to General Arnold, everyone had heard of the second-class-citizen fiasco, and though Rob had at first casually dismissed it, he suddenly found himself burning at the implication. Possibly, he thought with brutal honesty, because it held more than a grain of truth. And possibly because to be considered a second-class citizen in such a dismal country was too much to bear.

Like being in another world—a poor and primitive world. He took in the sights from the window of the moving car—a few blocks crowded with small structures of cinderblock or brick, houses or places of business. He noted the obvious poverty of the people who moved about on foot...the narrow stretch of road threading through a barren countryside...vultures feeding on animal carcasses that littered the roadside. Christ! He was second-class compared to *this?*

What the hell was he doing here, anyway?

The answer saddened him. He was bringing weapons, the gift of American taxpayers to a country that was in far more need of housing, hospitals, sanitation and food. This was a crazy mixed-up world.

However, as was always the case, the minute he entered the conference room, Rob was all business. The United States was replacing the Swedish propeller-driven Spads with their jet-engine-propelled F-86s. Ethiopian pilots who were to fly them were being trained in the United States. Some had completed training and were awaiting delivery of the aircraft.

Rob's task was to make sure the host country had the infrastructure and facilities to maintain the plane and its equipment.

The discussion was long and heated, the Swedes declaring that the Americans wanted too much too soon. The Ethiopian general, growing impatient and confused, turned to Rob. The critical point was the Americans' demand for a special environment and careful maintenance of the F-86 fire-control system. "Tell us, Mr. Metcalf," the general insisted, "why we must have this clean room you speak of."

Rob explained in detail that the system had to be maintained in a dust-free environment to accommodate the tolerances of the circuitry that assured a hit. "Otherwise," he concluded, "we're taking a six-hundred-thousand-dollar weapons system up for a joyride." Even as he said it, he winced. He'd wanted to design planes for travel and pleasure, not carnage and destruction.

From then on, the Ethiopian general questioned Rob on every detail, regarding him with respect.

Rob appreciated his new first-class status, but couldn't shake off the depression—because it was his expertise in the weapons of war that had earned him the status.

In April 1958 Rob had received a job offer from Colonel Marks—who was now a General and stationed at Langley Field in Hampton, Virginia.

"Marks is in deep trouble on some project and thinks you can bail him out," Chuck had said. "But hell, I need you here. You're not going to take it, are you?" Rob knew what he meant—jim crow territory. But he was acquainted with most of the leadership at the base, so it wasn't particularly a concern. Moreover, Joe Tillman, his old buddy at Stalag 109—now a full colonel—was stationed there, too.

"Well…" Rob had hesitated. He'd liked working with Chuck and hated to desert him, but there were other considerations. Jobs above the GS-13 level had a political dimension. Someone higher up had to want and sponsor you if you were to advance. You didn't turn down such an opportunity. "I'll check with Ann Elizabeth," he'd said. If she objected to a move to Virginia, he wouldn't take the job.

Much as she loved her life in California, Ann Elizabeth had been delighted. They'd be on the East Coast, much nearer her parents. And Hampton was familiar to her. She remembered going there with her parents, once for an NMA meeting—a national association of Negro doctors—and once for a bridge tournament. They'd stayed at the home of friends and been royally entertained.

The children would be all right, with Bobby in high school and Maggie just out of kindergarten and ready for first grade. No, she had not opposed the move.

But now... Ann Elizabeth's thoughts were in a disconsolate scramble as she stood in the kitchen of their house in Hampton, arranging gladioli in a low bowl.

She wished they'd never moved here. Wished they'd never bought this house.

At first it hadn't been too bad. Julia Belle had put her in touch with some of her old friends, and Ann Elizabeth's old classmate, Jennie Lou, now lived here with her husband, Dr. Allen Slater, whom she'd managed to capture after giving up on Dan. Jennie Lou wasn't one of Ann Elizabeth's favorites, but she'd renewed the acquaintance.

She'd expected living in Hampton to be fun. And yes, it could have been.

But it wasn't.

Rob was so stubborn. They hadn't needed to buy this place. She could have managed a little longer in the apartment they'd found to rent. At least until they could build. There was that big lot right next to the Slaters. And houses for sale in a fairly decent section that was going colored. But, she thought ruefully, Rob had changed. He wasn't going to buy and remodel an old house someone else had dumped. And he wasn't going to wait to build. Not when there were good solid brand-new ready-made houses for sale. Besides, he didn't want to commute from the colored section.

He was so stubborn! Somewhere he'd picked up a bug about "going first-class."

Ann Elizabeth stared out her kitchen window, remembering how, Sunday after Sunday, Rob had dragged her here. To Lansberg, a development of new custom-built homes located near the base. "Open for Inspection," declared the signs posted every few blocks.

For three Sundays they'd walked through every three- and four-bedroom model, staring enviously at the large family rooms with fireplaces, the beautiful tiled kitchens with built-in appliances. "Exactly what we need," Rob had said. But he knew as well as she that their tour was meaningless. Ann Elizabeth could still feel the humiliation. They were pointedly ignored by the salesmen, who eagerly approached white customers. She was embarrassed every time Rob cornered a salesman who smoothly lied through his teeth, "All our present models are spoken for. Try again in six months."

Then her mother had come for a visit.

"I don't see how you can stand being cooped up in this apartment," Julia Belle had said. "Haven't you found a house yet? You've got the money from selling the place in Sacramento, and with what Rob makes, surely you can find something suitable."

Ann Elizabeth mentioned the lot near the Slaters'. Rob talked about Lansberg, particularly the number 168 four-bedroom model, which had appealed to them. "But one look at us and they turn the other way."

"I think I'll go out there," Julia Belle said with a

conspiratorial smile. "Rob, find a chauffeur's cap and drive me."

"Oh, Mother! This isn't just a trip on a train," Ann Elizabeth said. Her mother and Aunt Sophie always sat in the section reserved for whites whenever they traveled by train.

"But it will do the trick," Julia Belle replied calmly. "I just bet they'll sell to me."

"But *we'll* have to live there!"

"In a house that's perfect for you. You deserve it, the same way I deserve the best accommodations on a train."

Ann Elizabeth thought of the beautiful homes owned by her white friends in Sacramento. Thought of how hard she and Rob had worked to make their Sacramento house livable. Thought of the bright new houses in Lansberg, and protested no more. Now, all these months later, she wished she had.

Surprise. Number 168 was available, explained the charming salesman. Julia Belle made out a check for the down payment, saying that her husband would be joining her later. Amazing how quickly business was transacted with Julia Belle's white face and the absent Dr. Carter's excellent credit rating. When the deed was signed, sealed and delivered, Rob reimbursed her for the down payment and Julia Belle transferred ownership to the Metcalfs and returned to Atlanta.

Ann Elizabeth sighed, for the first time in her life resenting her mother's fair skin. If they hadn't bought the house...

She stuck the last blossom into the bowl, brushed the leftover stems into the garbage disposal and put the clippers away. She leaned against the sink and surveyed her spotless kitchen—the gleaming beige tile counter, smooth birch cabinets, the bronze double oven, the matching bronze refrigerator and dishwasher. Things. Just things. Her feet sank into the plush carpet as she entered the formal dining room. She placed the flowers in the center of her mother's old Chippendale table, which looked as if it had been made for this room. The house had been so easy to decorate, requiring only a few extra pieces of furniture and a few pictures here and there. It was spacious, modern, new and clean. And she would exchange it in a minute for that old house in Sacramento with its crumbling plaster and leaky faucets.

She so longed for the sound of Bertha's husky voice that she called her long-distance one day.

"The children trying to reform me," Bertha told her. "Roberta and Racine got this big bottle and they want me to put in a nickel every time I cuss. Shit! I had to cut that out. I'd be plumb broke. How you all doing out there in that place with them peckerwoods?"

"Fine. Just fine." No need to tell Bertha how it really was. No overt violence, though they'd expected it and had come prepared. Her fears had increased that first night when she caught Rob hiding a gun under the mattress. She hated guns and was more concerned about accidental injury to or by the kids than anything else.

"Just a precaution," Rob reassured her. "And just for a few weeks until we settle in. Then I'll get rid of it."

They hadn't needed the gun. A neighborhood of decent law-abiding upper-middle-class citizens had taken a decent law-abiding approach. A committee had come from the housing developers, offering to buy back their house at a considerable profit for them. "We don't think you'll be happy here. We're prepared to assist you in finding a place somewhere else."

Rob insisted that they liked the house, it was near his work, and they were quite happy.

Happy? Ann Elizabeth was miserable.

It wasn't only the obscenities scrawled on their garage door, the eggs splattered against the windows—not even the cross someone had burned with some kind of acid right in the center of their new lawn. Nothing would grow over the spot. They'd called in a gardener, but so far had found nothing to erase that insignia that stated so clearly, "You are not wanted."

What bothered her more than anything else was the isolation. No friendly greetings, no coffee klatches, no place to borrow a cup of sugar. Except for the obscenities under cover of night, they were completely ignored.

No, that wasn't quite true. Old Mrs. Levin next door had become a friend. Maybe because Rob had changed her tire that morning he found her staring helplessly at the flat on the left rear wheel. The next day she'd come over with cookies, a welcoming committee of one. Perhaps, Ann Elizabeth thought, Mrs. Levin was also lonely in this bustling youthful community. She was a pale wisp of a woman, with gray hair and spectacles, crippled with arthritis. She lived with her divorced son, who was a traveling salesman and seldom at home. Ann Elizabeth was grateful to Mrs. Levin and really liked her. She knew it was difficult for the old woman to shop and always checked to see if she needed anything when she did her own shopping. Now, as she placed the flowers on the table, she was glad she'd bought a bunch for Mrs. Levin, too. She'd seemed so pleased.

But one crippled old lady was no company for two active children. That was what worried Ann Elizabeth most. The children. She was glad she'd let Bobby, then fifteen, go to Atlanta to live with her mother.

"Will hasn't been feeling so well," Julia Belle had said. "And Bobby always perks him up. He can attend University High. He's had so many visits here that he knows most of the kids, and it'll be good for him as well as Will."

Dear God, how glad she was she'd let him go. Bobby was a friendly outgoing boy and she wanted him to stay that way. She certainly didn't want him having to deal with bigotry all through high school. She wasn't going to let happy bouncy six-year-old Maggie be hurt, either. So far, she'd been able to protect her from the isolation of this community, driving her almost every day to play with the children of friends, who, like most Negroes, lived near the Negro college. Maggie was at the Slaters' now.

It was at the Slaters' that the subject of schools had first come up. "Where are you going to send Maggie to school?" Jennie Lou had asked.

"Good Shepherd," Ann Elizabeth answered. "You said it's a good school."

"Oh, it is. Tony loves it and the tuition's not bad. But you're so far away."

"Yes, I'll have to drive her in every day." If Rob couldn't commute, she could, Ann Elizabeth had decided.

"Long drive," was Allen Slater's comment.

"Worth it," was Ann Elizabeth's quick reply. "She's already met many of the kids."

Rob had been strangely silent. But on the way home he said, "Honey, don't you think it's rather foolish to drive Maggie all that distance when we have a brand-new school just two blocks from us?"

Ann Elizabeth glanced at the backseat. The exhausted Maggie was fast asleep. She turned to Rob. "You don't mean we should send her to the white school?"

"The neighborhood school."

"Same thing. *Their* school."

"*Ours.* We pay taxes."

Ann Elizabeth looked at him, shocked. Surely he wasn't going to saddle the children with his "first-class" obsession! "Robert Metcalf, I will never, and I want you to understand this, I will *never* let Maggie be exposed to the kind of treatment she would receive at that school."

"You're against integrated schools?"

"It's what *they've* got against us that concerns me. Look what's happening all over the country. In Little Rock—"

"They integrated, didn't they?"

"With all that rioting and having to call in troops! I tell you, I will *not* let Maggie—"

"It won't be like that. They brought in a whole bunch of kids at once. There'll probably be no fuss at all about one little Negro child in first grade. They wouldn't—"

"You don't *know* what they'd do! And I won't listen! All right, we moved to this neighborhood where I didn't want to be in the first place. But I don't have to send my child to school here."

"This is where we live."

"You call this living?"

"Listen, Ann Elizabeth, we've only been here a few months. You have to give people a chance."

"They've had a chance to throw eggs and burn that cross—"

"Just some rabble-rousers! Could be one person."

"The point is, Rob, you don't know who or how many."

"Look, honey, it's like my job. I know they didn't want me at first, but when they got to know me... I'm not resented. I'm respected, yes, even liked in some cases. I'm part of a team."

She reached over to touch his hand tenderly. "I know that. All you've done, this promotion, was quite an accomplishment. Don't think I'm not proud of you."

"But what does it mean if I can't share it with my family? If the money I make can't provide a good home, a good school for my kids, what good is it?"

"I know, Rob. And I do appreciate what you do for us, the...things. I love the house. I really do. It's just...well, you're a man. An adult. You can take it. I can take it. We can wait for people to get to know us. But Maggie's just a little girl. I want her first day at school to be happy. I don't want her hurt!"

"Do you think I do?"

"No, of course not. But—"

"I've got to think of her whole life, Ann Elizabeth. Not just one day. I'll never forget that Jewish doctor in Germany."

"Oh, Rob, no! Spare me the don't-let-it-happen-to-you speech! We're not talking about concentration camps. We're talking about a little girl starting school."

But Rob had become reflective and withdrawn. "He said it happens a little bit at a time. They take you out of the schools... Hell, we just got *in* the schools! What's the point of the Supreme Court decision if nobody integrates?"

That was their first argument on the subject. But not their last.

She didn't understand why Rob felt so strongly about

this. Bobby was safe in Atlanta, thank God. And she meant to enroll Maggie at the Catholic school near Jennie Lou.

Ann Elizabeth went into the family room and picked up a magazine. The jangle of the doorbell made her jump. There was always that prickle of apprehension every time a bell sounded in this silent house. She went to the door and squinted through the peephole. A white woman in a green shift was standing on the threshold. Another friendly neighbor? No. A car, probably hers, was parked out front and she carried a purse, not cookies or flowers. A saleslady?

Anyway, she looked harmless. Ann Elizabeth opened the door.

"Mrs. Metcalf?" The woman tossed back a mane of blond hair and smiled.

"Yes."

"I'm Marcia Wheeling and I'd like very much to talk with you. May I come in?"

"Yes, of course." Rather puzzled, Ann Elizabeth stepped back to admit her. She wasn't puzzled for long.

As soon as she was seated on the living-room sofa, Marcia Wheeling came to the point. "I want to talk to you about the possibility of enrolling your daughter in the Lansberg elementary school. I've already talked with your husband."

"Oh?" Ann Elizabeth sat up. When had she talked to Rob?

"Otis Pitts, president of the local chapter of the NAACP, brought him out to meet with me. Otis knows of my interest and experience in integrating schools."

"I see." And I see that my husband's been babbling to the NAACP and you and God knows who else about what concerns only me and him.

"I understand you're reluctant to send your daughter to school in this area."

"Yes."

"But don't you see? Your position is unique. You're not crossing district boundaries. You live in this area. And Robert is anxious to test the new ruling."

Robert? Ann Elizabeth felt a flash of resentment. Just how well does this woman know Rob?

Marcia Wheeling leaned toward her and spoke persuasively. "Surely you want to support your husband."

"In this case I must think of my child." Ann Elizabeth smiled, trying to mask her animosity. The woman meant well. "This will be her first day of real school. She's very excited and I don't want it to be a day of upheaval for her."

"I understand how you feel."

"Do you?" She wondered if Marcia Wheeling had children of her own. She glanced at her left hand. No wedding ring.

"Yes." Marcia brushed back a strand of hair. "I've been through this before."

"Here?"

"No. When I was living with my husband in Kansas. After the Supreme Court decision, I became aware of the appalling inadequacy of most of the Negro schools. I immediately joined the effort to integrate the schools and bridge the gap."

Ann Elizabeth heard the sincerity in her voice, the dedication, and felt a surge of admiration. "Could I offer you some refreshment? Tea, perhaps?"

"Oh, that would be nice."

As they sipped iced tea and munched on cheese and crackers, Marcia talked about her work. She described the situation in Kansas City—a small replica of the Little Rock episode, one of many such skirmishes being fought all over the country. The woman has courage, she thought, and perhaps that's what makes her…well, not beautiful, but attractive, with all that zeal and energy sparkling in those eyes. Arresting green eyes, as green as her dress.

"I think the hardest part was getting Negroes to cooperate." Marcia Wheeling smiled ruefully. "We often had to plead and beg. That surprised me. It was as if they didn't realize what they were missing."

"Perhaps they realized only too well what they were letting their children in for," Ann Elizabeth suggested.

"Maybe. But do you know who the biggest stumbling blocks were?"

"Who?"

"People in the black middle class, especially teachers. So afraid of losing their jobs."

"I can understand that."

"Well, they weren't the only ones. Those who'd made it and could send their children to private school didn't want to participate. I'm beginning to think that man is right—what's his name? He wrote that book about well-to-do Negroes."

"You mean *America's Black Middle Class?*"

"Yes, that's it. He says that those who've made it don't want to rock the boat. They've adopted the behavioral patterns of white America. As long as they can keep their good jobs, buy houses and cars, educate their children and—"

"Wait a minute!" Ann Elizabeth bristled. This kind of talk infuriated her. "Why are those virtues exclusive to whites?" she snapped. "Why is it that when a black man buys a house, a car and takes care of his family, he's emulating white men?"

"I didn't say it. I was only paraphrasing the author. What's his name…Stanley Robinson. He's a Negro. He wrote the book."

"And why is it that everything a black man says about another black man has to be gospel?"

"Just a minute, Mrs. Metcalf. You're taking this all wrong. What I meant and what Stanley Robinson meant is that Negroes who *have* achieved often forget those who haven't."

"In other words, a black man should either be wallowing in the ghetto or down there helping to pull his brother out!"

"No. I only meant that those who've made it have a certain responsibility to—"

"Do you have any idea how hard it is for a black man just to survive? To get a job, buy a house, feed his family? Then when he gets a little ahead, he's made to feel guilty for not bringing his brothers up with him!"

"Mrs. Metcalf, you're twisting my words."

"The words are not exclusively yours. They're the hue and cry of every disgruntled Negro. Another burden on the black men and women who've tried so hard and succeeded even slightly."

"Oh, please, Mrs. Metcalf. I didn't mean… Oh, I do know all this. That's why I want every school available to every child. And I know there are Negroes like your husband who are concerned about others of his race. I do so admire Robert. I know you can afford private school, and yet he's willing to send his child to—"

"He may be, but I'm not! I am not willing to have my child dragged through the kind of experience you've described."

"But it won't be, don't you see? One little girl will

hardly be noticed. Just quietly integrated into her neighborhood school.''

Ann Elizabeth stared at her. "You really believe that?''

"I do. And that will make it easier for others to follow. To integrate the school, the way you've integrated the neighborhood. Just living here, the example you set, will make it easier for another Negro to buy a house in Lansberg.''

Ann Elizabeth laughed. "Then I guess it's a good thing we don't brawl and have wild parties and break windows.''

"A darn good thing." Marcia's laugh joined hers. But her face sobered as she added softly, "Don't you see what it would mean to send your intelligent well-behaved daughter to school here?''

"I don't know about well-behaved. Maggie's a bit of a rebel. But she is intelligent, and most of all she's happy. And I want her to stay that way.''

Marcia Wheeling said she might be happy at the Lansberg school, too, and continued to urge Ann Elizabeth to try it.

But Ann Elizabeth was firm. "I know I can't wrap Maggie in a cocoon, shield her forever from life. But right now, just going into first grade is enough for a little girl. I want it to be a positive step for her.''

"I know how you feel," Marcia said, "and I'm sorry it has to be this way—one little girl, one little step. But don't you see? It would be such a big step for so many. It could open—''

"NO." Ann Elizabeth spoke with finality. "She doesn't have to battle in the race war yet.''

But as she watched Marcia retreat down the walk, she felt a twinge of guilt. Was she protecting Maggie or herself? For a moment she felt a longing so intense it startled her. A longing for the cozy segregated world of Atlanta's West Side with home and school and friends, the bustling colored business world of Auburn Avenue. A longing for the quiet uncomplicated life she'd known.

She remembered that night, twenty years ago, in the little Rockefeller Hall theater, when she'd looked into the serious face of a white boy with red hair and thought, *We're doing all right without your help.* She'd been so happy. She *was* happy! She had a good life. Now people like Marcia Wheeling were trying to force her out of it.

And Rob. Rob was on their side. He had no right to go behind her back and appeal to the NAACP and that woman!

19

Rob turned into his driveway, pressed the switch and watched the garage door open. Neat. He chuckled as he pulled his Mustang in beside Ann Elizabeth's station wagon. Hadn't even had a garage in Sacramento. Had to tear down that old shack.

He entered the house from the garage and went in search of Ann Elizabeth. He found her in the kitchen, her back to him, reaching for something in one of the top cabinets. He watched for a moment, enjoying the sight of her figure in lavender stretch pants, as she stood on tiptoe straining to grasp whatever eluded her groping fingers. He laughed and strode across the floor. "I'm here, honey. I'll get it for you," he said, his arms encircling her, lips nuzzling the back of her neck.

She swung around, shoving him away. "Don't you touch me, Robert Metcalf! Not after what you've done."

"What...what did I do?" he asked, stunned.

"You know what you did. You blabbed about our personal affairs to perfect strangers."

"What...who?"

"Oh, just everybody at the NAACP and that white woman do-gooder, and anybody else who'll listen. And sneaked behind my back to do it!"

"That's not true. I didn't—"

"I suppose you didn't go to the NAACP meeting and—"

"No, I didn't! Now, hold on, wait a minute and listen! Otis was at the poker game at Allen's a couple of weeks ago and asked me how we were getting along out here and—"

"And I suppose you didn't meet with a woman named Marcia Wheeling."

"Well, yes, I did. But—"

"A meeting you neglected to mention to me!"

"Because you blow up any time I say school! And yes, I'm glad I talked to her. Marcia Wheeling has had experience with this kind of thing and—"

"Knows all about forcing kids into hostile environments!"

"Goddamn it, Ann Elizabeth! You act like school integration is a crime!"

"As far as I'm concerned, it is! And I'm not going to change my mind about Maggie. So you can just tell your friends to stop bothering me!"

"My friends? What are you talking about?"

"I'm talking about Marcia Wheeling. She came to see me today. And take that surprised look off your face. You know you sent her!"

"No, I didn't. I swear—"

"Then why did she come?"

"Honey, that's not surprising. She's been working hard to implement the school-integration law. You'd be astonished at what she's accomplished."

"I know all about what she's done. And believe me, nobody's going to use my Maggie as a guinea pig."

Rob sighed. "Ann Elizabeth, listen. You can win all the decisions, get all the rulings and court orders you

like. But it's not going to mean a damn thing if somebody—''

''Not Maggie!''

''Look at it this way. Nobody's going to hand you
your rights on a silver platter. You have to walk two
blocks to get them.''

''You keep talking about rights! I'm talking about
hopscotch and jump rope and...and...'' Her voice
broke. ''And sharing peanut-butter sandwiches.''

He pulled her into his arms. ''I know, I know. You
want Maggie to be happy.''

''Yes, like I was,'' she said through muffled sobs, her
face buried against his chest.

He cradled her in his arms, knowing how she felt.
Christ, he wanted Maggie happy, too. And he wanted
Ann Elizabeth happy. She was his life.

He picked her up and carried her to their bed. The
outside world with its tensions and terrors was shut
away. The setting sun filtered through the long sheer
curtains that enclosed their world. With infinite tenderness and burning passion, he showed her how much he
loved her.

But during the following weeks the outside world did
not disappear. The problem remained, grew worse, tearing them apart. He didn't want it that way. He needed
her on his side. Especially now, when he wasn't sure
himself.

A little bit at a time, the old Jewish doctor had said.
That meant you had to fight it a little bit at a time, too.
But with your child? He didn't confess, even to Ann
Elizabeth, that he was glad Bobby was in Atlanta, away
from the furor. Julia Belle was right. Bobby was Randy
all over again, laughing at life with that teasing grin,

liking everybody. Rob didn't want that grin wiped away. *I'm glad he's there.*

But Maggie? Maggie's here. Next to Ann Elizabeth, Maggie was the joy of Rob's life. She was more excitable than Bobby, a joyous jubilant child.

"Daddy, read me a story." She curled up in his lap and pointed. "There's a *c*, there's an *a* and a *t*. That spells cat. See? I know my letters and I can read some words."

"You sure can, baby."

"How many more days?"

"Well, let's see. About forty, I think."

"That's a long time."

"No. Not too long." Not long enough.

"When I go to real school, I'll learn more words. Then I can read to you. Would you like that?"

"I'd like it very much." And I'd like it if all you had to learn were letters and words. Wasn't that enough for a six-year-old?

"Ann Elizabeth," he said later, "I do understand how you feel."

"Then why do you fight me?"

Why, indeed? Because he couldn't help it. Something was pushing him. Something about rights. Something about dues paid—taxes, military service, good citizenship. He would not be cheated. He would not let Maggie be cheated.

The Supreme Court decision hadn't come as one big momentous event. It had come a step at a time, school after school, case after case, child after child. It wasn't fair, but if that was the way it had to be, then that was the way it *would* be. And he had to be a part of it. Maggie, too.

He wished Ann Elizabeth understood his point of

view. She didn't. The chasm between them deepened. The dimple at the corner of her mouth appeared only with the tightening of her lips. The sunny smile was gone, only surfacing when she talked with Maggie.

He missed her cheerful chatter, her smile. *Her*. She went moodily about the house, keeping it in perfect order. He was beginning to wish they'd never bought the place. Often when he returned in the evening, it was silent and empty.

He couldn't blame Ann Elizabeth for escaping. For taking Maggie across town, where there was laughter and friendship. But he couldn't help feeling, too, that if she stayed home more, if people got to know her... How could anyone not like Ann Elizabeth?

"If you spent more time at home," he suggested, "Maggie might find friends here."

"Who, for instance? Those kids across the street? They stare, but they never speak or come over."

"Does Maggie ever go over there?"

"Of course not."

"Of course not. Of course not," he mimicked. "*Why* not?"

"I'll not have her traipsing over to be called names by bigoted brats!"

"You don't know how they'd receive her. Maybe if you got to know their mothers, made some gesture, they'd—"

"Make some gestures in return? They've made their gestures. Which reminds me—what do you plan to do about that unsightly cross in the middle of our lawn?"

"Oh, for God's sake, I'll take care of it!" Damn it, he had enough to take care of. All hell breaking loose at work, which was the reason Marks had sent for him in the first place, and he couldn't concentrate on it because of the school thing. If Ann Elizabeth would only… "Why do you have to be so standoffish? You go around with your nose in the air. Why don't you try—"

"To win friends and influence people? Among this group of godforsaken hypocrites?"

"Ann Elizabeth, they're people just like everybody else."

"I don't need them. I have my own friends."

"You know your problem? You're a snob!"

"I am not!"

"Yes, you are. It's that damn Julia Belle Washington Carter pride. If people don't count it a privilege to know you, if they don't cater to you—"

"Cater? Oh, no. I just want them to refrain from throwing eggs on my porch and burning crosses on my lawn."

"Ann Elizabeth, there haven't been any more incidents since the first week we moved in."

"But there will be if we take our daughter to their precious school."

"Not if they get to know you first."

"They don't need to know me. I know me. I'm Ann Elizabeth Carter."

"Oh, yeah, girl from the golden ghetto in Atlanta, Georgia."

"That's right!" she snapped. "And I wish I was there now."

"You had the choice. You could have married that pale-face doctor like your mother wanted you to."

"I wish to God I had!"

That was the night she moved out of their bedroom. She retreated to the sanctuary of Maggie's bed, where he couldn't follow. Maggie had asked if Mommy was mad at Daddy, but Ann Elizabeth had merely said, "Oh, no. I just want to be with *you*." At least the child would be protected from these anxieties and quarrels. A storm might be raging all around her, but Maggie must not know.

No way to reach Ann Elizabeth through the stony silence, broken only at mealtimes by gay trivial chatter for Maggie's sake. If Ann Elizabeth was even there. Almost every day she and Maggie were at the Slaters' or with other colored friends across town. The new modern house he'd so triumphantly purchased for his family now mocked him. Was it worth it?

He was frightened. She had said nothing, but he feared she might leave him. Go back to Atlanta. To that doctor Julia Belle had never stopped talking about. "Oh, yes, he's still single and back in Atlanta on the staff of that new hospital for private Negro patients. You should see it, Ann Elizabeth. Fabulous, with the latest equipment. Spalding, the tennis-shoe magnate, donated the money for it. Full name is Hughes Spalding Pavilion of Grady Memorial Hospital," she'd said importantly. "It's a teaching hospital, under the auspices of Emory University, so Dan's also on the university staff." Integration, elitist style, Rob thought. Quiet, dignified. Nothing like the hell we're going through!

Their problem was compounded by publicity. He had done as suggested at one of the private meetings. He had spoken with the principal of the school and Maggie's prospective teacher. The first-grade teacher, a Miss Agnew, was quite a person. Young, friendly, attractive. Of course she'd be delighted to have Maggie, she'd told him, and would do everything she could to make her happy and comfortable. She was sure things would work out.

The principal was a mealymouthed hesitant sort. "Well, yes, Mr. Metcalf, we will abide by the law, but I'm not sure the public is ready for this. Do you think it's quite the time?"

Damn right, it's the time! Rob was even more determined when a group of parents, probably encouraged by the principal, appealed to the school board, requesting a delay. The school board, bless them, had stuck by the law.

He couldn't let the school board down. Nor the NAACP. Nor the Supreme Court. Nor himself. Nor Maggie. There was no turning back.

He missed Ann Elizabeth. He needed her, needed the strength of her support, her bright smile, the warmth of her body next to his. He had never felt so alone in his life. Even POW camp hadn't been this bad, he reflected as he sat in the kitchen, munching a roast-beef sandwich and staring out the window at the rain.

He'd always liked rain, but now found it depressing. It wouldn't be raining in California this early in August. He wished to hell they were still in California. He and Ann Elizabeth had had some spats there. But nothing like this.

When he pulled out of the driveway, he noticed how fresh and green his lawn looked with the rain pelting down on it. Except for that brown spot in the shape of a cross. He would have to do something about that.

He didn't want to go to the NAACP meeting tonight. What good were all the meetings? In the end, it would just be him and Maggie alone. If Ann Elizabeth didn't take her away, he thought glumly.

"We'll meet at Marcia's," Otis had said. "There're some things we need to talk over."

Well, it looked as if Otis, Marcia and a couple of

other guys were all the support he had. He'd better show up at the meeting.

Marcia's place was on the outskirts of the city. The country, really, where the city hadn't encroached on farmland yet. It was dark when he parked his car in the driveway and made a run for the front door. Even in the dark and the rain, he could tell there had been some refurbishing of the old house. The shutters had been replaced and he could smell fresh paint. Looked as if Marcia, who'd apparently returned to her old home after a divorce, planned to make her residence permanent. Alone in this big house?

Well, it had probably been in her family since the time it was a plantation and Negro slaves were out picking cotton for her great-granddaddy. Otis said most of her land was now leased to a colored farmer who was doing quite well for Marcia and himself. Rob smiled, wondering what her great-granddaddy thought about that. He was probably turning over in his grave at the idea of this meeting. But Marcia was a rebel. So intense, and more dedicated than the rest of them. You almost forgot she was white.

Besides Marcia and himself, there were only four at the meeting. Otis, his wife, Cecelia, Jack Warren and another man Rob hadn't met.

"Reverend Williams is the pastor of the Abyssinian Baptist Church," Jack Warren explained. "He's brought out a very significant point. One we'd like to discuss with you."

Rob smiled as he greeted the old man, who appeared to be in his sixties. He wore a dark business suit, but his hands were gnarled and rough, as if accustomed to hard work.

"Most of his parishioners live in Innsfield, an area that borders the Lansberg tract," Jack said.

Rob nodded. He passed the area every day when he went to work. A squatters' community, a mix of make-shift houses and motor homes. Negroes who had come from the farms to work at the airfield had hewn out a community for themselves.

Even before they finished speaking, Rob knew what was coming. Why not include some of the Innsfield kids in the integration move?

My God, another Little Rock? No, he didn't want that.

Strangely enough, it was Marcia who supported his stand. "I'm thinking of Mrs. Metcalf," she said, "who, you know, is reluctant in the first place. I've assured her that the entrance of one little girl will not cause the furor that bringing in several would."

She managed to convince the rest of the group, and Rob was grateful. After the meeting he remained to tell her so.

"Thank you, Marcia," he said when she'd closed the door behind the others, "for understanding how difficult this is for my wife, and…well, just thanks. You have compassion, as well as dedication."

"Not compassion. Strategy. It's easier to break through with just one child who lives in the district than to… Oh, enough talk! You look bushed. Sit down and let me get you a cup of coffee."

He sat back on the sofa. He *was* bushed. Weary of the whole damn thing.

"This is difficult for you, too, isn't it?" she said as she handed him a mug of coffee.

"It sure is." He took a swallow, set the mug on the table, sighed. "I'm not sure it's right to force my—"

"Now wait a minute! Don't you back out on me!"
She put her mug on the table and sat beside him.
"There's nothing, no progress at all, without people like
you who are willing to take risks."

He thought about that. Had he taken risks? He
grinned and said, "Mostly it's just been pounding on
doors, trying to get in long enough to eke out a living,
take care of my family."

"Well, it seems you've done some pretty good eking.
And, look, it's like I told your wife—every step you
make is a step for your race. And when your child walks
into that school..." She talked on as if he and Maggie
were examples for the whole Negro race. It shouldn't
be like that and he didn't want the burden. He studied
the woman beside him, sparkling with zeal and determination.

"Why do you do it?" he asked.

"Huh?" She picked up her mug and drank some of
her coffee.

"Okay, so what I do is for me or my race. But you—
why are you knocking yourself out trying to open
doors?"

She smiled, but there was a sadness reflected in the
eyes that were looking at him but seeing something a
long way off. She put her mug back down on the table.
"Would you believe," she finally said, "that it started
when I was about your Maggie's age?" She didn't notice that he hadn't answered, but went on talking as if
to herself. "A circus came to town and my daddy took
me down to see the parade. There was a clown on one
of the wagons. He was joking and handing out candy
to all the kids, and my dad went rushing up to get a
sucker for me. But in front of us was an old colored
man. He had a little girl, must have been his grand-

daughter. He pulled her along and got to the wagon just before we did. He reached up for a piece of candy for her. And that clown, that stupid ugly painted clown…he spat in the old man's face. The old man just dropped his hand and stared. But I could see tears in his eyes and the little girl kept asking, 'Did you get it, Gramps? Did you get the candy?'"

Marcia took a deep breath and when she spoke again, there was a sob in her voice. "My daddy handed me a sucker and I started to run after them. I wanted to give it to the little girl, you see. But the old man was hurrying her through the crowd and my dad was holding my hand. I couldn't catch them. I didn't enjoy the circus. I kept looking around to see if I could find that little girl. But I didn't see any colored folks at all. Everybody laughed when the clown came out. But I didn't. I hated him." She picked up her mug again, holding it with both hands, as though its warmth gave her comfort. "That day haunts me. It haunts me every time I see the differences between white and colored schools. I can't help it—I get so mad!"

"Yes, I—"

"At everybody! At those self-righteous bigots who are fighting us every step of the way. The sanctimonious do-gooders who tell us to go slow. And yes, all the Negroes who try to pretend everything's jim-dandy if they just don't make any waves. It…it's like I'm giving a big party and nobody wants to come." She laughed, but he saw the pain in her face, saw a little blond girl holding out a piece of candy to a little black girl who wasn't there.

And he saw a warm loving compassionate woman. An attractive woman with expressive green eyes that could dance with zeal…or cry. Why had her husband let her go? Or was it the other way around? Suddenly he had to know.

"Your husband, Marcia? Did he object to your...this cause of yours?"

"Ken? Oh, no. He was definitely in favor. Felt the same as I do. Still does, I guess. He's a psychologist, and he testified for some of the colored plaintiffs in the integration suits."

"Oh? I didn't know that."

"People got the idea he resented my activities. But he was all for it."

"Then why did you—?"

"Divorce him? Because he's a bastard!" The coffee mug flew from her hand and crashed against the stone fireplace. The green eyes brimmed with tears. "Do you know what it's like to live with a bastard? To watch him chase one woman after another? And try to put up with it? Ignore it? Because you love him."

"Marcia, don't!"

"To lie awake at three in the morning, listening for his car? To wish...? To wait?" The tears were falling freely now.

"Don't do this to yourself. It's over now."

"Do you know why I left him, Rob?"

He shook his head, wishing he could say something. Wishing he hadn't started it.

"I left him because I couldn't stand *me*. Loving, wanting that cheating bastard! It's no good, you know. I still want him." She put a hand to her mouth, trying to stifle the choking sobs.

He took her in his arms. This vibrant lovely woman, as needful as he was...

20

September came too soon. The air was heavy with it, a nostalgic reminder of all the Septembers of Ann Elizabeth's life. May smelled like apple blossoms. December smelled of pine needles and peppermint candy. But September smelled like a tin lunch box with an apple in it. The aroma engulfed her, filled her nostrils, and tightened the band of fear around her heart.

Memories of a happy childhood stirred within her, at odds with the hatred. The hatred embraced them all. The NAACP, the Supreme Court, Rob. Yes, even the delightful anticipation in Maggie's big brown eyes. And that wasn't fair. When it was September and you were six years old and the beginning of school was only three days away, you had a right to be excited.

"I'm going to school on Tuesday. Did you know I'm going to school on Tuesday?" That was Maggie, outside, her voice floating like September through the open window. "It took me a long time to decide which dress I'll wear. At first I thought the pink one. But then I thought maybe that one with lots of red. On account of Daddy likes red. Do you like red?"

"Yes, I do, Maggie. I think red is very pretty." That

was Mrs. Levin. Ann Elizabeth often warned Maggie
not to bother her, but Maggie just as often forgot.

"I like pink. But Daddy says red is a brave bold
color. Not wishy-washy like pink."

Okay, so I'm wishy-washy. Ann Elizabeth swallowed
the lump in her throat. She didn't want to leave Rob.
She had delayed, hoping Rob would change his mind.
But now... She swallowed again, thinking of the two
plane tickets in her purse. Maggie didn't know it, but
she wouldn't be here on Tuesday.

"You wanna know which dress I decided?"

"Indeed I do. Which?" Mrs. Levin's voice was light
and cheery. But Ann Elizabeth could imagine the question in the piercing blue eyes behind the gold spectacles.
Where are you going to school?

"The green one. On account of it has a real leather
belt. The red one is pretty, but it has a sash like babies
wear. I wouldn't want to wear a sash the very first day,
would you?"

"No. I think I'd choose the green," Mrs. Levin said.
"My, my! Such a big day for such a little girl!"

Abruptly Ann Elizabeth shut the window. She
couldn't stand it. It *was* a big day for a little girl. And
she was not going to have it spoiled. The perfect case,
Marcia Wheeling had said. But Maggie wasn't a case.
She was an adorable child with thick black braids, fun
in her eyes and a dimple in her chin. She liked licorice
and raw carrots and Huckleberry Hound and people.
Especially people.

If only Rob would see it her way. But he was so
stubborn. And now...so detached. Her fault maybe.
Moving out of their bedroom. But he'd made her so
mad that day. And once out, there seemed no graceful
way to move back in.

Especially when he'd stopped pleading. No more arguments, just polite stilted conversations more deadly than the long silences. She didn't like living like this. And she didn't want to leave Rob. She would try one more time to convince him. Tonight.

She didn't think he'd change his mind. Numbly she went about doing what had to be done. She packed, set their suitcases in the back of the closet, washed Maggie's hair.

Rob was late. Probably went from work to one of those meetings. She and Maggie ate their dinner, watched television. She put Maggie to bed.

Ann Elizabeth paced the floor, waiting for Rob. She would do her best to convince him. She had to.

At eleven o'clock the doorbell rang, startling her. Rob had his key. Who could it be this late? She flicked on the porch light and looked through the peephole.

"It's me, Ann Elizabeth. Otis Pitts."

She opened the door, started to explain. "Rob's not here—"

"Yes, I know." Something in his tone frightened her. "Now, look, don't get excited. Everything's all right. But...there's been an...an accident."

"Rob?" Her heart stood still.

"Well...not exactly an accident. He's going to be all right. He's at the hospital. I came for you. Cecelia can stay with Maggie."

Ann Elizabeth turned her confused gaze to Otis's wife, for the first time noticing that she was with him. Cecilia put both arms around her. "Now you mustn't worry, Ann Elizabeth. It's not too bad. But you'll see for yourself. Go on with Otis and don't worry about Maggie. I'll be here."

On the way to the hospital, Otis told her what had

happened. A gang of men had apparently forced Rob's car to the curb and dragged him out and beaten him. "Thank God a passing motorist witnessed it," Otis said, "and had the good sense to get to the nearest phone and report it." By the time the police got there, the men were gone. "They found Rob lying in the gutter behind his car and took him to the hospital."

Stark terror gripped her. Rob, lying helpless, unable to move. "If he couldn't even…"

Otis's hand covered hers. "He'll be okay. He's been pretty badly knocked about, but no knife or club marks and no guns. I think they just wanted to scare him."

She shivered. "On account of the school thing."

"That's what the police think. What Rob thinks, too. He asked them to call me. Didn't want you coming down alone. He was so worried about you, Ann Elizabeth. When I got there, the sedative hadn't quite taken effect, and he gave me a message for you. Said to tell you that you were right."

Rob, hurt and bleeding, thinking of her. She wanted to take back the ugly words, erase the empty weeks. She stared out at the dark streets.

Jennie Lou and Allen Slater were at the hospital, and General Marks, Rob's boss, and Joe Tillman and Marcia Wheeling. Marcia was crying. That frightened Ann Elizabeth.

They gathered around to assure her that Rob was going to be fine. Some pretty bad bruises, a broken arm and a dislocated shoulder. They were lucky. His injuries could have been a lot worse.

It was a long time before she believed that he *would* be all right.

It was longer still before her fear for him was replaced by a hard cold anger. At men who roamed dark streets and brutally assaulted one lone man. Who thought *their* rights were the only rights.

With anger came determination.

They didn't expect it of her. "Of course you can't take Maggie to the school now. We didn't anticipate this kind of violence. But now…no. Too dangerous."

"I *will* go," Ann Elizabeth said. "We'll be at that school on Tuesday morning."

Marcia stared at her in surprise. "Don't be foolhardy. Rob wouldn't want you to go. Not now."

"I think that was what he meant me to tell you, Ann Elizabeth," Otis said. "He kept saying tell her she's right."

"We can wait," Marcia said. "We'll have another chance."

But Ann Elizabeth wasn't listening. More than a school was at stake. She knelt by Rob's bed. He looked so defenseless. Gingerly she touched the bruise over his left eye. He winced in his sleep. She wanted to throw her arms around him, but his shoulder was swathed in bandages, and there was a cast on his arm. She touched his lips lightly with her own.

"I won't let you down," she whispered. He couldn't hear, but she had to tell him anyway. He'd had a long journey—countless missions in a bloody overseas war, a German prison camp, the battle for jobs and dignity at home, a dark street in Virginia. "I won't let you down," she whispered. "Not when our rights are just two blocks away."

When they couldn't talk her out of it, they offered to come with her.

She said she'd go alone. Her mother had once told her, "Sometimes it's better for a woman alone."

* * *

She didn't tell Maggie that Daddy was in the hospital, only that he'd gone away for a few days—as he often did.

Tuesday morning it was almost as if she got Maggie ready too quickly. The last scrap of egg had disappeared from the plate, the teeth were brushed, the thick braids smooth and tied at the ends with crisp green ribbons. Nothing to do but buckle the green leather belt.

"Maggie," she said as she knelt before her, "Mommy wants to tell you something." Tell her what? That the children might not be friendly? That grown-ups might stand by and sneer? That somebody might throw a rock? What could you tell a six-year-old girl who was so eager and happy about her first day of school? The light in those big brown eyes almost blinded her.

"What, Mommy?"

"That you look very pretty. Like a very big girl. And I love you. Daddy and I are proud of you."

Then there was nothing more to do. She opened the door, took Maggie's hand and started the two-block walk. Like going the last mile.

"Hello," called a cheery voice. "So the big day begins!"

"Hello, Mrs. Levin," Maggie said. "Do you like my dress?"

"I do. It's just right for the first day of school."

"That's what I thought." Maggie smiled proudly.

"I'm on my way to market," Mrs. Levin said. "You don't mind if I walk along with you, do you?"

Ann Elizabeth's heart flooded over. Mrs. Levin never walked to market, and it was too early, anyway.

"Thought I'd like to see my girl start her big day."

Mrs. Levin's arthritic fingers gripped Maggie's other hand.

Ann Elizabeth couldn't speak around the lump in her throat. It was as if she and Maggie and Mrs. Levin, and nine robed judges and a million other Americans were walking together.

21

The only thing we have to fear is fear itself. When those words had come humming over the radio to a frightened nation, Ann Elizabeth had been a young girl.

Now, as they approached Maggie's school, she remembered and repeated the words. But she couldn't stifle the fear pulsing through her veins. They walked slowly to accommodate Mrs. Levin's arthritic knees. Children passed them, laughing, calling to one another, seemingly as oblivious as Maggie to this momentous occurrence. A few parents stared curiously and gave them a wide berth as they hurried past.

Ann Elizabeth saw that a noisy crowd had gathered outside the school, spilling into the street. Her heart pounded, and she glanced anxiously around for the promised police protection. They were there, but in plain clothes. Inconspicuous. Now she wished they were more in evidence, a controlling influence. The faces around them were belligerent. One husky man stepped in front of them as if to block their way. Mrs. Levin lifted her spectacles and surveyed him. He backed off, looking confused. There were a few catcalls and jeers, of which Maggie seemed blessedly unaware.

But no violence.

Something restrained them. Held them back. Was it the frail bent form of the gray-haired white woman who held tightly to Maggie's hand and glared defiantly at the crowd? Was it the presence of newspeople and the flashing bulbs of their cameras? Bigots who attacked in the night would not expose themselves in broad daylight, would not be photographed assaulting one defenseless white woman, one tiny colored girl.

As they entered the school, Ann Elizabeth thought she heard someone shout, "Atta girl, Maggie Metcalf!" She couldn't be sure, but it heartened her, anyway.

The principal, who looked as anxious as she did, was unsmiling but solicitous. The school clerk was openly curious but friendly. She quietly registered Maggie and gave directions to her classroom. At the door of the room, they almost bumped into a buxom woman who was going out. She looked at Maggie and smiled. "My, my! Such a pretty little girl. Are you going into first grade?"

Maggie nodded shyly.

"That's nice. But watch out for my Troy. He's the redhead over there. Don't let him pull your pigtails." She gave one of the braids a little tug and Maggie grinned. Ann Elizabeth could have hugged this stranger who'd spoken to her child in...such an ordinary way.

So Maggie was quietly registered in Lansberg Elementary and entrusted to the care of the friendly Miss Agnew. Maybe, Ann Elizabeth thought, as she walked home with Mrs. Levin, Anne Frank was right. What was it she'd said? Something like, *Most people are basically good at heart*. Maybe Roosevelt was right, too. Certainly the fear that had traumatized them for weeks struck a discordant note in their home, torn them apart, had been so much worse than the feared event itself.

But... Her heart pounded. Rob was in the hospital. There had been, still was, cause for fear.

Each morning Ann Elizabeth walked Maggie to school and called for her every afternoon. Each time, making no excuse, Mrs. Levin walked with her. The crowd outside the school diminished, finally disappeared altogether. Maggie Metcalf had quietly integrated Lansberg Elementary, and could now make the two-block walk alone.

"I'm glad I was the only one hurt," Rob said, still mulling over it on the day he was dressing to go back to work. "If anything had happened to you or Maggie, I could never forgive myself. I kept pushing you."

"Hush." Ann Elizabeth put a finger to his lips. "You made the right choice."

"Easy to say now. But that night, when those men came after me... Otis said they just wanted to scare me, and let me tell you, they did. Men I didn't even know hated my guts and were beating the hell out of me." He sat on the edge of the bed, put on his loafers, looked up at her. "Funny how you tend to forget what it's like. The hate."

She shuddered, remembering what she'd seen as a child when she'd gone with her parents to view the abandoned Williams farm. Crude boxlike cells, rusty chains hanging, the Yellow River flowing swiftly by.

"You get used to prejudice," he said. "You know it's there and you try to deal with it rationally." He paused. "It's something you have to maneuver around. And I don't know why you forget about the hate, the pure unadulterated hate that breaks out every now and then in brutal violence or lynchings. Why do you forget about that kind of hate?"

"Because you have to," she said, sitting beside him. "You have to, or you can't get through your life." She paused. "Personally I think the hate is outnumbered by love, by people like Marcia and Mrs. Levin."

"Mrs. Levin. Isn't she the greatest? Do you think she liked the cameo?"

"Yes." Ann Elizabeth laughed. "She liked the cameo. And the stole. And the flowers. And the candy."

"Okay, laugh. But I could never repay her for what she did."

"Nor I. You don't know how much it meant when she came out and took Maggie's hand."

"And you. God! I would've stopped you if I hadn't been so out of it."

"I just took up where you left off. You got the beating and I got the glory. Okay?" She was smiling, but his face was sober.

"It took guts. After what happened to me it took a lot of guts. You're some kind of woman, Ann Elizabeth."

The same thing he'd said the night he asked her to marry him. Did he remember? She caught the hand that held her chin. It was so good to have his respect, his love, again. The days of his convalescence had been like a honeymoon. At the hospital there had been other people. But at home just the two of them.

"I hate to see you go back to work, Rob."

He grinned. "I need the rest. Can't get any around here. You're wearing me out, honey."

Blushing, she brushed his hand away. "Robert Metcalf, if you—"

"Let me get back to work and revive. Tonight I promise—"

She threw a pillow at him. He laughed and seized her. "Come here, my lady in the parlor. Oh, what you do to me in bed. Ann Elizabeth, it's so good to have you back. I went a little crazy without you. Don't ever shut me out again.''

"Shut myself out, too," she whispered against his chest. "I'm glad this nightmare is over. If it is."

He tilted her face up. "Of course it's over. What do you mean? Maggie's been in school for two weeks now and there's been no disturbance."

"Yes, I know. Guess I'm just edgy." He'd been through enough. She wouldn't plague him with her doubts. It was never their hate she'd feared as much as their tolerance. Or rather, tolerance without acceptance.

As the days passed she grew more anxious.

Each morning as she wrapped the sandwich, placed the apple in the tin lunch box, she prayed Maggie would share them with someone. Each afternoon she watched children hurrying home from school, laughing and playing together. Watched Maggie walking alone.

Then one day, one glorious happy day, Maggie came up the walk holding the hand of another little girl. The child's socks were falling down, one shoe was untied, the hand that kept pushing the hair from her freckled face was grubby, and her broad smile exposed a gap where two front teeth were missing. She was the most beautiful child Ann Elizabeth had ever seen. "Hello," she said. "What's your name?"

"Lisa. Lisa Aiken." The child stood on one foot and rubbed the back of her leg with the other. "Can Maggie come over to my house to play?"

Beautiful words. But… "Hadn't you better check with your mother?"

"My mom don't care."

"You'd better ask. Where do you live?"

She lived across the street, three doors down, and her mother really didn't care. Too ill to care much about anything, Ann Elizabeth decided when she was admitted by a uniformed nurse into a spotless house heavy with the odors of medicine and illness.

Her heart went out to the wasted woman on the bed, who gave her a feeble smile. "Lisa needs a playmate."

"Maggie, too," Ann Elizabeth said. "But perhaps they should play at my house."

"No," Lisa said, glancing first at her and then at her mother. "We'll be quiet. I want to show Maggie my dollhouse."

Her mother nodded. "Let her stay," she whispered. "Lisa has so little."

Ann Elizabeth stayed, too. To be sure the children kept quiet, but also compelled by a need she sensed in the other woman.

"Cancer," Clara Aiken told her. "They say I have only a few months to live." It all spilled out as if the two women had been friends for years. She related it in a matter-of-fact voice—her husband's job transfer from Florida, the happy move to the new house, the surgery that had come with no warning and much too late. "And now this," she finished, with a small gesture Ann Elizabeth read all too well. This. The painful helpless waiting…to leave a loving husband, a child she would never see grow up.

Tears burned in Ann Elizabeth's eyes, but she held them back. This woman, who hadn't had time to make friends before illness struck, needed a friend. Compassion filled Ann Elizabeth's heart and she decided to be that friend, to do all she could for Clara. A book, a flower, a cup of soup or just a visit to talk, to listen, to share.

Perhaps she did more for Lisa, substituting for a mother who was ill and a harassed father who worked a full shift and spent the rest of his time maintaining a household and caring for his dying wife. During the following weeks Lisa spent most of her after-school time at the Metcalfs', playing with Maggie, staying for milk and cookies and often dinner, going over her schoolwork. Ann Elizabeth tied the laces of the scuffed shoes, brushed the tousled hair, washed the freckled face and loved her.

Perhaps it was the giving, the close association with Lisa and Clara, that made Ann Elizabeth open up to others. No longer did she see her neighbors as simply whites, belligerent or friendly or indifferent, but as people like herself, with problems of their own.

Troy's mother was getting a divorce and worked full-time, so he had to remain at school for after-hours care. Once when she had to work late, she asked Ann Elizabeth to pick him up, promising to reciprocate any evening by baby-sitting Maggie. Another child, Todd, had a learning disability, and his mother really appreciated the extra help Ann Elizabeth gave him, and in exchange here were a couple of books she'd bought for Maggie. Some doors were still closed, some people still looked the other way when the Metcalfs approached. But Ann Elizabeth began to feel that most people were too busy dealing with the vicissitudes of life to spend their time hating.

Determined to help Maggie adjust to school, Ann Elizabeth began attending the PTA and volunteering as a classroom aide two days a week. About the middle of the year, a few children from the Innsfield area entered the Lansberg school, quietly, as Marcia Wheeling had predicted, with no fanfare. Yes, Ann Elizabeth thought, with a touch of pride, Maggie had taken a big step for many others. Here, too, she determined to do her part.

She found herself mothering them, taking a special interest. "What? No lunch today? Here, I have an extra sandwich." Or, "Now that's no way to talk. Of course you can do it. Like this." She was glad she was there. There were no Negro teachers and most of the Negro mothers worked.

"Why are white girls the prettiest?" Maggie asked one day.

"What? No, they're not. You're very pretty and so is Sara and…" Ann Elizabeth faltered. Her daughter's question had come out of left field and she didn't know how to respond. "Anyway, it's not what people look like. It's what's inside that counts."

"I bet Karin will be fairy queen," Maggie said.

"Fairy queen?"

"'Cause she's the prettiest and she's got yellow hair and blue eyes. Just like a real fairy queen." The story of the spring play came out then. Most of the children were to be flowers, sleeping, and the fairy queen had to go around with her magic wand and wake them up.

The next day there was another question out of left field. "Mommy, are there any black fairies?"

"Of course. Just as many black as white ones." So there!

"Troy said there wasn't. And he made Lillith cry."

"Oh?"

"'Cause Miss Agnew picked her to be the fairy queen."

Bless you, Miss Agnew. Lillith was the other colored girl in first grade, and the teacher was probably trying to prove a point.

"Nonsense," Miss Agnew said the next day. "It's because the fairy queen has to do a solo and Lillith has the best voice."

But Lillith wasn't fairy queen, after all. For some reason the roles were switched. Karin became fairy queen and Lillith was one of the brown-eyed Susans.

Troy said, "I *told* you so."

"Maybe you were wrong, Mommy," Maggie said. "Or maybe there are no colored fairy queens."

"Oh, yes, there are," Ann Elizabeth said firmly. "Just as many as white fairy queens. This is just play-acting, and sometimes people get cast in roles for the wrong reason."

"Like parent intervention," she told Rob. "And it bugs me that Maggie has to face it."

"Par for the course," he answered. "And it's not always color or parents. People get shoved around for lots of reasons, and Maggie has to learn to deal with it."

"I know."

"Anyway, it's not Maggie this time, it's Lillith."

"I know," Ann Elizabeth said again, and wondered that she worried as much for Lillith as for Maggie.

Gradually they felt integrated in the Lansberg community. Rob helped build the booths for the street fair, and Ann Elizabeth directed the play for the PTA spring luncheon. They still visited colored friends across town, but not as often. It wasn't Sacramento, but Ann Elizabeth was beginning to enjoy Hampton.

June 1959

Until that Tuesday bridge at Jennie Lou's.

As usual it was a lovely affair. Jennie Lou loved to entertain. Ann Elizabeth smiled, remembering Rob's comment, "She's trying to be another Julia Belle. Mrs. Dr. Allen Slater, doing her duty as grande dame of Hampton's black elite." And doing a pretty good job of it, in Ann Elizabeth's opinion. She surveyed the elegant setup in what Jennie Lou called the sunroom of her spacious home. After a delicious luncheon, linen tablecloths were whisked away and three tables of fashionably attired women settled down for a round of bridge.

Pleasantly complacent, Ann Elizabeth chewed on mints and nuts, and tried to concentrate on the bidding through the wide range of table talk—politics, people, gossip. Mary Jean Adams, at the next table, called over to ask how Maggie was getting on at Lansberg Elementary.

"Just great," Ann Elizabeth said. "I'm beginning to feel a little foolish about all the fuss I made."

There were murmurs of understanding. Definitely something to make a fuss about, some of the women agreed. "Look what happened to Rob," Mary Jean said. "How's he doing?"

"He's fine now," she answered. "That was the worst part. But—" she sighed "—I guess all's well that ends well."

"Right," Jennie Lou said. "I think even all those nasty rumors have finally been squelched."

Something about the way she said it, something about the sudden quiet, something about the way Cecelia hurriedly broke in with, "Let's see. Whose bid? Ann Elizabeth, did you pass?"

"Yes. I passed." She called over to Jennie Lou, "What rumors?"

"Oh, you know. Same thing they always say—black man, white woman. That the real reason those men attacked Rob was because he—"

"—was trying to integrate a school," Cecilia interrupted hastily. "Everybody knows that."

"Of course, but…" Jennie Lou hesitated. "I suppose it was his leaving Marcia's house at that time of night."

"You mean they're saying that Rob and Marcia Wheeling…? That's disgusting!" Mary Jean Adams— open, naive and a little slow—was oblivious to the distracted throat clearing and who-bid-what attempts to shush her. "Why they drag that sex bugaboo into every attempt at integration is beyond me!"

Jennie Lou persevered. "I suppose it was because Rob was out there so often."

"As we all were," Cecelia said. "Rob was so anxious to protect Maggie, to make the right moves, and you know Marcia's experienced in these maneuvers. It's only natural that he'd consult with her."

"Of course," Jennie Lou said. "And now that he's not there nearly as often, like I said, the rumor's died down. I'm thankful for that."

So why are you digging it up? To inform me? Ann Elizabeth wanted to slap her. "I'm glad, too," she said, and managed to keep her voice steady. "Marcia's a staunch friend and has been a tower of strength to *both* of us during this whole ordeal. There are few enough whites like her. It's a shame to slander her with lies." But the rumors were true. She knew it. *Rob…how could you?* "Now, let's see, I'm dummy, huh?" Ann Elizabeth laid out her cards. "Hope you can make it," she said to her partner. "I overbid. But we may as well chance it." Nothing mattered, anyway. Nothing but the thoughts thrumming through her head. Rob. How many times had he said it? "Gotta run out to Marcia's." Or not said it. *Leaving Marcia's house at that time of night.* The hospital… Marcia had been crying, and she'd thought… God, she'd been a fool. A blind stupid fool!

Never before had she thought that Rob… She felt bereft and a little sick.

"Good going, partner! I knew you could make it. If you hadn't played that heart…"

Rob parked his car in the driveway and got out to inspect his lawn. Rick Travis, two doors down, had told him what to put on that spot. By golly, it was working! Green sprigs were showing through. That ugly cross would soon be obliterated. *Ugly* cross? One of his mother's favorite hymns was "That Old Rugged Cross." Ironic, he thought, how good symbols could be twisted into something evil.

The front door slammed and Maggie ran out and leaped into his arms. "Hi, Daddy!"

After a hug and a kiss, he put her down and smiled at the girl beside her. "Hello, Lisa."

"Hi. We're going to play at my house."

"So late?" He looked at his watch.

"Just till dinnertime," Maggie said quickly. "Mommy said so. On account of she's got a headache," she added as they sped away.

Headache? Ann Elizabeth never had a headache. He went inside, letting the screen door slap shut behind him. "Honey?"

No answer and no sounds from the kitchen. He went to their bedroom, loosening his tie, shedding his coat. She was lying on the bed, still in the green silk dress she'd probably worn to bridge. That was unlike her, too.

He threw his coat aside, sat on the edge of the bed. "What's wrong, sweetheart? Don't you feel well?"

"I'm okay," she said, not looking at him, staring at the ceiling. He moved toward her and she shifted away, stood up. "Didn't know it was so late. Better fix dinner."

"No. If you're not feeling well, I'll..." But she'd already disappeared. Still in the silk dress, in stocking feet. Something was wrong. He pulled off his tie, rolled up his sleeves and followed.

She was yanking things from the fridge, throwing them on the counter. Chops, frozen beans, lettuce, tomatoes. She stopped, as if confused, uncertain what to do next.

"Ann Elizabeth, what's wrong?" He took her by the shoulders, turned her toward him—and was shocked by the hurt in her eyes.

She pushed him away.

"You know what's wrong. Everybody knows but me!"

"What are you talking about?"

"I'm talking about Marcia Wheeling."

"Marcia?" His blood ran cold. "What...what about...?"

"About *you* and Marcia." She gazed steadily up at him, her eyes boring into his, reading the truth. "So. It is true." Her pain squeezed at his heart.

"Ann Elizabeth, I... It's not...wasn't like you think."

"How was it, Rob? You tell me."

"It was..." Comfort. Two ships passing in a stormy sea. Needing each other. "Ann Elizabeth, you've got to understand. It was when you shut me out. It was nothing. Just—"

"Oh, I do understand." Her voice was sharp with sarcasm. "She was helping you with Maggie. And you...what were you, Rob? Her black stud?"

"Jesus, Ann Elizabeth!"

"Or is it true what they say? That all of you are just itching to get your hands on a white woman?"

"That's ridiculous. Let me explain." He moved toward her.

"Don't touch me." She picked up the salad bowl, held it like a weapon.

He watched her anxiously. "Sweetheart, listen—"

"I'm not your sweetheart. I'm nothing to you. Nothing!" She hurled the bowl to the floor, smashing it into bits.

"Ann Elizabeth, don't!" He remembered another night. A cup crashing against a fireplace.

"Don't what? Don't tell it like it is?" She reached into the cabinet and a plate shattered into pieces. Then a glass.

"Honey, don't!"

"Don't what? Don't break up our pretty things?" He stepped aside, just missing a flying cup. "Don't break up our pretty things? You've broken up our marriage, our lives, our—"

"Mommy, I'm back. I— What's the matter?" Maggie stood in the doorway, eyes wide.

Ann Elizabeth brought a hand to her mouth, turned and ran from the room. He heard their bedroom door shut.

"Daddy, what's the matter with Mommy?"

"Mommy's not feeling too well."

"Oh, should I—"

"Wait, honey, stay away from that glass. Let Daddy do it. You bring the dustpan." He stooped to pick up the larger pieces. It had started this way with Marcia, flinging that cup against the wall and calling her husband a bastard. Jesus! Now he was the bastard.

"Why did Mommy throw all those dishes? Was she mad?"

"Yes." And hurt. But he hadn't meant to hurt her.

"What was she mad about?"

"A misunderstanding, honey. Don't. Let Daddy pick it up. You might cut yourself."

"There's a piece right there, Daddy."

He picked up the larger pieces, ran the vacuum.

"Daddy, I'm hungry. Aren't we gonna have dinner?"

He fixed Maggie a peanut-butter-and-jelly sandwich, prepared her bath.

"Want me to read to you, Daddy?"

"Not tonight, honey." He gave her a kiss and switched off the light. Ann Elizabeth was already asleep, or pretending sleep, in Maggie's bed. She knew they couldn't talk in front of their daughter.

Tomorrow, when he got home from work, he would make her understand.

When he returned to their room and saw the bottle of sleeping pills on the bathroom counter, he panicked. Ann Elizabeth never took sleeping pills, but she'd been in such a state... The pills had been prescribed for him when he left the hospital. No one had touched them in all these months. He realized the bottle was almost full and sighed with relief. Still, he flushed the rest down the toilet.

He didn't sleep well. How could he explain it to Ann Elizabeth? He wished he could stay home the next day. He couldn't—there was an important meeting; he had to be there.

He was up early the next morning and stopped by Maggie's room. They both appeared to be sleeping. He touched Ann Elizabeth's shoulder.

"I have to go, honey. I'll come home early. Please…we need to talk."

She said nothing.

When he returned home she and Maggie were gone. There was a note on the kitchen table. The car was at the airport, it said, the key at the airline counter.

22

"I was so lonely for Bobby," she told her mother. "Talking to him on the phone once a week wasn't enough. And I'm anxious to see one of his baseball games before school closes." She turned to her son. "Oh, Bobby, honey, you've grown so tall. Are you still pitching? When's the next game? You haven't been neglecting your schoolwork, I hope."

"Fat chance!" Bobby grimaced. "Grandma's worse than you. Even threatened to take me off the team, and we're in first place and I'm top pitcher." He launched into an enthusiastic play-by-play description that caught at her heart. *Doing what he wanted to do and having fun at it.* Like Randy.

"Maggie's out of school already?" Julia Belle asked as soon as Bobby left for practice.

"Just one more week. She won't be missing anything. I picked up her report card before we left. All *A*'s and *B*'s." She glanced at her daughter, who was absorbed in a television show. "She's really bright. Miss Agnew, her teacher, says she wishes all her kids were as quick as Maggie. She's already reading second-grade books."

"How's Rob?"

"Fine. Just fine. Really busy right now. Something's wrong with some planes the Air Force purchased. A whole pile of them. Wouldn't you think they'd check them out beforehand? Anyway, the whole trouble has landed in Rob's lap and he...he's real busy." She noted her mother's scrutiny, and her voice trailed off. She was talking too fast. She drew a deep breath. "Dad's looking well." He had picked her up at the airport, but had been too full of Bobby's doings to ask any questions, thank goodness. He'd dropped them off and gone on his way. "I take it he's back to his old busy self."

"Yes, working too hard again as usual." Julia Belle sighed. "I hoped he'd lighten his load since he's closed the hospital. Closed it as soon as the Hughes Spalding Pavilion opened and he could take his patients there. Isn't it wonderful, Ann Elizabeth? A teaching hospital for black doctors and Dan's been appointed the head of obstetrics. Dan also has an office at Emory, you know."

"That's what he wanted and worked for." She thought of the long talks with Dan and Sadie about the lack of training facilities for black doctors. She thought of Bobby and Children's Hospital. "Is it well equipped?"

"Is it! The very latest in everything. They say Spalding insisted on that. There are some good white folks in this land, Ann Elizabeth."

"Yes." She thought of Marcia. She tried to swallow the lump in her throat.

"You must see the hospital. Sadie's working there, too, a supervisor. Dan's says she's an excellent nurse. Did you have dinner on the plane?"

Ann Elizabeth said she had and, to her relief, their conversation stayed on Atlanta and there were no questions about her sudden arrival.

Maggie was given the guest room and Ann Elizabeth

was ushered into her old room. "Had it done over. How do you like it?"

"Very much," she said. "I like the beige and brown tones with just a splash of orange. And you changed the bed."

"For Rob," Julia Belle said, laughing. "That frilly canopy didn't seem to suit him."

Ann Elizabeth's heart lurched. Rob. Would they ever share a bed again? She was glad Maggie was in the small guest room. She was grateful for the privacy. Alone in the new bed, she could let the tears flow unchecked, could pour out the hurt and the anger. She'd taken refuge in flight, but her torment had only grown worse. A broken record repeating... Jennie Lou's cruel remarks, Cecelia's kindly meant protests. The truth in Rob's eyes. Rob. The image of him holding Marcia in his arms burned in her brain and her heart like hot coals that couldn't be smothered, no matter how hard she tried.

Downstairs with the family, she was cheerful. Sometimes too silent or too talkative, but never expressing her inner turmoil. The children were no problem. Bobby, already ensconced in the Carter household, had his school, his friends, his baseball, even a part-time job in his grandfather's office. Maggie spent most of her time with Helen Rose's family. Helen Rose now had three lively children and a big house in a new section called Collier Circle. Negroes were moving farther out, covering more territory. Their houses were bigger, the furnishings plusher, the acreage surrounding them more expansive. Millie had married an insurance executive and their home included a guest house with a wide deck overlooking a mammoth swimming pool. The deck was the setting for the bridge party Millie hosted for Ann

Elizabeth. There was a series of such parties, and as Ann Elizabeth was entertained in one beautiful home after another, she remembered Rob's calling her "girl from the golden ghetto." It seemed the ghetto had grown larger and more golden. Yet there was a certain sameness about it. Same social cliques, same parties over and over again.

Ann Elizabeth loved parties, loved renewing old acquaintances. So why was she feeling stifled? Bored, even. Would she feel that way if she'd remained a part of it? If she'd married Dan? Dan and Sadie were busy at their new posts and she saw very little of them. She was glad about that. It was hard to put up a front with such close friends. However, she did tour the hospital and was impressed. She was especially proud of Dan, so efficient, self-assured and at ease in his position. As for not marrying him...no, she had no regrets.

All jealousy, all regret, was centered on Rob. She was miserable. It was harder and harder to remain cool, detached and noncommittal when he phoned. Her longing for him battled with the hurt and humiliation she felt at his betrayal. Because betrayal it was, of the most fundamental kind.

"We should all go to the Morehouse graduation ceremonies," Dr. Carter said. "Martin Luther King, Jr., is the keynote speaker. He's an alumnus, you know."

"Will we be able to get in?" Ann Elizabeth asked. After that unprecedented bus boycott, the man drew a crowd wherever he went.

"You forget. Your mother has connections."

Julia Belle's connections got seats for all of them, including the children. When the president of the college introduced Dr. King, Ann Elizabeth's only hope was that he not speak too long. It was hot in the auditorium. Even in her sleeveless chiffon, she felt sticky and uncomfortable, and Maggie was already fidgeting by her side. She fanned herself with her program and prepared to hear the Montgomery story all over again.

Nothing she had heard or read prepared her for Martin Luther King, Jr. The nondescript brown-skinned man who spoke with the rhetoric of a Rhodes scholar and the delivery of a Baptist preacher reached far beyond Montgomery and carried his audience with him. Under the passion and power of his words, no longer was she just Ann Elizabeth Carter. She was one of twenty million Negroes caught in the trap of racial discrimination. King spoke of a tactic that would free the American Negro from this trap—nonviolent direct action. "It's hard to fight a man," Dr. King declared, "when he is clothed in right and the only weapons he carries are courage and honor."

"Nonviolent direct action," Julia Belle repeated later that afternoon as the family sat under the magnolia tree sipping iced tea and musing about the speech. "Why didn't we ever think of that before?"

"Because it wasn't the time," Dr. Carter said.

"Guess we never really had a strategy," Ann Elizabeth suggested.

"Oh, we had plenty," her father said. "There was Marcus Garvey who advised us to leave the country, and Booker T. Washington, who—"

"He was an Uncle Tom." Bobby spoke with all the wisdom and vehemence of his nearly sixteen years.

Dr. Carter regarded him with interest. "What do you know about Booker T. Washington?"

"I been reading about him. He started all this segregation."

"Wait a minute, son." Dr. Carter held up a hand. "It was the white man who started segregation, and don't let anybody tell you different. Old Booker T. just tried to deal with it."

"By Uncle Tomming! I ain't never gonna Uncle Tom!"

"No, I don't think you'll have to," his grandfather said.

"What do you mean?" Bobby's face fell, as if he regretted he was to be denied this challenge.

"I mean there's a lot of difference between a man with nothing in his pocket, standing on the land of the man who used to own him, and a man with money in his pocket, living in a house that belongs to his father."

"Huh?"

"In order to survive, that former slave had to make a deal with the man who'd owned him. There's been a lot of dealing, a lot of Uncle Toms between that slave and you. Between him and Martin Luther King, too. You don't think Dr. King just popped out of thin air, do you? How do you think he got his education? Morehouse, Crozier, Boston University. How did he get to India and how did he get the chance to study Mahatma Ghandi's tactics?"

Bobby considered. "Well, I guess his daddy..."

"Right. His bread, butter and books all started with his father. Martin Luther King, Sr., is a minister, supported by his congregation. Many of those parishioners ride on segregated buses and earn their meager wages by working at menial tasks for white folks. They have to Uncle Tom every single day. They live decent uncomplaining Christian lives and take their pennies to their segregated churches on Sundays."

Bobby looked a little puzzled. "Granddaddy, don't you like Dr. King?"

"Oh, my child, of course I do. All I'm saying is that it took a lot of so-called Uncle Toms to produce him." The ice in his glass rattled as the old man shook it. "Ah, yes. In my opinion, Martin Luther King, Jr., might very well be the greatest man this century has produced. I think it was Toynbee who said the American Negro would make a living fire from the ashes of the white man's Christianity."

Ann Elizabeth looked at her father. "Did he really say that?"

"Something to that effect—and I think King has handed us the torch." His eyes twinkled as he glanced at his wife. "I bet you thought such a fire would come quietly and sedately from the Congregationalists. Not from a roaring Baptist."

"Oh, hush up!" Julia Belle laughed and slapped him playfully on the knee.

Ann Elizabeth sighed. "He did all right in Montgomery. But…does he propose to tackle the whole South?"

"I think so. And I think this is the time."

"Well, I'm with him in spirit. But I'm chicken." Ann Elizabeth sighed. "I'm not taking any direct action, violent or otherwise."

"You already have," her father said. "What do you think you did when you walked Maggie to that school?" He stood up. "Come on, Bobby. Time to make hospital rounds. Want us to drop by Helen Rose's and pick up Maggie?"

"Oh, yes, please," she said, and watched them depart, thinking about what he'd said. "Guess I never thought of what I did in those terms," she said to her mother.

"Didn't you?"

"No. Actually I didn't even want Maggie to go to that school. Then, that night, when Rob was hurt...by those men, I was so mad." Mad because he'd been beaten over the school issue when all the while... Her eyes clouded with tears and she blinked rapidly. "So that's why I did it. For Rob."

"Well, well." Her mother drew a deep breath. "It's about time."

"To integrate, you mean?"

"I mean it's time you mentioned Rob's name without being prompted."

"Oh." Ann Elizabeth stood up and began to gather the glasses.

"Sit down, Ann Elizabeth."

"I thought I should take these things in."

"Sit down."

Ann Elizabeth sank back on to the glider, averting her face.

"What's wrong, honey?"

"It's... Oh, Mother, I don't want to talk about it."

"I think you need to talk. What's wrong?"

"Rob. He...he...doesn't love me anymore."

"Oh? Did he say that?"

"No."

"Does he neglect you? Abuse you?"

Ann Elizabeth shook her head.

"Another woman?"

"Oh, Mother..." Now the tears began to flow. "I was such a fool. All I was thinking about was Maggie not going to that stupid Lansberg school. And Rob...all the time he...I had no idea..." The truth tumbled out, along with the tears. Ann Elizabeth felt relief at finally telling the story. Here at last she would find understanding and comfort.

"I'll say you were a fool," Julia Belle said.

Ann Elizabeth nodded. "Yes. Because everybody, all our friends, knew, and I didn't have any idea."

"No. Because when you did know, you ran away. Sent the fox right back to the henhouse."

"What?"

"This Marcia person gave him sympathy and sex when you moved into the next bedroom. What do you think she's giving him now that you're five hundred miles away?"

Ann Elizabeth stared at her mother. "I...I hadn't thought about that."

"Well, think about it."

"Oh, she's so deceitful!" Ann Elizabeth said in a sudden burst of fury. "All that talk about getting our children into good schools when she had her mind on something else entirely. Tossing that blond hair and flashing those green eyes. Talking about integration when what she wanted was—"

"Now wait a minute, Ann Elizabeth. Just wait a minute. Let's not buy the white man's rhetoric that integration leads straight to the bedroom."

"Well, it does—at least in this case."

"My dear, we've always been in each other's beds. Where do you think I came from?" Julia Belle laughed. "You know, there's a rumor in this country that anybody named Washington is colored and they all descended from you-know-who. Another name under question is Jefferson."

Ann Elizabeth sighed. "Oh, I know we're all mixed up. And it doesn't matter what color she is. It's really

Rob, Mother. I never thought he'd…he'd be unfaithful."

"I'd say you've been pretty lucky."

"Lucky?"

"Helen Rose has been through hell since the first day she married. They say Clyde makes a pass at every woman under thirty who sits in his dental chair."

"Oh, Mother."

"Well, that's an exaggeration. But he's had his share of affairs."

Ann Elizabeth was shocked. No wonder Helen Rose had that lost look and filled her time with bridge parties, charities and children. "I couldn't stand that," she said.

"No. You're lucky you haven't had to. Now, after sixteen years, he takes one look at another woman and you take off, ready to throw your marriage out the window."

"It wasn't just one look and I didn't…I'm not…" She stopped. She hadn't thought beyond the hurt. "Mother, you're sounding like I should have ignored the whole thing!"

"Oh, Ann Elizabeth, honey, I'm not belittling the fact. I even admit that it might be more serious because Rob isn't the philandering type." Julia Belle hesitated. "What does he say?"

"Not much." She hadn't given him a chance. "That it wasn't like…like I thought. That I'd shut him out."

"You had."

"Well…but you don't know what I was going through, and he… He didn't have to go running into someone's else's arms!"

"Oh? He probably didn't go running. The arms were just there and he needed them. I suspect the decision to send Maggie to that school was as hard for him as for you.''

"Oh, no, Mother! He didn't have any qualms until—''

"He was probably putting up a front for you. Weren't you pulling in the opposite direction?''

"Yes, but—''

"He certainly wasn't going to let you know he had doubts, too. How do you suppose *he* felt? You pulling him back, others pushing him on, and bigots fighting him every step of the way. He needed someone to say, 'You're okay. You're doing the right thing.'''

"Well, why couldn't he see it my way? I'm not convinced, even now, that it *was* the right thing.''

"Oh, Ann Elizabeth, of course it was.''

"But, Mother…one little colored girl in one school.''

"Didn't you say other coloreds came later? Didn't you tell me how much they needed you? How you helped them make the adjustment?''

She nodded.

"That was a great contribution, Ann Elizabeth.''

Ann Elizabeth looked at her mother. She hadn't thought of it as a contribution. "Well,'' she said slowly, "it was just that I was the only Negro parent who…who was there.''

"Exactly. You were there. It was a big step for those black kids and you made the transition easier. I bet your college education came in handy. You can thank your daddy for that, and you can thank Rob that you were there to use it.''

"Yes, it was Rob who insisted that we integrate.''

"I'm not talking about that.'' Julia Belle twisted her wedding ring around her finger. "You haven't shared

Rob's letters, but I noticed there was a book of checks in one of them.''

"He said he didn't want me to run out of money."

"Uh-huh." Julia Belle smiled. "Money. And time to volunteer at that school because your husband supports you."

"But that's not what counts."

"No. These are things we take for granted. You and I are considered part of a privileged class—with privileges we are purported to use for our pleasure. But we all make our contribution, wherever we have the good luck or the bad luck to be."

"Good Lord, Mother, you keep talking about contributions and privileges and all that stuff. I'm talking about my husband having an affair with another woman."

"Sometimes we take our husbands for granted, too." Julia Belle seemed to be musing. "I remember when your father was in medical school and being a waiter in a dining car during his spare time. We lived in a rented room and I was teaching school and felt, I guess, a little put-upon. At least, I wasn't paying too much attention to that pretty little nurse who was helping him with his studies. When I did look up, I found he was spending more time with her than with me, and much of it at her apartment." Julia Belle laughed and pushed back the streak of gray hair that only enhanced the shiny black framing her still-youthful face. "Well, I broke that up!"

"How?"

"I just strolled up to the doctors' lounge one morning when the two of them were having a little tête à tête over juice and coffee. He looked like a boy caught with his hand in the cookie jar. I was supposed to be at school, you see. I just sat down, leaned close and whispered very sweetly, 'If I see this again, there'll be hair pulling and screaming and juice dripping from the ceiling.'"

"Mother, you wouldn't!"

"Your daddy didn't know whether I would or not. He sure couldn't risk it in front of all his professors. That put a stop to the little meetings. And to the affair—if there was one."

"Just like that?"

"Not exactly. I got a medical dictionary and I helped him with his studies. Besides that, I gave him so much sex and sympathy, he didn't have the energy or the inclination to seek it elsewhere."

Ann Elizabeth, still trying to picture her mother as a brawling wife and voracious sex partner, sighed. "You sound as if Rob's betrayal was all my fault."

"I'm just trying to make you understand something, honey. I once read a card that said marriages aren't made in heaven, they come in a do-it-yourself kit. I'd like to add that they need constant maintenance. And I want you to understand something else. Every day our men are taking it on the chin—hard knocks from the outside world. Perhaps that's why they need more coddling, more 'You're wonderful' than most. If they don't get it at home…" Julia Belle gave a significant shrug.

Ann Elizabeth thought of Rob's words. *Par for the course. People get shoved around for lots of reasons.* She knew how often he'd been shoved or banned. But he'd never griped. He even joked about it. Her father had once said, "Your mother has made me a comfortable retreat." Had *she* done that for Rob? Always instinctively she'd acted as she thought she should…as a wife, a mother. "I had to think of my child, too," she said now. "I wanted Maggie to be happy with friends around her. Like I was at Oglethorpe."

"Maggie's at a different place, in a different era. Everything changes, Ann Elizabeth."

Do you want things to stay the way they are, Mrs. Moonlight? Who'd said that? Was she still holding on to the past?

That night when she went to bed, Ann Elizabeth was still hurt. Still angry. But more frightened. What had her mother said about sex and sympathy and being five hundred miles away?

The next time Rob called she wasn't as cool and detached. "Ann Elizabeth, we need to talk."

"Yes, Rob. We do."

23

Rob arrived two days later, and Ann Elizabeth drove alone to the airport to meet him. She stood by the gate, feeling unsettled and anxious as passenger after passenger descended. No Rob. Then there he was, in a dark-blue business suit, sophisticated, distinguished and somewhat aloof. He searched the crowd, and when he saw her his eyes lit up. He smiled, a warm intimate questioning smile that deepened the creases in his cheeks and sent her pulses racing. She flew into his arms, buried her face against his chest and clung, oblivious to the people around them.

"You drive," she told him. But not home, not yet. Washington Park. It would be deserted this early in the morning and they would have privacy.

He parked under a big oak tree in the almost empty park, switched off the engine and turned to her. Her breath caught and for a moment she could only look at him. He had shed his coat and tie, and his deep brown skin so like her father's was beautiful against the crisp white shirt. He was unbelievably handsome to her. Deep-set dark eyes, long lashes, full lips so often curved with laughter or puckered in a whistle. That was what she loved about him. He was always cheerful. And yet he was strong, tough and…lovable, she thought as she began to cry.

She hadn't meant to cry, but everything set her off these days. And one look at Rob… He was *hers*. How could he…how could he…? She couldn't hold back the gulping sobs. All the pent-up hurt and anger came gushing out.

He pulled her close. "Oh, honey, don't."

"I can't…can't…stop," she choked. "I…I'm so mad." She hadn't meant to be mad. After that talk with her mother, she'd meant to be calm and understanding. "I'm so mad. You don't… Obviously I'm nothing to you. If you loved me, you couldn't…wouldn't…" The words seemed to be stuck in her throat and her tears soaked his shirt.

"*If* I loved you! Oh, honey, if only you knew how much I love you. You're my life, Ann Elizabeth." He hesitated, as if carefully choosing his words. "That thing with Marcia was just—"

"Don't!" Blind rage checked the sobs. She sat up, pushing away the arms that had held that…that hussy! "Don't mention that woman to me. I hate you. And I hate her. Pretending to be so concerned for all the poor little colored children, so dedicated, when all the while she was scheming to get her hands on you. She's nothing but a tramp and I hate—"

"Stop it, Ann Elizabeth!" He shook her, not too gently, shocking her into silence. "Stop acting like a crybaby and listen!"

"Don't you talk to me like that. Not after what you did!"

"All right, I screwed up." Suddenly Rob looked very

tired. "I'm sorry. Sorrier than you'll ever know, damn it."

"You don't sound sorry! And I think we've talked long enough. Why don't I take you back to the airport so you can go back to your tramp."

Rob drew a deep breath. "I *am* sorry. But that doesn't solve anything. Neither will screaming and name-calling. Can't we talk?"

She rubbed the back of her hand against her wet cheek but said nothing.

"Listen, Ann Elizabeth, all hell's breaking loose at the base, and Marks is pissed off at me for leaving. But I happen to think that you...our marriage is important. When you said you'd talk... Anyway, I promised to get right back. I'm scheduled to leave tomorrow night. Will you listen for a minute? Please."

She nodded.

"First of all I want you to understand something. Marcia Wheeling is no tramp. She's a fine human being. She's sincere, warm—"

"And so?" Her voice was cold, sarcastic, hiding the panic. ...*might be more serious because Rob isn't the philandering type.*

"In the second place, she wasn't scheming to entrap me. She was just...there. I..." His eyes changed focus, stared into the past. "I was so scared. Really scared, Ann Elizabeth, scared for Maggie. And confused. Maybe you were right and I was wrong. Marcia kept assuring me that Maggie would be safe—one child, already living in the neighborhood. And she gave me a different perspective, made me see it as an opportunity, something bigger than you or me. She really is sincere, honey. She believes in our cause and works hard for black children."

"That's no reason for you to...to fall into her arms."

"No. And that's not... Oh, Ann Elizabeth I can't explain why it happened." He turned away from her, his face reflective. "Like I said, she was there. I liked her, admired her, I was grateful for her support, and...well, I guess I was sorry for her, too."

"Oh?"

"She's all confused herself. Her own life is in a shambles."

"How?"

"She's madly in love with a husband who's cheated on her with one woman after another, it seems."

Ann Elizabeth thought of Helen Rose, living in misery—too much in love or too embarrassed to leave Clyde. "I thought Marcia was divorced."

"She was, is, I guess. Only now she's thinking of going back to him."

Panic surfaced again. "You're still seeing her?"

"Good God, no! I saw her at an NAACP meeting Sunday and—" he hesitated "—okay, she phoned me last week. Heard you were out of town and she was concerned that rumors had reached you." His mouth twisted. "Said she'd hate for another woman to be in her shoes. I lied. Said you were just visiting your parents and would be home soon. Then...well, she wanted to talk. We're still friends, and I guess there was no one else she'd told about her husband. Anyway, he's promised to seek counseling, and she wanted to know did I think she should return, that sort of thing."

"What did you tell her?"

"To go back to him. That living without the person you love is hell on earth. God, Ann Elizabeth, you don't know what it was like. Trying to talk with people and deal with that crap at work when all I could think about was you. I couldn't concentrate. I didn't give a damn about anything. And then when I got off that plane an hour ago and saw you standing there, waiting...it was like everything fell into place and I was on solid ground again."

A comfortable retreat. Do I do that for you, Rob?

"Ann Elizabeth, do you know how beautiful you are?" The adoration, the consuming love in his eyes answered the question she hadn't asked. "Just to see your smile. I'll never make you cry again. I promise." Willingly, eagerly, she returned to his arms.

Later that night when they were finally alone again, in her room, she smiled at him. "Do you like the new bed? Mother said the old one didn't suit you."

He glanced up as if looking for the canopy, then back at the bed. He chuckled. "I hadn't even noticed. Maybe it's because anyplace *you* are suits me, my lady in the parlor." His words were warm and engulfing, a prelude to rediscovery. And more. A consummation, more passionate and powerful, greater than what they'd almost lost.

The next morning she was busy on the kitchen phone, trying to get reservations so she and Maggie could return with Rob, when the operator cut in with an emergency call. For Rob. She handed him the phone.

He answered, then gave her a complacent nod. "The office." But as he listened his expression became grave. He scribbled a number on the pad. "Thanks. I'll take care of it and I'll be in touch," he said, then rang off and picked up the phone again. "My mother," he explained as he dialed. "An accident."

"Those damn stairs!" he exclaimed when he'd completed the call. His mother had fallen down the stairs

and broken her hip. Hank Stevens, the tenant downstairs, had taken her to the hospital. He'd wanted to call
earlier, but Thelma wouldn't let him. The doctors had
found no internal injuries, but were unwilling to release
her unless there was someone to care for her at home.
Hank's wife was out of town.

"I'll call and change my flight," Rob said.

"No." Ann Elizabeth put a hand on his arm. "You
need to get back to work. I'll see to Thelma."

"And the children can stay with me for the present,"
said Julia Belle, who'd been wiping the counters.

That night Ann Elizabeth and Rob left at the same
time, flying in different directions.

Ann Elizabeth was glad to look after the indomitable
Thelma, who had welcomed her so graciously all those
years ago. She kept the place clean, lugged flowers and
groceries up the stairs, prepared delicious meals and ba-
bied her mother-in-law as much as the older woman
would allow.

She was a little disheartened at the way the Watts
neighborhood had deteriorated. Thelma's well-kept
house was of sturdy brick, the wood trim newly painted
and the yard carefully tended by Hank Stevens. But
many of the surrounding houses were beginning to look
unkempt. Sagging steps, broken windowpanes, cluttered
yards. Stevens said there were frequent muggings in the
neighborhood now. The corner store had been robbed
three times, and the last time the owner had been shot
and wounded, but was still hanging on. The men around
the pool hall were younger, noisier, less courteous.

Ann Elizabeth was concerned for Thelma's safety
and suggested she come to live with them.

"No, I'm gonna stay right here," Thelma said firmly.
"And you can stop fretting about me. I done got the

swing of these crutches, and Lizzie's back now. She'll
be up here every day. You go on back and see after
Robert and the children.''

"If I do, you'll get back to work as soon as you're
off those crutches. And you don't need to work. Besides, I don't like leaving you alone, and I know Rob
would feel better if you were with us.''

"No. That ain't never gonna happen. Ah, now, don't
look like that. It ain't you. You just like a daughter to
me and I know I'd be welcome—spoiled, I 'spect. I
ain't ready to just sit.''

"Oh, I'd keep you busy. And you'd love Virginia.''

"That's another thing. Virginia.'' Thelma grinned at
her. "Honey, I promised myself when I left Alabama
I'd never go back to the South.''

Ann Elizabeth smiled and didn't say what she
thought. If Thelma's "South'' meant segregation and
poverty, this run-down section of Los Angeles was just
about as South as you could get.

August 1959

"Ann Elizabeth, I have a surprise for you,'' Rob said
when he met her at the Hampton airport. "We're leaving here. I waited until you got back to tell you.''

"You should've told me before I left.''

"Well, I wanted to be sure first. I thought I should
wait until all the details were ironed out.'' He hesitated.
"I...I thought you'd be glad to leave.''

"Oh, I am.'' She reached up to caress his face, wishing she could wipe away all the anger, pain, torment
and anxiety of the months spent in this city.
"But...well, the past is past, Rob, and I don't care
where we are as long as we're together,'' she told him.
"I was only thinking of Thelma.''

"Mom?" He looked puzzled as, arms around each other's waist, they walked to the baggage carousel.

She described Thelma's misgivings about moving to the South. "I might have persuaded her if she knew we were moving to—" She stopped to confront him. "Where *are* we going?"

"Germany."

She stared at him, mouth open. Never in her life had she imagined traveling to Europe, much less living there. And in Germany? Would Rob...? He hadn't said much about his stint as a POW, but there was a certain look in his eyes whenever that country was mentioned. "Rob, how do you feel about this move?"

He waited a beat. "Well, it's a prestigious position. A special project with NATO, involving several countries."

"But?" she prompted, seeing his harried expression.

"But nothing. It's a good move," he said. "As you know, I've been back and forth on short trips. And...it's a different country now. They're still busy repairing, rebuilding, clearing up the scars left by the war."

He's not thinking of scars to the cities, but to people, she thought as she watched him trying to convince himself. "When? And for how long?" she asked.

"We'd have to leave almost immediately. And for two years," he answered. "It'll be good for the children. You'll get in some travel, sweetheart, and it's a good step for me." Now he sounded like he was trying to convince her.

She sighed dramatically. "Guess I'll just have to settle for traveling, shopping and living the good life abroad. Just one of the hazards of being married to a big nigger."

Rob grinned. "Now are you glad you married me?"

"Well, I don't know about that. I'll have to let you know after I sample Germany. See how it rates against the medical conventions I've missed."

"What you've missed is jim crow, baby, and don't you forget it," Rob said as he reached for her bag.

"Touché!" she said, laughing.

As she prepared for the move, she was surprised to discover that she was more than a little sorry to leave the Lansberg community. Sorry to desert the children, black and white, she tutored as a volunteer at the neighborhood school. Sorry she wouldn't see the installation of the park's playground equipment she'd helped to fund. Sorry to leave the friends she'd made, especially Mrs. Levin and Clara, who had both become like family.

One bright spot. Unexpectedly Clara was getting well. The treatments she had endured had miraculously sent the cancer into remission.

"You look great," Ann Elizabeth told her friend, admiring the new crop of blond hair, the bloom in her cheeks. "Isn't it wonderful what doctors can do!"

"Not just the doctors," Clara said. "You. Taking care of Lisa, driving me back and forth…"

"You would have done the same for me," she said, knowing Clara would have.

"It wasn't just the driving and everything. It was *you*. You were always so cheerful, talking up a blue streak, with some jingle popping out that would make me laugh even when I was really down and—"

"Oh, no! Don't tell me," Ann Elizabeth said. "My mother says I talk too much, and Rob gets pretty fed up with my silly quotes and little lectures."

"Don't you call them silly and don't you ever stop saying them! That one about holding on when there's nothing to hold to… Honest to God, Ann Elizabeth, you kept me going with them…'' Clara's voice was choked, and her eyes brimmed with tears.

''Hey, cut the crying.'' Ann Elizabeth lightly tapped her cheek. ''This is eat, drink and be merry time. Take another cookie and I'll pour us more tea.''

She was glad Clara was recovering. It would have been doubly hard for Lisa to lose her mother and her best friend. Ann Elizabeth had the children travel home alone from Atlanta, so Maggie would have a few days to say goodbye to Lisa.

After the packing and goodbyes at the farewell parties, a large one with their Negro friends at Jennie Lou's and a smaller one at Mrs. Levin's with their Lansberg neighbors, they were on their way.

24

November 1959

Three months later in Cologne, Germany, Ann Elizabeth, drowsy from her stay in the sauna, relaxed on the massage table and surrendered herself to the soothing manipulations of the expert masseur.

"Been on holiday?" he asked.

Ann Elizabeth nodded, then almost laughed as she realized why he'd asked. His admiration for her smooth golden skin was expressed in an excited mixture of German and English.

"Natural," she explained. "I was born this way."

The masseur only smiled, and she gave it up. "With his poor English and my poor German," she said to her friend, Rachel Shapiro, as they left the spa, "how could I tell him, yes, I'd been on holiday to Italy, but the skin I had on was the one I was born with!"

Rachel laughed. "Let him eat his heart out. He'll spend his next holiday trying to acquire your tan. Then in two weeks it'll be gone."

"I thought he'd know I'm a Negro."

"Trouble is, you all come in so many colors, you keep us whiteys confused."

Ann Elizabeth chuckled, appreciating, as always, Rachel's tart humor. She liked Rachel and her husband, David, a colonel in the U.S. Air Force. He, like Rob, was on loan from the USAF to the Belgian, Italian, Netherlands and German air forces. All were engaged in a sensitive high-priority project that had to do with air superiority over central Europe; it involved a NATO commitment to supply the recipient countries with the necessary planes and weapons. The effort had the additional objective of rebuilding each participant's industrial and economic base.

Rob and David were two of the five-man detachment assigned to do the job on time and within budget. The procedure was compounded by picky, sometimes petty, military doctrine, political dogma and social protocol. Rob and David were inextricably swept up in the latter, since they were accompanied by their spouses.

"All these parties throw me," Rachel complained. "Sound like the Tower of Babel and I can't distinguish which language is which, much less the meaning."

"Yes," said Ann Elizabeth. "Wish I'd majored in foreign languages."

"Oh, you don't need it. You just stand around smiling and passing out canapés and looking gracious and they love you!"

Ann Elizabeth said nothing, but she breathed a silent thank-you to Julia Belle who had trained her well for this kind of role.

One of the parties being held at the German air base was to honor Rob and David for service above and beyond the call of duty. Walking together through the large entryway of the Officers' Club, the two couples stopped to view the portraits of German fighter pilots that lined the walls.

David chuckled. "I'll bet Hitler's turning over in his

grave," he said to Rob, "seeing that a nigger and a Jew are being feted by his air force."

"Hush," said Rachel. "Not so loud. We're all passing as Americans."

They laughed, but Ann Elizabeth reflected that there was truth in the joke. For the first time in her life she felt more American than Negro.

To Ann Elizabeth, these years were a holiday. She traveled to Spain and Switzerland, stood atop the Eiffel Tower in Paris, explored the Coliseum in Rome, raced from one theater to another in London, sometimes with Rob and more often with Rachel or Julia Belle, who came over twice. Thelma also came and stayed a month, but she steadily resisted Ann Elizabeth's urging to live with them. "Lord, child, I ain't ready for the rocking chair yet. And I've got to get back. That church social we have every year for the handicapped is next month and I'm in charge of it."

Ann Elizabeth was surprised to find that, except for London with its theaters, Germany, their temporary home, was her favorite. Perhaps it was the privileged setting in which she lived, one of the comfortable apartments in Plittersdorf, the diplomatic community near the American Embassy Club. Other facilities were conveniently adjacent—American chapel, base exchange, commissary, beauty shop and garage.

Perhaps she felt this way because it was so great for the children. Maggie was enrolled at the International School on the Rhine, the elementary school maintained for children of diplomats. Bobby, along with other high-school students, was transported back and forth weekly via a special bus to an American boarding school at

Weisbaden, eighty miles away. His senior trip was a ten-day excursion to Italy.

Perhaps it was their automatic membership in the exclusive Embassy Club, with access to its swimming pool, tennis courts, bowling alley and racquetball court. Frequently they dined and danced at the club, rubbing shoulders and conversing with people from every country in the world.

Or perhaps, she thought with stark realism, she was simply experiencing a sensation that was new to her. The sensation of feeling absolutely colorless.

"I love it," she told Rob. "I didn't expect this."

"What did you expect?" he asked.

"Oh, grim gray buildings, lots of cement and..." She choked back the words *concentration camps*. "The German people are so friendly and the country so beautiful," she finished.

"And peaceful," he said, a faraway look in his eyes. "So different from my first time here."

They had been strolling along the walkway that bordered the Rhine. Now they turned and walked across the grassy bank to the steps of the Embassy Club.

She nudged his arm. "I want to tell you something," she whispered.

"Yes?"

"This has medical conventions beat all to pieces."

"Well, ma'am, we do our best," he quipped, but she could tell he was pleased.

"I feel like a queen. I didn't know people lived like this."

"All at the expense of the United States government. Live it up, baby. White folks been doing this for years.

And now…just a few of us niggers.'' He chuckled. ''Those big enough or smart enough, you understand.''

She stood on tiptoe and kissed him full on the lips. ''What I understand is that I'm very glad I married one!''

''Me, too, honey,'' he said, sweeping an arm around her and almost carrying her up the steps. ''Anyway, you're stuck. No pale-face doctor still waiting for you back in that golden ghetto.''

''No. Isn't it wonderful?'' She beamed, thinking of Sadie's letter. She followed the waiter to their table, a bemused smile on her face as she recalled every word.

Ann Elizabeth:
Dan and I are getting married. We wanted you to be the first to know because you'll be happy for us, and because you're partly responsible—you and Randy. If it hadn't been for you, I would probably never have met Dan. Oh, Ann Elizabeth, I know that part of Dan will always love you, just as a piece of my heart will always belong to Randy.

If it hadn't been for Randy—do you know he told me I was beautiful? Even made me believe it. Me with my black skin and kinky hair! And that was long before this ''I'm black and proud'' refrain that's going on now. I can't help it, I'll always love Randy. He made me what I am, the woman who will make Dan a good wife. We'll be as happy as you and Rob, Ann Elizabeth. I promise.

We're keeping the ceremony quiet and secret until it's over because, well, you know Atlanta! Thanksgiving Day at my house. Your parents and just a very few close friends. Your dad's standing up for Dan. I wish you could be here to stand with me.

I hope you're having a grand time in Europe, and I hope you'll forgive me for going on and on about me. If I sound garbled and mixed up, it's because I am. Crazy and happy, and trying hard to believe it. Isn't it strange how things happen?

Love to Rob and the kids, and most of all to you.

Ann Elizabeth was so pleased about this union of her two best friends that she immediately placed an overseas call to share her elation with them. The next day she sent them a whole set of the most beautiful German crystal she could find.

A few days after the big event, she received more particulars from other sources. From Helen Rose:

Girl, have I got news! Knowing how close you and Sadie are, you've probably already heard it from her, but it hit Atlanta cold! The whys and wherefores are flying all over the place. Our prized, sought-after, most eligible bachelor in town has been hooked! And by whom? Sadie Clayton. The whole town is shocked and more than a few seditty females are quite seriously burned. How could a gal like Sadie catch what they couldn't get their hands on?

Well, all I've got to say is more power to her!

From Julia Belle:

It was a simple but beautiful and touching ceremony. They both seem happy.

Of course, the news has set the town on fire. But Will says it's an excellent match. I quite agree. Sadie's been working with Dan all these years and will certainly make him a better wife than some of these featherheads who know nothing but how to play bridge, and not too well at that. Some people are quite upset, but I'm glad and I am sponsoring her for the Ladies.

It was in Amsterdam in Anne Frank's attic room that Ann Elizabeth confronted the spectre of what it had been like in Germany twenty years before. Was it because one Ann was a Negro and the other a Jew? Both from relatively privileged backgrounds? Or was she contrasting her own full happy life as a young girl with what life had been for another?

As she stood in the narrow little attic room that had shielded a young girl for a short while, she knew she identified with her. She gazed at the portraits of movie stars, torn from a magazine and pinned on the wall by Anne herself. From the tiny window she saw the street below, teeming with cars, bicycles and hurrying people, as it must have looked long ago to a young girl, so eager, so full of life—and shut away from it all.

"I feel like I've been dancing on somebody's grave," she told her father a few weeks later. He'd flown over with Julia Belle for a visit. The two of them were alone, lunching on the patio of the Embassy Club, while inside, Julia Belle took Ann Elizabeth's place at the Tuesday bridge session.

"I know how you must feel," he said. "But the past is past and you can't change it by grieving. As my mother used to say, 'Leave it lay where Jesus flung it!'"

She pondered this. Of course one could do nothing about what had passed. But the present?

She might be isolated, but she couldn't ignore what was happening in the United States as the battle for civil rights escalated. The news visibly reported how nonviolent direct-action groups were taking to the streets en masse, marching, holding sit-ins, demanding their rights to restaurants, hotels, hospitals, schools, jobs and the ballot box. The rabid segregationists, traditionally violent, fought back. Marchers were met with police dogs, electric cattle prods and fire hoses. One unforgettable TV newscast showed a small child being washed down a Birmingham street by the powerful force of water from a fire hose. Twenty ''freedom riders,'' testing their rights to interstate travel, were set upon by a mob in a Montgomery bus station and beaten. One man was permanently paralyzed. A church was bombed, killing four children attending Bible school.

A burst of laughter and a small uproar from inside the club broke into her thoughts. It sounded as if Julia Belle had made a slam. Ann Elizabeth smiled at her father. ''I'm glad she's having a good time.''

''But?'' he prompted.

She shouldn't be surprised. He could always read her thoughts. ''Oh, I was just thinking…it's so peaceful here and so ugly back home.''

Dr. Carter gave his daughter a keen look. ''Feeling a little guilty about your good life?''

''Maybe,'' she said, glad she didn't have to spell it out. ''It just seems that…'' She hesitated, as the comfortable chatter and laughter of the bridge ladies drifted toward her and she heard the *thump-whack* of a tennis ball from the not-too-distant court. She gestured helplessly toward the tall trees that shaded the beautiful grounds. "Oh, that they're *there* and I'm *here*."

He took a sip of wine, gazing through the trees toward the river. Suddenly he put down his glass and pointed. "Look," he said. She saw a barge sailing swiftly down the river. On its deck was a woman hanging clothes on a line suspended between two poles. Nearby a child was swaying on an improvised swing. "That woman is doing a terrific job of making do where she is," he said. "You have to take your life where you're flung. You might be luckier than most, Ann Elizabeth, but this is where you are."

"I know."

"Anyway, what would you do? Have Rob quit his job so you can go home and march in the streets and possibly end up living on welfare?"

She laughed. "I know," she said again. "Anyway, marching in the streets—I don't have that kind of courage."

"You're not the only one. It seems like a lot of people, but in reality there's just a small percentage of blacks, and a few dedicated whites, bravely marching for the rest of us."

"I guess you're right."

"Didn't you tell me both you and Rob have life memberships in the NAACP?"

She nodded. "And we just bought one for Bobby."

"Good. The battle is really won in court. Do you have any idea of the money it takes for court costs and to get the street people out of jail?" When she shook her head, he added, "Nothing wrong with being a success, either. You know, during the famous Montgomery bus strike, they bought vans to transport people to work, and the white insurance companies refused to insure the vans. It was a successful black insurance broker in Atlanta who secured insurance for them through Lloyd's of London. Success and know-how are powerful tools, honey."

She nodded slowly.

"Someone once said that one man dies nobly for a cause while another lives humbly to achieve it." He turned to look at her. "That's true, you know. A black maid who does a good job of cleaning her white employer's house makes a statement, too. 'I'm reliable and trustworthy.' Your Rob makes a powerful statement when his black face appears at a conference negotiating with international officials. And they didn't exactly roll out a red carpet for him, don't forget."

"No. Quite the opposite."

Dr. Carter beamed. "He's come a long way. I'm proud of him. I'm proud of you, too, kitten. You do your part just rearing your children to be decent contributing citizens, and you make a step forward when you integrate a neighborhood. Which reminds me, what about the house you're planning to build back in Sacramento?"

She frowned. They'd be returning to California next year, when the assignment here in Germany was finished. "Dead end. We got the lot. Rob gave the cash to Chuck Samples, who bought it and turned it over to us on a quit claim deed. But we can't live on an empty lot, and we can't build. Every loan agency we contact turns us down. No fire hoses, but they don't want that area integrated, either."

"Guess what?" Rob greeted her when he returned from a trip to the States a few weeks later. "We almost got our house scot-free!"

She raised one brow. "Quite a distance between almost and scot-free!"

"Right. But that's the way it was. I have to admit I was kind of tempted."

"Oh?"

"Well, you know we were making a twelve-million-dollar decision on the installation of this refueling system on the 104."

"Yes," she said, though she didn't.

"Three competing companies," he said, "and yours truly happened to be the major decision maker."

"Yes?"

"Well, I knew Al Simmons, who's with Kenco, one of the competing firms. He was at McClellan when I started there, one of the few whites friendly to me. Got snatched up by Kenco and he's head honcho there now. We happened to board the same plane to Chicago, where we were both making a change—he was going to Ohio and I was coming back here. We sat together and he asked how much longer I'd be in Germany and I said not too long and—" Rob stopped, stared at her. "Damn. I wonder if he thought I was hinting."

"Hinting? At what?"

"Well, I started talking about the house we wanted to build in the States if I could ever cut through the financing runaround I was getting. Al looked down at his drink and said, plain as day, that wouldn't be a problem if Kenco got the refueling contract. Everything free and clear, no mortgage."

"Rob! What did you say?"

"Nothing. I was too stunned to speak. When I did get my thinking cap on, I just said, 'I didn't hear that.'"

"And what did he say?"

"Not another word. He knew that if I did hear him,

I'd have to report it. It really burned me, Ann Elizabeth. What does he think I am?''

"It's what *he* is," she said, her heart swelling with pride. Her husband had refused a bribe, but given the perpetrator an out. "Maybe he's used to buying his way in," she said.

"Well, he ought to have more confidence in his product." His mouth twisted. "The irony is he got the contract, anyway. I recommended him." He frowned. "You see, his really was the best deal. The only one, in fact, with the safety features we required."

"Don't explain to me." She laughed and held up a hand. "I don't know a thing about refueling and such. But I know if you say it's the best, then it is. Now come on, eat your dinner. And, oh, yes, there's mail from home." She made a face. "One letter you won't like."

He read it, then crumpled it and threw it aside. "Another rejection. And they don't even bother to make an excuse. I've got the down, I've got the credit—" He shook his head. "But as soon as I come in to sign the application, they see my black face and…"

"Ssh. Don't get upset. You'll spoil a good dinner. I found some frozen mustard greens in the commissary."

He was still fuming when he picked up his fork. "Maybe I'm the fool. All I had to do was nod my head and I wouldn't have to worry about a mortgage. What the hell's wrong with me?"

She smiled. "I think it's called integrity."

In July 1961, when the luxury liner *United States* pulled into the New York harbor, Ann Elizabeth, standing on deck, felt a surge of joy. She was excited about being home, anticipating the pleasure of decorating her new house in Sacramento.

Rob had secured financing, she'd gleefully written her father, through a successful Negro insurance company in Los Angeles. One of its directors was Greg West, a former Tuskegee airman.

Rob had checked on their home's construction on business trips to the States, and the house was now finished. Ann Elizabeth's mind was full of landscaping, carpeting, textures, colors and the rush to ready a son for college.

She looked at Bobby, standing next to his father at the railing, and thought how much alike they were. The same curly black hair and deep-set dark eyes, but Bobby's skin was a lighter brown and he was an inch or two taller. Thank goodness, he'd filled out. The endless search for jeans small enough in the waist and long enough in the legs was over.

Ann Elizabeth smiled when Bobby grabbed Rob's arm and pointed to something. The two of them had grown close during the past two years. Men don't always become pals with their sons, she thought. Rob's travels had been somewhat curtailed while they were in Europe, and he'd had time to play tennis with Bobby, attend his football games, take him to soccer matches and to races in Nuremberg. The Weisbaden school had been good for Bobby, too, and he was all set for college.

College! Incredible that she, Ann Elizabeth Carter, had a son old enough for college. It seemed only yesterday that she was at her debut and Rob, so tall and handsome in his uniform, had come into her life. Now their son would enter the same university complex where she'd spent four happy years.

She drew in a quick breath. Would Bobby be happy there, too? More important, would he be safe? Students from the seven Negro colleges and universities were determined to integrate Atlanta, and had joined the scores of sit-ins and marches that were sweeping the country.

She'd talked it over with Rob. Of course, she'd always wanted Bobby to attend Morehouse, but in view of the possible risks in Atlanta, should they send him to a California college instead?

Rob, in his direct way, had said it must be Bobby's decision. Looking at her grave face, he'd added, "Time marches on, honey. This is a different era."

Bobby, with no hesitation, had chosen Morehouse, "where Grandpa went," he said.

But things really *were* different now, and she wondered...

"What's the matter, Mom?" Maggie, fresh and pretty in the simple navy dress with its crisp sailor collar, gazed anxiously up at her. Strange how that sensitive child caught her every mood. "What are you thinking, Mom?"

"I was thinking I'm getting old."

"Old? You're not old. That lady in the lounge last night said my mom was sure young and pretty."

"I hope you thanked her." Ann Elizabeth, pleased, glanced down at the black sheath that complemented her slender form. The exercise and massages had paid off.

"I like your hair cut short like that," Maggie said. "I'm glad you and Daddy aren't fat and old-looking."

Ann Elizabeth laughed. "I love you, too," she said, reaching down to tighten the blue ribbon that held Maggie's ponytail in place. "Don't lean over the rail," she cautioned as Maggie started to do just that.

She sighed. Once a mother, always a mother. And, like most mothers, she wanted her children safe and happy.

25

As summer gave way to that fall of 1961, the house was finally beginning to look like it was theirs. The children seemed happy, Maggie at a neighborhood school and Bobby at Morehouse in Atlanta. Now that the decorating was complete and the landscaping underway, Ann Elizabeth could relax a bit. She was doing some volunteer work with the Red Cross and the YWCA, and had rejoined her old bridge club, as well as another with Cora Samples and some neighbors. She had never been more content.

No, not content. How could she be content when her son was marching, attending sit-ins, facing jail in the campaign for civil rights? The television coverage was so explicit. Ann Elizabeth watched and suffered with the demonstrators, feeling every blow—the whack of the billy club, the sting of the cattle prod, the propelling gush of water from a fire hose. Her heart turned over as she watched a bleeding boy, about Bobby's age, being dragged and shoved into a police van.

When the students began to march in Atlanta, Ann Elizabeth was frightened for her son.

"Rob, let's bring Bobby home," she said, urgently. "He could transfer to Berkeley."

"And what's to guarantee he'd be safe there?" Rob answered. "Students are agitating all over the place."

He put an arm around her. "Anyway, honey, this kind of brutality isn't happening in Atlanta. Not one student there has been hurt or even mistreated. I have to give it to those kids. Their campaign is well-organized and orderly."

"Stop saying that!" she cried. "How do you *orderly* break the law? *Orderly* go to jail?" But she'd heard it all before—from Julia Belle and the newspaper clippings she sent. How students of the seven institutions that made up the Atlanta University complex had banded together, drafted "An Appeal for Human Rights," which they sent to city officials, all the news media and other interested parties. They addressed existing inequities and announced their intention to act, to gain the rights inherently theirs as human beings and citizens of the United States. The edict was so concisely and eloquently written that it elicited praise from members of the press and a comment from some high-level bigots that "it couldn't possibly have been written by a bunch of ignorant niggers. More likely it was inspired and drafted by communists."

However eloquent, the appeal also alerted authorities that the students meant to act. And act they did. The campaign was in full swing before the Metcalfs returned from Europe.

She phoned her mother and was surprised to find her complacent. More than complacent. Excited. "Oh, for goodness' sake, it will be a wonderful experience for Bobby!" she said. "The students are behaving so beautifully. The whole thing was their idea. But we're behind them one hundred percent."

"We?"

"The whole community. We're boycotting the stores."

"Oh." What did that have to do with what those kids might encounter? "What does Dad say?"

"That his bank balance might increase for the first time in years. And that it might do some good."

"But, Mother, I'm worried about the kids. The police—"

"Yes, honey. I was concerned, too. But the college president has been in touch with Police Chief Jenkins, and the students have promised to submit quietly to arrest."

"Arrest!" She couldn't believe her mother was being so calm about this. "Mother, I don't like it."

"Oh, honey, Bobby will be perfectly safe. Don't worry."

She called the college president.

"Yes, Mrs. Metcalf. I sympathize with your concerns. But I contacted Police Chief Jenkins, and he's been out to confer with the students."

"The chief himself?" An unheard-of precedent.

"Yes. And everything's been orderly. No brutality."

So far. The words caught in her throat as she recalled that long-ago night at the Subers' when the police had wanted to throw two innocent Negro boys in jail. And that day in the car with Rob.

The president sighed. "Frankly I can't stop the students. And I don't think I would if I could."

You don't have a son there, she thought as she replaced the receiver.

Yet according to his letters, Bobby was happy at Morehouse.

Stan Archer's sister was visiting here from Fisk. She's a stone fox and I'm trying to persuade her to switch to Spelman. Wanted to take her to the frat dance but I already had a date. Took her to Grandma's for dinner.

Don't worry about that math deficiency. I'm making it up.

And Mom, stop worrying about the police—they haven't beat up on us. Anyway, if they do we're ready.

We practice beating up on each other, so we learn how to remain non-violent no matter what happens.

Statements like that last scared her. And the horrors happening to demonstrators in other cities, so vividly shown on television.

"Rob, do you have any travel plans?" she asked.

"Not for a while. Why?"

"Then you'll be here with Maggie. I thought I might spend a couple of weeks with Mother and Dad, and check on Bobby." *I'll see for myself,* she decided.

"It doesn't matter what anyone says!" Sophie exclaimed. "The students don't intend to give in." She and Julia Belle sat in the breakfast room having coffee with Ann Elizabeth and bringing her up to date. Ann Elizabeth listened, hearing a replay of what she'd seen on television as students in other cities invaded facilities banned to Negroes. Atlanta students were employing the same strategy. They invaded restaurants, lunch counters and theaters. Negroes with fair skin would buy several theater tickets, which they would pass to their darker companions. They would check to see when the tearooms were open and then notify the other students, who would go in and occupy every seat. When one group was arrested, the second moved in, although they were always refused service. Most of the tearooms were forced to close, and one five-and-dime store removed the stools from around the lunch counter.

"No better for them," chuckled Sophie. "When I think of the money I spent in these stores and they wouldn't even serve me a cup of coffee, I feel downright ashamed."

"You shouldn't be ashamed," Julia Belle said. "Will said we had to show them how much money we spent before we could withdraw it. Well, we've withdrawn it now," she told Ann Elizabeth, explaining that Negroes no longer patronized any of the downtown stores. "Do you know sales in the department stores are down twenty-two percent?"

"I believe it," Ann Elizabeth said, thinking of all the shopping trips with her mother for her college wardrobe, her debut, her wedding and so on. When you multiplied that by all the Negro shoppers in Atlanta, it must amount to a pretty hefty sum. And it wasn't only Atlanta. How much money to how many merchants in how many cities for how many years? Ann Elizabeth, like Sophie, began to feel ashamed. How often had she entered these stores, searching eagerly for the right outfit for some planned function, spending money freely, knowing before she spent it that she wasn't permitted to eat lunch or use the ladies' room there? Why hadn't she thought then of how unfair that was? She'd considered herself privileged, encased in her own private world, never realizing how much she was contributing to a larger world where she was treated like scum.

Negroes were right to withdraw their money, she thought now, glancing at her mother and aunt, sharing their enthusiasm.

Still, it was the students who'd had to make them

aware, these young people who were refusing to take it anymore, who were pushing their way in, demanding respect. If she was honest, she'd come here to stop her son, not just to see what he was doing. But now she couldn't. She remembered Bobby, sitting with the Carter family under the magnolia tree not long before the Metcalfs had gone to Germany, saying, "I ain't never gonna Uncle Tom!" As clearly as if it were yesterday, she remembered her father's answer. "No, I don't think you'll have to."

Yes, these kids had more to bargain with. But not enough to shield them from avid segregationists, who meant to maintain the status quo and had never even pretended to be nonviolent. The visions of what had happened in other cities still haunted her. She tried to stifle her fears, even mouthed the moral support she knew Bobby needed. "You're right, son. I'm proud of you."

But she was scared.

So far, no student had been hurt. "Police Chief Jenkins said if we played fair with him, he'd play fair with us," Bobby said. "You know, give him notice where we plan to protest, submit quietly to arrest."

But Ann Elizabeth simply couldn't reconcile this attitude.

"Oh, yes," her mother said. "Chief Jenkins has been very sympathetic and supportive. So has Mayor Hartsfield. But Governor Vandiver is a different matter."

"A dyed-in-the wool racist," her father added. "Says he'll never submit to a passel of nitwit niggers calling themselves students."

So when the students determined to confront the governor, Ann Elizabeth panicked. It started out simply enough—a planned march from the West Side through downtown Atlanta and up Auburn Avenue to Martin Luther King, Sr.'s Wheat Street church.

Auburn Avenue. Once that was all we wanted. Ann Elizabeth remembered happy treks down Auburn—the colored library, the Citizens' Bank, her debut on the roof of the Odd Fellows Building. But now, against Chief Jenkins's direct orders and warnings from college administrators and parents, the students planned a demonstration at the state capitol where Police Chief Jenkins had no jurisdiction and where the governor and his state troopers would be waiting, guns and billy clubs raised.

Ann Elizabeth's heart almost stopped. What did anything matter if Bobby was maimed or killed—which he certainly might be if those crazy students tangled with the governor and his state troopers.

"Don't go," she begged him. "Not this time."

"Aw, Mom, it's just a march. Not a sit-in where we'll be hauled out."

"All right," she conceded, "but not to the state capitol. If they decide to go there—"

"I'll go," he said, his voice steady. "I wouldn't let the others down."

So on the morning of the march Ann Elizabeth stood with the crowd in front of the university library, the rallying ground for the protesting students, as they listened to pep talks from their leaders. She'd come hoping that someone would dissuade them from confronting the governor. But she felt helpless, lost in the mass of young people all around her, out of place in her yellow sundress and sandals. Like Bobby, they were clad in jeans, pullovers, low walking shoes. Like Bobby, they were young, eager and excited. She heard them laughing, making jokes, her Bobby—like Randy—the chief clown among them. The laughter faded and they became silent when a tall brown-skinned boy stood on the top step, raised his hand and began to speak.

Ann Elizabeth heard and didn't hear. She was watching the serious faces around her and remembering how it had been twenty years before. She had sat on those steps on such a day as this, a warm Indian-summer day, when the sun was hot and the smell of fall was in the air. She'd faced the beautiful vista between the library and the Atlanta University administration building as she laughed and flirted, talked about dates and frat dances, the homecoming game and exams. And that was what she wished for Bobby. That he should sit on these steps, stroll serenely about this campus with his "stone fox," whoever she was, that he should be content and peaceful. Not this...

The voice of the speaker caught her attention. "...planned a stopover at the capitol to pay our respects to Governor Vandiver." He paused as the students broke into cheers, then continued, "It seems the governor has made special arrangements for us. He's brought in hundreds of state troopers, who have surrounded the capitol." Here the cheers and boos exploded and Ann Elizabeth's heart plummeted. The speaker went on to say that he'd been asked by the college presidents and Chief Jenkins, who had no jurisdiction over the capitol, to exclude it from their march. He concluded, "I told them the decision would be yours. Do we go?"

Ann Elizabeth's heart sank further as the enthusiastic YES from the crowd turned into a chant. "We will go! We will go!"

Ann Elizabeth hardly heard the speaker's impassioned plea urging that "only the pure in heart should go, those committed to nonviolence, those dedicated to

ending injustice, those brave enough to bear sarcasm
and physical violence and not strike back.''

An image from a TV report remained in her mind—
a bleeding boy lying on the pavement, passively sub-
mitting to abuse. Shaking with fear, she looked at the
young people all around her.

Not one student hung back. They jostled each other,
preparing to move out, as if to a picnic. Their laughter
was like a death knell to her ears, and tears ran down
her cheeks. Still, a line the leader had quoted from the
manifesto drummed in her ears. ''Every normal human
being wants to walk the earth with dignity.''

Oh, God, she wished she were back in Germany. No
problems, no manifestos. There they'd walked the
streets with dignity and without all this hullabaloo.

Then she remembered. On those same streets, not so
long ago, Jews had been humiliated, beaten, murdered.
What was it the old Jewish doctor had said to Rob? *A
little bit at a time.*

But how important was it to sit in a restaurant, to
defy a governor? Important enough to get your head
bashed in?

She looked at Bobby, still beside her. So young, so
handsome. A nice kid. Her only son, her first child.
She'd almost lost him. She would have if Dr. Benson
hadn't sneaked him into that hospital. Sneaked... She
lifted her head, thinking. It wasn't just a restaurant.
*Every human being has a right—to a hospital...a
school...dignity.*

Bobby bent down, brushed her cheek with his lips.
''We're off, Mom.''

''Wait,'' she said. ''I'm coming with you.''

But her heart wasn't in it. *I don't have their kind of
courage,* she thought as she moved with the throng of

students, now singing "We Shall Overcome." She thought of the troopers waiting at the capitol. Would she shame Bobby—turn on her heel and run or, more likely, wind her arms around him and hold him back? She took off her sandals and marched with the cheering crowd, feeling the heat of the pavement on her feet and a cold chill running down her spine.

The sun glinted on the twirling red light of the Atlanta police car parked across Hunter Street, burned against the motorcycles and helmets of the policemen who stood quietly by. Deputy Police Chief Frank Malloy took off his helmet, wiped the sweat from his brow and watched Chief Jenkins pace. They waited. This was the intersection where the students planned to make their fatal turn toward the capitol.

Damn fool kids! Those troopers would beat the hell out of 'em. Just as soon kill a nigger as swat a fly! Something between wrath and pain burned in Malloy's gut, formed a tight band around his chest.

One of those students was his son. Luke Matthews. The boy didn't know it. No one knew except Luke's maternal grandma, who had taken him in when Gussie died. Gussie. He'd loved that skinny black gal... Anyway, he couldn't quite abandon their son. Not even after he married Maybelle and started a legitimate family. God, Maybelle would skin him alive if she even suspected. Not that he'd had any direct contact with the boy since he was two. The grandma, grateful for the support money, was sworn to silence. Frank, watching secretly, found himself growing proud of his nigger child. Hell, he hadn't been to college himself. Luke was a senior now, with a part-time job in that nigger bank and a scholarship to Harvard for a master's degree in business. *If he doesn't get his head busted today!*

Crazy kids. Guts, though. Pushing in and thumbing their noses at everybody, even the Klan. Frank chuckled, thinking of the day the Klan had marched outside that restaurant while the kids were being evicted. The Klan had been in full regalia, carrying signs reading SEGREGATION FOREVER, INTEGRATION NEVER. The police force was set for riot alert, and he'd expected a riot for sure when the kids jeered at the Klan, especially when that guy threw a white tablecloth over his head and yelled, "Boo!" But it didn't happen. The Klan had just stood there looking foolish, and the police had had one hell of a time getting those niggers into the paddy wagons. Not that they'd resisted. They'd just stretched out prone on the ground. Dead weight.

Yeah. Guts. But if they didn't have the chief and his police force between them and the Klan, between them and everybody else, for that matter... When I think of the crap we're taking, especially when the merchants gang up on us. He thought of the meeting he'd attended a couple of week ago. The chief had been away on an emergency, and Frank had sat in for him. The meeting had been held in the conference room of the most influential merchandiser in town. Tough? No, hell!

"These sit-ins have got to stop," Les Abbott had growled.

"Yes, sir. We're trying, sir."

"Well, you'all ain't trying hard enough," Les had said. "What are you—a cop or a damn baby-sitter?"

"I like to call myself a peace officer, sir."

"Well, your peacekeeping is messing with our profits."

"Hear, hear!" the others chimed in.

Les frowned. "Sales are down twenty percent since this mess started."

"That's them boycotting niggers," boomed Mr. Bailey, CEO of a dime-store chain. "Ain't there a law against that?"

"Nothing on the books forcing people to buy, sir."

"Well, there's a law against niggers sitting in white folks' restaurants."

"Yes, sir. State law."

"So call in the state troopers if you can't handle it."

"Some of those boys can get pretty rough, sir."

"Good. It's time to bust some of them kinky heads."

"Hell! Can't hurt a nigger in the head." Mr. Craft of Pickways Buffet laughed. "Bust their legs and they stay home where they belong."

Thinking fast, Malloy countered, "Sir, a lot of violence might upset your lady shoppers. And you sure wouldn't want your tearooms busted up." At that point the merchants had looked pretty frustrated. One of them, Stanley Hutchinson, the owner of a men's clothing store, had said, "Why don't you try serving them?"

They'd burst out laughing like he'd plumb lost his mind.

Malloy's musings and recollections were halted. Chief Jenkins stopped pacing, stood in front of his car, head lifted. Frank heard it, too.

Marching feet. Singing voices. "We shall overcome..." If he heard that damn song one more time! Damn fool kids.

He looked at his chief, who so far had kept the peace. Who'd been keeping the peace for a long time—before some of these kids were born. And keeping it while trying to be fair to both sides. Hell, he'd integrated the golf courses—quietly, with no fanfare. He'd cleaned up the Klan-dominated police force, instituted training classes, even hired a few niggers.

But these kids… Damn! Didn't they know he was on their side? Didn't they have any idea what he was going through? Catching hell from the merchants, niggers and politicians. Working like hell to hold off the Klan. Working overtime trying to dispatch the right men to the right place at the right time. Not easy, when the students kept popping up all over the place. Got us jumping like cats on a hot tin roof!

Now, here they come. All ready to march up to the capitol, as much as to say, *Here I am. Kill me.* Shit! Didn't they know those troopers might do just that?

Despite his apprehension, pride swelled within him as the crowd of students marched up, their eager young faces alight with brave determination. Malloy's own eyes lit. There, right near the front on the right, was Luke. He almost felt like pointing him out. That tall boy, the one in the yellow T-shirt—that's my son. But he couldn't do that any more than he could stop the fear that was almost choking him.

Damn! He did not want a bloodbath.

He wasn't a churchgoer. He never prayed, but he guessed that was what he was doing now. And maybe, just maybe, somebody up there was listening. He hoped so.

He saw Chief Jenkins climb to the hood of his car and point a commanding finger down Hunter Street, away from the route to the capitol. The leaders of the mob halted respectfully, and Malloy moved closer to hear.

"Sir," said a tall brown-skinned young man, "I have to report to you that we took a vote and we have decided to go by the capitol."

"Didn't you get my message?" the chief asked.

"Yes, sir," the youth replied. "But you see, sir, it's a matter of principle with us."

"Principle, huh?" the chief growled. "Suicide, more likely."

The boy raised his head and two others slipped in beside him. "We are not afraid to die, sir."

Damn, Malloy was thinking, maybe the chief should call out the riot squad. Then he saw a woman move forward. Not one of them, obviously, in that yellow sundress and with the sandals in her hand. Older. He'd bet a dollar she was somebody's mother. Anyway, she talked like one when she confronted the three leaders.

"So you're dedicated to nonviolence, are you?" she asked.

Looking a little surprised, they nodded.

"Then tell me, why are you so determined to invite violence?" The boys started to talk about courage and she scoffed. "So you just want to prove you can take it, huh? What are you trying to do—integrate a city or thumb your nose at bullets?"

She had them. Malloy could tell they were listening. Maybe the riot squad wouldn't be needed, after all.

Now she gestured toward the chief. "Chief Jenkins has played fair with you and you ought to play fair with him. Especially since he's just asking you not to get yourselves killed. He cares about you. He cares about this city. He wants to keep the peace for all citizens and you ought to help him!"

That got them; they looked at one another, nodded. Then the tall boy saluted the chief. He beckoned to the crowd and they proceeded down Hunter Street as the chief had directed, singing as they went.

Frank Malloy sighed with relief, surprised to find

tears staining his cheeks. Surreptitiously he wiped them away.

Ann Elizabeth walked fast to keep up with Bobby's long-legged stride, one hand clinging to his, the other swinging her sandals. The warm pavement felt good on her bare feet. *She* felt good. They were walking with dignity through the streets of Atlanta. No bullets or billy clubs. No battered and bruised young people. Yes, she'd played a part, but it was really due to Chief Jenkins. If he hadn't stopped them... Shivering, she suddenly wanted to run back and thank him. A white police chief. Once again she remembered her thought when she'd looked into the serious face of that white boy with red hair so long ago. *We're doing all right without your help.* It wasn't true. We do need each other's help. If she could see that boy now, she would tell him so.

Stanley Hutchinson stood at the window of his office on the top floor of the men's clothing store that had borne his family's name for three generations. He stared down at the busy streets of midtown Atlanta and thought of the bravery and dedication of those college students, who were about to bring the city to its knees. Only the young had such zeal.

Once he'd been that young. He was older now, his waist a little thicker, and a few specks of gray had appeared in his red hair. But he could still remember that feeling, the belief that he could do something to make things right. Only he hadn't known what.

His mouth twisted wryly as he thought back to his own college years and those black-white seminars. He thought of his father, dead three years now. Always a cantankerous man, he'd become downright belligerent when he heard Stan was going to attend one of those seminars on the race question. That was back in 1942, but he remembered the conversation well.

"What you doing discussing anything with a bunch of uppity niggers? In the first place it's against state law. Second place, what you gonna say to 'em? They're all lazy an' ignorant. Ain't worth a tinker's damn!"

"That include Lucy?"

"Oh, shit, don't you go bringing Lucy into this. She's a good nigger. Knows her place, right in the kitchen. She ain't out here trying to tell me to treat her like she's white."

Stan had defied his father and gone to the meetings, anyway. Not that it did any good. Everybody talked about what was wrong, but nobody knew what to do about it.

Funny. The person who had impressed him most was a girl who'd said nothing at all. A Negro girl from Spelman. She'd sat there, looking aloof, as if she resented the whole thing. It was as if she'd said, "How dare you sit here discussing how to treat me? I'm a person. Treat me like one."

He'd seen her later, in a play at Spelman. She was a good actress; he'd told her so. She'd said she had no desire to be a movie star. He wondered what had happened to her, what she'd become.

He turned away from the window and his musings. Time to get to the meeting. Time to decide what to do about these college kids who did more than talk. Yes, sir, this was a new breed of Negroes and it seemed they'd found the solution. He chuckled. All the merchants were frustrated as hell. But they'd acted like it was some kind of joke when he suggested they simply serve Negro customers.

"You expect *me* to serve niggers?" Les Abbott had croaked.

"Not you personally, Les. Aren't all your waitresses colored?" That was a low blow, and Red knew it. Of course they were colored, handpicked by Les, just the way he liked them—smooth chocolate or golden tan and very shapely. His favorite locker-room talk was of how many he'd seduced.

Red picked up his briefcase and started for the meeting. It had been a couple of weeks ago that he suggested they serve colored, and they'd laughed. They weren't laughing now. They were hurting too much. Not only from the Negro boycott, but from a drop in white sales, as well.

Red smiled as he got into the elevator. Yes, sir, those kids had got them where it hurt most—smack-dab in the cash register. Not only would all the merchants attend today's meeting, so would a contingent of Atlanta's leading and most influential Negroes, there to reach a viable solution.

Yes, sir, it was going to be very interesting!

The protests, in their various forms, lasted eighteen months, until Atlanta was fully integrated. Not such a long time, Julia Belle contended, considering how long segregation had been the law of the land.

September 1962

At an American air base in Seville, Spain, Robert Metcalf sat with Colonel Lemons, briefing him on some details of the most important assignment Rob had received since his entry into government service. The Soviets' erection of the Berlin Wall had compelled the NATO allies to act quickly to ready themselves for any emergency resulting from the blockade. The project assigned to the U.S. Air Force was the transfer of certain weapons and planes from the States to bases at Seville and Ramstein, Germany. The aircraft had to be partially disassembled for transportation to the respective bases, where they'd be reassembled, test-flown, armed and readied for combat within thirty days.

After his meeting with Lemons, Rob, as project manager, returned to the States for quick stops at participating bases to inform officials of plans and procedures. When he arrived at Tinker Air Force Base in Oklahoma, he was greeted by the commanding officer, General McCall, with easy familiarity and his usual, "Two hearts, partner! Two hearts!" The two men had often worked and traveled together, and the greeting was an inside joke, dating back to a bridge game on a flight from Hawaii a couple of years earlier, when the general, as Rob's partner, had missed a two-heart cue bid and a grand slam.

At Tinker further details of the project were made known, and the command's YC-97 transport was assigned to carry the ninety mechanics and technicians to the assembly sites. General McCall briefed the team members, wished them Godspeed and informed them that Robert Metcalf would manage the show.

The pilot of the YC-97 was Captain Banks, a hefty ruddy-faced young man with a blond crewcut and pale blue eyes. As the general talked to Rob at the steps of the transport, Banks absented himself to do flight-check chores—deliberately, Rob noted.

The general, however, seemed oblivious and tried to get the pilot's attention. "Say, Banks, I want you to…"

Banks lifted a hand, polite and deferential, but clearly indicating that he was out of earshot and motioning that

the crew chief required his attention. The general nodded and turned back to Rob. "Anything you need during the flight, tell Banks, and keep us informed of the
project's status every step of the way." Rob noticed that
Banks stayed some distance off until the noisy start
carts were fired up. Talking over that racket was impossible, and this, he decided, was exactly what the pilot wanted. Banks was not about to allow the general
to command him to obey a nigger. Rob shrugged, as if
to knock a chip from his shoulder. He could be wrong.

But he didn't think so. He'd encountered this kind of
maneuver too many times. And although irritated, he
was also amused at the pilot's attempt to maintain protocol while avoiding the command. He watched Banks
nod to General McCall and yell over the noise, "You
were saying, sir?"

"It's too noisy," the general yelled back. "Metcalf
will fill you in. Have a good trip." Then he got into his
car and departed.

Rob waited for Banks to reappear. His suspicions
were confirmed when the pilot strode up and looked him
in the eye. "Get on board, boy, if you're going. We're
leaving now." He left Rob to follow as the crew chief
pulled in the steps.

Rob shook his head and muttered under his breath,
"This is going to be a long hard ride." He kept his
cool, however, and stifled any small talk about the next
stop at Brookley Field in Mobile to pick up the aircraft-
handling equipment people.

At Mobile they were ready. The last ten men were
boarded, and Rob met with the leadership and was
driven back to the aircraft for takeoff. When he arrived,
the engines were running and the ramp was about to be
removed.

Colonel Wilson, who was driving, got out and asked, "Where's the captain?"

"He's aboard," the ramp operator said. "He told me to button up, but I saw you coming and waited."

Rob got out and spoke to Wilson. "No sweat. He's got a problem for some reason. Did you want to speak to him?"

"No. Just to say good luck to our guys."

"I'll tell them," Rob said and he hustled up the steps.

Rob was annoyed by the pilot's attitude, but too consumed by the project to worry about it. On the flight to the Bahamas, he found it difficult to explain the necessary details to the captains of the three groups over the noise of four four-bladed propeller-driven reciprocating engines and ninety talking passengers. He went up to the flight deck and requested that Banks unlock the crew rest area to make it available for this purpose.

Banks's response was curt and unequivocal. "Request denied."

"Listen, you—" Rob bit back the "son of a bitch" and made an effort to control his rage. The roar of the engine was nothing compared to the blood pounding in his temples, but he tried to keep his voice rational. "It's impossible to talk back there, and I have instructions I need to convey to the team captains. I'd appreciate it if you would allow—"

"Regulations provide that the crew rest quarters be limited to crew members. Your request is denied."

Rob made one more attempt. "You do realize that this is a matter of national security and—"

"You do realize that I am the captain of this ship," Banks replied, smirking.

Rob turned away. No use arguing with an ignoramus. The pilot's taunting words followed him. "Furthermore, when I announce takeoff and departure time, that's it! There will be no exceptions.''

Rob got the message. *I'm in charge, not you!* The only way Banks could maintain his white supremacy. He resented "driving a nigger" as surely as had the woman who'd driven off in front of Rob's face years before. But Banks was stuck with Rob.

More to the point, I'm stuck with him, Rob thought, trying to stifle his wrath and frustration. He had a job to do, and no time for this racist crap. Maybe, when he got to Ramstein, he'd request another pilot.

Meanwhile he'd manage as best he could. He had his meeting with the group captains in the dining room of the Bachelor Officer's Quarters when they stopped in the Bahamas for a refueling and rest stop. He made sure they all understood that takeoff time was as announced and not a second later.

Many of the hard-drinking mechanics, however, took advantage of the cheap booze available, and two hours into the flight, the noise of the drunken team members drowned out the noise of the engines. Banks attempted to bring about order, but to no avail. Rob pretended not to hear his remark to one of his flight crew. "Them goddamn drunken civilians! But what can you expect from a crew managed by a boot!"

Two hours later all was quiet. The drunks were asleep, the sun was up and they were over land. Another hour later, Banks greased the YC-97 onto the runway and taxied to Operations at the American base in Seville, Spain. Here, forty-two of the technicians disembarked and Rob hustled off to headquarters, where he briefed the leadership on their piece of the action and left schedules and other necessary data. He also had to brief the Spanish officials, and this took more time.

Then he had coffee with Colonel Lemons while finishing his consultation about accommodations for the technicians. Business completed, they climbed into the colonel's car to drive to the flight line for Rob's departure to Ramstein. As they approached the area, both saw the four-engine transport some distance away, already lifting off the ground.

Lemons slowed the car and looked at Rob. "That's your airplane! What the hell is going on?"

Rob said nothing, but he knew exactly what was going on. That dumb son-of-a-bitch pilot had finally managed to dump him. His blood boiled. This was one hell of a time to be caught in a racist game.

Lemons sped to Operations, jumped out of the car and ran into the office. Rob followed and stood, cooling his heels and fuming, while the colonel took the ground-to-air communications console and contacted the aircraft. The loudspeaker was on, and the conversation clearly heard by all in the room.

"Captain Banks, this is Colonel Lemons. What's going on? You left behind the team leader of Project Brass Ring!"

"Sir, as you know, I am captain of this flight. I told that guy we were to take off at 09:45. He wasn't there and, as aircraft commander, I departed on schedule."

"Captain, don't give me that crap! That aircraft *and you* were assigned for this project. Fly your ass back here or I'll have your bars!"

"Sorry, sir. My orders read to take YC-97-1191 to Seville, Spain, and then to Ramstein and return. I have made the Spanish stop and I am proceeding as ordered."

The Ops office was in shock. The irate colonel called Air Force Headquarters in Weisbaden and got General

Langston, who knew Rob from other duties. He told Rob to stay put, that he'd be picked up by another air-craft. "Sorry it turned out this way," he said, adding, "We'll take care of Banks. We know his problem."

And it's a big problem, Rob thought. Big enough to risk losing your bars. But prejudice wasn't limited to Banks, and Rob was skeptical. Would the pilot really lose his bars or even get a reprimand?

He dismissed the thought. More important things to worry about.

A few hours later Rob was in a C-54 on his way to Ramstein. The aircraft was met by the duty officer, who drove Rob to headquarters where further briefings were given and information exchanged. Then Rob immedi-ately sought out the flight-line chief, knowing from ex-perience that he was the one who'd help marshal the forces and provide the equipment to facilitate any ex-ercise. On an operation as big as Brass Ring, the line chief would be the man in the know, and Rob asked to be taken to him.

He was driven down runways, artfully hidden be-tween rows of trees, to an unobtrusive driveway, which led to a two-room shack. It was a chilly evening and Rob was grateful for the electric heater that gave wel-come warmth when he entered.

"Sergeant Felton," said Rob's driver, "this is Mr. Metcalf."

Rob moved ahead to quickly shake Felton's hand, gripped by the exultation he always felt when he en-countered another black man in charge of an important project. And this time an old friend. "Well, I'll be damned. It's been a few years."

"Lieutenant Metcalf! It sure has," said the sergeant. The driver retired, and the sergeant and Rob became reacquainted and reminisced about the old Tuskegee days.

"So you're a chief master sergeant now," Rob said. And in charge of the flight line at Ramstein Air Force Base, the largest such installation in the NATO system.

"And you..." Felton reached into a drawer and took out the wire regarding Brass Ring. "I thought it might be you when I first got this. Then I said no, this is a civilian." He grinned. "Man! Not only are you a civilian. You're the MFWIC of Brass Ring, the biggest operation we've had since the shooting war!"

Rob looked blank. "The M... What did you say?"

Felton's grin grew wider. "Just something we noncommissioned officers use to put things in perspective. Okay?"

"Okay," Rob said, still puzzled. "But what—"

"The motherfucker what's in charge, man!"

As they both laughed, there was a knock at the door, followed immediately by the entrance of a two-star general in full regalia—Major General Richard Brewer, Commander of the Eighteenth Air Division, USAFE (United States Air Force, Europe).

Felton stood erect and saluted. "Come in, sir," he said to the general, who was already in.

"At ease, Sergeant," the general said as he grabbed Rob's hand. "Rob Metcalf! I'm damn glad you're the guy running this program. Heard about the Banks fiasco. Put it behind you. There'll be no more glitches like that, I guarantee it. This is my command and you'll get what you need when you need it. I've already promised the boss that the planes'll be ready in thirty days. Right?"

Rob assured him they would indeed. They discussed more details, then Brewer secured a car from the motor pool and departed, leaving his staff car and driver at Rob's disposal.

Felton grinned at Rob. "You know, I'm gonna have to change what I said."

"Now what?" Rob grunted.

"You're the MFWICC."

"Meaning?"

"The motherfucker what's in *complete* charge."

They were still laughing when they heard the telltale whine of the C-124 that had landed and was taxiing in. Felton picked up the phone and swung into action, contacting all components and issuing orders. He gave crisp detailed instructions concerning the assembly and storage of the pertinent cargo.

Rob experienced a rush of pride as he watched Felton's expertise at his job.

We're not marching in the streets, Felton and I. But we, and others like us, also make a difference.

26

On a hot day in August 1963, more than 250 thousand people, black and white, invaded the city of Washington, D.C., in a mammoth march for civil rights.

Rob, his eyes glued to the TV screen, said, "Television sure brings the world to you."

"Whether you want it or not," Ann Elizabeth said. She'd been rather negative about the planned march.

With such a mob there was surely going to be a measure of disorderly conduct, even rioting. Possibly a bloodbath. Anyway…another march. What would it accomplish?

She certainly didn't intend to be there.

But she *was* there—irrevocably caught up in the enthusiasm of the orderly throng, the eager excitement on the faces of so many people, pressing together, reaching across racial barriers in a plea for human justice. Yes, she was with them, heart and soul.

Others, in other living rooms, must have been as moved as she was. As captivated and inspired by Martin Luther King's dynamic "I Have a Dream."

And maybe the dream was coming true. President Kennedy met with leaders of the march and pledged his support for a civil rights act.

"He means it," Rob said. "We've got a good president."

"And a great first lady," Ann Elizabeth said, recalling the TV vision of an elegant Jackie Kennedy describing the rooms of the White House she'd refurbished.

"Yep," Rob said. 'We hit the jackpot when we got John Kennedy!"

Yes, she agreed. A young vibrant president, dedicated to human rights. He could make a dream come true.

Three months later, on a crisp November day, Ann Elizabeth was deep in plans for Fran and Pete and their two kids, who were to spend the holiday weekend with them. Pete, a colonel now, was base commander at Hamilton Air Force Base, only eighty miles away, and the two families often visited back and forth. *If the weather holds, the men can get in some golf,* she thought, lifting fluffy towels from the dryer. She smiled as she heard the whir of the vacuum cleaner suddenly cease. Mrs. Lindsey, her weekly cleaning lady, did an excellent job. But she did it during commercial breaks between her soap operas. *Must be "General Hospital,"* Ann Elizabeth decided as the television's volume increased.

Then she heard Mrs. Lindsey scream. She rushed in to find the woman staring at the television, murmuring, "Oh, my God! My God! They done killed my president."

Ann Elizabeth sank to the sofa, hugging the warm towels as a cold chill crept up her spine. She didn't want to believe it.

But the horrible truth flashed before her, over and over again. Tears rained down her cheeks.

Day followed day, blending into an endless grief-stricken blur. Jackie Kennedy in her bloodstained suit...Lyndon Johnson, standing in a plane, taking the oath of office…little "John John" bravely saluting…the long funeral procession that tore at her heart.

"The dream didn't die with Kennedy," Phil said when they dined with the Masons a couple of months later. "We'll get the legislation he promised."

Ann Elizabeth's spirits lifted. Phil was in the political know. He had campaigned for Kennedy, and he and Laura had twice been entertained at the White House.

"I hope you're right," Rob said. "But wasn't Johnson on the ticket to get the Southern vote?"

"Oh, he's a Southerner, sure enough, and he knows about discrimination. And doesn't like it!" Phil added, grinning. "More to the point—he's an astute politician and he holds a lot of due bills. Trust me. He'll push through legislation that Kennedy couldn't have gotten out of committee!"

Phil's predictions were right. In 1964 President Lyndon Johnson forced through and signed into law the Civil Rights Act, which ended discrimination in public accommodation. The Voting Rights Act was passed a short while later.

It was phenomenal that such changes had come about in her lifetime, Ann Elizabeth thought the following June, when they drove to Atlanta for Bobby's graduation. They'd driven across country, staying at motels and eating in restaurants without being turned away once. They'd actually been treated with courtesy—just like any other customer.

"I'd like to go out to the Fox this afternoon," she told Rob a few days after the graduation ceremonies. "That's where we went the night we got engaged. Remember?" It was true that Atlanta had been integrated for two years, but she hadn't been to the Fox since that

night, more than twenty years before, when they'd sat
in the jim crow section.

Now how could such a hard fight for change suddenly
seem so simple and easy? Never would she have believed it possible, she thought as they stood in the main
lobby of the Fox Theater. *And nobody paid them any
attention!*

No, that wasn't exactly true. The usher smiled as he
took their tickets. The girl at the popcorn stand said
"Thank you, sir" as she handed Rob his change. The
fat man who jostled against her murmured, "Sorry,
ma'am. Kinda crowded, ain't it?" But nobody stared or
shied away or even looked uncomfortable.

Rob glanced down at her. "Are you all right,
honey?"

Ann Elizabeth nodded and loosened her grip on his
arm, tried to stem the tide of emotion sweeping through
her.

When they were seated, she glanced around the darkened theater. It was magnificent. Encased in niches
spaced along the wall and illuminated by tiny lights
were sculpted figures almost as exquisite as those she'd
seen in Rome. Above, simulated twinkling stars and
floating clouds gave a masterful interpretation of open
sky. It was like sitting in the great courtyard of a me-
dieval castle. She hadn't known the Fox was so beautiful.

She'd missed so much beauty.

The tip of the floating cloud, glimpsed from the jim
crow balcony, had only hinted at the opulence below.
And so, of course, had the building itself, viewed from
outside. That wide stone staircase Negroes had to
climb—up and up and up, to the colored section.

Dear God, was it so long since she'd climbed those

steep outside steps with Rob? Had stretched her arms
to the real sky above? She'd felt like a princess looking
down from the balustrade of her father's castle. She was
incredulous that she'd given no thought to what was
missing.

There had been so much joy.

The movie started, but Ann Elizabeth shut her eyes.
Remembering.

She couldn't recall the name of the film they'd
viewed that long-ago evening, but she remembered it
was a love story that had followed them out into the
night. She remembered the ride home, her head on
Rob's shoulder. The shrill sound of the police siren. The
taunting eyes and nasal drawl of the redneck policeman
that had seemed to strip Rob of his dignity.

It wouldn't be that way now. A policeman, and he
might be black, would be more likely to treat them with
respect.

Respect. They could call it whatever they wanted.
Integration. Civil rights. But it was respect for you as a
person. A person who had the right to sit in a theater,
eat at a restaurant, stop at a hotel, go to any hospital,
attend any school.

Emory. Hard to believe that Bobby had been accepted
by the medical school at Emory.

In her day no Negro could get near the place.

Well, yes. Once. She remembered sitting in a classroom at Emory, back in her student days. She'd sat,
planning a homecoming outfit, while others talked about
race relations. Thinking of those serious dedicated
faces, she felt a little guilty. So complacent she'd been.
It was as if she'd sat by while others propelled her into
a fuller life.

Well, she *had* participated, hadn't she? Okay, but she'd done it reluctantly, especially in Maggie's case.

And how had that affected Maggie? It was hard to be a first and therefore considered different. And in the places they'd lived, Maggie had often been an only or at least one of the few. And now... It bothered Ann Elizabeth that Maggie was so withdrawn, that she buried herself in books.

Funny, she never worried about Bobby. Boys, maybe because of sports, seemed to adjust more easily. And Bobby, with his Randy-like carefree ways, seemed happy wherever he was. Dad was so excited about Bobby's admission to Emory. "Opportunities, facilities, training that were never available to me," he'd said.

Ann Elizabeth smiled. Why did she always consider *happy* more important than *opportunity* when it came to her children?

She tried to concentrate on the film, but the memories kept crowding in.

Later she was quiet as Rob drove across town and up through the familiar curving driveway to her parents' house. The lawn was as carefully groomed as ever, the woodwork freshly painted. But the house somehow seemed smaller, perhaps in contrast to the fabulous residences of younger and more prosperous Negroes. Someone had told her that Grayline now hosted a tour through the black residential district. Worth seeing, Ann Elizabeth thought. Helen Rose's new house was incredible! But she liked Sadie's better. It was smaller and cozy, yet still large enough for the entertaining they had to do, both in Dan's capacity as a department head at Spalding, and for the black social elite, who were kowtowing to Sadie now that she was Dr. Trent's wife. Ann

Elizabeth grinned. Sadie was handling it. She and Dan seemed very happy.

Bobby's voice floated through the screen door as they reached it. "Don't give me that old line 'What matters is how you play the game.' It ain't true. The name of the game is *win*, boy. Win!" he said as he needled Butch, his faithful but unathletic friend. His infectious laugh rang out. Randy. Bobby might look like Rob, but the wit, the humor, the braggadocio was Randy all over again. No wonder people loved him.

Rob grinned at his son. "I take it you won the tennis match."

"Better believe it. Three straight sets. My man here needs to work on his backhand."

"Come, sit down and have a bite to eat," Julia Belle said. "We've just finished but there's lots left. Everything's still hot."

Ann Elizabeth glanced around the table at her parents, Aunt Sophie, Butch and Cindy, Bobby's girlfriend. "Where's Maggie?"

Julia Belle smiled. "Where else? Upstairs, reading."

Sophie's charm bracelet jangled. "Helen Rose tried to get her to go with them to the Jack and Jill picnic, but she refused. You need to do something about that child, Ann Elizabeth."

"That child is just fine!" Only to Rob and Julia Belle would she admit her concerns about Maggie.

"Sit here, Mrs. Metcalf." Cindy relinquished her chair to Ann Elizabeth and began to clear the table. The sandals on her bare feet fairly danced as she sped back and forth, and the ruffled hemline of her pink sundress swayed provocatively about long slender tan legs. Ann Elizabeth sighed. Surely she wasn't jealous of her son's girlfriend!

Cindy tossed back long black hair, not entirely secured by the pink band, and told Bobby to get up and
let his dad have the chair.

Rob said no, he was going into the family room to
watch the baseball game.

"Has it begun?" Dr. Carter glanced at his watch.

"Five minutes ago."

Dr. Carter followed Rob. The boys also started toward the family room, but Cindy called Bobby back.
"Wait until I fix this tray for your father."

Bobby waited.

That's what I don't like, Ann Elizabeth decided. That
proprietary air, telling Bobby when to come and when
to go. She smiled graciously as Cindy handed her a
plate heaped with turnip greens, fried corn, sliced tomatoes and cucumbers, corn muffins.

Julia Belle half rose from her chair, but Cindy protested. "No, Mrs. Carter. Sit still. I'll stack the dishwasher. Shall I put the rest of these greens in this container?"

By the time Ann Elizabeth finished eating, Cindy had
stacked the dishes, stored the leftovers, wiped the
kitchen counters and summoned Bobby from the baseball game to take her home. She had to have time to
wash her hair if they were going to the frat dance tonight. Bobby, with Butch in tow, followed her out.

Sophie, watching Bobby's car go down the driveway,
remarked that he might as well have a collar around his
neck, the way that girl led him around.

"My sentiments exactly," said Ann Elizabeth.

Julia Belle laughed. "A little bossy perhaps. But
she's quite sweet."

"Too sweet!" Sophie mimicked, "'Let me do this,
Mrs. Carter. I'll get that!' You mark my words, she'll

have Bobby's ring on her finger before he gets into medical school! She's trying to wheedle her way into this family, just like her ma wheedled her way into the Ladies.''

"Oh, Sophie!"

"You know that's true, Julia Belle. Essie Campbell was over here every day, bringing you flowers or a cake and inviting you to this or that. Licking your behind until you sponsored her for membership.''

"Oh, Sophie, don't start that again!''

"Don't start what?'' Dr. Carter asked as he and Rob returned to the kitchen.

"Nothing,'' Julia Belle answered. "Sophie's talking about the Ladies.''

"Oh, the *Ladies*,'' Dr. Carter said.

"What are they?'' Rob asked.

"Not what, my boy. Who.'' Julia Belle rolled her eyes at her husband. "I thought you were watching the ball game.''

"Seventh-inning stretch. We came for our ice cream before the eighth inning.''

"Let me get it for you.'' Ann Elizabeth moved toward the ice-cream freezer. "Rob, lift this into the sink for me. It's getting soft. I'd better pack it.''

Rob picked up the freezer as Dr. Carter continued, "Rob, my boy, your social education has been sadly neglected if you don't know who the Ladies are.''

"Tell me,'' Rob said as he took out the inner canister, poured the ice into the sink and rinsed the bucket.

"A most select society culled from the cream of colored women. Those wellborn, well padded, well married or all three.''

Sophie rattled her charm bracelet vehemently. "You may say what you like, Will Carter. But we are a national organization with important responsibilities, and we have high standards for membership. We have to be careful who we take in.''

"I thought the emphasis was on who you could keep out!'' Dr. Carter winked at Rob. "I want you to know that many a heart has been broken, many a bitter tear shed over a rejection.''

Julia Belle put a hand on his sleeve. "Will, stop teasing Sophie.''

"Oh, I don't mind,'' Sophie declared. "Take in, keep out—what's the difference? All I say is that Essie Campbell was certainly not Ladies caliber!''

"Well, now, you have to admit, she's well padded. In the physical, as well as the monetary sense.'' Dr. Carter grinned as he took the dish of peach ice cream from Ann Elizabeth. "Thank you, honey.''

Sophie sniffed. "Well padded with tainted money!''

Turning to Rob, Dr. Carter laughed. "That means, my boy, that Hern Campbell's got no letters behind his name—just dollar signs and a whole lot of numbers.''

"Oh?'' Rob lifted an understanding brow. "A numbers man?''

Dr. Carter nodded. "Yep. Made his money and got out before the white folks caught on and took it over, calling it a lottery.''

Rob smiled. "Smart guy, huh?''

Sophie sniffed. "A racketeer!''

"Now, Sophie, what's wrong with the numbers racket?''

"Will,'' Julia Belle said, "you know it was illegal. And he was put in jail.''

"Yes.'' He sighed. "Seems the white folks don't want the niggers to make any money.''

"What do you mean by that?'' Sophie asked.

"You don't see anything wrong with the stock market, do you?"

"Now, Will," Julia Belle said, "you can't compare the stock market with the numbers game."

"I certainly can. Mr. Rockefeller puts a few dollars into some stock, trying to make a few million, and a poor Negro puts a few pennies on a number, trying to make a few bucks. What's the difference?"

"It's illegal," Sophie said. "Exploiting people."

"You might call it exploiting. Some regard it as an opportunity."

"Call it what you like. I don't care to hobnob with people who made their money outside the law," Sophie said decisively. "Ann Elizabeth, I think I'll take a dish of that ice cream before you put it away."

"Truth is," said Dr. Carter, "many folks just like to hobnob with money."

"You're right about that," Sophie agreed. "A lot of people know very well that the Campbells' money came from the numbers racket. But as soon as she built that fine house and gave those big parties, they all went trotting over. They tell me folks were there eating her food, drinking her drinks and asking, 'Now, which one is Mrs. Campbell?'"

They all laughed. Dr. Carter kept teasing and Sophie kept defending the Ladies. "The Ladies would soon become nothing at all if they let just anybody in. We'd be in the same category as all these other clubs that keep jumping up."

"I know just what you mean, Sophie," Rob said in mock sympathy. "When it was just Jackie Robinson and Campanella, we were solidly behind the Dodgers. Now there's so many of us on so many teams, we don't know who to root for!"

They laughed again as Dr. Carter said they'd better get back to the game. Ann Elizabeth washed the churn and slipped quietly upstairs to find her daughter.

Maggie lay on her stomach on the bed, head propped on her elbows, as she read a book.

"Maggie, you should—" No, she wouldn't remind her about turning the spread back. "Hi, honey."

"Hi, Mom, how was the movie?" Maggie rolled over, her lips curved in a welcoming smile, even white teeth against smooth chocolate skin. No braces, no sign of acne. Ann Elizabeth crossed her fingers. How lucky could you get! Maggie was beautiful, small-boned like herself with Julia Belle's fine aristocratic features and Rob's dark deep-set eyes.

"Oh, the movie was great. What are you reading?"

"Anna Karenina."

"Oh." Good heavens! Heavy reading for a twelve-year-old. What had *she* read at Maggie's age? *The Five Little Peppers, The Secret Garden…*

Maggie stretched and yawned, long lashes fluttering. "She was so silly."

"Why?" Ann Elizabeth, who hadn't read the book, tried to recall the movie. "Because she left her husband?"

"No. After she left him. Why didn't she just go on and be happy, instead of practically going crazy because those society ladies wouldn't speak to her?"

Ann Elizabeth studied her daughter. She had never before heard the book discussed from that perspective. "Speaking of society, why didn't you go to the Jack and Jill picnic?"

"Ugh!"

"That's a funny way to describe a picnic." Ann Elizabeth sat on the bed and pushed back a strand of Maggie's hair. It was darker and coarser than hers, and quite unmanageable out of braids. Bertha had shown her how to run a warm comb through it, so that it fell in soft waves about Maggie's shoulders.

"I was reading."

"Sweetheart, you can read any time. We're on vacation. This is a time to enjoy yourself."

"I am enjoying myself."

"With other people."

"I don't know any of them."

"Margaret Ann Metcalf! Your very own cousins!"

"They're so silly. Giggling about who likes who and somebody kissed somebody."

Ann Elizabeth laughed. "I guess that's the way kids are at this age." She thought back. Wasn't she thirteen when Ambrose Phillips had kissed her at the Sunday-school picnic? She'd slapped him, but had been secretly pleased. Ambrose was the best-looking boy in their set. How grown-up she'd felt, telling Helen Rose all about it in this very room. They had certainly giggled. But Maggie... What made it difficult for her to fit in? Even here, she was withdrawn.

Integration. Ann Elizabeth was beginning to hate that word. All of Maggie's young life had been spent in integrated schools, sometimes the only black child in her class. There, but not quite in. Oh, she had friends, in Brownies, then Girl Scouts. But it wasn't the same.

Ann Elizabeth had tried to compensate. She'd joined the Sacramento chapter of Jack and Jill, the national organization formed by Negro parents to bring their children together for a proper social life. But that was artificial, too—infrequent meetings with kids scattered all over town, not the cozy easy everyday contact Ann

Elizabeth had enjoyed as a child. Her heart ached for her daughter.

Later, propped up in bed with a book on her lap, she watched Rob as he peeled off his shirt. He was still lean and handsome, and could still beat Bobby at tennis. He seemed so complacent. He never worried about the children the way she did.

She sighed. "Rob, I'm concerned about Maggie. She's so...so out of things. Always has her nose stuck in a book."

"Nothing wrong with that."

"Well, yes, I'm glad she reads. But she ought to be out having fun."

"Seems happy enough to me." Rob took off his watch, laid it on the dresser.

"She's not happy."

He looked at her. "What do you mean?"

"She's so out of things," Ann Elizabeth repeated.

"Like what, for Christ's sake?"

She watched him drop one shoe and tried to explain. "She doesn't even want to go to Susie's party tomorrow night."

"Can't blame her for that. Those silly girls of Helen Rose's are as shallow as their mother."

"Robert!"

"Oh, I know she's your cousin, but there's always so much damn crap about who's invited to what and who belongs and who doesn't."

It struck her that his remark was uncannily similar to Maggie's complaint about the cousins. *Giggling about who likes who...* But she had to make him understand.

"Oh, Rob, it's only natural to try to select the right friends for your children."

"It's not natural."

"Well, it's certainly natural for Maggie to be comfortable with kids her own age."

"She's comfortable enough."

"Not really. You know, I think that always being in an integrated environment—"

Rob laughed. "Oh, oh! Here we go again. Mrs. Moonlight, who wants things to stay the way they always were."

"That's not true! I'm glad we've made progress—glad about integration. But—" she sat up, put the book aside "—I just feel for Maggie. She's never really had a chance to develop socially. She's never really felt a part of anything."

"Don't know why. You sure did your best to see that she was in all kinds of groups. Brownies, Girl Scouts, chasing all over town with the Jack and Jill." Rob yawned, unbuckled his belt, dropped his pants.

"You think that's wrong, don't you? To want Maggie to have what I had." That sense of security, never feeling different. She blinked. Rob just didn't understand.

She was surprised to find his arms around her. "What you had..." he crooned as he rocked her. "My little princess who's traveled all over the world and never left Atlanta."

"Maybe that's why. What I had here, I mean..." She fumbled for the words. "Maybe that's why I was never uncomfortable—wherever we went. The way Maggie seems to be."

"You mean you can't integrate Maggie with the Ladies?"

"The Ladies?"

"You know. That select organization dedicated to keeping out whoever they can."

"Oh, that. Dad was just teasing Aunt Sophie."

"But it's true. Somebody's always going to be left out of something. Even in your precious Atlanta."

"I don't want Maggie's life based on what she can or can't get into. That's not what I mean, Rob."

"That's not what you mean to mean, I know. Let Maggie alone. She'll get more out of a book than she will out of any party Susie's giving."

"But she's so withdrawn, so uncomfortable."

He kissed her. "I'm not worried about Maggie. She's her mother's daughter."

She stared at him.

"Now what?" he asked.

"You made me remember something Dad said a long time ago." *You're definitely your mother's daughter...that same core of inner pride, that sense of knowing you're somebody.* Did Maggie have that? She shook her head. "I don't know," she said. "I just don't know."

27

September 1965

Thelma Metcalf was tired and she kept getting that sharp little pain in her chest.

"Why don't you stay here tonight, Thelma?" Mr. Tyler said. "It's late and you have a long drive home."

"No. I'll go on. Don't seem to get no rest 'cept in my own bed. I'm not going to put these dishes away, though. You can do that tomorrow." She didn't work for Mr. Tyler anymore. Didn't need to. Her social security and the check Rob sent every month were more than enough, especially since she'd paid off the duplex. But she did come sometimes to help out, like tonight, when the Tylers had a dinner party.

She panted a little as she got into her old Buick for the drive back to Watts. It had been a long day. She still liked to get her groceries out here and she'd come early to shop at the super. She'd loaded up on staples for the Stevenses and herself. Didn't know when she'd get back this way.

As she made the turnoff from the freeway into the Watts area, she heard sirens. A fire somewhere. She could smell the smoke and saw a big blaze. Wasn't near her place, thank goodness. She crossed herself and said a little prayer for the person whose house was burning.

It's more than a fire, she thought with some fear as she started to make her turn into the main street and found the way blocked. Something had happened. People running back and forth, cars just standing in the street, some turned over. What on earth?

"You can't get through, Mrs. Metcalf." Stoney, a stringy teenage boy from her Sunday-school class, stuck his head in the window.

"I can see that, Stoney. What's happened?"

"Don't know, but all hell's done broke loose. Peoples gone crazy. Somebody broke into Mr. Ben's pawnshop and they just helping themselves—watches, radios, clothes and everything."

"I hope you—"

"No'm. I'm just watching."

"You shouldn't be out here." Thelma tried to speak calmly, tried not to be frightened. "Get in the car. I'm going to park it in Mr. Grant's garage and walk home. You'd better go straight home, too. No sense being out here in all this mess. Somebody's going to get hurt."

She managed to back up and maneuver the car into the lot at the garage, which was closed. She hoped the car would be safe. Stoney helped her unload her groceries and they started home through an alley, each carrying a bag. Thelma walked as fast as she could, but the pain was back and she was having trouble breathing. They had almost reached the street when they were blinded by the headlights of a squad car as it turned into the alley. Thelma and Stoney backed against a building wall to avoid being hit but, brakes squealing, the police car stopped a few feet past them and two policemen got out and advanced toward them.

"Halt there, boy! What you got?"

"Nothing," said Stoney. "I'm just helping Mrs. Metcalf."

The policeman cursed, and whatever else he said was lost as three motorcycles roared past.

Thelma, startled by the noise and the sight of the helmeted patrolmen, was momentarily stunned, but immediately came to when she saw the policeman moving toward Stoney, his billy club raised. "Don't lie to me, boy. We ain't gonna stand for this looting."

Without stopping to think, Thelma grabbed his arm. "Don't. Stoney ain't done nothin'. He's just…just…" She tried to catch her breath, tried to talk, but the words wouldn't come out. The pain was sharper, and spreading down her arm, her back…and everything was fading….

On the day of Thelma Metcalf's funeral, Shiloh Baptist Church was packed. The funeral had been delayed until the furor had subsided, the helmeted troopers no longer needed, the riot officially over. Over but not forgotten, Ann Elizabeth thought as they drove toward the church and she surveyed the battle-scarred area. Buildings boarded up or gaping open, all the contents gone. Rubble and ashes where a building had been. What had happened? she wondered. What trivial incident had set a torch to the tinderbox of frustration just waiting to blow?

The church, however, except for one broken window, was untouched—a haven of peace and order amidst chaos. The service was surprisingly inspiring. It was as if Thelma was still with them, her smile warm and welcoming, her lovely contralto blending with the voices of the choir in the gospel songs she had so loved. The teenage boys from her Sunday-school class were pall-bearers. One former member, Charlie Gates, delivered the eulogy. He told how, within the class, she had organized WIS, Watts Improvement Society, inspiring the boys to clean up the area and start community projects to improve their standard of living. He ended by declaring, "It was because of Mrs. Metcalf that I stayed out of trouble and am now a student at Stanford."

Then, one by one, other members of the community stood to talk about Thelma. She had brought fresh vegetables from Belair for one, organized the deaconess board to take meals to the sick, assigned her boys to run errands for others.

It's as if her loving giving spirit is still alive. Ann Elizabeth remembered her father's comment about making the best of life "wherever you're flung."

Maggie, sitting next to Ann Elizabeth, was leaning against Rob's chest, sobbing openly. Both the children had loved Thelma. Ann Elizabeth was glad Bobby, just getting settled in medical school, had not come. It's so awful for all of us, she thought, glancing at Rob. She had never before seen him cry. She reached over to gently squeeze the arm that was wrapped around Maggie.

"I wish to God I'd made Mama come to us," he said later, when they joined other mourners in the church hall where dinner was served by the women's auxiliary. "She'd still be alive."

"You can't be sure of that," Ann Elizabeth said. "You know it was her heart." This had been confirmed by the doctor at the hospital where the policemen had taken her. They'd done so immediately, Stoney had said, as soon as they realized she was ill.

"I know," Rob said. "But it was what happened here. All that excitement. If she'd been with us…"

"Then she wouldn't have been here." She shook him a little. "And so many good things happened just because she *was* here."

Am I making the best of life where I'm flung? Ann Elizabeth wondered when she returned to Sacramento. *I'm involved with me and mine*—the Jack and Jills for Maggie, the Officers' Wives Club for Rob, her two bridge clubs for her own enjoyment. Thinking of Thelma, she had an urge to reach out to others.

With a burst of energy she volunteered two mornings a week at a local hospital, read books to the blind and was soon an active member of several civic organizations, pulling many of her friends, black and white, in with her.

"I don't know why I let you get me into this," complained Cora Samples as they addressed mailers for the League of Women Voters. "I may as well have a job. Anyway, I'm not the volunteering type."

"Nonsense." Ann Elizabeth smiled at the woman who'd been her friend since that first dinner party when they'd labored together over a broken bowl of gravy. "You're the perfect volunteering type." It was true. Her rather shy anxious-to-please personality, coupled with dependability and willingness to work, had gained her quite a reputation. "If you want something done, ask Cora." Probably that was why this Mr. Wimbush had called her.

"Out of the clear blue sky, from somewhere in Arkansas," she told Ann Elizabeth. "He said I'd been referred to him, that I was the best person in the city to do the recruiting."

"Recruiting?"

"For the White Citizens' League. He wants to start a chapter in Sacramento."

"Cora." Ann Elizabeth felt her blood run cold. "They're just like the Ku Klux Klan. More sophisticated and probably more deadly."

"I know. I was appalled. I didn't know what to say."

"What *did* you say?"

"That I couldn't of course. I was too busy. And then he wanted to know if I could suggest someone else, someone, he said, who was active in various city organizations. He went on and on about how they want members who are well-known and respected in the community. I was shocked, but I couldn't shut him up. I didn't want to be rude, but—"

"You should've just told him to go to hell!" Ann Elizabeth retorted. "But not you, Cora. You couldn't be rude to a rattlesnake." Rage hammered at her. This group, with its venomous racial bigotry poised to strike at all the rights, all the goodwill, was more dangerous than a rattler. "People like you, Cora, have to speak out. You can't just sit complacently back and let a group like this get its hooks into our city!"

"Ann Elizabeth, calm down. I told him I was too busy. You know I wouldn't participate in such a venture."

"But you didn't tell him—" She broke off. If the man couldn't get Cora, he'd just get somebody else. An idea began to form in her mind. "Cora..." she said softly, tentatively.

Cora was still trying to recover from her friend's outburst. "I know I should have told him off, but—"

"No, no. I'm glad you didn't. Is he planning to call you back, or did he leave his number?"

"Well, no. That is, yes." Cora stared at her as if trying to decipher this change of mood. "He did say he'd call back, even though I told him I couldn't recommend anyone."

"No, you won't," Ann Elizabeth said decisively. Now the idea was fully formed. "You'll do the recruiting yourself."

"What? You want me to…to…" Cora trailed off in bewilderment.

"I'll help you." Ann Elizabeth laughed as she explained. This was going to be fun.

It so happened that Julia Belle came for a short visit on the day before the initial meeting.

"You can't be serious." She stared at her daughter. "You surely don't expect me to attend a meeting of the White Citizens' League."

"Oh, yes, I do. We need as many people as we can get." Ann Elizabeth's eyes twinkled. "I wish I could pass. I'd just love to be there."

When the plan was explained to her, Julia Belle agreed to go, albeit rather dubiously. At seven o'clock the following evening she was picked up by Tony Ross and his wife, Alice, both of whom, Ann Elizabeth said, had been active in the recruitment. Alice Ross was a blond buxom woman, very talkative and enthusiastic about what they'd accomplished.

"Ann Elizabeth is so clever," she said. "It was her idea. I never would have thought of it, but I'm sure for it. My maiden name is Bernstein. Did you bring the tape recorder, Tony?" she asked. Her quiet unassuming husband nodded and she turned back to Julia Belle. "I'm going to tape the whole proceeding for Ann Elizabeth. Don't want her to miss all the fun."

Julia Belle felt a little nervous when they entered the

meeting room in one of the city's major hotels, but everyone was cordial. There were about sixty people, and all of them seemed to know the Rosses, who received friendly nods and greetings as they settled in their chairs.

"That's the organizer from Arkansas," Alice said of the tall cadaverous man at the head table. Seated beside him was Cora Samples. "Cora agreed to serve as secretary," Alice whispered.

When Mr. Wimbush got up to speak, his voice was a surprise to Julia Belle—a clipped, almost British accent. He started out mildly enough, expressing appreciation for their presence, saying he knew they were concerned, as he was, with maintaining the American way of life. However, as he continued, Julia Belle became shocked, indignant, incredulous. How could anyone with such intellectual bearing spew such racist venom! Be so bigoted! She hoped the rage wasn't showing on her face as he went on to talk about "the lechers on our economy, the lazy ignorant niggers, who swell the welfare rolls and increase the taxpayers' burden." It seemed the "money-grabbing Jews were conniving, cheating and taking over most of the businesses in the city." This all had to be stopped, he said.

Julia Belle sat tense, almost unable to contain herself, and wondered how the people around her could be so...so relaxed. There were even chuckles and murmurs of agreement every now and then.

Mr. Wimbush finished his speech and opened the meeting for discussion.

Tony Ross stood up. With a perfectly straight face, he suggested that one way to get back at the Jews was to refuse to work in any of their establishments.

A woman in the back agreed. "Many white Protestants hold important executive positions in stores owned by Jews,'' she said. "If they all resign—"

"Er, just a minute." Mr. Wimbush looked a little confused. "We don't want to be too hasty. Cut off our noses, so to speak," he said with a chuckle. "There's a bit of a dilemma here, a conflict of interests."

Tony persisted. "Look at it this way. What's best for us? We sure don't want to help Jews be successful."

Wimbush promised to take his view under consideration.

Another man stood. "Sir, I think we should work to ban restrictive covenants."

Mr. Wimbush seemed even more confused. "Ban them? We're having enough trouble keeping them from being broken. Some of the Realtors are ruining good neighborhoods by selling to inharmonious groups—Negroes, Orientals and Mexicans."

"But don't you see?" the man said politely. "If they're living around us, we can keep our eye on them, prevent riots and that sort of thing."

Enlivened by the look on Mr. Wimbush's face, Julia Belle stood. She might as well join the fun. "I think that's an excellent idea. It would stop some of the agitation. I have another idea that will put an end to all that abominable picketing at our stores."

"Yes?" questioned the dazed Wimbush.

"Give them jobs," said Julia Belle. "Then they'd have no reason to picket."

"Good thinking," Tony Ross said. "They'd be too lazy to take the jobs, but they wouldn't have any reason to agitate. Have you got all these ideas down, Cora?"

Cora nodded, trying not to smile.

A tiny woman in the front stood up. "Mr. Wimbush, I think this is a wonderful organization and I have an excellent proposal to make.'' When the chairman, who seemed to have lost his voice, only stared at her, she continued, ''Why don't we take Negroes and Jews in as members? Then we'd *really* be able to keep an eye on them. Of course, we might have to change the by-laws a bit, but—''

By this time Mr. Wimbush had caught on and was glaring at his now-laughing audience in disgust. ''This is a farce!'' He gathered up his papers and stormed out of the room, followed by only one man.

Alice Ross was almost hysterical. ''Did you see his face!'' she cried as they all gathered around to congratulate one another. ''I can't wait for Ann Elizabeth to hear this tape,'' she told Julia Belle. ''She'll be proud of us.''

January 1968

It was raining hard, a cold winter rain, that Wednesday morning when the phone rang. Early, before the alarm went off. Ann Elizabeth picked it up with trepidation.

It was Bertha. ''Ann Elizabeth, they got my Sammy.''

''No! Oh, no!'' Her mind flew back twenty-two years to a cuddly dark-skinned toddler. ''I'm so sorry...I...'' She fumbled for some comforting word.

Bertha wasn't listening. Her rage bounced, sputtered and spun through the wire. ''It ain't right! It ain't right! My baby lying in some slimy swamp in that godforsaken shit-ass country where he didn't have no business to be! On account of these crazy white folks' god-awful war, which he didn't even know nothin' about. They didn't ask him, neither! Just here's your number, put on this suit, take this gun and go out there and shoot some po' ass fool that don't know why he's there, neither. Ann Elizabeth, you know Sammy.'' Her voice broke. "He couldn't hurt a flea. You know that.''

She did know. The other boy, Hodge, a year younger, was still at college on his football scholarship. But Sammy— "He ain't tough like Hodge,'' Bertha had said, "and not all that bright, neither, but he's a good boy, got a good job at that nursery'' —Sammy had gotten swallowed up by the draft and Vietnam. It was 1968 now and the war was still going on!

But this wasn't the time to be bitter. "I'll be right there,'' Ann Elizabeth said.

She drove through the rain and the morning traffic, her heart aching for Bertha. She was a mother, too, and she couldn't help being glad that Bobby was safe in medical school, safe from that dreadful war. Would it never end?

Later that year she wondered if it really was true that bad things happened in threes.

Sammy's death was personal, of course, and a terrible blow, but he was just one of a great many. Martin Luther King's assassination, however, was a blow to the whole world—"though they might not know what they've lost,'' her father said.

Bertha said the same thing in a different way. "Killed him 'cause he was trying to tell 'em what they don't wanna believe—ain't no difference between black and white. There's po' white folks, too, and don't nobody, black or white, want their kid killed in a crazy war we ain't got no business in, anyway!''

Ann Elizabeth just felt very sad, especially when the assassination triggered riots across the nation. "I can understand the anger,'' she said to Rob. "Their grief must be as great as mine. But the violence and destruction are insults to his memory. This man accomplished so much for all of us—and did it while keeping to the Christian principles of nonviolence.''

A few months later Senator Robert Kennedy, campaigning for president, was assassinated in the hallway of a Los Angeles hotel.

''What's happening?'' Ann Elizabeth asked as she and Rob watched a repeat of that dreadful episode in the peace of their living room. ''Here in the United States where we've always had open and peaceful elections.''

''Which, in spite of everything, is still the best place in the entire world to be,'' said Rob, who had just returned from a trip to the Middle East.

In the spring of 1969, Ann Elizabeth helped Maggie fill out her college applications.

28

They were still at it. Rob hadn't stopped nagging his daughter since she'd turned up with that short Afro hair-cut Friday afternoon.

Ann Elizabeth sighed. "I'd better put the food away," she said, and fled to the kitchen.

No escape. Rob's voice boomed from the living room. "I don't get it! Why you do your damnedest to look like something the cat dragged in is beyond me. Beat-up jeans and scrubby Keds are bad enough. But when you practically scalp yourself to—"

"Oh, Dad, you just want my hair long and straight like white girls!"

"And you want it short and nappy like the gals in that gang you run with!"

"I want it like it is!" Maggie said. "Natural. Just wash and wear! It's easy this way."

Certainly easier than all that straightening and setting, Ann Elizabeth thought, smiling as she spooned rice into a Tupperware container. Still, Rob was right. Maggie was just trying to conform to the new Neg—*black* image. Lord, would she never remember to say black, not Negro or colored?

"Anyway, what's wrong with my gang?"

She heard the defiance in Maggie's voice and her smile faded. Be careful what you wish for, woman. You might get it!

How she'd longed for Maggie to have a gang. How she'd ached for the daughter who kept her nose buried in a book, with never a group of friends to talk and laugh and have fun with.

Maggie had found her group at Berkeley. Black classmates, like herself, and she was clinging to them like mad. But they weren't the happy laughing group Ann Elizabeth had hoped she'd have. These young people were angry, rebellious, demanding. Worse, Maggie had begun to emulate them.

Poor kids, Ann Elizabeth had mused. They don't know how far we've come, and they're not good at listening. Rob seemed to enjoy the debates, but Ann Elizabeth shuddered every time Maggie brought Ted, Sue or any of her new friends home. Not that it was any better when Maggie came alone, she thought now as the argument continued.

"I'll tell you what's wrong with you and your gang," Rob said. "You think you're supposed to run things— the school, the state and the whole damn country!"

"We're *involved!*" Maggie countered.

"Right! And you don't know shit from shinola!"

Ann Elizabeth shut the kitchen door. She'd heard it all before. She filled a box with fried chicken, rolls and most of the cookies she'd baked the previous day for Maggie to take back with her. College kids were always hungry. When she had the counters clean and the dishwasher going, she returned to the living room.

The heated discussion had switched to the subject of black history.

Ann Elizabeth wished she'd stayed in the kitchen.

"Do you realize that blacks have been eliminated from history altogether? In books? In history courses?" Maggie said.

Not quite, Ann Elizabeth thought, remembering the required course in Negro history at Washington High. She'd learned that it was a Negro who'd died first in the revolution, a Negro doctor who'd performed the first heart surgery, a Negro who'd designed the Capitol in Washington, D.C. But her mind had been more on dances and boys, and she hadn't been very interested.

Unlike her daughter. "We're demanding that we be included," Maggie said.

"Right," Rob agreed. "But you should want to be included in the whole thing. We're just beginning to crawl out of the separatist shit, and you want to shove us back into it! Black students' union, black dormitory, black whatever. And now you want a whole black-history department!"

"Because we've been neglected for too long," Maggie declared, and launched into a diatribe about the lack of pride felt by blacks, the lack of knowledge about their African heritage.

Rob clapped his hands. "Excellent!" he said when she was done. His voice dripped with sarcasm. "Great rhetoric! Courtesy of Mr. Oola Bunga, I take it!"

Maggie stiffened. "His African name is Lamumba!"

Rob snorted. "His real name is probably Willie Jones. And all he knows about Africa is what he's read in a book."

"At least he's not ashamed of his blackness!"

"Hell, no! He's trading on it. This department of black studies you kids are getting your heads busted for, won't he be the nigger in charge?"

"Oh, Daddy, I wish you wouldn't use that horrible n-word! Yes, Professor Lamumba is the right person to head the black-studies department we're advocating. But there's no use discussing his qualifications with you." Maggie threw up her hands. "You don't understand."

"You're damn right I don't understand. And what's it to you? I thought your major was political science, not niggerology!"

"There's that word again. You can't stand to say black, can you? And you're probably ashamed of your African roots!"

"My roots are here, not in Africa. And you know something? I *like* it here."

"Of course you do. You get pretty good pay, sending those planes and guns to Vietnam, don't you?"

Ann Elizabeth gasped when she saw Rob wince. Working on the weapons of war had not been his career choice, and she knew Maggie's jab had hurt. She braced herself for his outburst.

But Rob only smiled. "Don't knock it, girlie. That pay keeps you in those cashmere sweaters you don't wear and at that college you're so bent on tearing apart."

Ann Elizabeth swallowed the lump in her throat, even as she felt a rush of pride. It was so like Rob to whistle away his hurt, to laugh it off. Just as he had through so many episodes of discrimination.

Maggie, unlike Rob, bristled.

"We are *not* bent on tearing it apart. We're trying to ensure that we have a part in the administration and decision-making, and that there's an emphasis on black, as well as white, culture!"

"Right on! I see Professor Mumbo Jumbo has it all figured out. He's got you all fired-up to take over!"

"Oh, I'm wasting my time talking to you." Maggie grimaced in disgust and left the room.

Rob chuckled as he sank back in his chair and returned to his newspaper. "I'm the one wasting time. I should know better than to try to reason with a know-it-all college sophomore."

Ann Elizabeth envied him. She wished she could take things as lightly as he did.

But she didn't like Maggie being mixed up in all the anti-this and anti-that activities. She could get hurt.

Nonsense, she told herself. Maggie wasn't at San Francisco State where the confrontations were vicious and several students badly hurt. But if the rallies at Berkeley continued and they brought in the city police…

She felt a real stab of fear and started toward her daughter's room, her mind resolutely searching for some happy conversational topic.

Plays. Like mother, like daughter, she'd thought when Maggie joined a theater group. But an all-black group?

"We want to participate, Mom! Like act. In some of the major roles! Anyway," Maggie had added, "wasn't your group all black?"

Ann Elizabeth had found herself involved in a hot debate over why a black theater group in a black university was part of the whole, and the same thing in an integrated university was separatism. There was another altercation later, when she criticized their first performance and the repertoire of future plays.

"We're telling it like it is!" Maggie had insisted. "We're not hiding behind Shakespeare!"

"No, but you're hiding *from* Shakespeare. And that's a shame," Ann Elizabeth had said, for once losing her own temper. "Exposure to the classics is one of the major offerings of a university. Furthermore, if you must limit yourself to black culture, why portray only the seamiest side and in that foul language that turns my stomach?"

No, she decided as she went into Maggie's room, drama wasn't a good choice.

She found Maggie stuffing jeans and sweatshirts into a duffel bag. Fashion was not a safe topic, either.

"Packing already?" Ann Elizabeth sat on the bed, took out the jammed-in clothes and began to smooth and fold.

"Yeah. I need to get back." Maggie knelt to reach under the bed.

"Who cut your hair?"

"Dena." Maggie's voice was muffled as she fumbled under the bed, finally emerging with a pair of scruffy tennis shoes.

"I like it." The hair was much shorter, but Rob was wrong about Maggie's looks. No hairstyle could spoil her classic beauty. Not that Maggie cared. With no hint of vanity, she strode across campus without makeup and in clothes that might have come from Goodwill. Intense, resolute and defiant in the battle for…for whatever it was they were after. These kids! Last year at Kent State four students had been killed and nine others injured. Ann Elizabeth shuddered. She didn't want Maggie's pretty head bashed in.

"I hope you're not planning another one of those campus rallies," she said, repacking the folded clothes.

"Oh, Mom!" Maggie tossed in the shoes and bent to kiss her mother's cheek. "You're just an old scaredy-cat. We can't just sit around like you and Dad. Some of us have to fight for social justice." She threw in a comb and zipped the bag shut. "There. I gotta scram."

Ann Elizabeth followed her into the living room and handed her the box of food she'd prepared.

Maggie kissed her again. "Thanks, Mom." Then she bent to hug her father. "See you later, alligator."

"In a while, crocodile," he answered. Their usual farewell. Ann Elizabeth marveled that they could be in a shouting match one minute and a joking mood the next.

She watched from the doorway as Maggie backed her Volkswagen out of the driveway and headed toward Berkeley. Back to the agitation and the rallies.

Maybe if she'd gone to Spelman…

No. According to Mother, the students there were rioting, too. The Atlanta University regents had been locked in the boardroom for twenty-four hours. "Wanting us to adhere to the stupidest demands," reported Julia Belle. "Change the name from Atlanta to Martin Luther King University. Lord, don't they know white folks have been trying for years to buy the Atlanta name? Well, we're hanging on to it, and we're not banning whites from the board, either. As if they weren't our most influential, not to mention richest, members! I don't know what in the Sam Hill these youngsters are thinking!"

Ann Elizabeth smiled. The use of her harshest cuss, "Sam Hill," meant her mother was really upset.

I'm upset, too. "Don't college kids know how to have fun anymore?" she asked, turning to Rob.

"It's marching fever!" he said, and chuckled. "But pretty soon they'll have to march to a different drummer."

"Oh?"

"Like doing some schoolwork. They'll find out. Hey, it's time for the game." He put down the paper and switched on the television.

Ann Elizabeth, shaking her head at his complacency, returned to Maggie's room and began to strip the bed. Her kids were working. Maggie might be agitating, but she was still on the dean's list. And Bobby had marched and demonstrated right through medical school and halfway through his internship without missing a beat.

An intern at Grady—where black doctors had been banned only a few years before. And already accepted as a resident at Children's Hospital, where he'd been practically smuggled in when he was a baby!

She went to the linen closet for clean sheets, thinking of her father, who was about to burst with pride. "We'll have a celebration when you come for the wedding," he'd said.

The wedding would be held early in June, the one month Bobby would have free before beginning his duties at Children's. Cindy, teaching in an elementary school, would be on vacation then. "Perfect timing for a honeymoon," Cindy had said. "And I'll have the whole summer to settle us in.'

She had to admit that Cindy planned things well. Like her mother, she thought. Cindy's mother was planning, as Sophie said, "to put on the dog" at the biggest wedding Atlanta had ever seen.

So? Atlanta's social-minded mothers, her own included, had been trying to outdo one another for years.

It wasn't that. It was...

An old nursery rhyme flitted through her mind. "I do not like thee, Doctor Fell. / The reason why I cannot tell. / But this I know, and know full well, / I do not like thee, Doctor Fell!''

She shook out a sheet and began to make the bed. She didn't know why she didn't like Cindy Campbell. The girl was attractive, charming and smart.

Bobby loves her. And she must be good for him. Keeps him laughing, teasing, still his happy-go-lucky self, despite all the long hard hours at the hospital.

And I'm ashamed of myself. Possessive of my son and jealous of any other woman in his life!

The wedding was held at the Methodist Church where the Campbells were members. But it took Ann Elizabeth back to that day, more than thirty years before, when she'd walked down the aisle at the Congregational Church.

She held Rob's hand, her eyes misting as their son waited at the altar for his bride. Cindy was a lovely bride in the best creation of tulle and lace money could buy.

But not as beautiful as Maggie! Ann Elizabeth's eyes focused on her daughter, standing with the other brides- maids. Maggie's short black curls accentuated the per- fection of her features, and her deep-tan skin was strik- ing against the pale lilac of her dress. Lilac! *The exact shade of my debut dress the night I met Rob.*

It seemed only yesterday. Dear God, where had all the years gone? *I'm getting old.*

''Maybe I should dye my hair,'' she'd said to Rob earlier when she'd slipped into her own dress of deep lavender and inspected herself in the mirror.

''Don't you touch it!'' he'd said. ''That gray kinda highlights the brown. I like it.''

That made her feel better. Not too much gray, and

her skin was smooth, her figure slender. She still re-tained a youthful look—she hoped.

And why, for goodness' sake, was she thinking about herself? This was Bobby and Cindy's day. She listened as they exchanged vows and prayed that they'd be happy. Prayed that Bobby would be as loving, as steady, as Rob.

When the wedding party filed out, her thoughts were again on Maggie. That young man escorting her—Michael somebody. Wasn't he the one who'd stuck to her like glue at Dan and Sadie's party?

Ann Elizabeth was glad she and Rob had come early enough to enjoy some of the prenuptial parties. It had done her heart good to see Maggie talking and laughing, even flirting a little. She'd spotted Maggie sitting by Sadie's pool, apart from the others, dimpling up at him as if she really liked him.

I like him. I like that rich dark coloring like Rob's, his handsome clean-cut look and well-bred manner. He was one of the four blacks who'd finished with Bobby's class from Emory. Bobby says he's going into cardiology. I must ask him where—

"Stop it!" she whispered to herself. She wasn't one of those pushy matchmaking mothers she despised!

A soft rain had fallen while they were in the church, and the clean earthy scent still lingered. Ann Elizabeth smiled as she breathed in the sweet familiar smell of Atlanta. Some things never change, she thought as she hurried into a car.

But many things *have* changed, she had to admit as they reached the biggest hotel in Atlanta and she was whisked by a glass-sided elevator to the roof. There they sat at tables laden with wedding memorabilia, sipped champagne, munched on hors d'oeuvres and wedding cake served by smiling courteous *white* waiters, enjoying the festivities as the carousel roof went round and round, offering splendid views of Atlanta.

In her lifetime! It was still hard to believe.

Ann Elizabeth chuckled. Essie Campbell was outdoing all the Negro—oops!—black society matrons. None had ever before held a wedding reception in such a spectacular place where blacks had only so recently been admitted. Anyway, few could have afforded it.

Dr. Carter apparently had the same thought. "Campbell must've made a pile in that numbers racket," he whispered.

"And must've known what to do with it. Smart man," Rob said, grinning as he added, "Glad he's joined the family."

Sometime during the evening, Bobby and Cindy left to take a flight to Florida, where they would board a cruise ship to the Bahamas for their honeymoon. And suddenly it was all over. But they were still talking about it when they got home—her parents, Rob, Maggie and the young man whose name, she'd discovered, was Michael James.

"We must have a nightcap to toast such a fantastic affair," Ann Elizabeth said, bringing out chips and wine, and engaging the young man in conversation. Simply being gracious wasn't being a pushy matchmaker!

"I hope the marriage will be as wonderful as the wedding," Julia Belle said.

"It will be," her husband murmured. "Those two are made for each other."

Ann Elizabeth looked at him.

He nodded in answer to the question she hadn't asked. "Bobby has the brains and Cindy will handle the budget. She—'' He suddenly gasped as if trying to catch his breath. He stumbled and almost fell.

The young man moved quickly and helped him to the sofa. ''Nitroglycerin?'' he asked.

Dr. Carter shook his head. ''No. Could be...'' He couldn't finish the sentence.

''Call this doctor,'' Michael said to Maggie, scribbling a name and number on a pad. Then he turned to Rob, who was already lifting Dr. Carter. ''We'll take him to Georgia Baptist.''

Ann Elizabeth ran after them as they hurried out, but Rob gestured over his shoulder. ''Your mother.''

Ann Elizabeth turned back to Julia Belle, who had not moved. She was so still, so pale. Obviously in shock.

''I'll get you some hot tea, Mother.'' With lots of sugar, she thought. ''Then we'll go to the hospital. Maggie...''

But Maggie was on the phone.

Ann Elizabeth tried to support her mother, but she could hardly hold her*self* together. She had never known her father to be sick, even with a cold. She was terrified.

Afterward she always believed it was Michael James's quick thinking that saved her father's life. Dr. Sutherland, the surgeon he'd told Maggie to contact, met them at the hospital. After a thorough examination he told Dr. Carter, ''You need a bypass, two in fact, immediately.''

Dr. Carter, despite being in a hospital bed, was quite his old self again. He seemed to understand and he nodded in agreement.

Ann Elizabeth and her mother, who had never heard of a bypass, were extremely apprehensive.

Michael took them aside and carefully explained.

"Two of Dr. Carter's blood vessels are defective and not enough oxygen is reaching his heart. Dr. Sutherland will replace them. And don't worry!" he said to their dismayed expressions. "Bypass surgery is relatively new, but it's almost always successful, even when five vessels are replaced at once. And you're lucky. Dr. Sutherland is an expert heart surgeon, the best in the business. That's why I wanted him."

The best surgeon. The best hospital, with all the necessary facilities and equipment. Available to her father who had served so many with inadequate facilities for so long.

Thank you, God.

Even so, she was still scared, and her mother had fallen apart. She didn't know what they would have done without Rob.

And Michael. "This is a good thing. He'll be better than ever," he kept saying. "You'll see."

He was right. In almost no time, it seemed, her father was home, and feeling so well it was hard to keep him on his limited exercise routine. As soon as he was out of danger, Rob returned to Sacramento and work. Ann Elizabeth and Maggie stayed to administer tender loving care.

Maggie was wonderful with him. "Sit out here, Grandpa. I'll read to you... I'd better walk with you... Are you crazy? I threw your cigarettes away!" He loved Maggie, and she seemed to have more influence on him than anyone.

"Don't worry so much," Michael said. "He's a doctor. He knows his limits."

Michael James. Such a nice young man. "A brilliant young man," Dr. Sutherland had confided, adding that he was very pleased Michael was to begin his residency under him at Georgia Baptist the next month.

"Maggie," Ann Elizabeth said, "I'd better go home to Rob. But why don't you stay and help Grandma? You've been doing most of the grocery shopping and you're so good with Grandpa."

Ann Elizabeth went home, glad that Maggie had agreed to remain. If she was there and Michael continued to haunt the house... Anything could happen.

She was dismayed when Maggie came home early in August. "Grandpa's fine and they don't need me anymore. And I have to register early to get the classes I want."

"Yes, but—" she hesitated "—you were enjoying Atlanta so much. I thought you might transfer to Spelman."

"Oh, Mom! You, too? That's what Michael asked me to do."

"He did? So you'd be near..." She caught herself, cleared her throat. "Do you like Michael?"

"Oh, sure. He's nice."

"But?"

Maggie frowned. "I get the feeling he wants to get serious and...well, I don't like him like that!"

Ann Elizabeth said nothing. She wasn't a pushy matchmaking mother, after all.

But she sighed. Now, she thought, I know how Mother felt when I refused to marry Dan.

29

November 1971

"How you spell yestiddy, Maggie?" The little boy looked up from his desk and licked his pencil. His kinky uncombed too-long hair stood out like a bush, his clothes were rumpled and none too clean, but the look on his face was intense, his eyes bright with enthusiasm. Maggie smiled. That was what drew her to these after-school study sessions. The eagerness of the youngsters who came.

"Yesterday," she said, enunciating it clearly and loudly enough for him to hear over the din of the others in the room. Dena was helping with math problems, and Leland was tutoring a group of fifth graders in history. "I'll write it for you." She wrote the word on the board, then pronounced it again, underlining each syllable as she did so. She watched while he laboriously copied it in the cursive writing he was just learning. "That's a mighty big word for a third grader. I'm proud of you, Ricky."

He grinned. "We got to write 'bout our trip to the park yisti—yes-ter-day. I want to get a *A*."

"Good for you. I'll check it when you finish," she said, and turned to help Marylee with spelling.

Maggie had been up since six that morning, as she was every Monday and Wednesday, her volunteer days. From seven to eight she stood in line at the school cafeteria, helping to serve the hungry kids who came for the free breakfast. Then back to campus for her two morning classes, lunch and her one afternoon class. After that she returned to Martin Luther King Elementary in Oakland for the after-school tutoring.

"Christ! You could skip it today," Sue Jekels, secretary of the Black Students' Union, had urged. "You'll miss our meeting. Anyway, you must be beat, hauling your ass over to that school every fucking minute."

But Maggie wasn't tired. She was bursting with energy. She moved about the small desks, perusing scattered books and papers, explaining, correcting and praising, invigorated by the air that reeked of chalk dust, pencil shavings and the damp clothes of children who'd braved the rain to get there. She felt refreshed, full of zeal. Given the right start, these kids could make it!

"That's very good," she said when she returned to check Ricky's paper. "Only you should capitalize the Y because that's the beginning of a sentence. And maybe we should change two words. We *went*, not *been*, to the park. And I saw, not seen, a duck." She then gave a short English lesson, explaining verb tenses as simply as she could, wondering all the while if this was too much for a third grader to absorb.

"You're not supposed to do that," Leland said as he and Dena climbed into Maggie's Volkswagen for the ride back to Berkeley. Leland was a slightly built young man with a creamy brown complexion. He was from Washington, D.C., where his parents were both teachers. Like Maggie, he was at Berkeley on an academic scholarship. He was bright, sincere and genuinely concerned about the plight of those who lacked the advantages he'd always had.

"Do what?" Maggie asked as she put the car in gear.

"Correct the way they say things. That's putting them down."

"Wrong. That's raising them up. Which is the point, isn't it? Why we're here?"

"Oh, Maggie, you know what I mean. This is their environment. If they use black English—"

"Don't give me that crap, Leland. That's poor English. Right, Dena?"

Dena, in the backseat, nodded vigorously. Dena was Maggie's roommate and they had made a bargain. She cut Maggie's hair and Maggie corrected her papers— particularly in English.

"And as long as I'm tutoring them, I mean to correct it," Maggie said. "I want them equipped to compete in the real world."

"The world they live in is pretty damn real," Leland said, "and if this is how people talk..." The argument continued all the way to the campus, with Dena, in the back seat, looking from one to the other, saying nothing.

As soon as Maggie parked the car, the three tumbled out and headed for room 3A in the Student Center, where the meeting was being held. They went in the back door and Bud Wilson gestured to Maggie. "Over here, babe."

She slipped into a seat beside him, mostly to avoid Jake Adams, who had also gestured. Jake had wandering hands.

Sue, at the front desk, gave her that I-knew-you'd-be-late scowl. She nudged Ted, the BSU president, who glanced at the latecomers and yelled, "Quiet!" over the din their entry had caused. "Okay, Sue. Let's wrap it up. Read the petition so everyone'll know what's happening.''

The petition was read, but not without interruptions.

"Fifty additional black professors?"

"You heard it, man. No token shit, you dig?" Sue, the fair-skinned daughter of a Denver dentist, seemed compelled to prove herself with proper gutter lingo.

"Yeah, but fifty? You're asking for that many?"

"Not asking. Demanding."

The talk flowed around her, and Maggie sat quietly listening, enveloped in the warmth of a fellowship she'd never before known. She was part of this. Not the odd one out in a class full of blondes, the last to be chosen or shunted off with the doofus rejects. And not like her Atlanta cousins' who-got-invited and who's-kissing-whom silliness. This group was real. Feeding and tutoring poor kids, petitioning for more black professors, expanding black studies, increasing the enrollment of black students, even those like Dena, who hadn't received the right preparation. Maggie was euphoric, exhilarated by the plans, the expectations. They were going to make the world better for black people. She was glad to be part of it and she reveled in the camaraderie.

The session ended with Ted reminding them that he wanted "every black ass on the quad at ten tommorrow morning when we're gonna bring our petition to the attention of the motherfuckin' head honky!"

Maggie filed out with the rest, refusing Jake's invitation to "take in a movie." She knew what *that* meant. She also refused Bud's suggestion to go to a bar. She joined Leland and Sue and a few others at a coffee shop where they continued the discussion. Leland wasn't exactly a boyfriend. More like a pal she enjoyed arguing with. A safe pal, too. Not as pushy as Ted or Bud, who always wanted to get into her pants.

The quad was full. There weren't that many black students at Berkeley. Maggie looked around. These were people she'd never seen before.

Dena nudged her with an elbow. "There's that guy."

"What guy?"

"You know. Black leather jacket. Chains. He's always at the breakfasts."

"Oh." Yes. She recognized that tough stance, legs apart, arms folded. He winked at her and she gave a wary smile. Of course he'd be at the breakfasts. It was his gang who had the idea of feeding the poor kids in the first place. "What's he doing here?" she asked.

"Leland says they got some of the people from the community to join us."

"I guess that makes sense," Maggie said. The more people, the greater the impact. But she felt uncomfortable. She didn't like crowds. And this was a noisy bunch. She couldn't even hear what was being said. She stood on tiptoe, trying to at least see. Her view was blocked by heads, shoulders and gesturing hands.

"Wanna see what's happening, babe?" In an instant she was hoisted onto Bud's wide shoulders. "That better, little mama?"

Well, not much. She had trouble maintaining her balance, and she didn't like the way he nuzzled her thigh. Yes, now she could see. But she still couldn't hear the exchange between Ted and the college president, drowned out as it was by calls from the audience. "Right on!" "You heard him, motherfucker!"

This wasn't right. The hostility bothered her. Maybe they should have chosen a committee to discuss issues with the president in his office. Not this angry shouting crowd. She could tell the president was a little scared. And who could blame him? Ted was shaking his fist at him. And Sue...my God, Sue had spit on him. Maggie, appalled, saw his face contort, saw him back away, then turn and enter the administration building. The crowd moved forward, but two guards emerged from the building, rifles raised, and Maggie was almost knocked from Bud's shoulders in the crush. She saw Ted lift one hand in a "follow me" gesture as he started to run. With a great roar, the crowd followed.

Maggie had no idea where they were going and kept saying, "Let me down, Bud, let me down!"

"I gotcha, babe! Don't worry," he answered, and taking a firm grip on her legs, jubilantly ran with the crowd. "Hold on, kid."

Maggie, truly scared, held on. If she fell from her perch, she would surely be trampled.

Now she insisted. "No! Put me down."

He did so, but clutched her hand tightly, pulling her along.

The bookstore. That was where they were heading. Someone inside shut the heavy glass door. But someone else—that guy in the leather jacket—smashed it with something hard. A gun? The crowd broke through. Bud's long legs had carried them ahead of the others and they were among the first to reach it. She felt a jab of pain in her arm as they surged through the door, but she paid it no mind as she struggled to free herself from Bud's grip. This time he didn't resist. "Go to it, babe," he yelled, and started yanking books from the shelves. Everybody seemed to be in a frenzy. Books were dumped, torn, trampled. The cash register flew from its hinges and a file cabinet was knocked over, its contents scattered.

This was madness. Maggie tried to make her way to the door, but was pushed back every time, jammed against the wall. She didn't know how long she stayed there, trapped, watching the destruction around her, helpless to stop it or to walk away. Then she heard the siren. Police whistles. She felt relief, but not for long. They'd be after her, too.

"The pigs! Split, mothers!" The crowd rapidly dispersed, each on his or her own, running in all directions. Maggie ran, too. At last the way had been cleared and she made a dash for the door. But the riot squad had arrived now and they were entering the store, penning those they could surround for formal arrest. Frantic, Maggie ducked under a blue-coated arm and made her escape. He turned to follow, but someone tripped him. Maggie heard him curse as he fell. But she'd gained precious seconds. She ran faster, not sure where she was going, just away from the shouts, whistles and pounding feet.

The feet were gaining on her. She had to hide. Please, God, she prayed. As if in answer, she rounded a small building and an open door yawned before her. She tumbled through it, almost knocking over the young man on the other side. She slammed the door shut and gasped, "Hide me. Please. Quick!"

Steve Pearson wasn't sure why he did it. He'd heard the police sirens and figured there was another disturbance on campus. Either the peaceniks or the blacks protesting, raising hell about something. He was damn sick of these disruptions.

"Please," she said again, clutching his arm.

It was something about her, the terror on her face,

the appeal in her eyes, the human need that touched the human in him. "This way," he said, and led her into an adjoining room, grabbed a white smock and helped her into it. He pushed her toward the sink and handed her a test tube, funnel and pitcher of water. "Pretend to be measuring something," he said just as the door burst open and they were confronted by a scowling policeman.

"Anybody come in here?" he demanded.

The girl never turned. She concentrated on pouring the clear water through the funnel into the test tube, as if her life depended on measuring correctly.

Steve tried to register astonishment. "Nobody here but us," he said, gesturing toward the girl.

"Damn! She got away," the policeman muttered. "Sorry to disturb you, sir," he added, giving a little salute as he hastened off.

Steve crossed to the girl. Her hands were shaking, still fiddling with the water.

"It's okay. You're safe now. You're—" Seeing the blood, he stopped.

She turned to him. "Th-thank you," she whispered just as the pitcher and tube slipped from her hand and crashed into the sink. He caught her just as she started to fall.

There was a funny monotonous sound like the hum of running water and a very strong smell she couldn't identify. Maggie opened her eyes. She was lying on a leather couch and a young heavyset man with very blond hair and a very freckled face was peering down at her.

"Like I told you, man, she's okay," he drawled. "She's coming to."

"Good. How do you feel?" Another young man moved nearer. Tall, sandy hair, blue eyes. The man she'd bumped into and— Oh, God! She tried to sit up.

"You're okay," he said. "Lie still."

"Nah," said the other man. "Let her sit up. Fix that coffee now and put in lots of sugar," he said as he helped her to a sitting position. "Don't want you to go into shock," he explained.

"I won't," she said. "I'm okay."

"Yeah, but that was a deep gash. You lost a lot of blood. Sorry I had to cut your shirt."

She gasped. Her left arm was bandaged; the bloody sleeve of her shirt hung loose. She remembered that jolt of pain when Bud had pulled her through the door. Broken glass. "I think I cut myself."

That seemed to amuse him. "She thinks she cut herself," he said to the tall man who held a mug of coffee to her lips.

"Sip slowly," he commanded, sitting beside her.

"What y'all doing, anyway?" The freckled man asked in what she now realized was a distinctly Southern accent. "You think you gonna bust up the war by busting up one puny little bookstore?"

"Shut up, Roy," the other guy said. "Don't be agitating."

"I ain't agitating. And I'm with 'em on 'Nam. It's one mixed-up hellhole that somebody ought to squash. But that's got nothing to do with the bookstore and—"

"Shut up," the other man said again, and smiled at her. "Feel better?"

She nodded. The hot coffee did make her feel better.

"I'm Steve Pearson," he said. "And this tub of lard," he added, pointing to his friend, "is my scuba-diving buddy, Roy Jackson." He gestured at her bandaged arm. "When you fainted and I saw all that blood, I panicked. But I didn't think you'd want to go to the clinic."

"Oh, no." A tremor of fear ran through her.

"So I called Roy. He was a medic in Vietnam."

Roy grinned. "Yeah, I done my time in that goddamn place and now Uncle Sam's paying me off. Premed. And if you guys would just protest somewhere else and not bust up this fine insti—"

"Roy, why don't you get us some food?" Steve broke in. "Aren't you hungry?" he asked Maggie.

Surprisingly she was. Steve dug into his pocket and sent Roy for burgers, despite his protests. "Don't see why I have to be the errand boy when the whole damn campus is crawling with cops."

While Roy was gone, Maggie managed to get a good look at the room. There were a half-dozen aquariums containing plants, as well as fish and other sea creatures. Shells, rocks, funnels, test tubes, measuring and monitoring devices. And that very strong smell. Formaldehyde.

Steve told her this was a marine-biology lab. He was doing graduate work at Scripps and was temporarily based at Berkeley for a special project on the northern waters.

Roy returned with hamburgers, french fries and shakes, which the three hungrily devoured. He said cops were still patrolling the campus and she'd better stay put for a while.

"That butterfly bandage ought to hold if you don't mess with it," he said. "You should be okay. But if you have any problems," he added in the voice of a professional, "take a couple of aspirins and call me in the morning."

"Get out of here!" Steve ordered.

"Wait!" Maggie called. "Thank you, Roy. You've been a real lifesaver."

"Piece of cake."

Yes, she thought, compared to what he must have dealt with in Vietnam.

After he left she turned to Steve. "It's really you I have to thank. For saving me from the police, for calling Roy and—"

"Piece of cake," he mimicked.

She glanced toward the windows. The sky was darkening, threatening rain. And the campus was still teeming with police. "Is it all right if I stay here a little longer?" she asked hesitantly.

"Sure. Stick around. I'll enjoy the company."

"But you were leaving when I burst in."

"So, I've changed my mind," he said, smiling. It was a sweet smile—warm, boyish and altogether genuine. She liked it. And she liked his manner. Casual, friendly, as if she really wasn't interfering with whatever he'd planned to do. She wondered what that was. "So you're at Scripps in La Jolla" she said. "Is that your home?"

"Not really. I'm from Boston."

"So how come you don't sound like Ted Kennedy?"

"Aha! A linguist, are you?"

"Doesn't take a linguist to recognize a Boston accent—or to know that Roy comes from the Deep South. But you..." She studied him, attracted to his clean-shaven face, strong rugged features, the keen direct gaze of his blue eyes. He really was handsome. "You...you have one of those all-around could-be-from-anywhere accents."

He laughed. "You got it. That's me."

"But I *don't* get it."

"Boy from a broken home. Mom's married to a Boston lawyer, and that's where she lives when she's not traveling or wintering in Florida. My dad's usually in New York or San Francisco, but he has a little place in Monterey. I've been kicked around from one place to another since I was ten."

She considered. "Broken home? A rather privileged one, I'd say."

"Yeah. You got anything against privileged white males?"

"Of course not," she said, and wondered if she was lying.

"Good. How about a game of gin? You play?" he asked, producing a deck of cards.

"Sure."

Seated on the old leather sofa, her feet curled under her, his jacket over her shoulders, the rain beating against the window, the hum of six aquariums, and a man laughing as he beat the socks off her in a card game, she felt a strange sense of contentment.

And joy.

30

Only Dena knew when Maggie, still wearing Steve's jacket, returned to the dorm late that night. Only Dena, sworn to secrecy, was told where she'd been.

Dena herself was full of news. "I thought you were gone for sure. That cop almost had his hands on you. But that guy in the leather jacket tripped him. What's his name—Ken something? Anyway, he just stuck out his leg and that cop went down. When he got to his feet, Ken had disappeared. And so had you, thank goodness! Me? I was just standing on the science building steps watching the whole thing like I didn't know nothin' 'bout it. I was way behind, you see, never got into the bookstore, for which, as my ma says, I wants to thank the man upstairs. When I heard the sirens I ran to the science building fast as I could, 'cause I knew the shit was gonna fly! Ted and Lucille and Jake and some others got arrested, and Sue's collecting bail money. But the honkies are mad as hell, and some kids are likely to be expelled."

Before she got out of bed the next morning Maggie was accosted by Sue. "Girl, where'd you go? The fucking pigs were all over the place."

Maggie displayed her bandaged arm. "I got cut. Had to—"

"Hope you didn't go to the clinic!"

"I'm not crazy, Sue. I, um, had it taken care of. Privately."

"Good. You got any cash? I mean real cash." Sue knew Maggie was always good for a touch. She wasn't into drugs or even clothes, and hardly spent any of that hefty allowance she received. "Ted and some of the others—"

"I heard." Maggie gave her a good-size check. There, but for the grace of God...

After lunch she went to the marine-biology lab to return Steve's jacket. She was surprised to encounter several people going in or out of the various rooms in the small one-story building. Last night, sitting in that room with Steve while the rain hammered the window, it was as if they were the only people in the entire world. She felt a peculiar sense of anticipation as she opened his door.

He wasn't there. A girl in a clean white smock stood by one of the aquariums and appeared to be feeding the fish. She turned and smiled. "Hi," she said, giving Maggie a questioning look.

"I just wanted to return this. It's Steve's."

"Oh. Just dump it over there." The girl waved toward the sofa and returned to her task.

"Please tell..." Maggie hesitated. She'd already thanked him. What else was there to say? "Thank you," she said, and the girl nodded.

Well, that was that, Maggie thought, and wondered why she felt so disappointed. He was nice and he'd done her a big favor, but... Marine biologist. White. This was a big campus. She'd probably never see him again.

She saw him two days later. She was coming down the library steps with a big group—Sue, Ted, Dena,

Leland and others. They had just learned there were to be no reprisals. Word was the administration felt it unfair to punish only the few who'd been caught when so many others were involved. Professor Lamumba said the honkies didn't want to be accused of racism, since not one white student had been suspended when they'd held that peace march last month. Whatever the reason, they were off the hook with only a stern warning. The group was going to a coffee shop to celebrate.

Maggie was walking with Leland, a little ahead of the others, when she saw Steve coming up the walk.

"Let's hurry or all the booths will be taken," she said, clutching Leland's arm and hurrying right past Steve as if she didn't see him. She fixed her eyes on Leland and began to talk like crazy, hardly aware of what she was saying. She thought she heard Steve halt and call out, but she couldn't be sure. She hurried on, hoping he hadn't seen her.

Mostly she hoped he hadn't seen her see him.

It bothered her. If he knew she'd seen him... She sat with the others in the coffee-shop booth, not hearing anything that was said.

Late that afternoon she again made her way to the lab, this time knocking softly on his door.

"Come in." His voice. She entered, feeling ashamed and uneasy. How could she explain? Thank goodness he was alone. He was wearing a white lab coat and peering at something through a microscope.

"Hello."

He turned quickly, his face beaming. "Hi! I'm glad you came back. Sharon said you brought my jacket. Sorry I missed you. How's your arm?"

"Okay. It's fine." Overwhelming relief. He didn't know she'd seen him.

"Good. I wanted to phone you but... Do you know that all you told me was that your name's Maggie? Not Jones or Brown or which dorm or anything." He smiled. "Not much to go on when you want to call a girl for a date."

"Oh." Warm bubbles of delight. Apprehension?

"I thought I got lucky this morning when I spotted you at the library. But you were in a hurry and totally involved in your conversation. Anyway, you didn't see me and—"

"I saw you." She couldn't lie to him.

He seemed stunned. "You saw me? But you didn't...speak."

"I didn't think it was wise."

"Oh?" He was plainly waiting for an explanation, which she found hard to give. How could she tell him that if he'd stopped to talk about her arm or the other night and maybe lingered, Sue and the others would have interrogated her and she didn't want to get into it with them.

She fumbled for the right words. Fraternizing with whites was strictly forbidden.

"It would've been...awkward."

"Why?"

"It's...well, we blacks don't...oh, you know how things are with us."

"No. How are they?"

That made her angry. "Prejudice! Discrimination! We've had to fight like mad for just a little bit of progress."

"Right."

"So we're still fighting."

"And?"

"You..." She paused. "White people don't really

understand the problem. It's up to us blacks. We have to stick together if we're going to put a stop to racism."

"I see." His smile was unamused. "How racist can you get? If you can't even speak to a white person?"

"It's not that! Oh, you *don't* understand."

"Right. I don't. Just tell me one thing, will you?"

She waited, poised to defend the stand her group had taken.

"What's your last name?"

"Metcalf," she said, thrown off balance.

"Maggie Metcalf. And where do you live, Maggie Metcalf?"

"Why?"

"So I'll know how to get in touch with you."

"You didn't hear me, did you!"

"Sure. You said—"

"Then you didn't get it. It isn't... They...well, you're white. I can't date you. All hell would break loose if my friends found out."

"Then we can't go public, can we?" This time his smile was real, and it reached out to her.

Enchantment. Maybe it was the secrecy of the courtship. Sneaking off in separate cars to meet someplace they weren't known. Coded messages over the dorm's public phone. Making plans that involved only the two of them.

Maybe it was the magic of San Francisco, just across the bay but a world away from Berkeley. They walked in Golden Gate Park and stopped for tea at the Japanese Tea Garden, once spent a whole day at the aquarium where she was fascinated by Steve's stories about the lives and habitats of sea urchins. They went to the latest plays and to the opera.

She took Steve home with her for Thanksgiving. Dena, too, because she'd already invited her, and Dena knew about Steve.

"What about your parents?" Dena asked. "Won't they object to your dating a white boy?"

"As many white friends as they have, I doubt they'd object. Anyway, they'll probably think he's one of those blacks who looks more white than black—like my cousins—and I don't think I'll tell them any different," she said, and wondered why. Was she ashamed of Steve? Of dating a white guy?

Ann Elizabeth reacted just as Maggie knew she would. It was a lovely quiet weekend. No explosive arguments like they got into whenever she brought Ted and Sue. Steve golfed with Rob, and she and Dena went shopping with Mom. They sat around the fire at night, watching television, playing cards or Scrabble. A delightful weekend.

But just before they left, Rob took Maggie aside. "What's going on? You deserting us poor niggers?"

"Stop using that word! And what are you talking about?" she asked, although she knew.

He grinned. "Well, I thought I was giving one of our poor black but almost white brothers a treat. You understand—taking him out to this nice golf course where don't many of us go. We get to talking. New York, Monterey—winter golfing in Florida, for Christ's sake! I get to thinking what is this? This cat's sure enough one of them. Way up the ladder, too! And I ask myself what's my little black-power daughter pulling here? Has she deserted us for the big bad white establishment and—"

"Oh, Dad! I should have known you'd say something like that!" Now she knew why she hadn't mentioned

Steve's race. "What's wrong with my having a white friend?"

"Absolutely nothing. In fact, I haven't had such a pleasant weekend with you since you entered Berkeley. Glad you're joining the big picture. Does this mean we won't have any more knock-down-drag-out black-only rhetoric from the great Professor Mumbo Jumbo?"

"Oh, for goodness' sake! My dating…being friends with Steve has nothing to do with what we— Oh, stop laughing! There's no use talking to you, and I gotta go!" She stormed out to kiss her mother and join Steve and Dena for the ride back to Berkeley.

One week when Steve's dad was in town they had dinner with him at the Top of the Mark. He was an older handsomer version of his son. Steve will look like that, Maggie thought, when his sandy hair is tinged with gray. James Reginald Pearson, of Pearson Associates, was the epitome of a mover and shaker—dynamic, alert and affable to all of them. To Steve, Maggie and the young actress who was with him. He was particularly attentive to Maggie, however, often directing his conversation toward her. When they parted he kissed her on the cheek, said she was "a stunning beauty," and Steve "a lucky guy."

She began to see Steve more frequently, at least four times a week. They talked and talked, lingering over candlelit dinners at quiet exclusive out-of-the-way restaurants. It wasn't enough.

"It seems so…unfinished," Steve said. "I hate it every time I put you in that Volkswagen and you drive away from me."

"Me, too," Maggie admitted.

"How about Christmas? Couldn't we spend it together? Just the two of us. We could stay at my dad's little place in Monterey.''

She hesitated. Christmas was family time. They'd planned to go to Atlanta, visiting with her grandparents. But to be with Steve…alone together…just the two of them. Two whole weeks. No driving away in separate cars.

Explaining to her parents would be difficult. She decided to do it by phone and at the last minute.

''Mom, I'm calling to tell you I won't be home tomorrow.''

''But you have to be here then!'' Ann Elizabeth, in the middle of a bridge game with Rob and Chuck and Cora Samples, had picked up the phone in the living room. ''My daughter,'' she said in apology to the others, and then to Maggie, ''You know our flight's for six the next morning. You have to be here to—''

''I'm not going.''

''What?''

''I'm going to Monterey. I've been invited to spend Christmas with…friends.''

''What friends?''

''A friend, really. Steve.''

''Ste…'' Good Lord! If Rob knew Maggie was going off with some guy, he'd blow his top! Ann Elizabeth shot a glance at him. He was deep in a discussion with Chuck about the last hand. ''Listen, Maggie, we need to talk. I'll call you tonight.''

''You can't, Mom. I'll be gone. We're driving down and—''

''Wait. Let me get to another phone.'' She told Rob she couldn't hear and to please hang up when she picked up the other phone. In Rob's den she listened for the click that shut off their voices before she spoke.

"Maggie, isn't this a last-minute decision? One that you haven't thought through?"

"No. I thought about it. I just didn't tell you because I knew you'd try to stop me." That was Maggie, honest to the bone. "And, Mom, I want to go." A cry from the heart. Ann Elizabeth had met Steve just that one weekend. He seemed nice, but... "Oh, honey, you see Steve all the time. Your grandfather—"

"I don't see him all the time and we never... Oh, Mom, I'm sick of this sneaking off to San Francisco and sneaking back and—"

Ann Elizabeth's heart stood still. Sneaking off. "To motels?" she asked.

"No, Mom, not to motels. Just to talk, to be together."

She felt a wave of relief. But... "I don't understand. Sneaking?" Apprehension cut like a knife. "He...he's married?"

"Oh, no, Mom! You know I wouldn't go out with a married man. It's just...well, you know the crap I'd get if Sue and the rest of them knew I was dating a white guy."

"Steve's...white." She'd assumed... Well, it just hadn't crossed her mind. Maggie was so involved with everything black.

"I thought you knew. Dad does, and he doesn't care."

"He cares about you going off alone with some boy, black or white, and I don't like it, either! Maggie, listen to me, you—"

"Ann Elizabeth!" Rob called. "Let's get on with this game. Talk to Maggie later."

"Maggie, we need a chance to finish this conversation."

"I have to go, Mom. I'll call you at Grandma's. Love you." Maggie hung up.

Ann Elizabeth dialed the dorm.

"Maggie Metcalf? Oh, she left at noon."

So she hadn't called from the dorm. She was already on her way. It was too late.

"Ann Elizabeth!"

She went back into the living room, picked up her cards. Why, in every major crisis of her life, was she in the middle of a bridge game? The talk flowed around her, but all she heard was Maggie. *I'm tired of sneaking.* All this fighting for integration and she had to sneak—

"It's your bid, Ann Elizabeth."

"Oh. What did you say? A club?" She studied her cards. "One no trump." Anyway, she didn't care what color he was. Or did she? She thought of Michael James—such a nice young man. If only...

An old oft-repeated phrase surfaced in her mind: White men have no respect for black women. A white man was taking her nineteen-year-old daughter off and... Oh, God! She and Maggie had talked about sex, condoms, birth control. They'd laughed and agreed the best prevention was abstinence. But now...oh, dear, things were different now.

More important for the moment—what would she tell Rob? "Christmas in Monterey," she said, "with friends. Lots of friends."

She could lie even if Maggie couldn't.

Maggie had been to Monterey several times with her parents. They'd driven along Carmel's famous seventeen-mile drive, marveling at the spectacular view of sea, sand and rocks. She had wondered about the people who lived in those grand houses that seemed to melt into the cliffs—remote, isolated, barely visible through the eucalyptus trees that surrounded them. She shouldn't have been surprised when Steve turned into a circular drive leading to one of those houses. But he was such a regular down-to-earth guy she'd forgotten he was more privileged than most.

"This is your father's 'little place'?" she asked.

He nodded, apparently not noticing the sarcasm. He touched the remote control and drove into an underground four-car garage.

"All ours for now," he said as he led her up the steps and into the house. "Dad's housekeeper is on vacation. Come on, let me show you where everything is."

It was so well designed that it seemed smaller than it really was. Three bedrooms, each with its own bath, a well-equipped kitchen, dining and living rooms.

"You can have any room you want, but I thought you might like this," he said, leading her into what was obviously the master bedroom. Spacious, with so many built-ins—window seats, cupboards, bookcases—that the only furniture needed was the big bed and the small sofas on either side of the stone fireplace. Everything— the carpet, the walls, sheer curtains and spread—was a pale green, all beautifully matched. "Like it?" he asked.

She nodded. The room seemed to invite her.

He pulled her to him, kissed her on the nose. "It gets a little cool at night. You'd be cozy here with a good fire. And me?"

An invitation. No demands. No urging. "I'll think about it," she said. "After I've checked out the other rooms. Or maybe I'll take this and you can have one of the others."

He chuckled. "Your choice, my sweet. Let's look in the fridge first. Dad told Mrs. Mack to leave it stocked."

It was. They made sandwiches, heated the cream of mushroom soup and opened a bottle of wine. They took their meal to the round coffee table in the sunken living room and ate before a roaring fire.

Maggie kicked off her shoes and sat cross-legged on the floor. She ran a hand over the thick pale-green carpet. Somebody sure liked that cool serene shade. His father or some impersonal decorator?

"Does your father spend a lot of time here?" she asked.

"Hardly." He added another log to the fire and dusted his hands. "Maybe a day or two, three or four times a year. Sometimes a week or so."

She looked around. "And all this just sits and waits?"

He laughed. "With the able assistance of Mrs. Mack." He refilled their wineglasses and sat beside her.

She took a sip of wine, pondering. "Nobody really lives here. Or even comes very often. That's a shame. It's so lovely."

"And lonely."

"You think so?"

"I know so. It's a great place to dump a kid when one parent's touring Europe and the other's running to meetings or chasing his latest lady."

"Oh." So that was how it had been. Her heart ached for a poor little rich kid shut away in this grand isolated house. "There must have been other kids," she said. In those other isolated houses.

"Yeah. I'd see them on the beach. They had their own friends. I never seemed to fit in."

"Like my cousins in Atlanta," she said. "I never fit in with them, either."

He smiled at her. "So you were a misfit, too? Anyway, I found the fish more interesting."

"Books were my escape," she said, and added reflectively, "Places aren't lonely. People are."

"Yes. Until they find the right person to be with." He set both their glasses on the table and took her in his arms. "I'm not lonely now."

Neither was she. That night, lying in the wide bed in the pale-green room, lit by the flickering fire, with the sound of the ocean pounding against the rocks, she responded to his gentle caresses with a passion she hadn't known she possessed. Cried out his name and reveled in the wonder of fulfillment.

Steve awoke the next morning feeling a rush of tenderness for the girl beside him. He knew it had been the first time for her. Yet she'd never hesitated, had responded with an ardor that touched his heart. He felt her stir against his chest, stretch, and open those big brown eyes to look at him.

"Hello," he said.

"Hello."

"Lonely?"

"No. Oh, no!" The glow in her eyes, the feel of her hand on his cheek, told him much more.

He kissed the palm of that hand, brushed his lips against hers, against the lobe of her ear, and whispered, "I'm glad you're spending Christmas with me and I... What's the matter, sweetheart?"

Did the guilt show on her face? Christmas was family time. Grandpa would miss her.

But this...Steve...last night. She wouldn't have missed it for the world. She wanted to make Steve as happy as he made her. "A Christmas tree!" she said, kissing him. "I was thinking we don't have a Christmas tree."

They went into town and bought a small tree that filled the house with the pungent odor of pine. They bought tiny white lights, golden bells and ornaments, two tiny white birds and an angel for the top. They decorated the tree and placed their presents under it.

"Is there a church around here that has a candlelight service?" she asked, wondering why it was so important to retain the family traditions.

They found one. The church was small but filled to capacity and rich with the Christmas spirit. They sang the traditional hymns, lit their individual candles and held them up like stars in the darkened church "as your light, your love, shines in a darkened world," said the minister. It was all very moving, she thought as they walked out with the smiling throng, each carrying a little scroll tied with a red ribbon—their own personal messages. Maggie's read, "Whatsoever things are good, think on these things."

They opened their gifts on Christmas morning. For him, a sweater and two books, one a treatise by a marine biologist that she knew would fascinate him. The other...

"Edna St. Vincent Millay?" he asked.

"I want to introduce you," Maggie said. Though he was as avid a reader as she, he never read poetry.

For her, a gold charm bracelet with a tiny gold fish dangling from it. Which she loved. And several boxes containing all the gear she'd need for scuba diving. Which scared her.

"I don't even swim very well, and never underwater! I couldn't."

"You have to. I want to introduce you to my fish. Don't worry. You'll be fine. I'll teach you."

He did teach her. A few times in the swimming pool first, "so you'll get used to the face mask and breathing from the oxygen tank." He was patient and gentle as he strapped the tank to her back and explained everything. "Trust me," he said. And she did trust him as she went under.

It was a wonderful sensation. Everything in slow motion. She felt a keen awareness of touch, of breathing. She could hear the bubbles each time she exhaled. She gained confidence. This was fun. And once again, she was glad of her natural hairstyle.

"Ready for the ocean?" Steve asked a few days later.

"Yes!" Ready and eager, even though it meant getting used to wearing a wet suit.

"We'll go out to the point," Steve said.

Point Lobos. The wind-whipped cypress and pine trees bending forever landward, the tall rugged cliffs with crevices, rocks and hidden coves forever descending into the sea, the endless churning ocean stretching toward a distant sky. There were a few people about, snorkeling or walking along the cliff, a few birds fluttering near the edge of the water, sea otters sunning themselves. And yet... "it seems so untouched," she said to Steve, marveling.

"Not quite untouched," he said, and told her how a thriving abalone business had stripped the spot of its abalone and how its beaches had once been the site of a processing plant for whales brought in from the ocean. "Thank God it was saved from a would-be developer by a farsighted millionaire who bought the land and donated it to the state."

"I'm glad," she said as she followed him down to

one of the hidden coves. To destroy such natural beauty would be sacrilegious.

Why wasn't she more frightened? she wondered as Steve strapped the tank to her back, adjusted her face mask, helped her slip on the fins. Because Steve was there beside her, his eyes smiling at her through his own mask, promising wonders that made her excited and eager to explore. She felt safe with him holding her hand as they waded out into the surf, going deeper and deeper. There was a moment of panic when she went under and the water closed around her. But Steve was with her, eyes smiling, fingers raised in an okay sign.

It *was* okay. Her wet suit was comfortable and surprisingly warm in the cold ocean. A wonderful sensation of freedom possessed her, and her breathing became rhythmic and hypnotic as she gazed about at a strange new world, mysterious and intriguing. A school of fish, a shimmery stream of liquid silver in their togetherness. Splashes of color—purple and orange starfish, and vibrant vegetation. One plant, with tendrils of a greenish iridescent color, like baby fingers all in a circle, seemed to draw her. When she reached out to touch it, it closed in on itself.

Amazing!

She was reluctant to go when Steve signaled that it was time to surface.

Roy and his girlfriend came down for a couple of days. They all went scuba diving, made a fire and had a picnic on the beach. She enjoyed their company, but was glad when they left and she was alone again with Steve.

Alone together. Days walking on the beach, exploring the ocean. At night they spent long hours lounging by the fire. Talking. He told her about the mysteries of the sea and the wonders of nature. "The plant that closed when you touched it was an anemone. Do you know we can tell time by them? Their petals open at different times, the red ones at two, the blue at four and so on." She told him about her tutoring sessions, about Ricky and Marylee. They read aloud from the book of poetry she'd given him.

It was as if their hearts were stretching, reaching into each other's worlds.

31

Ann Elizabeth paced the floor, glancing out the front window now and then. Waiting for Maggie. *We're gonna have a come-to-Jesus meeting!*

Taking off like that with some man we don't even know.

That one time he was here for Thanksgiving—why didn't I ask about him, his parents, his background?

Oh, no, not me! I'm not like my mother who always gave my friends the third degree. Who's your mother, father, who are your grandparents, and what does your father do? She had poor Sadie Clayton squirming, and if it hadn't been for Dad...

My daughter's away with some man I don't know anything about! Who he is, how he feels about her— *nothing!*

Christmas was a nightmare. Two whole weeks of pretending I was happy when I was worried sick!

Worried about Maggie. Some of those kids are into heavy drinking and drugs and I don't know what else. Maggie's a sensible girl, but...what was it Mother always said? *Lie down with dogs and you'll get fleas.*

Oh, Maggie! Maggie!

And I lied to Rob. "These young people... It's only natural that Maggie wants to be with her friends."

I'm not sure he believed me. I saw that thoughtful forbidding look even before he asked, "What friends?"

Ann Elizabeth hadn't found it easy to lie and pretend, when her insides were topsy-turvy with apprehension.

And now... She and Rob were back from Atlanta, and Maggie had phoned last night, sounding casual and relaxed. Lighthearted. "Wonderful Christmas, Mom! I'll tell you all about it when I get home. Tomorrow. I've got a couple of days before school starts again."

Ann Elizabeth had tried to seem just as lighthearted. "Great, honey. We're looking forward to hearing about it," was all she'd said, because Rob had been sitting right there looking at her. Now she glanced at the clock, hoping Rob would still be on the golf course when Maggie got in. And before she had to go to the airport to pick up her parents, who were following them to Sacramento.

"The weather's milder there, and Will's patients won't be able to call him," her mother had said. "They don't seem to know that he needs to rest."

Life's become a juggling act, Ann Elizabeth thought. I've got to give Maggie hell, while at the same time shield my parents from Maggie's problem, and Maggie from Rob's wrath.

If I possibly can!

But just wait until I get hold of her! How could she be so inconsiderate! So foolish! So stupid! Oh, here she is!

Maggie jumped out of her car and ran into the house, dragging her duffel bag, just as usual. "Oh, Mom! It was wonderful!" She dropped her bag and threw her arms around her mother, swinging her round and round.

Ann Elizabeth, trying to catch her breath, gasped,

"Maggie, wait! We need to talk. Do you know how *worried* I've been? And your father—"

"I told you where I was going. There was no need to worry."

"Oh, sure. No need to worry. My daughter's just gone off I don't know where, probably sleeping with this guy—"

"Don't, Mom!" Maggie put her hands over her ears and shut her eyes. "I've just spent the happiest two weeks of my life and I won't let you spoil it."

Oh, Maggie, Maggie. Ann Elizabeth felt a surge of tenderness for her daughter. For her trusting innocence, her joy. She didn't *want* to spoil it, but she had to make her face facts. "Honey, you don't know…men. Maybe it was that way for you. But for him, it might have been just another weekend, another—"

Maggie shook her head. "Steve isn't like that."

"You don't know—" She broke off. "Maggie, listen to me—"

"No. You listen." Maggie took her hand and drew her to the sofa. "Sit down and let me tell you how it is. This wasn't a spur-of-the-moment thing. Steve and I have been dating for over two months now and—"

"Two months! You think you can know everything about a person in two months?"

"You fell in love with Dad the first night you met him, didn't you?"

Love? Ann Elizabeth, stunned into silence, stared at her daughter.

She couldn't believe this was her solemn intense Maggie. Not deep in a book. Not ranting about the plight of blacks or the injustices of the world. Not even quietly laughing and flirting, as she had in Atlanta—but she'd been unmoved and uninvolved then, Ann Elizabeth realized. She was involved now. Radiantly alive, bursting with the kind of happiness that comes once in a lifetime—if you're lucky.

Ann Elizabeth, seeing the stars in her daughter's eyes, hearing the joy in her voice, couldn't bring herself to diminish that happiness. But her heart ached with fear.

Maybe, if she'd stopped her from going...

As if she could have! Maggie had already been on her way when she called.

She followed Maggie into her room and watched her pull out the clothes she'd brought home to wash. "It's so unbelievable, Mom!" Maggie took out a pair of jeans and sand flew everywhere as she shook them.

"Maggie, you shouldn't...!" Well, no use stopping her now. She'd get out the vacuum cleaner and—

"When you look at the ocean... Oh, you know, there are fish of course, but I'd always somehow thought that, underneath all that water, everything else was dead. But it's not. It's so alive! Even the plants. And so much color. You just can't imagine! Steve kept saying the sea was murky and I couldn't see like I would if I was in a place like Bermuda or Hawaii. Steve says the waters there are so clear that..." Ann Elizabeth listened to her daughter's chatter, punctuated with "Steve says." Steve. He was the joy. Like Rob had been for her that very first week. As if it were yesterday, she remembered him saying, *You are a princess. You live in a grand castle, surrounded by a high wall.* She had responded with the same teasing rapport, *I hope a prince can rescue me.* She had touched the wings on his shoulder. "I thought he came swooping from the clouds..."

She'd known how to tease and flirt. She'd been doing it since she was twelve.

But Maggie didn't know the game. Steve was her first

real boyfriend. And things were too deep, too soon. Too
complicated. Dear God, things were so different now.
When she was nineteen, no single couple would have
dared go blithely off together for a weekend. Certainly
no black-white couple. She thought of her mother's
comment: *We've always been in each other's beds.*
True. But at nineteen I was protected by both segregation and convention. And I'm not equipped to deal with
now—all this sexual freedom and integration and a
daughter with her head in the clouds. Dear Lord, how
much does Steve mean to her?

More important, what does she mean to him?

"You just can't imagine the beauty! Steve says it's
even more incredible down deeper, but he only let me
go down fifty feet. He—"

"Fifty feet!" Ann Elizabeth exclaimed, grappling
with a new fear. Underneath the surface of the ocean!
"Weren't you scared?"

"With Steve right there? Oh, Mom, he's so protec-
tive." Maggie paused, gathering up her laundry. "Gentle and caring," she whispered, as if she spoke to herself.

The words echoed in Ann Elizabeth's heart. Like
Rob, that first night in Tuskegee.

But I was married! And Maggie…

No, Maggie wouldn't be scared. Solemn and intense,
yes, but never scared. Even when she was twelve. What
had she said of Anna Karenina? *She was so silly. Why
didn't she just go on and be happy, instead of practically going crazy because those society ladies wouldn't
speak to her?* No. Maggie would plunge right in. Into
a swirling ocean or—against convention—into bed with
a man she cared about. No matter that they weren't

married or that he was white. Not caring what anybody said.

Only...she did care. *I'm tired of sneaking around.* She cared what her peers, her black radical friends, thought, didn't she? And now... What was going to happen now?

"Mom, can I wash this with the other things?" Maggie held up a bright red sweatshirt.

"Set the dial on cold water, and I think it'll be okay," she replied automatically, her mind focusing on how to say what she needed to say. But there wasn't time now. She glanced at the clock on Maggie's bedside table. Ten-forty-five. Rob would be back from his golf game any minute.

"I'm glad you came home this morning, Maggie. Your grandparents are arriving today."

"Grandma and Grandpa? Great!" Maggie paused in the doorway with her bundle of clothes. "When?"

"Plane's due in at noon. So, as soon as you get those clothes in the washing machine, come back here and vacuum up all this sand. And change the sheets in the guest room for me, will you?"

"Sure, Mom."

"And Maggie?" Maggie turned, waiting. "Listen, there are some things..." No, she couldn't rush it. "We'll have to talk, but later. I'd better get the vegetables ready now." She knew she'd have to be careful of what she said to Maggie and how she said it. This was the first time she'd seen her serious daughter so full of joy. She didn't want to break her heart with warnings and dire predictions. She wondered at herself. How ironic that she should be more concerned about a daughter's broken heart than her lost virginity.

Rob came home just as she was preparing to leave

for the airport. "You're picking up the folks? I'll get the meat on the spit. Dinner about four, huh?"

She nodded and was picking up her purse and car keys when Maggie, having thrust her clothes into the dryer, burst into the kitchen.

"Hi, Dad!"

"Hi. So the prodigal has returned." Rob put down the rod that was to hold the pork loin and glanced over his shoulder. "How was Monterey?"

"Great."

"And who were these friends you deserted us for?"

Ann Elizabeth paused, holding her breath.

"Friends?" Maggie's apprehensive glance at her mother indicated that she, too, was worried about Rob's reaction. But, being Maggie, she plunged right in. "Just Steve. Most of the time. He…we stayed at his father's house in Monterey."

Rob abandoned his task and turned to face Maggie. "Steve? That guy you brought here at Thanksgiving?"

Maggie nodded.

"Alone? Just the two of you?"

Again she nodded.

Rob's nostrils flared. "You needn't be so damn blasé. I don't like this one goddamn bit and you know it!" He looked at Ann Elizabeth. "You knew about this." A statement, not a question.

She flinched, but couldn't help reaching out a hand in a silent plea. *Don't say things that will hurt her.*

"No! Mom didn't know."

"Don't give me that! Your mother can't lie any better than you can. She's been a zombie this whole Christmas."

"Okay. Mom knew I was gone, but she didn't know

I was going until I'd already left. And Dad, it isn't like you think. It's—"

"You don't know what I think. Maybe you don't give a damn. But I'm sure as hell gonna tell you." He glanced at the clock, then at Ann Elizabeth. "Hadn't you better go?"

"Yes." Still she hesitated, torn. Not wanting to keep her parents waiting, wanting to remain as a buffer. She looked at the two who faced each other. Maggie, frail and small, her eyes on her father. Rob, tall and stiff, waiting for Ann Elizabeth to leave.

This was out of her hands. She went out to her car, reminding herself that no matter how the sparks flew between them, those two loved each other. Hoping that things would simmer down a bit by the time she returned with her parents. She particularly didn't want her father upset. Not with his heart condition.

In the kitchen Rob gazed down at his daughter, reminding himself that she was no longer a child. He should have been prepared for this. But was any father ever prepared? He took a deep breath. "Who else knows about this?"

"Roy and Kate, friends of Steve's. They came to visit during my stay. And Mom. I called her as I was leaving Berkeley and I really didn't give her a chance to say no. Because I was afraid she would and I wanted so much to go. And I'm glad." She said it all in one breath and slumped into a chair, eyes downcast.

Rob read it: *I've fessed up. There's no more to say.*

The hell there wasn't! He walked over to stand before her, his arms folded. "As usual I'm the last to know. And make no mistake, I'll be the first if there's a disaster or if a rescue is required. Maggie?" He waited, silent until she looked up. "I've been on your side and have supported you all your life. Why would you not talk to me about boy-girl, man-woman things?''

Her eyes widened, but a slight shrug was the only answer.

"We've talked about everything else, haven't we?"

She nodded, her gaze hypnotic.

"This sex thing—" he pulled on his ear, took a deep breath "—it's not something you enter into lightly. You not only compromise yourself, but...well, I needn't name the risks. And if the guy is just out for a piece of ass, you're nothing but another notch on his dick.''

"Dad!" The stricken cry, the tears in her eyes, nearly broke his heart. She'd never heard such gutter talk from him. But he had meant to shock her. She needed to know what she might be in for.

Rob almost backed away when she raised her head, defiance showing through the tears. "It isn't... Steve... our relationship isn't like that.''

Rob mimicked. "Our relationship isn't like that. How the hell do you know?"

"I know." Her gaze was steady, confident. "I know Steve, and I know me.''

"Did he ask you to marry him?"

She looked surprised. "No, but—''

"Hell, no!"

She stood her ground. "Because we didn't even think or talk about that. We talked about...other things.''

"I bet." His mouth twisted. "There's something else. He's a white boy, you know, and even if—''

"You knew he was white. You didn't care that I was dating him!"

Rob pulled on his ear again, sighed. "No. To tell the truth, I was relieved to see you branching out. I was fed up with your rapping black.''

"And now?" she challenged.

"Dating some dude is one thing. Sleeping with him is another. And sleeping white...well, it's an even bigger complication."

"Why?"

"Don't look at me like that. I don't give a damn about his color. But there are many who do. And even if your relationship is as you say—" He stopped himself, swallowing his own doubts. "I repeat, there are those who do care, including his parents, I'm willing to bet."

Maggie sat up abruptly, opened her mouth as if to speak, but for a moment, nothing came out. When she did speak, it was almost a whisper. "Okay, Daddy. You've got a point. And you might be right. About...about everything. But you know something?" Her voice broke now and the tears began to fall. "I don't care. It...Christmas...Steve...was so...so... I didn't know it could be like that." She mopped her face with the back of her hand. "No matter what, I'm glad it happened."

Rob felt a lump in his throat and his own eyes filled. He reached down and drew her into his arms. "Honey, don't cry. I'm still in your corner. I'd just hate to see you hurt. But if this is what you think it is—" *and even if it isn't* "—your daddy's right here as always. Just mark my concerns, okay?"

She nodded against his chest. He held her for a long time before he kissed her cheek and resumed his cooking chores.

Ann Elizabeth was anxious as she drove back from the airport with her parents. Rob loved his daughter, but he wasn't the type to bite his tongue. He'd tell her exactly what he thought, confront her. Ann Elizabeth felt a nervous quiver in the pit of her stomach as she wondered what really was going on between Maggie and this Steve. She hoped Rob hadn't been too harsh. And she hoped the explosion was over before she arrived with her parents.

Everything seemed to be all right—at least for the moment—as she pulled into the driveway and a smiling Rob came out to haul in their bags. Maggie, too, was smiling as she ushered them into the guest room, which was ready for them, the bed neatly made. Good. Maggie had changed the sheets.

"Haven't seen you since the wedding! Prettiest bridesmaid in the place," Dr. Carter said as he hugged his granddaughter. "Deserted us at Christmas, didn't you? Some handsome swain? Someone special? Come on—tell your old grandpa."

Ann Elizabeth saw Maggie's mouth quiver and was glad Julia Belle cut in.

"Oh, for goodness' sake, Will. Leave the child alone. Don't start badgering her before we even get in the door."

"Put the kettle on, Maggie," Ann Elizabeth said. "I'm sure they'd like a hot cup of tea. It's turning colder and I think it's going to rain."

Maggie fixed the tea, then retired to her room to "work on a paper."

Rain was falling now, and Rob started a fire in the family room where they sat to drink their tea and catch up on family doings.

"You know Cindy's dad's wedding present was a lease on a condo," Julia Belle said. "Near the hospital. I think they're the only colored in the complex, but they've settled in quite nicely."

"That's good," Ann Elizabeth said. "It's so convenient for Bobby."

"Yes. Of course he's hardly ever there. But one thing I must say for Cindy—she never complains about his long hours at the hospital."

"'Course not." Dr. Carter chuckled. "She's too busy putting hubby through. He'll be a pediatric surgeon and she'll have that fancy house and all the trappings if it kills her."

"Oh, hush, Will," Julia Belle said. "You're always knocking Cindy."

"As the kids say, just telling it like it is. And it's more good than bad. Bobby's got the brains, a surgeon's fingers and that easy manner. Too easy. He needs Cindy's prodding to make him the splendid surgeon he can be."

He's right, Ann Elizabeth thought, feeling a little shock of guilt. Not the wife she would have chosen, but probably the best wife for him. Anyway, you certainly had no say about whom your children chose. She hardly knew this Steve person Maggie was so wild about. Or where the affair was headed.

She had no more control over Maggie than her mother had had over her when she went happily off to a wider and different world with Rob.

Happily? Oh, yes!

In a penthouse apartment high above San Francisco Bay, Steve Pearson faced his father.

"Marry her?" James Pearson nearly choked. "Are you out of your mind?"

"I thought you liked Maggie."

"What the hell has that got to do with anything? Okay. I was impressed. She's classy. Got a lot on the ball. Pretty, too. Good figure. I'll bet she's a damn good lay. But—"

Steve took a step toward his father. "Let's get this straight. Maggie's no lay. She's—"

"All right, all right. Simmer down!" The older man threw up his hands. "I didn't mean it like that."

Probably didn't, Steve thought. Just his way of assessing women. "Look, Dad, you've got to understand. Maggie is special. I've never felt this way about any other woman." So excited and yet so at peace.

"Fine. I do understand. And I'm not objecting to the relationship. Just to... Good God, son, you can't marry her!"

"I can. And I will—if she'll have me," Steve said, suddenly remembering Maggie's reluctance, her insistence on secrecy.

"If she'll have you!" James Pearson snorted. "You're Stephen Elliott Pearson, heir to two considerable fortunes, and she's just... Oh, for Christ's sake, you're from two different worlds. Your lifestyle and hers are miles apart."

"I kinda like her style," Steve said musingly. For a moment he was back in Monterey, decorating a Christmas tree. His mother always had a professional decorator do that. "Do you know, we went to church on Christmas Eve—a quaint little church just before you turn off for the drive. I hardly noticed it before and—"

"Come off it, Steve! Let's be realistic. She's a black woman. A marriage between you would never work."

"Why not?"

"Damn it, come out of the ocean and face the real world. What about children? Have you thought about that?"

"Sure. I'd like at least two, maybe three."

"Good God!" Pearson shook his head in disgust. "You don't live in this world by yourself, you know. What would your friends say?"

"I don't give a damn."

"Well, you better give a damn about me. I'm not letting you mess up your life. Forget this marriage. I won't have it."

Steve's gaze was steady. "I'm not asking your permission, Dad."

"Oh?" James Reginald Pearson, of Pearson Associates, was not accustomed to being thwarted. His face turned crimson. "I'm warning you. If you persist in this course, you'll not get one red cent from me."

"Keep it. I don't need it."

"You needn't look so smug. You won't get the Elliott fortune until you're thirty. And not then, if your mother can break the trust. She won't like this union any more than I."

"I'm twenty-five, Dad, old enough to make my own decisions. Anyway..." Steve shook his head. "You really don't understand, do you? This isn't about money. I think I can earn whatever I need. But I don't think I could live without Maggie." He picked up his jacket.

His father grabbed his arm. "Wait, son. Promise me you won't do anything in haste. We'll talk about this later. We're not through."

"We're through on this matter. You can be sure of that," Steve said, and departed. He was anxious to get away from his father and to a phone. He wanted to catch Maggie before she left Sacramento.

Maggie was just about to leave when her mother called her to the phone.

"Oh, Steve!" Just hearing his voice seemed to make everything right.

"Maggie, we need to talk."

"Sure." Was he having doubts? Her heart sank.

"When are you getting back?"

"I'm leaving now. Have to get there for a meeting." The black students were planning another rally, and she wanted to be part of it. Their destruction of the bookstore rankled.

"Okay. Where will you be and what time is it over? I'll meet you there."

"No!" She almost dropped the phone. "Not there."

"Maggie, it's time we went public."

His words sang in her heart—like a promise. Still... "I don't think that's wise, Steve."

"Don't you fight me, too." He sounded tired.

Instinctively she knew. He must have had a row with one or both of his parents. About her. And he had chosen. Her. Elation soared. Plummeted. She didn't want him to have to choose. Didn't want him estranged from his parents.

"Maggie, are you there? Where's the meeting?"

She told him, but quickly added, "We should be through about five. I'll phone you when—"

"I'll be there at five," he said, and hung up.

She worried all the way to the campus. She worried more when she got to the meeting and found the place jammed, standing room only.

"What's going on?" she whispered, pushing in to share Dena's seat.

Dena shrugged. "Ted invited people from the community. He says if they're gonna participate in the rallies, they should know beforehand what's going on."

Maybe. Or maybe Ted wanted a bigger crowd to act

out his agenda. Ted had some crazy ideas. With his hate rhetoric and this irrational crowd, anything could happen.

She didn't like it. She was even more apprehensive when she saw that Ken and some of his cronies were there. Ken was standing, leaning against the wall and cleaning his fingernails—with a switchblade.

Steve had picked a heck of a time to go public. Maybe she should get out of here now, head him off.

Oh, she was being ridiculous. Nobody was going to do anything physical. And if she got a lot of flack about him, so be it.

Besides, she'd wanted to make this meeting for a special purpose. She had some ideas to present and maybe this was a good time to present them. She kept her seat.

Ted's rhetoric had his usual fervor, and the audience, as always was swayed. Maggie, waiting for an opportune time to make her suggestions, listened politely to Ted's complaints about the status quo, the evils of complacency and "how to get the honky's attention." The need to shock. Tension. A rally. A disturbance. Everybody was clapping and cheering Ted on before she realized that the next target was the library.

The library. Vandalize the library! She had a horrible vision of books scattered and torn, records forever lost.

"No!" Before she knew it, she was on her feet.

"No!" she cried. "No! You can't do this." So loud was her cry, so impassioned her plea, that the room grew quiet. Everybody was staring at her.

She had their attention. "I thought our mission was to make things better, not worse. To build up, not destroy. And certainly not a library, which contains the history of our past, the nucleus of—"

"Honky history!" Sue broke in, trying to shout her down. "Shut up, Maggie! You sound like a freaking honky. Fuck the honky history, the honky books—"

"You shut up!" Maggie, furious, shouted louder. "You don't even know what's in those books. You've never looked." The room rocked with laughter and Sue seemed mad enough to spit. But Maggie didn't care. This was a good time to talk about her ideas. "You want to destroy books," she said, "when others are starving for them." She told about her tutoring sessions, how she'd found that most of the kids had no reading material at home—not even a newspaper. She said if they collected used books, maybe they could raise funds to buy children's books and distribute them. She talked on, carried away by enthusiasm and the feeling that her audience was receptive.

Until Ted broke in. "Bullshit! We been begging and groveling for years. The honky owes us."

"And it's time to collect!" Sue stood up, urging on a raucous response.

"Right on!" several voices chorused.

Maggie's heart sank.

"Cut the crap!" The voice boomed loud and rough, demanding, threatening. The room was suddenly quiet. Everybody stared at Ken. "The sister's got a point. Let's hear it."

Only Sue was brave enough or mad enough to challenge him. "Shit, Ken! She's one of them Toms. Think they got it made. Think they're white. She don't know what the fuck's happening down in—"

"She knows what's happening in the breakfast line. She's always there." His eyes focused on Sue. "More'n I can say for some." He looked at Maggie. "Go ahead, sister."

"Well—" Maggie bit her lip, her eyes on Ken as if she was appealing to him alone "—that's it, mostly. Only I thought we could maybe throw in some learning games like Scrabble. And we could teach the kids to tune into educational channels. Everybody's got a television, even if they don't have books." Understanding chuckles reverberated, and the atmosphere changed. To her relief quiet talk and good sense prevailed. "The games could be prizes for attendance at the tutoring sessions and might encourage more participation."

There was faint applause as she took her seat.

Dena moved that Maggie's proposal be accepted and Maggie head the committee for the project. The motion carried—just barely. Maggie felt an eerie elation. Had she turned things around? At least the library trashing was on hold. She could hardly wait to tell Steve.

Steve! She glanced at her watch. Almost five. She tried to push through the departing crowd, but was stopped by people eager to discuss her project. The room was almost empty when she found herself hemmed in by those on the other side.

"Okay, asshole!" Ted planted his bulky frame in front of her. "What's with you? Fucking up my meeting with all that do-gooder shit. Taking charge like whitey!"

"Oh, yeah!" Sue sneered. "Didn't you know? She's making out with that white dude." She turned to the others, her words thick with menace. "She ain't with us. I say we trash the bitch."

Maggie tried to step back, tried to stifle the fear.

"Cool it!" Ken's voice was quiet this time, but just as threatening. "Any trashing around here comes through me and the brotherhood. Thought I already told you this sister works her butt off for the kids. I ain't seen you down there.'' He pointed at Sue.

"Another thing!" Ken held up a hand. The people who'd started to melt away froze in their tracks. "The brotherhood don't give a damn who's screwing who. You all doing it," he said as he flashed a look at Ted.

Maggie would have laughed at the expression on Ted's face had she not felt so faint with relief. She stared up at Ken, wanting to speak, but she couldn't swallow the lump in her throat. Timidly she touched the sleeve of his leather jacket.

He gave her a thumbs-up. "Right on, sister."

She smiled at him and walked from the room.

Steve was waiting in the hall. Together they walked down the hall, out of the building and across the campus.

Going public.

_____ Epilogue _____

August 1999

Ann Elizabeth stood alone in the kitchen, trying to remember where Cindy kept the coffee. They had come to Atlanta for Helen Rose's granddaughter's wedding and were staying, as always now, with Bobby and Cindy in their fabulous house on the lake. A *real* lake, with their own small dock and boat, convenient for sailing and visiting their neighbors, black and white. She smiled. Dad had been right. Cindy's house was grander than most.

The coffee...

She remembered. The Swedish coffee was in the fridge in this everything-in-its-place house. Thank goodness she didn't have to grind coffee beans. She had breakfast almost ready when Rob came in.

"Bobby gone?" he asked.

"Long ago. Early surgery." She always felt proud when she said that. Like her mother, she thought. *Your dad's at the hospital.* Well, she had a right to be proud of Bobby! "Sit down. I'm just doing the eggs."

"I'll bet Maggie's mad at you for stealing her daughter," Rob said when she joined him at the sunny breakfast table.

"She's been with them all summer." In the Greek Islands, where Steve was heading some project, doing whatever marine biologists do. Whitney, their nineteen-year-old, had flown in to meet her grandparents in Atlanta—at Ann Elizabeth's request.

"She'd have had to come back early, anyway, to register."

"Bull. Stanford doesn't open till mid-September." Rob chuckled. "You just want her with you."

"I need someone to shop and go visiting with while you're on the golf course."

"And who else but your favorite grandchild."

"Nonsense. I love all six of them—equally!" She did. Bobby's handsome sons. Jerry, the oldest, a contractor who had a big stake in all the real-estate development going on in Atlanta. Todd, a broker in New York. And Lyndon, who'd decided to follow in his father's footsteps. *He's only just finished his Residency in brain surgery, of all things. Dear me, seems only yesterday that he was a wriggling baby in my arms.*

It seemed they had all grown up so fast. Maggie's eldest, Robbie, with his own family in New York, was deeply involved in the Pearson family business, which had never interested his father. Ann Elizabeth chuckled. Robbie was busy building up the family fortune while Richard, the younger son, was busy giving it away. Emulating his Uncle Bobby, Richard had also become a doctor. But like his mother, Maggie, he was full of compassion and generosity. He spent more time at the free clinic he financed in Harlem than in his Fifth Avenue office.

Anyway, they were all doing well and that was what mattered. "Do you ever think how lucky we are?" she said now. "To have children and grandchildren who are all successful and happy in such varied careers?"

"And taking it all for granted!"

She knew he was thinking of the struggle he'd endured just to fly a plane. She touched his hand. "They're so young. But they're taking advantage of what's available to them, and I'm proud."

"Me, too," he said, getting up. They'd both heard Jerry's horn outside. "Gotta go. Tee time." He kissed her and went out.

Might as well catch the news, she thought, and switched on the television. A commentator was interviewing Rosa Parks, who had received the Congressional Medal of Honor in June. She's still beautiful, Ann Elizabeth thought, and she certainly deserves the honor. Hers was the first step. Toward the marches and sit-ins. Toward change. Toward our entry into all hotels, hospitals, schools, new careers and neighborhoods and public parks like the one where Rob's playing golf right now, instead of that crummy one we'd had at our Lincoln Country Club. She gave the television a little salute. *Thank you, Rosa Parks.* One woman alone. That took guts!

One person alone often made a difference in this crazy mixed-up world, she thought as she refilled her coffee cup. If it hadn't been for that doctor who took Bobby to the white hospital in Atlanta, or Mrs. Levin who'd walked Maggie to that school, or Captain Jenkins in Atlanta...

My goodness, why was she thinking backward? She should concentrate on what she and Whitney would do today.

She smiled. Rob was right. Whitney was her heart. Maybe because she'd come a bit later than the boys, when Ann Elizabeth had despaired of there ever being a granddaughter. It never ceased to amaze her that Steve and Maggie, who lived like Gypsies, jumping from one underwater project to another, could produce such a sedate, sophisticated and very sweet daughter. Never mind that they'd named her Whitney Alyson Elliott Pearson after her paternal grandmother. At least they hadn't tacked on Richardson, her second husband's surname.

And I'm grateful to Whitney Richardson. Had it not been for her, Steve and Maggie might never have married!

That had been one of the tough times. Only a week or so after that fateful Christmas, Maggie had announced that she was transferring to Scripps, where Steve was on a fellowship. We both knew she was also transferring to his condo, and nobody had said anything about marrying!

To tell the truth, I was glad to get her out of that turmoil at Berkeley, and it seemed we could do nothing about making things legal. Especially after the talk Rob had with Steve. He was on our side. It was Maggie who wasn't sure she was "ready." That really gave me a turn. Had Maggie been so brainwashed by those black rebels at Berkeley that she couldn't face marriage to a white man? Even if she couldn't live without him?

Had it not been for Whitney Alyson Elliott Richardson… She was a *Boston Elliott,* "Too far above everyone else to give a damn about race or color," Rob had said. However, she was a devout Protestant, committed to the sacred institution of marriage, and determined that her son not follow in the footsteps of his father. Maggie had to shape up or ship out!

Ann Elizabeth smiled, remembering. It had been a small family ceremony on a Mendocino Beach. But more touching than any other wedding she'd ever witnessed.

"My, you were up early," Cindy said, entering the kitchen. "Whitney still asleep?"

Ann Elizabeth nodded. "I made breakfast for Rob. He had an early game with Jerry."

"And there's still coffee. Good!" Cindy poured herself a cup. She looked pretty, energetic and still young enough not to worry about putting on weight, Ann Elizabeth thought enviously as she watched Cindy reach for a cinnamon roll.

"Only five days before the wedding, and there are still so many things to do," Cindy said, and began to list them.

Ann Elizabeth, listening, marveled that some things never changed. Cindy, grandmother of the flower girl, Jerry's three-year-old, was as involved as Helen Rose, grandmother of the bride, each determined that this wedding should outdo any other.

And you're being spiteful, Ann Elizabeth Metcalf! You can see for yourself that your dad was right. Cindy *has* been the best wife for Bobby. Perfect with the social life, the boys and the budget.

But Bobby made himself what he is—one of the most famous and respected pediatric surgeons in the country. People brought special cases to him, and he lectured everywhere, and experimented with new techniques. Last night, he said that the time was coming—and soon—when most surgery would be done by computer without the necessity of cutting into the body at all! Ann Elizabeth could hardly imagine such a thing. But she was glad her son was part of it all. She thought of her dad. *Wherever he is, he's smiling!*

Cindy left to get dressed. She hadn't been gone five

minutes when Whitney, her sun-kissed cheeks glowing, bounced in, wearing a crisp chocolate-brown shirt over matching shorts. Simple and smart, Ann Elizabeth observed. Probably straight from a Paris salon.

"Hi, Grandma," Whitney said, kissing her.

"Hi, honey. What do you want for breakfast?"

"Just cereal. I'll get it."

She may have her other grandma's name, Ann Elizabeth thought, but she looks like me. The boys, with their fair skin, could be mistaken for white. But Whitney... Well, her hair is black and straight as a poker, but she has my exact coloring and features. Oh, she's just a beautiful example of a child of mixed genes.

"Where are we going today, Grandma?" Whitney looked up from her bowl.

"I thought we might take in the Sweet Auburn Heritage Festival. There's an item in the *Journal* about it."

"Good. You can show me your dad's office."

Ann Elizabeth kissed her on the forehead. She was so sweet, so willing to do things with her old grandmother. Yesterday they'd toured the university complex that had grown bigger and more crowded than it was in 1992, when she'd come for the class of '42's fiftieth reunion. All the Negro institutions had merged now, with the addition of Morehouse Medical School. There were new stadiums and dormitories from the Olympics in 1996, and a new library and other buildings paid for by philanthropists and entertainment stars whose children had attended one of the colleges. It was all so much bigger.

With a pang of nostalgia, she remembered what it had been like more than half a century earlier. She'd sat on the old library steps—

"We didn't go by your old house yet."

"No. Not yet." That too gave her a pang. She'd avoided going down Hunter—oops! Martin Luther King Drive, past her old house, although Bobby said the current owners had refurbished it and the neighborhood hadn't deteriorated that much. And goodness, Mom and Dad had sold the house in 1975 and moved into that beautiful senior citizens' home on Peachtree. They'd enjoyed three years there before Dad died, and Mom a year after.

Feeling tears in her eyes, Ann Elizabeth reminded herself that both her parents had retained fairly good health and complete mental clarity before their sudden deaths. She was grateful they hadn't lingered like Aunt Sophie, who lived five years longer, unable to recognize even Helen Rose.

Senior citizens' complexes were popping up everywhere now. Rob had retired and they'd bought into one. But they weren't moving yet. Not as long as Whitney was at Stanford and bringing her friends up almost every weekend.

But she wasn't bringing home all that organized dissension of Maggie's time. More of a mixture now. Not just black and white, but all those immigrants—from Vietnam, Bosnia, Russia, Haiti, you name it. Still, so many of them were pursuing new separatist agendas—ethnic this and ethnic that.

As Rob put it, everybody was beating it to the big melting pot, but they didn't want to melt when they got here!

Anyway, Whitney's not interested in any of that. She's interested in tolerance, in live and let live—and in opera. Had the lead in the college production of *La Bohème* last year.

Imagine. Opera, and most in some foreign language,

which she handles like a native. Guess that comes from living in all those places with her parents. But she got her voice from Thelma. Oh, she's a soprano, not contralto, but the range, the clarity, the color—that's Thelma Metcalf.

"Grandma! You're not listening."

"Oh!" Goodness, her mind was rambling again. "I'm sorry. What did you say?"

"I was reading this article, and I was wondering why they call it *sweet* Auburn."

"Wesley Dobbs, the man who coined the name, said it was because the nucleus of Negro business was contained in those four blocks. Lots of fun and cultural life, too. And it *was* sweet," Ann Elizabeth said, remembering the treks to the library, swimming at the Y....

"And now the slogan is 'Making Auburn Sweeter'?"

"Because they're renovating and refurbishing the old, and adding so much that's new—the Martin Luther King Center, a performing Arts Center, the new bank and insurance buildings and more. And they're expanding." Just as our lives have, she thought, Rob's and mine and our children's, as well as the lives of so many others.

She grinned at her granddaughter. "We're moving right uptown with everybody else," she said. "It's bigger. Better. *Sweeter!*"

If you enjoyed what you just read,
then we've got an offer you can't resist!

Take 2 bestselling love stories FREE!

Plus get a FREE surprise gift!

New York Times Bestselling Author

JAYNE ANN KRENTZ

CALL IT DESTINY

Successful businesswoman Heather Strand strategized, calculated and negotiated every aspect of her life—including her engagement. Marriage to powerful Jake Cavender could only strengthen her control over her family's resort. It's a perfect arrangement...until she learns that Jake has other plans. When business is mixed inextricably with pleasure, Heather finds herself caught between ambition and passion, dreams and desire. But Heather's not a woman who will relinquish the upper hand easily, especially to a man who wants her on his own terms.

"A master of the genre...nobody does it better."
—*Romantic Times*

Available the first week of February 2000 wherever paperbacks are sold.

MJAK563

It will take everything they possess to face
the truths about to come to light under
the California moon.

CATHERINE LANIGAN

Shannon Riley is living in the shadows of a past she cannot
face. Gabe Turner is her patient, a man lying in a coma—and
the prime suspect in his business partner's murder. Just outside
the door, Officer Ben Richards stands guard, watching as the
woman he is falling in love with falls in love with his prisoner.

Then the unthinkable occurs. Gabe awakens and flees the
hospital, taking Shannon hostage in his desperate attempt to
piece together the deadly mystery threatening his life.
They are on the run from ruthless men who want them
dead—and from Ben. The three soon find themselves
trapped in a dangerous game with no clear rules—
except survival and courageous love.

CALIFORNIA MOON

MIRA®

"Lanigan knows her genre well." —*Publishers Weekly*

On sale mid-February 2000 wherever paperbacks are sold!